A FRAGILE HEART

That night, Anna tossed and turned during a terrible storm. She was not yet used to the frightful howls and shrieks of rage, when the wind bent the trees to the ground and great bolts of lightning split the earth around the house. Usually she held on to Mario afterwards and shook with fear. But this was a dream that refused to let her wake up. She felt as if she were being drawn inexorably into the maw of something evil. Whatever the monster was, it had her leg and was pulling her away from all those people who loved her.

She half managed to wake up, but was so firmly held by the nightmare that, although she knew she was dreaming, she couldn't escape.

'It's all right, Anna, I'm here.' Mario kissed her gently on the neck.

She clung to him. 'Don't ever leave me, Mario. Promise you'll never leave me.'

'I'd rather die than ever leave you, Anna. You know that.'

ATTENTION: ORGANIZATIONS AND CORPORATIONS

Most HarperPaperbacks are available at special quantity discounts for bulk purchases for sales promotions, premiums, or fund-raising. For information, please call or write:
Special Markets Department, HarperCollins*Publishers*,
10 East 53rd Street, New York, N.Y. 10022.
Telephone: (212) 207-7528. Fax: (212) 207-7222.

For the
Love of a
Stranger

Erin Pizzey

HarperPaperbacks
A Division of HarperCollinsPublishers

HarperPaperbacks *A Division of* HarperCollins*Publishers*
10 East 53rd Street, New York, N.Y. 10022

A paperback edition of this book was published in 1994 in
Great Britain by HarperCollins*Publishers*.

Cover photograph by J. Inove/Photonica

First HarperPaperbacks printing: March 1996

Printed in the United States of America

HarperPaperbacks and colophon are trademarks of
HarperCollins*Publishers*

10 9 8 7 6 5 4 3 2 1

Dedication

To everyone in San Giovanni d'Asso. To Danielle and Rocco and their mineral baths at Bagnacci where we all swim, and to Letizia and Elizabeth and their cottages where my friends stay. To Lea and Rocco, my friends and neighbours, and to Sylvana and Giacomo, as well as his mother who is such a good cook. For Luana and Nicoletta and her parents. To Ottavio, always captain of his boat. To Roberto Capelli, our mayor. Lida, who does my hair, and Antonella, who organizes me.

To all my white knights: Christopher Little, David Morris, Allen Cohen, John Eltham, Alan Hubbard of Lloyds Bank, Christopher Sauter, and Graham Harper. To David Robbie, who flies kites — as does Christopher Butler, Eddie Saunderson, who is a marvellous photographer, Graham Harper of Ashgreen Travel, who organizes my trips: they all make my world a better place to live in. To Larry and Walter, my next-door neighbours at last!

Finally, to the Savoy Hotel and to St James's Court, two of the best hotels in the world. To Mr Kelly and Sonia Potter at Fortnum and Mason's, who send me hampers, and to Stella Burrowes at Harrods, who sends me clothes. God bless you.

To all my children everywhere I send my love.

'For there is a virtue in truth;
a virtue in truth; it has an
almost mystic power. Like radium,
it seems to give off forever
and ever grains of energy,
atoms of light.'

VIRGINIA WOOLF

BOOK ONE

IRELAND

One

The fire burned low in the grate. The smell of the peat
gave an ancient sense of history to a people and their
love of the soil. The sweet, delicate fumes, which over
the decades had impregnated the rustic, whitewashed
cottage walls with yellowy brown stains, seemed to
shield this simple, ageless human scene from the tumul-
tuous reality outside. Almost exactly a year after the
nationalistic indignation of the Republican rising of
1916, the waves of discontent and provocation were
now lapping the heartlands of rural Ireland. The worst
was soon to follow. But for now the peat smouldered,
its gentle heat providing an enveloping, caressing oasis
in a chilled February landscape.

The baby was a long time coming. 'No matter,' said
the village midwife, singing quietly to herself. ''Tis your
first and, God willing, it will be a boy.' Although she
thought to herself what chances a new-born baby could
have in a country overrun by Britons intent on genocide.
Another Scotland.

The young girl's face was flushed with effort and
pain, but the old midwife noticed she did not scream
and yell like the other young women. She did not cry
out against God and the Virgin Mary or the priests
who forced the women to bear yearly on pain of hell's
eternity. Rather she relaxed between the contractions
and lay back on her fern pillow. The ferns came from
a bog and were picked by the old women and prepared
for childbirth. When bruised by the suffering body,
they released a calming oil which soaked the hempen
sheets. Joanna, the midwife, had birthed and laid out

the whole village. She remembered birthing Mary, this young mother, twenty-one years ago. Mary was no pink mass of wriggling flesh, not she. She was white and calm as if nine months in her mother's stomach had been a mere yesterday. Today the same smile wreathed her lips. 'She will not be a boy.'

'How do you know?' Joanna said, feeling the huge swollen stomach.

'I know. I have always known. Her name is to be Anna, the same Anna that recognized baby Jesus when he was carried in the arms of his mother Mary.'

Mary smiled, her wide blue eyes undimmed by the long hours. Her hair, tied on top of her head, picked a hint of red from the glow of the fire. 'Check on Daniel,' she said. She giggled. 'He wants a boy. I know he does. He'll be surprised, but what he doesn't know is that I spun my wedding ring tied to a piece of silk over my belly on St Mansueto's Feast, and the saint told me it would be a girl, and he said she'd be born on his birthday.' Her last words were high and shrill. 'My!' she said, her brow wrinkling. 'I think she's coming, Joanna. I can feel her moving.' Mary took great gasps of air.

The room filled with women. Mary's two sisters-in-law, behatted, hovered bat-like in the air. Aunt Kitty, the singer of the family, shook like a tree in the wind. 'Are you all right, Mary? I mean, you're not goin' to die like your mother, are you?'

'You stop that, you big cow you!' Joanna's eyes shone with rage. 'Don't you women come in here and frighten the lass. She's a brave girl. No fuss. No fuss at all.'

Martha, the dancer, slim and fey, the one who saw the wee fairies and keened at the family deaths, came up to the bed. 'You have nothing to worry about, darlin',' she said, and put her hand on Mary's now contorting belly. 'Your child will be with us in a few minutes.'

'She will be here.' Mary corrected her sister-in-law. 'Daniel will be disappointed.'

'Disappointed?' Kitty said. 'Why on earth he should want another man-child is anybody's guess. All men's balls are owned by their mothers. I should know!'

Martha laughed. 'Daniel will not be disappointed, Mary. Once he looks at the little one's face, he will fall in love with the third woman in his life.'

'Humph! The first woman being his mother, I suppose?' Kitty's ample body shook with rage, now it was being warmed by the fire. 'Like I said, all men's balls are owned by their mothers, and then there's precious little to go round.'

Mary tried to laugh, but could feel the crown of her baby's head and then a gentle whoosh as the perfectly formed child fell into Joanna's waiting hands. There was a moment of such reverent silence that Mary strained her head forward. 'Is she all right?' she faltered, crossing herself.

The three older women breathed in unison. The room filled with feathery, gentle words, the crooning of women stunned into silence by great beauty. 'Tonight,' Martha said, 'a child of light is born and that light shall never be put out, except when God takes it away.' The words hung in the air. They sparkled and they spangled and then they popped, one by one.

Joanna put the baby, wrapped in a white knitted shawl, into Mary's arms. 'You can come in now, Daniel! See what the good Lord has sent you.'

Daniel walked into the room. He was embarrassed by the number of women around him, although all close family. He was a shy and quiet man. His eyes were only for Mary, his beloved wife. Daniel felt his life did not begin the day he was born. It began when he first saw Mary in the school-house sixteen years ago. She was five and he was two years older. Their eyes met in the playground on that momentous first day and their love fused over the water pump in the backyard. Now, he leaned over and kissed her. 'Are you all right?' he whispered. He had expected the murderous groans that he had heard so many times from his mother. His birth, he had been assured, had been the worst, and it was then that she became famous for her loud screams during delivery. 'Ah! It's the Kearneys again,' the villagers would say. Maybe that was why Daniel was such a quiet boy. But when the other boys had called him a sissy for spending his time playing with Mary, he had reacted with surprising, immediate force. Then there was no turning back. Mary knew his quiet strength, his loving ways, and she was glad for it.

'I'm afraid it's not a boy,' she said, shyly putting the child into her father's cradled arms.

Daniel pulled back the shawl and looked into the radiant sea-change of his daughter's eyes. 'I thought all babies looked like little lambs when they were born,' he said, puzzled. 'But this one . . . her eyes are perfect. Look!' He held the child up to his face and turned his head. 'She can see me quite clearly.'

'Yes, she can.' Martha smiled. 'She's an old soul. She has been here before.'

'None of your heathen rubbish, Martha,' Joanna said. 'This is a good Catholic child and she'll be baptized by Father O'Brian like you were.'

Martha grinned at Joanna. 'She'll be baptized right enough, but she will take after me and see the ghosts and the witches. She'll know how to keen for the dead. I tell you, she's been here before. Mark my words.'

'What would you like to drink, darling?' Daniel sat down on the chair. The other two women, seeing the three of them wrapped in a cocoon of love and light, withdrew.

On Kitty's face lay a sad shadow. She had once

loved like that, but it had not been returned. The empty grate of the failed relationship was still with her and sometimes she felt it always would be. Still, Mary was all a woman could wish for. And now they had another girl-woman in the family. Unlike her gentle mother, this one would be strong, but the mother's hand would be a quiet guide, so the girl need not waste her destiny rebelling against her parents like so many of the modern generation.

Joanna, carrying a hot flagon of sugared tea, brushed past Kitty. ''Tis well done.' She grinned her toothless smile.

Kitty nodded. 'And he'll not force another one on her soon,' she said. 'He's a good man.' Kitty walked into the smoke-filled inner room and adjusted her face. 'Now, lads!' she said, her head thrown back, and rolling her blue eyes. 'Which of you is it tonight?'

The men roared and slapped their knees. No man had Kitty, and they knew that. Only Kitty had Kitty, and each man could lust after her in his heart, and go safely back to his wife and sleep the sleep of the faithful, even if a little confused by dreams of soft, fat white knees and feet with a kissable instep.

Two

Martha kept a strict but loving eye on her little niece. Mary, Anna's mother, tried as hard as she could to keep a gentle leash on her boisterous daughter. Daniel made no attempts to restrain the child. His love for her was as boundless as the skies that hung over his dreamed-about America. His dream was the dream of not only his generation, but those before him. Daniel had been weaned by his father and uncles on first-hand stories of famine and rural injustice and how relatives and friends had been driven broken-hearted to find opportunity elsewhere. By the time he was able to decide for himself, his yearning for America was natural, unquestioned, almost a predestination.

Anna's first memories were the clear, soft Irish rain falling on the bright, emerald-green valleys. Aware of the sexual softness of the soil, she dug her little fingers into the loamy grains and wriggled them pleasurably. The warmth of the feeling spread from her fingers and raced in little joyful explosions until it reached a pitch of released excitement between her legs. Puzzled, she put her hand in between her legs, trying to find the source of such intense feeling. She encountered a soft fold of flesh. Martha, who was in the garden with her, laughed.

'Aye, little one! You are growing up too fast.' She removed Anna's hand. 'There's time for all that later. Be a child. Come, let's go and pick apples.'

September in Mayo and the trees pregnant with fruit. Anna wandered the dusty roads around the village, well known and well loved. The gaunt hens scrambled out of her way. Anna was a persistent, delinquent egg thief. Not for her the pristine boiled egg for breakfast. Her mother had to chase her around the house to get her to eat. There was far more adventure in stalking a hen and lifting the tail just as the perfectly formed egg fell into her hand. Then, proudly, she took it to her mother for cooking.

Her relationship with her Aunt Kitty was a little troubled. She loved her big, flowery aunt with all her passionate nature, but she was aware of a compressed rage in the woman. Rage that never really exploded, but seeped through the powder on her aunt's face and leaked into the bitter words spoken about men. Anna was three and a half when she first understood the extent of her aunt's disillusionment. 'All men are dogs,' her Aunt Kitty announced, sailing through the little front door of Anna's cottage.

'Not all men,' Mary replied gently, setting the table for high tea.

'All men,' boomed Kitty, her majestic bosom heaving at the thought of all abandoned women clinging to the main spar of their sunken relationships.

'Daniel is not a dog,' Mary said in a determined voice. The cup clattered on to a saucer with a clink of annoyance.

Anna looked up, unfamiliar with the tone of Mary's voice. 'A dog is a dog,' she said, looking uncertainly into Kitty's face. 'My daddy is not a dog. He's my daddy.'

Kitty, sensing that she had frightened the child, swept her up in her arms and began to waltz around the tiny room. 'I'm just one of the ruins that Cromwell knocked about a bit.' Kitty's rich contralto tone throbbed through the cottage.

Kitty stopped mid-waltz, still clutching Anna. Anna leaned from Kitty's arms, reaching for her father's safe embrace. Mary, recognizing the tension in her daughter's face, gently prised the child from her aunt's possessive arms. 'Have a cup of tea, Kitty.'

Kitty snorted. 'A cup of tea is your answer for everything.' Her pale blue eyes swept the room. She heaved a huge volcano of a sigh. 'Oh, very well then,' she said, and flounced to the table. Mary winced as Kitty's huge bottom buffeted one of her little Victorian chairs.

'I'll just wash up, darling, and I'll be with you.' Daniel had a smile hiding in the corner of his mouth. He was used to the little wars waged by women. Daniel was the third child. He adored his diminutive mother who, arms akimbo, could cause his father, a huge bulk of a man, to cower in a corner. His father died when Daniel was twelve. Mary never raised her voice, but her power was such that Daniel could tell she was annoyed by the way the hairs on the nape of her neck stirred. His daughter had inherited the same ability, he observed, as he ruefully washed his hands in the kitchen sink. Most men went to the table with mud clinging to their shoes and grime under their fingernails. Not in Mary's house. Any man who entered her house wiped his feet, washed his hands, and minded his manners. If anyone breached her code of honour, they were politely shown the door.

Daniel sat down at the table with his sister and his family. 'Martha is back from town this evening,' he said.

The three adults sat in silence for the moment, unwilling to reveal to Anna the news that the unruly bands of English mercenaries were getting closer. The ink on the declaration of an Irish Free State was hardly dry and was still judged no more than a politically expedient act by those for whom the bloody battle for self-determination had become an accepted lifestyle. Daniel's elder brother was already dead, buried in the cairn near Ballyglass. 'Darling,' he said gently to Mary. 'I think we'd better pack. I'll not be offered a golden guinea.'

Mary offered a troubled, strained smile. Anna, watching the faces of the adults, saw thunderclouds in their eyes. She also saw drums, like the ones she heard in the village when they all gathered together to dance. It had been a long time since her father had carried her on his high Irish shoulders to the village, her mother trotting on her small feet to keep up with Daniel's long strides. Those days were no more, and Anna missed them. Aunt Kitty always sang 'Danny Boy' and a hush would fall over the audience. Once the hush was a reverent, peaceful pause, but the last time Aunt Kitty sang, Anna felt the village and all its inhabitants tremble with sorrow. Even Aunt Martha danced quietly and listlessly.

Anna began to cry. 'What is it, darlin'?' Mary lifted her and cuddled her.

'We must go, Daniel. Anna is agitated.' Kitty leaned across the table and stared at Anna. 'Does she have the gift, like Martha?' Kitty's voice was incredulous.

'Aye.' Mary sighed. ''Tis not a gift I'd wish on my worst enemy. The future is best left on its own.'

Kitty sat back.

'You'd best go and see if Martha has returned and tell her to pack,' Mary said, standing up. She went to a drawer in the kitchen. 'Here,' she said, holding out a little bundle to her husband. 'My da gave me this before he died.'

Daniel took the little package. He unwrapped it and then smiled. 'It's gold sovereigns, Mary . . .' His eyes held wide.

'Sure,' she smiled. 'It's for us to go to America. You've always wanted to go there. Let's go, Daniel, while we can get out. If we wait, we'll all be massacred.'

Kitty got to her feet. 'I'll go and warn Martha, and Daniel, you'd better go to Mother's house. She'll not go, I'll tell you that.'

'She will.' Daniel's mouth was set in a hard line. 'She will go if I have to drag her. I'll not leave her to be raped and murdered by the bastard English.'

Anna loved her grandmother Biddy. She wrapped her legs firmly about her father's knees. 'Me too,' she said. 'Me too.'

'All right, child.' Daniel picked Anna up.

'Put a coat on her, Daniel, will you? These November nights are cold.'

Outside it was dark by now, and the approaching winter heralded its arrival with a whitening of their breaths and the cracking of hoar-frost under Daniel's feet. As they made their way to the centre of the village, people passed furtively, their heads down. 'The news is not good, Daniel.' Father O'Brian, wrapped in a big black cloak, stood beside the well in the centre of the village. There was a hubbub and a shouting to the east of the village. 'Daniel, get your brothers, and we will go and negotiate with the heathens, even if it's not possible. Even if they'll murder us all it will give the women and children time to hide in the woods.'

Daniel nodded. 'I'll leave Anna with my mother, and then I'll come.' He strode across the square and pushed open the door of his mother's house. In the sitting room Biddy sat knitting with Raymond and Sean. 'I need you both,' Daniel said. 'Father O'Brian needs us to go and negotiate with the English.'

Sean, the youngest of the family, looked up from the fire. 'Will the Holy Father be carrying the sacraments?'

'Aye.' Daniel nodded. 'He will anoint us with Holy oil so that, if we do not come back, our souls are safe.'

Biddy's eyes filled with tears.

'Don't cry, Mother.' Daniel's voice was brisk. 'You know the cave in the woods? It's all set with food and wood. They'll never find us there. Get Donald and Peter Shaw next door, and let's go.' He kissed Anna very gently. 'I'll see you soon, little one.'

Anna nodded. Nothing was going to happen to her father. She knew that.

Daniel put his arms around his frail mother. 'Pack little and go to Mary, and then be away before they get here.' He grinned at his mother. 'Mother, haven't I always been able to talk myself out of anything?'

Biddy nodded, a wry smile on her face. 'That you have,' she admitted.

'Well then. Expect to see me back again in the cave.'

Mary, Biddy, and Anna, together with Martha who had just arrived, watched the men of the village line up behind Father O'Brian. Sean carried the incense. The father then made the sign of the cross on the foreheads of the men now kneeling on the cold ground. The sounds of battle were closer. Martha put a shivering hand on Anna's shoulder. Anna smiled at her aunt. 'It's going to be all right, isn't it, Anna?' Martha was amazed. Under her hand she could feel the psychic energy of the child. 'You're a wise child, aren't you?' she said, remembering the light around Anna when she was born.

Anna just smiled.

The men got to their feet and Father O'Brian returned the body of Christ to the glass case set in a simple wooden cross. He carried with him the sacristy bells. Each note played on the three bells. Anna loved the sound of those bells. Each note in the clear night air was like the striking of golden coins. She heard the noise in the marketplace when the poor trussed hens changed hands, as did eggs, pigs, and vegetables. Now the little handbells pealed loudly for peace. The men, ready to give their lives for their loved ones, moved out of the village. Sean tenderly carried the oil, the priest the cross which he held high. 'Hail Mary, full of grace. The Lord is with thee.'

'Amen,' rumbled the men in answer.

Biddy took Anna's hand. 'Come, child. We must go,' she said.

The women all picked up their bundles and then, in the shadows, they stole away into the night. The only noise in the silence of the night was the sound of a baby crying. 'Whist,' its mother said, 'or the English will take your soul away.'

Three

The forest was silent and so were the women. They walked steadily, cat-like. This moment had been long-rehearsed. Anna, from when she was a baby, knew this secret path into the forest and she approved of it. In the summer they picnicked here. She swam in a pool just below the cave. A stream leaped and tumbled by the mouth of the cave. Anna always thought of the cave as a smiling face, the mouth open and welcoming. Lumbering behind the women came Joanna, she, too, carrying a commodious carpet-bag.

Finally, Kitty set Anna down in the centre of the darkened cave. 'Whew!' Kitty said, straightening up. 'You're a lump of a child, Anna.'

Anna giggled. She shuffled her feet in the soft soil. 'Light,' she said.

Biddy pulled out a box of lethal cooking matches. She put the flame to the waiting fire. 'I never thought I'd see the day we'd need to light this fire to save our lives,' she remarked.

Kitty opened her bundle. 'We have plenty of food and all the warmth we need. We must just pray for the men.'

The women crossed themselves and then set about laying out their blankets for the night. Mary made gruel. She stirred the oats and she sang to herself. 'Mellow the moonlight to shine is beginning.' Her courtship song to Daniel. The marvellous moment when their lips met for the first time. That gentle touch of his face and the smell of new-mown hay just harvested. 'Close by the window young Eileen is spinning. Bent o'er the fire the blind grandmother is sitting . . .'

'I'll not be blind, Mary.' Biddy, determined, parked her little body on a blanket. 'But I'll be all skin and bone before you serve a drop of that gruel. Here.' Biddy pulled a pewter hipflask from her capacious pocket. 'Have a drink, Kitty. Take that mournful look off yer face. They'll all come back.'

'They don't *all* come back,' Martha said quietly. 'Joseph didna' come back.'

Biddy's eyes snapped as fast as a sea-turtle's beak. 'I know,' she said, taking a swig of her homemade potheen. 'He lies in a far country under grey skies.' She sighed, her arm around Anna. 'But he died in a good cause and his soul is in heaven. But there's not a day I don't miss him, or a time I don't think of him. He was a beautiful boy, and they say only the good die young, and he was good, he was.'

Anna was lying sleepily by her grandmother. 'Is he an angel?' she asked, thinking of the angels painted on the church walls.

'Yes, he is that,' Biddy agreed.

Mary handed Biddy an enamel mug with two wooden spoons. 'You feed the child, Biddy.' She tried to distract the old lady from her memories. 'They'll not be long,' she said as she handed out plates to the other women.

They sat in a circle around the fire. Not much was said. Against the walls of the cave lay piles of potatoes and onions. From a stalactite a string of pork sausages sent shadows on to the walls.

Anna, her stomach full of warm porridge, lay back beside her grandmother. Everything was not all right. She could feel that. But it soon would be. She knew that.

Four

§

Daniel did not return to the cave for days. The women were desperate for news of him and his brothers.

'Surely they'll no' kill a priest?' Kitty looked across the fire at Biddy.

'They'll do anything they like.'

Mary's mouth tightened. Through all the agony of waiting, she showed no sign of strain. Her one thought was that little Anna should not be afraid. The child asked after her father, her soft dimpled arms around her mother's neck.

'He will come back,' the child said.

And Mary wondered at the blaze in the child's eyes. 'How can she be so certain?'

Kitty shook her head. Martha smiled a warm, comforting smile. 'The child is right. Here, let us go down to the pool and gaze in the water and I'll see what I can see.'

The women hurried down the path, Biddy hobbling behind, holding Anna's hand. The water in the pool was lying silken under an early morning sky. The moon extinguished herself that morning in disgust at the carnage taking place below her skirts in Ireland. Really, she thought, the English are a savage crowd. She far preferred to sail serenely over the Far East, but even there the English and their American offspring were destroying those countries that she so loved. She withdrew her skirts with a sharp snap of disapproval and sailed over the horizon on her way to comfort the English convicts marooned in Australia. Her much gentler sister, the sun, put out a gentle finger of light towards the waiting women. Slowly, as her emblazoned head rose over the mountains, the water shifted and moved.

The light illuminated small frogs in their frozen chambers, waiting for the spring to come. It sparked on little patches of ice. Anna laughed as she caught sight of slight explosions of purples, greens and blues as the refracting crystals took their full fill of sunshine. Martha stood silently at the edge of the pond. Mary and Biddy waited. Kitty was bored.

'All of ye put so much store in all this hocus-pocus. Next ye'll be digging up those toads and frying bats.'

Martha looked up at her truculent sister. 'I'll do no such thing,' she said firmly. 'I'm a white witch and I'll kill no living thing.'

Anna tugged at Martha's arm. 'Look,' she said, pointing at the middle of the pond. 'Daddy.' She was laughing and clapping her hands. 'Daddy's coming.'

Martha gazed at the picture that slowly began to form around Daniel's face, at least unharmed but sombre with suffering. All around him there were ricks, and behind him crouched another figure. Martha couldn't tell who it was. The face was covered with a white bandage and stained with blood. Blood, a rust-brown colour.

'An old wound,' Martha whispered. Daniel was hiding and frightened, but safe. Martha made a motion with her hand. 'Where are the boys?' she quietly asked the water.

Daniel's face disappeared, and in its place she could see Raymond and Sean walking with Donald and Peter. They were on a country track, making their way to a farmhouse. Martha smiled for the first time.

'The boys are unharmed. They are going to the Williams' farm where they'll be hidden.' She shook her head. 'Thank the Lord they're all safe now. It's just a matter of waiting for Danny.'

'And Father O'Brian.' Biddy was worried. Hopefully

the man behind Daniel was Father O'Brian. 'I know Daniel will take care of the man of the cloth.'

'He is hurt though,' Martha said.

Biddy slipped her arm around Mary's waist. 'Let's get the bandages out. I'll collect the moss from the banks and heal the wound.'

Mary nodded, her face radiant. 'I have my digitalis for the heart with me, and I have brought a bottle of verlain for the pain. Then we can set up a variable apothecary when we get to America.'

Her raised voice caught the echoes of the tops of the hills. 'When we get to America,' they sighed. 'America, America, America.'

Mary danced up the hill on the way back to the cave, carrying Anna. 'We'll have meat and potatoes,' she announced to the joyful little crowd.

'I'll make dumplings,' Biddy declared.

'And I'll sing,' Kitty offered.

'It would be nice if you offered to wash the dishes, such as they are,' Biddy said sharply.

'But Mother, I'll ruin my hands, and then who's a rich man in America to marry me?' Kitty spread out her long fingernails. 'I'll have to wear my hands in gloves tonight,' she mourned. 'I have some chicken fat with me.'

Martha laughed. 'Kitty, for sure you'll be the belle of New York.'

'I will,' Kitty replied complacently. 'Sure I will, and if any bitch thinks she's going to outshine me, she's got another think coming. Here, child, let me just show you the dress I'm bringing with me.'

Anna dropped to her knees by Kitty's bundle. It was the largest of them all.

'Did ye pack any food, Kitty?' Martha asked. 'Or matches, or plates . . . ?'

'No, Martha.' Kitty's large, noble brow wrinkled. 'Not at all. Why should I? I have yours, don't I?'

'You're hopeless,' Martha said in mock disgust.

'I know.' Kitty lifted her head and gazed at Anna. 'Look, darling,' she said, raising her bare arms in the now warm sunlight. 'I'm all right until the flesh under me arms looks like tripe. If I'm not tucked up with a rich man by then, I'll go into a convent.'

Anna was fingering the dresses on the ground. She loved the feeling of the silks and satins between her fingers.

Kitty sat down beside the child. 'There's talk of films being made in America. I'd love to be in films.'

Mary was busy with pots on the fire. Biddy was moulding lumps of grey dough on a flat rock. Martha sat with her arms around her knees. Beside her was a small pile of moss and a roll of white sheeting. 'You know,' she said, stretching her knees. 'Even if we are fugitives, this might be the happiest we are going to be for a long while.'

A passing rook agreed loudly and settled busily into his perch of bare sticks. 'People-people-people!' he warned.

Anna dozed by her aunt's side.

Five

Anna sat up. Where was she? For a moment she panicked. And then she consulted this restless movement in her chest. What was it? The sound of drumming.

Around her the women were lying huddled on the ground. They had waited up late by the dying fire. Anna wanted to go back to sleep. She slipped away from her mother's side and stood up. Her father was coming. She could feel it. That was what the drumming was. The links made of silken emotional cords that grew between herself and her parents were taut, pulled tight by the chaos of the events. Anna could see Kitty's cord lying snipped by her side, oozing out of her belly. Kitty severed her cord years ago when she ran away to catch men. Martha's cord was still intact and twined very firmly to her brother Daniel: there was another she had grown to bind Mary to her. Anna sent a message down Martha's cord. 'Don't wake Ma. She's tired. You wake up and we'll go into the forest together.'

When Anna used her cord to communicate, she was talking from her old soul, a communicant so ancient that it resided only as a crystal in the back of the iris of her right eye. The gene that transferred the secret of the DNA molecule. The sound that was there before she was. The great round rolling sound spoken by the Creator of the Universe. Not an old man with a beard, but the slice of space between the two-fingered Buddha. The moment before conception when the tailed male seeks his own female soul and, once buried, there belongs for ever.

Martha stirred. Her cord pulsed with life. Lights flashed along it as she stretched. Rays of electricity shot from her hands and feet. Anna closed down her third eye. It was too distracting. Besides, she was a three-and-a-half-year-old child in this life, and she must meet her father and the man who was so hurt. 'Come along, Anna.' Martha took her by the hand. 'Thank you for waking me up.'

The earth beneath them was shimmering in the early morning light. 'Why does the earth shake so?' Anna stood looking down at her feet.

'Oh, that's the energy of people waking up and making love, darling.'

Anna smiled at Martha. 'It feels wonderful.'

Martha laughed. 'It was wonderful,' she said. ''Tis a holy communion, and when you're old enough you'll understand it, though I know you understand more than most.'

They walked to the edge of the clearing and then up the path. Far away Anna could hear things cracking. It was not the sound of a large deer. They knew how to brush the twigs noiselessly. Nor was it the sound of a big bird. They knew how to glide without sound through the branches. She knew it was the sound of a labouring human being carrying an unfamiliar burden. It was her father.

They broke into a run. White with strain, Daniel staggered up the path. He had lost much weight and his face was stubbled. Across his back was slung the long still figure of the priest. A white, ragged, blood-soaked bandage over his face. 'Don't let the child see,' he gasped as he fell to the ground. 'Don't look, Anna. Don't look.'

Anna leaned down and touched the bandaged face. 'No nose,' she said, looking at her exhausted father. Anna felt waves and waves of sorrow wash over her. She felt the awful moment when the English sword sliced the nose clean through, as she did the time an ear was sliced from a man's head two thousand years ago. He was able to touch the ear and make it heal. Anna knew she would never achieve that perfection, yet she sorrowed for the priest and she heard his shriek of pain and then the sting of prayers from his mouth to his God's waiting ear. 'I bear this pain for the burden Your Son bore for me.' God heard the prayer, and the touch of the little girl's hand on the stricken man's face erased the pain. But the nose was gone for ever.

The priest opened his eyes wide with surprise. 'Who touched me?' he said.

'Anna,' Martha said simply. 'She has the healing power.'

Anna watched the colour come back into her father's

face. He took his daughter's little hand and looked at the left palm. 'See?' he said, sitting up, his head bent studiously. 'She has the line.'

The priest cautiously lifted himself from the ground. He clung to Martha. He crossed himself. 'So she has,' he said. 'So she has.'

Anna looked down at her hand. Indeed, a clear line did stretch from the wrist straight up the hand to her fingers.

'Destiny,' the priest said.

Anna's strange eyes burned into him. 'I'm hungry,' she said.

Mary took Father O'Brian to the back of the cave. Though the pain had been lifted, his face was in bad shape. 'Fortunately,' Mary muttered to Kitty, who was holding the good Father's head, 'the nose must have been removed by a clean blade-cut.' Though infected, the septum was neatly sheared into two round holes.

'Aargh!' Kitty was appalled. 'I didn't think I'd be holding a mutilated priest's head,' she moaned.

'Quiet, Kitty.' Mary dipped the moss into some water and wiped away the accumulation of pus. 'I'll take some moss along for the journey,' she said, patting the Father's face dry. 'There, Father, you'll do. You won't be a pretty sight, but you'll live.'

Father O'Brian attempted a smile. 'I never was a pretty face, Mary. I was always for the Church. My mother said no woman would ever have me, with my long face and straw in my hair. But nearly to die concentrates a man's mind wonderfully. I'll be a happy man if I can see the New Country and celebrate Mass in Boston. I have family there.'

'Don't we all?' Kitty said. 'All those who had the sense to get out years ago. I should have gone. They're short of women out there in the West. Find me a rich land baron.'

Mary looked at Kitty's face. Always the dreamer, she thought. She was impatient to get to her husband's side. She could see him back by the fire. He was lying on his side, his head on his hand, talking to Anna. Those two, she thought. What do they say, so intent they are together? 'You take care of the Father for me, Kitty. I'll go and see to Daniel.' She lifted her long grey woollen skirt and moved over to the fireplace.

Biddy was roasting her homemade pork sausages on the embers. She stroked the sausages with twigs of fresh thyme. Bubbles of scented oil smoked invitingly. Charred black potatoes awaited the cooking of the sausages. Daniel watched the fire and the food hungrily. Anna held his free hand in hers. 'I saw you,' she said, 'in Martha's water picture. Bad bad men.'

Daniel nodded. 'Yes,' he said and then he smiled. 'But they're gone now. We are safe to leave in a few days. After a while we will get a boat, Anna, and go on the water, and then we will be safe.'

'Sweet Jesus!' Father O'Brian called from the back of the cave. 'I sure hope so!'

Biddy forked the sausages with a bent piece of oak and lifted them on to pewter plates. Daniel laughed. 'You'll not leave your pewter behind, Mother,' he said.

'No,' said Biddy. 'Neither will I leave behind my best linen. There'll be none of your new-fangled ideas in my house, young man.'

Daniel shook his head, sat up, and then encircled Mary's waist with his arm. Mary curled up beside her husband, and smiled at Anna. 'He's back,' she said contentedly.

'He's back all right.' Martha awoke from her nap. 'He's back and he's hungry.'

'Kitty,' Biddy called. 'Take the Father his plate.'

Kitty looked down at the priest's noseless face. 'He's

31

sleeping, Mother,' she said, 'poor man. What a thing to happen!'

'I have a scarf for him in my bundle,' Biddy answered, 'to cover his face.' She put the priest's plate by the fire. 'You, Daniel, say Grace.'

Daniel bowed his head and prayed for the food, for their rescue, and the journey ahead.

The pigeons which circled the cave, their wings sounding like the clap of many hands, were startled at the fervent 'amens' that closed Daniel's earnest prayer.

Six

It was a good long time before Anna smelled the early morning aroma of sausages cooking on an open hearth. Mostly she was carried, but often she trotted behind the tall figure of her father. Daniel carried as much of the luggage as he could bear on his back. Kitty, still complaining, with Martha helped the priest to walk. Slowly Father O'Brian's health returned. He came to appreciate Kitty and Martha in a way that he never had before. To him, brought up in a strict Catholic self-denial of things sexual, both women had been a source of torment for him. The sight of Kitty's fleshy underarms in the hot Mayo summer days caused him to wedge his fingernails into the palms of his hands so fiercely they drew blood. The villagers whispered among themselves that the Holy Father manifested the stigmata of the Lord when they saw the bleeding patches on his hands. Father O'Brian, to his eternal shame, failed in his confession to the local bishop to mention that the stigmata on his hands were nothing other than the sins of the flesh. Martha, for all those years, exercised a strange fascination for him. She had a broken-lipped smile that made her face at once both virginal and sensual. Father O'Brian, in the secret of his sacristy when removing his alb and his robes of office, wished secretly that he might run a finger across Martha's full lips and touch the moment when the mouth broke away from the radiant smile of innocence and dissolved into untold depths of promised passion. The flower that beckoned, he imagined, between her smooth strong thighs was like a delicate purple orchid, opening and closing, its tongue thrust out, full of pollen-flecked promise.

Now, stumbling between the two women, much of the mystery was gone. No longer did he yearn far off for their company. Kitty he knew as an impractical dream. Her strong body was ready to heave him up and help him down the road. Martha, he discovered, seemed almost emotionally stunted. She still smiled like a divine whore, but her actions were totally practical. Apart from the child who had inherited her aunt's broken smile, Martha seemed close to no one. In the long, forced marches from one village to another, the family talk consisted of nostalgic tales of what had been left behind. Before the little group of people lay the bleeding, betrayed soil of their beloved country. The English had swept all before them. They had looted, murdered, raped, and burnt not only the countryside and the villages but men, women, and children.

They passed cottages burnt to the ground. Anna watched the bodies lying rotting. She saw children of her own age sprawled in the unnatural sleep of the dead. Most of all she was aware of the silence. Only the crunch of the feet of her family and Father O'Brian's slow, solemn step. The silence. No sound. 'Where are the chickens?' she asked her father.

'The English took them, Anna. They took every living thing for their cooking pots.'

Now Mary's bundle of food was running short. They relied on Daniel to find the odd turnip in an abandoned field. A potato or two, and one heaven-sent day, a rabbit. Desperate for food for the family, Daniel had chased the big buck rabbit across the field. The rabbit, aware of the pursuit and the big man who could outsmart him, screamed with terror. Anna turned and saw the moment Daniel's finger squeezed the life from the animal. Its bulged eyes pleaded to Anna for its life, its mouth drawn back over its teeth. Anna buried her face in her hands and cried. She cried for all she had seen far too early in life.

That night, while the adults lowered their faces into their bowls of rabbit stew, Anna ate gruel. She knew that around her lay the unburied bodies of children frozen on the ground. She could not eat the rabbit.

'Not long now and we will reach the Liffey, the river that runs into Dublin. If we follow along the banks, we can keep out of the way of any English mercenaries.' Daniel sounded pleased. The meat had given him strength, and so far the journey had been uneventful.

They slept that night in the open, wrapped in old flour-sacks, Anna close to her mother's warm body.

A week passed by before Daniel saw the outskirts of Dublin city. Away across the meadows he could see the bells of Dublin Cathedral. By now they passed other groups of dishevelled travellers like themselves. Greetings rang out. 'Where are you from?' 'From Tipperary.' 'From Wexford.' 'From Killarney.'

''Tis as if the whole of Ireland is on the move,' Mary remarked.

'There's nothing here to stay for,' a young man said as he strode past, his bundle tied to the end of a long stick resting on his shoulder.

Anna was enchanted by him. 'I want a stick and a bundle like that,' she said.

Laughing, Daniel obliged. He was pleased to see the smile come back into Anna's face. He was grieved that he was unable to protect his young daughter from witnessing the dreadful sights they saw on their long journey. So far the English had not seen fit to sack the city of Dublin. Sure, there were rumours floating like black clouds through the assemblies of people on their way in and out of the city. Those leaving it for the country were, for the most part, those who had made their peace with the English and now worked for them. The dreaded rent-collectors, turncoats, and traitors. But even they had their uses. Often taken by Anna's sweet smile, they would part with a sweetmeat or a loaf of bread for the child. Mary received all donations gracefully. She had a few pence left and the one golden guinea, their passport to America.

They all felt lost, once in the heart of the city. The great roar of people rushing to and fro. Carts and wagons careering about. People yelling and screaming. The streets teeming. It reminded Daniel of a medieval scene out of one of his school history books. Decades of turmoil, neglect and exploitation had maintained a mantle of poverty over the city, seemingly barring it from the twentieth century and the social advances it had brought. His country had been handicapped by foreign domination and, despite recent pacts, would remain lame for many years to come. The chaotic scene before him filled him with a hopeless misery. His heart would always be here, but he knew his future was elsewhere. He put his arms about Mary and Anna. Martha, Kitty, and Father O'Brian stood in a tight little knot. 'What do we do now, Daniel?' Biddy hung off the back of his coat.

35

'I'm not sure,' Daniel said. 'This is the Dublin Post Office. Look. It says so.'

'We're not here to post a letter, Daniel.' Kitty's voice was tart. 'I thought you knew where we were going.'

'Aye,' Daniel said, gazing about him, his eyes wide with wonder. An elegant coach flashed by. Six black horses with manes threaded with scarlet ribbons. The door of the carriage was adorned with a rampant lion, its claws ready for war, facing a white unicorn, its horn glinting gold in the sunlight. Anna gazed at the white, terrified face of the woman inside. She sat next to an impassive black-eyed man, his arms crossed, his tall brow halved by a thick fur hat. The eyes of the woman implored Anna for help. For the second time Anna felt helpless. First the rabbit, and now this nameless woman. Anna shook Mary's skirt. 'Look,' she said, pointing at the carriage. But it was gone in a flurry of small stones that fell at Anna's feet. 'Poor lady,' she said to her mother. 'Sad lady.'

As they stood bewildered, Father O'Brian hailed a passing fellow priest. 'We are up from County Mayo!' he yelled, waving a long arm. 'Tell me, sir, where may I find lodgings for myself and my family?'

The priest, seeing another man of the cloth, leaped as nimbly as his fat little dangling form allowed, in and out of the traffic, and arrived quite breathless in front of Father O'Brian.

They shook hands. 'You're from Mayo then,' the newcomer said. 'Welcome to Dublin.' He vigorously shook hands with everyone. 'What brings ye here?'

'We're off to America,' Daniel replied.

The priest looked startled. 'Not going to risk your lives in those old rusty boats, are you?' he said.

Father O'Brian put a restraining hand on his new-found friend's arm. 'We must go,' he said urgently. 'Do you know what's been happening in the countryside?'

The priest frowned. 'Well, I've heard tell that most of the stories are greatly exaggerated. The bishop says that the troubles are mostly with the tenants in the big estates refusing to pay their rent. The English have been sent in to restore law and order.'

''Tis not like that at all.' Father O'Brian's voice was low and angry. 'It suits the Dublin government to tell these lies, and they *are* all lies. The English landowners refuse to accept they no longer totally control us and our land and are driving the tenants from their properties. And any reluctance is met the same way they've always confronted it – with the wanton violence of an arrogant, domineering race.'

The young priest stood uncertainly before them. Upon his face was confusion. His bishop had told this obedient servant one thing, but faced with the vehemence of the older priest, whose white face was wrapped in a black scarf, and this little motley crew of people stranded in a strange city, he asked, 'Have you any evidence for what you say?'

Father O'Brian pulled back the scarf. 'The English took my nose,' he said.

The young priest went white. The two holes, ringed with yet unhealed scars, gazed back at him. 'I see,' the young man gasped. 'Come. I'll take you to the bishop. He should hear these things.'

The young man turned and led the group through the narrow streets. Daniel carried Anna on his shoulders. From her vantage point, Anna could see down on the top of the milling crowd. Now she felt safe. This man was sent to help them. She knew that. Above her, gulls cried their full-throated cry. 'Turn of the tide! Turn of the tide!' they yelled at each other. 'Fishing boats landing at the jetty!' 'Soon, soon!' they encouraged each other. Anna laughed. She loved their beady black eyes and their gossipy ways.

'Come.' The young priest hurried the group around the back of a big church. 'Here,' he said. 'Before I go and find my bishop, I'll get cook to give you a decent meal, and he'll organize some hot water. I've no doubt you could do with both.' Mary nodded and the others burst into a chorus of consent. 'By the way,' he said, as he ushered Mary first into an old arched door, 'my name is Father Benedict.'

They filed past him as he held a big door open for them. Daniel, nervous but hopeful, cast his eyes around the room ahead of them. Their feet clattered on tile floors leading to a long room with a welcoming fire glowing at one end. 'Brother Ionedes, I have brought you travellers for some food and some hot water.'

'You are always bringing me travellers, Father Benedict,' grumbled a huge fellow. He wiped his hands on his big white apron. 'What is it this time, lad? Last time 'twas a bunch of tinkers, and we all had lice for a week.'

'They're not tinkers, Brother. They have come from County Mayo. They say the English have run them off their land.'

By now Father O'Brian was spearheading the group and gazing upward at the man who was evidently in charge of the kitchen. Behind his vast form various becowled monks could be seen scurrying about.

'I'm sure the bishop can't know of these conditions, Brother Ionedes.'

'Father Benedict,' the cook said softly, 'of course the good bishop knows all about the atrocities. I'm afraid you're still a bit wet behind the ears, my son. Everyone knows that the English are still sacking Ireland.' He looked over Father O'Brian's shoulder. 'Come along,' he said, examining the pale, exhausted faces. 'Bring the child to the table and eat. I'll see that beds are prepared for you. Where are you going?'

'To America,' Anna said. 'We're going on a boat to a new place. We will have another house for Mummy and Daddy and Grandma.' She skipped beside the great giant and she said, pulling him to a stop, 'Aunt Kitty is going to sing and dance until she finds a very rich man. And then she'll keep us all.'

Brother Ionedes bellowed with laughter. 'Sure, your Aunt Kitty must be a fine singer. And how about you?' he said, looking at Martha.

'Oh, I'll just see that Anna is kept safe,' she said, smiling.

They passed through the kitchen into a long, dark-panelled room. A shiny refectory table took up most of the space. Chairs lined the table and Father Benedict motioned for them to sit. Brother Ionedes disappeared. They could hear him clapping his hands and shouting orders. Feet clattered and a procession of young monks carried in bowls of soup and porridge, stews, platters of meat and vegetables, until Daniel waved his hands at them. He was the last to stop eating. 'If I eat this apple pie, I'll bust,' he said to Mary.

'Don't then,' she said.

Brother Ionedes reappeared like an Arabian genie. 'Your beds await you,' he said. 'The women go to the dormitory on the left side of the abbey, and the men follow me.'

Daniel looked perturbed, but Mary pushed him away after a kiss. 'We'll be fine,' she said. She picked Anna up.

Anna lay her weary face on her mother's neck. The last she remembered was being washed in warm water and then lain in a clean robe in a soft bed. She clung to her mother and drifted into a deep, oblivious sleep.

Seven

Anna had never seen a real live bishop before. Her entire knowledge of her Catholic faith was inculcated by Father O'Brian. 'Who made you, Anna?' he asked her as soon as he realized that she was capable of speech.

'God made me, Father,' Anna lisped back. They were almost her first words.

'Why did God make you?' Father O'Brian asked when she was four.

Pausing to reflect that adults asked silly questions, she said, 'To know Him, to love Him, and to serve Him, of course, Father.' From then on, Anna took off like a starling when she saw the thin figure with the flapping, snapping cloak come sailing towards her.

Now she could see that Father O'Brian was sweating with unease. The small group had been called for an audience with the great man. 'You kiss his ring so.' Father O'Brian had instructed the women and Anna on the niceties of a formal curtsey.

'I will not so,' Anna said fiercely.

'You must,' Mary said, concerned. 'Bishop Staleybrass is the representative of God Himself, Anna. You must kiss his ring.'

'No,' Anna said, and she meant it.

Mary sighed and shook her head. 'I don't know, Danny, where she gets her stubbornness from. It must be your Kearney blood.'

Daniel crossed himself. 'I hope not,' he said. 'But who knows?'

Now they stood, uneasily aware of their motley

clothing and humble origins. Martha, who minded the most, gazed at the ornately tiled floor.

Sitting on a gold throne, the bishop gazed at the little scene before him. At least they didn't smell, he thought, stifling a yawn. He had just eaten stuffed lamprey for lunch with a big elkhorn cup of malmsey sent from his estate in Devon. 'Definitely a surfeit,' he whispered to his page who also shared his bed. 'We shall have fun tonight, dear boy.'

Anna watched his fat stubby hands, bejewelled and beringed, stray to his fat little mouth. And his small piggy eyes blinked at her. He has white eyelashes, Anna observed, and a big black hole around his belly. He is a bad man. She wanted very much to warn her mother and father.

'What can I do for you?' The bishop leaned forward.

Father O'Brian cleared his throat. 'We want to tell you about the British, Holy Father.'

'Come closer. You may kiss my ring and I will bless you. Where are you going?'

'To America,' Daniel said firmly. 'We are going to make a new life for ourselves. We've nothing to go back to,' he said. A note of bitterness crept into his voice.

Father O'Brian bent over the bishop's hand and Anna watched him tenderly kiss the large red ruby that was embedded in a roll of fat. The bishop made a vague effort at the sign of the cross. His wrist flapped feebly. 'Next,' he said.

Kitty ran up to the throne and outdid herself as she sank to the ground, her head nearly touching the stone floor.

Over the top, as usual. Martha rolled her eyes at Anna.

My God, these Irish louts. The bishop was bored. His new page had a delightfully tight little sphincter and it needed to be explored. Pink, juicy, fruity flesh after lamprey . . . What could be better?

One by one they took their turns. Anna watched and felt a rage welling in her throat. 'Now, about the British – ' Father O'Brian began.

'Oh, the damned British,' the bishop interrupted. 'I know all about it, dear boy. A little bit of looting, a little rape here and there. Nothing really to worry about.'

'But . . .' Father O'Brian was speechless. 'Look at my face,' he stuttered. He pulled back the scarf and stood straight and still.

'Put it away. Put it away! That is not a pretty sight, Father . . . what did you say your name was?' With a shuffling big toe, the bishop was searching for a button under the carpet to summon Father Benedict to rid him of these louts. A sight like that quite discountenanced his newly forming erection and, goodness knows, at his age he needed all the stimulus he could get. 'An accident, Father. Must have been an accident.'

Father O'Brian stood stunned, too shocked to speak.

'Come, little girl.' The bishop waved his hand at Anna. 'You may kiss my ring.' What a stunner, he remarked to himself. Pity I'm not into girls. Well, at least not yet. The child has amazing eyes.

Anna glared at him. 'No,' she said. 'Don't like you. You're a bad man.' This last remark was made at the top of her voice.

'Well, really!' The bishop stood up. 'I think you should take that little minx of yours back home and thrash the living daylights out of her. How dare you speak like that to me?' The bishop felt his heart beginning to beat faster and then faster. He could hear a roaring in his ears and then blood rising up to mist his eyes. The last thing he saw before he hit the ground was Anna's face, and she was beaming. Why, the little bitch . . . *Bitch rhymes with witch*, he tried to scream, but it was too late. He lay stretched out on the carpet.

His page knelt over him. Sod it, the page thought. I'll have to go back to work. The tears welling in his eyes were not for his master but for himself.

Father Benedict ran into the room breathless. 'I'm sorry, My Lord,' he began, and then he saw the prostrate figure. He crossed himself and then he cast a wild glance at the little group of people he had so recently left for an audience. 'What happened?' he said, his eyes raking the ashen faces.

'I didn't like him,' Anna said. She was smiling. 'Bad man.'

'You'd better go,' Father Benedict said. 'Go quickly. Here . . .' He drew out a handful of coins. 'The ship sails on the full tide in two hours' time. If you hurry, you'll just catch her. Tell the captain I sent you. Here . . .' He pulled a ring off his little finger. He handed it to Anna. 'Show this to the captain. He knows the ring.'

Anna held the ring in her hand and gazed down at it. In the clear blue stone she could see the sea and waves heaving, a ship straining, and then something tall with a light at the top.

'An aquamarine,' Kitty said, admiring the ring.

Father Benedict was making shooing gestures with his hands. 'Go. Go,' he implored.

Slowly they trickled out of the room. The bishop lay motionless. A feeble shaft of sunlight pinned him to the ground. He was dead, the page realized. Very dead. The only sound in the room was the sound of the boy's bereft sobbing.

Eight

Anna leaned over the side of the ship. She watched as the bulging sides of the boat sank into the waves. Within an hour the wind had changed and huge rollers were falling down on to the prow as the boat tried to make headway in the storm. Beside her Daniel stood immobile. Under the deck the rest of the family and Father O'Brian lay racked with nausea. Daniel could not bear the stench of the vomit and unwashed bodies that lay in rows along the floor. He took Anna by the hand and they chose this little oasis, a small deck with a ladder ascending to first class. 'One day, my girl, you and I will be up there. No steerage class for us.'

Anna looked at her father. She was surprised at the vehemence in his voice. Talk on the ship had been predictably concentrated on the disarray the refugees had left behind. In the grubby communal rooms below deck, filled with cheap tobacco smoke and reeking with whisky, news of unrest throughout the country slowly, like an intricate jigsaw puzzle, had painted him a complete picture of national madness. War had turned civil. Irishman against Irishman, each with his own solution to an ancient dilemma. Daniel had listened to the impassioned debates, the fiery rhetoric, and had contributed tears of desperation. Why, he had thought, was his country still at war with itself at a time when the world had just earned peace after four bitter, sanguineous years? America had saved the world, and now it would save him and his family. But he felt strangely bitter that it should be so.

Anna climbed a little way up the ladder, the metal

rung ringing in sympathy with the iron cleats of her sturdy boots.

Away down the other end of the deck she saw a girl about her own age standing next to a very tall woman. The woman wore a thick black bombazine coat, her hands wrapped in a blue velvet handwarmer. The little girl had shoulder-length dark hair. Her skin looked translucent. She was laughing wildly at the wind. Her coat was a fur. Anna watched and wished she could be wrapped in fur. How wonderful not to feel the icy grip of the wind or the bony fingers of the frost pinching at tender flesh! The boat reared up on end and the girl and the woman half-fell, half-slid down the deck, the girl shrieking with laughter. Anna held on to the railings tightly and the girl careened down the stairs, knocking Anna off her step and breaking her hold on the railings. 'Whoa there!' Daniel shouted.

He picked up both girls off the deck. 'You saved my life,' the strange girl said rather dramatically. 'What's your name?'

'Anna.' Anna decided she must be older than she looked. 'How old are you?' she asked.

'I'm nine. My name is Mary Rose Buchanan and I'm not afraid of anything.'

'I wish I was nine,' Anna said, inspecting herself. She seemed to be all in one piece.

'Mary Rose? Mary Rose?' The tall lady's face was framed by the stairwell. 'What are you doing down there? Come here at once. You can't talk to those shanty Irish down there. You don't know what you'll catch.'

'Oh shut up, Prinny. Don't be so boring. I'll come up when I feel like it.'

Anna was aghast. 'Do you always talk to her like that?' she demanded.

Daniel said nothing.

'Yes.' Mary Rose stood balancing with the leap-frogging boat under her. 'She's just my nanny, and a very boring one at that. The last one was sacked for the gin, but at least she was fun. This one has no vices.'

'Vices?' Anna asked.

'Yes. You know, men friends, drink, cigarettes, all those fun things.'

Anna felt she was being educated by the minute.

'I think we'd better get back to the others,' Daniel said firmly. 'Say goodbye, Anna.' He took her hand.

Anna looked over her shoulder at her new-found friend.

'I'll see you here tomorrow,' Mary Rose mouthed behind Daniel's back. Anna nodded.

'Mary Rose!' The nanny's voice floated across the deck.

'Mary Rose, Mary Rose!' mocked the gulls, riding the currents.

Mary Rose was in Anna's thoughts that night as she curled up to sleep, the sleep of the very young and very contented. Mary Rose looked like a beautiful flower surrounded by soft leaves. And she is my friend, she thought.

By the next afternoon, Kitty was well enough to be cajoled on deck. Anna knew that Aunt Kitty had a soft spot for little girls, and an even softer spot for pretty furs. 'Let's go to my secret place,' Anna said, pulling her aunt along quickly.

Anna felt a little guilty. She was sneaking off to see Mary Rose and she knew full well her father didn't approve of her friend. Not that Daniel said anything, but something in him drew back when Mary Rose spoke harshly to her nanny. The usual warm light that surrounded him gave a flicker of dissent. Even when he recounted the story to Mary, Anna could see red flashes

46

in his aura. Still, I'll just talk to her. That can't do any harm, Anna reasoned.

Kitty stood by the ladder, the scene of yesterday's drama, and looked out to sea. 'One fine day,' she sang, the melody swelling up over the water. Quite oblivious to the rest of the world, Kitty sang her heart out. Indeed, the thrill of her voice caused the people going about their daily business on the boat to stop and listen. Kitty sang the Puccini aria with all the years of her sorrow and disappointment in men, causing her voice to etch the feelings deep upon the souls of the listeners. They, too, could hear in her music their own trials and suffering. Their eyes filled with tears. She sang of the triumph when the two lovers meet and then the terrible moments of her dying. Anna was always transfixed by her aunt's voice. To her it was the most glorious sound in the whole world. When the voice stopped, normality returned, but for a while the world without Aunt Kitty's voice was dull and flat.

Anna drew a deep breath and smiled at her aunt.

'That was wonderful.' It was Mary Rose. 'You have a really excellent voice, whoever you are.' Mary Rose's cool, imperious little figure stood on the middle rung of the ladder.

'I am Anna's Aunt Kitty.' Kitty shook the child's hand. 'And you must be Mary Rose. My brother Daniel told us all about you yesterday.' Kitty liked Mary Rose, Anna could tell. Kitty was exuding warm blue feelings.

'Where's your nanny?' Anna asked.

'Oh, I've given her the slip. She'll be running about looking for me.'

A voice floated down through the hatch. 'I say, are you the lady who was singing just now?'

Kitty looked up. A fresh-faced, very embarrassed young man looked down at her. 'Yes,' Kitty said simply. 'I was singing.'

'Well, I'm the purser,' he said, and he slid elegantly down the ladder. He bowed from the waist and removed his gold-braided hat. 'The captain sends his compliments and asks that you might be willing to have a cup of tea with him.' He glanced at the two girls. 'You can bring them with you as chaperons. Miss Mary Rose will be a welcome find for her nanny.' He tried not to grin. Here was Mary Rose Buchanan, the richest girl in Ireland, hob-nobbing with the poorest little tyke he'd ever seen. Mind you, he'd be hard-pressed to guess who would be the more beautiful when they were full-grown. Mary Rose, with her dark smouldering ways and her cold but intense eyes, or this little girl, so old in her ways but a fair beauty, with Irish blue eyes. 'Come then,' he said.

Kitty blushed. She wished she'd had time to change, or at least apply some rouge.

'You look lovely, Aunt Kitty,' Anna said, and sent her aunt a surge of approval. Kitty felt herself glow. Really, Anna was such an odd child. It was almost as if she could read people's minds.

Kitty followed the purser up the stairs. Mary Rose took Anna's hand. 'Maybe the captain will ask your Aunt Kitty to sing in the ballroom tonight. That would be wonderful. I'll ask my mother if you can come.'

Anna looked at Mary Rose who walked behind Aunt Kitty and the purser as though she owned the boat. Anna felt very dull and very dowdy beside her. 'I don't have your sort of clothes, Mary Rose.'

'Oh, never mind. You can borrow some of mine. I've got far more than I need. Father is always bringing me back frocks, mostly because he feels guilty.'

'Why does he feel guilty?' Anna asked.

'Because he chases other women and he knows I know.'

'Does your mother know?'

Mary Rose nodded. 'Yes, she does. But she loves

him very much, so I suppose she just puts up with it.'

Anna trotted after her aunt and was grateful that, though they had no money and no fine linen, her father adored her mother and Mary never looked at another man. What an odd world Mary Rose inhabited!

Nine

Kitty returned to the stinking dormitory with good news. Her fleshy, handsome face was flushed. Anna, after reluctantly saying goodbye to Mary Rose, skipped beside her aunt. Anna was so happy she felt like a tennis ball that regularly bounced poc-a-poc on the deck above her head. 'I am going to sing in the first class ballroom tonight,' Kitty said. 'And even better than that, the captain is giving us a big cabin of our own. It's the ship's old hospital bay at the end of the boat, so we will have our own bathroom and a proper bed each. Imagine!'

For a moment there was a stunned silence. And then Biddy and Mary burst into tears. 'Thank you, Lord!' Biddy said loudly.

'Mind your fucking mouth, woman.' A man turned on his back, his breath reeking with whisky. 'What's God got to do with this God-forsaken tub?'

Mary looked at the man and said quietly, 'Let's just pack our things. Here, Anna. You help me.'

Kitty was wildly throwing her belongings into her bundle. Father O'Brian quietly collected his. 'Bill the purser will meet us with the key,' Kitty said. 'He's such a nice man. 'Tis a pity he's married. And the captain is as handsome as a Mayo morning, with a ginger beard.

49

But marrying a captain is no good. He will always be at sea and have a woman in every port, no doubt.'

Martha smiled at her sister. 'Well, you could always play around too, you know.'

Kitty sighed. 'Martha, the Kearneys are the most faithful women in the world, and well you know it.'

Martha laughed ruefully. 'I do know it,' she said. She straightened her back and put her hand out to take Anna's bag. She looked around the dormitory. 'Thank God we're out of here,' she said.

Daniel put his arm around his wife. 'Yes,' he said.

The drunken man spat as they passed him. 'Too big fer yer boots, ye are,' he snarled.

'Bog Irish,' Kitty replied, and they swept out. Father O'Brian crossed himself.

Once away from the smell and the dirt, before they were half-way up the deck, Kitty's feet began to tap. She broke into a jig. It wasn't long before Martha was beside her, followed by Daniel, Mary, and Anna. Father O'Brian watched with amusement.

They arrived at the back of the ship, hot and flushed with laughter. The purser stood by the locked door, his eyebrows ascending his forehead. 'Well,' he said, 'what are you going to do for an encore? Do you always dance like that?'

'Always,' said Kitty. 'It's the Kearney blood. It makes your tonsils tickle until you have to sing and your toes itch until you scratch them with a dance.'

Bill looked at Kitty and wished his wife was such a fine figure of a woman. No, his wife was a good wife and an excellent mother, but she didn't sparkle and shimmer like Kitty. Martha gave a duller light, but the child was like a flame in a storm. He had never seen such entrancing eyes. Anna blinked at him and he came out of his trance. Scary, he thought as he unlocked the door. She could put a spell on you if you weren't careful.

Suddenly his quiet life seemed to be very attractive after all. Living with them must be like being in a perpetual hurricane, he thought as he pushed the door open. Mary smiled at him and took Daniel's hand. She walked into the hospital bay and looked around. Bill felt as if Mary's presence was the binding force of the group.

Kitty and Anna rushed around the room. Martha headed for the bathroom. 'Oh look! A real bath, Mary!'

Biddy sat alone and forlorn on one of the beds. 'I'm just an old woman far away from me home in Mayo,' she said to Father O'Brian.

Kitty swooped down on her mother. 'Come on, Mother,' she said. 'I'll run you a real hot bath. I'll throw in some scent I have, and you'll feel like a million dollars.'

'More like a million pounds, if you ask me.' Martha was grinning with delight.

'I'll leave you now,' Bill said, withdrawing politely. 'Shall I come and fetch you at seven, Miss Kearney?' Kitty nodded. As he closed the door behind him, he heard Anna plead with her father.

'All right, Anna. But you be sure to leave at eight. I will wait by the stairs for you,' Daniel said after conferring with Mary.

'Oh good.' Anna was delighted. 'Mary Rose is going to give me a proper dress to wear and shoes. She has ten pairs of shoes. That's more shoes than I've ever had in me life.' She looked at her mother. 'Oh, Mummy, don't look like that.' She threw herself into Mary's arms. 'I don't want clothes like that. I'd much rather be me. Mary Rose hardly ever sees her mother.'

Mary smiled. 'I know that,' she said. 'One day we'll be able to give you whatever you want. But you'll never lack for our love, and that's much more important. Now, let's see what we can do about a dress for Kitty. We can use the lace of my best nightdress for a start.'

Kitty was rifling through her belongings. 'I've got an old black silk dress I last used for Mr Thompson's funeral,' she said. 'Do you remember that day, Father O'Brian? The sexton was so drunk I thought he'd join the coffin.'

Father O'Brian had chosen a bed in the far corner of the room. He nodded. Since losing his nose, a change had come over him. He felt different, a new man. Instead of fretting about leaving Ireland, he found himself dreaming of his new parishioners. He was excited by the idea of a new land. Usually he spent his waking hours lost in a reverie of his childhood. Chained in the past, he never felt he had a future. But the sharp surgery of the sword severed not only his nose but also cast the chains of the past adrift: slowly they sank to the bottom of the ocean, and Father O'Brian was free at last. 'Will you be paid for singing?' he asked Kitty.

'Not by the captain,' Kitty said, watching Mary, Martha, and Biddy busily stitching away. 'If the people in the audience wish, they can give me a tip, and I'll sing till they tip me to stop!' She grinned. 'I know how to do that well. I've told Bill that I want a basket of whatever's left from dinner. We're not proud like some folk, I told him. To be sure, we've eaten the pig-swill before in the bad times and then eaten the pig in the good times. So I'll have some good food for ye without a doubt.'

Anna's heart was racing. She set her hopes on a pair of shiny black shoes just like Mary Rose always wore.

Ten

Anna sat with Mary Rose and the girl's mother and father. The mother Rosaleen was beautiful, more beautiful than pictures Anna had seen of the German film star called Frau Helena. Only Rosaleen's eyes were a deep blue, not pale, and her hair was as dark as her daughter's. 'Call her Lady Roswell, and my father is Lord Roswell,' Mary Rose had instructed while she had fitted numerous dresses upon Anna's slim frame. To Anna's great joy, Mary Rose had given her just the pair of shoes she had dreamed of. 'You can keep these clothes,' Mary Rose had said, stuffing a selection of dresses into a big bag.

Now Anna sat quietly between a real live lord and lady, and she gazed at her Aunt Kitty who was singing the 'Connemara Cradle Song'. Father O'Brian muttered a little in his beard about heathen singing. But that didn't still the thrill that Anna experienced when she heard her aunt's voice lift the little crystals on the chandeliers that hung over her and made them tinkle and tremble. Soon, as the lullaby soothed the watchers, the trembling and the tinkling caught hold of the jewels on the women sitting watching. The diamonds on the men's cuffs flashed back at the chandeliers. The whole room pulsated with music. The plump, plush chairs swelled with importance as song after Irish song fell from Kitty's lips. Again Anna could feel her eyes filling with tears. She looked at Lady Roswell, who was biting the corner of her lip. All around her, Anna realized that, though they were the rich and famous, they, too, were going into exile away, far away, from the country they loved.

From his privileged vantage point as purser, Bill watched the sincere joy and warmth that radiated from Kitty as she sang. There was something religious about the event, as if it were a private communication between her and those who watched, blissfully mesmerized. His past years spent largely out of Ireland had accustomed him to the latest and more popular profane entertainments of the Twenties in America: lyrics still wet with paint and dry in culture. He realized just how much he missed the songs of his ancestors.

Soon, far too soon, it was time for Anna to slip away to her waiting father. She leaned forward and whispered to Mary Rose, 'I must go now.'

'Must you?' Mary Rose said. 'He can't wait?'

Anna shook her head. 'I can't keep my father waiting,' she said. 'He'd be worried sick about me.'

Mary Rose nodded. 'I'll see you tomorrow,' she said. 'Same place, same time?'

'Sure.' Anna slipped off her velvet seat and picked up the bag. 'Thank you, Mary Rose,' she said. She put out her hand to Lady Roswell and curtseyed. 'Thank you, Lady Roswell.'

For a moment Lady Roswell looked startled. 'I'm sorry, dear,' she said in a sweet, high-pitched, girlish voice. 'I was miles away.'

Anna turned to Lord Roswell. 'Good night, Lord Roswell,' she said.

He leaned forward and said, 'Good voice, your aunt has. Tell her it's excellent.'

Anna threaded her way through the crowded room, oblivious to the hundreds of pairs of watching eyes that saw a fair, curly-haired little girl dressed in black velvet with white lace ruffles, her eyes ablaze with excitement. I'll sleep with my shoes on, she promised herself as she let herself out of the dining room.

Anna awoke much, much later to hear Aunt Kitty

recounting the evening's events. 'And I'm to sing every night until we get there.'

Anna smelled a wonderful smell. Food, she thought. Real food. She sat up in her bed. 'Come, Anna,' Mary called. 'We are having a midnight feast.'

Anna climbed out of her warm bed and listened to the sound her shoes made on the teak floor. She tried to tap her way across to her aunt's bed and then she stood looking down at a wonderful display of cakes and sandwiches. Slices of lobster in a funny white sauce. Crabs' legs in a pile looking like her father's collection of little saws, only they were bright pink. Dublin Bay prawns bursting from the shells swollen with fresh sea water. Several fish, their tails tucked coyly into their mouths, gazed at her with their bland, dead eyes. Hurriedly Mary was handing out plates.

'Are you going to come and have some of this heathen food or not, dear Father?' Kitty called.

Father O'Brian smiled. 'Well, it might be food given to heathens,' he said as he got out of bed in his white woollen nightshirt, 'but at least I can bless the food and it all comes from God. You don't happen to have a decent drop of wine, do you?'

'Not only do I have a decent drop of wine, Father, I happen to have a more than decent bottle of champagne. I much prefer to drink Dom Perignon at night. I have three admirers and one of them is in champagne.'

'Stop your blethering, Kitty,' Martha said, 'and start pouring. I'm parched.'

Anna watched Kitty fill the tin mugs with champagne and the bubbles explode against their white enamel. She had to admit the champagne looked better in the beautiful tulip-shaped glasses upstairs, but here she sat, her mouth full of lobster. Biddy chewed loudly on the crabs' legs. Father O'Brian and Daniel were munching on chicken legs cooked to perfection, and Mary, Martha and Kitty were cramming meringues into their mouths. 'I can't remember when I've had such a good time.' Kitty's mouthful of meringue fluttered like snowflakes on to the bed. She sloshed more champagne into everybody's mugs. 'Here's to us,' she said, standing up and swaying. 'Here's to the Kearneys who will never be dowdy. Here's to all those who are with us.' She raised her glass and the others, caught by the solemnity of her voice, stood up quite unselfconsciously. They all raised their mugs. Anna raised hers. 'To us and those who are with us,' Kitty said in a loud, clear voice. She tilted back her head and drained her cup.

'Amen,' they all answered.

'To those who are agin us . . .' Kitty spat on the floor.

Anna followed suit.

'Who are you cursing now, Kitty?' Martha was laughing.

'The old man that gobbed on us when we left to come here,' Kitty said.

'Leave him be, Kitty. He's just an old drunk. You don't believe in all that pagan nonsense, do you, Kitty?' Father O'Brian looked surprised. He saw the look in Kitty's eyes. 'Well, maybe you do,' he said, and hobbled quickly off to his bed. 'Thank the Lord I'm a priest,' he muttered as he lay chastely in his bed. Women, they bring nothing but trouble.

Anna went back to bed, had a quick polish of her new shoes, removed them, and put them under her pillow. Her stomach was full of good food, and tomorrow she would see her friend Mary Rose. The champagne made her sleepy. She could see her mother in the bed beside her, and her father on the opposite side. Flanked by the two people she loved best in the world, she fell asleep.

BOOK TWO

AMERICA

Eleven

In the excitement of Ellis Island, Anna forgot everything. She saw Mary Rose and her family swept through the waiting lines. No hard wooden benches for them. She watched other people, some dejected and crying, for they had been refused entry. She saw a small, shabby group of men and women standing shackled together surrounded by guards. Rumours spread like the plague. The fleas of malice whispered that they were anarchists and terrorists, being sent into exile. They were a danger to this new promised land. Some people spat at them and cursed them as they passed. Anna felt a sadness for these men and women. One of the men was a kindly-looking person. He had a shock of hair on his head and a sweet face. Another short, squat, toad of a woman was just an exhibitionist.

Anna could feel and smell the fear in her parents. Father O'Brian would be all right. Priests were always made welcome. Daniel, with all his many talents, was sure they were all right, and so it was to be.

To most people the little flat that Father O'Brian found for them was no more than a slum, but to Mary and the family, the three rooms with an inside bathroom were a joy. Even if there was no hot water, after the hovel in Ireland they felt rich. Anna missed the pigs and her dogs, but not for long. Kitty immediately got a job in a local Irish beer-hall, and brought home a little pug for Anna. 'She's come all the way from China just to be with you,' Kitty said as she put the tiny bundle of fur into Anna's waiting hands.

Father O'Brian very soon got his first parish up the road, but he still came every Sunday for dinner. Martha went to the local hospital and got a job nursing the elderly. Mary stayed at home while Daniel turned his hand to anything anybody in the area wanted. Mary took Anna to her school in the morning. The area in which they lived was mixed, partly a Jewish neighbourhood and partly Irish. Anna had Mary Rose's address in the pocket of her coat, and as soon as she could she sent off a letter giving Mary Rose her address.

Anna settled well at school. She enjoyed the early morning routine. The house was a-bustle by six-thirty. Mary was at the stove cooking bacon and grumbling. 'It's not like Irish bacon,' she announced on Anna's first morning at school.

'No,' Biddy agreed. 'But we're not Irish now. We're Americans.' Biddy grinned and drawled her words. 'We must sound like Americans.'

Anna, too, became truly American. She fell in love with New York and American hamburgers. She had never seen so much food. Even Mary put on weight and was all the lovelier for it. Her first school morning made Anna nervous. But she had a new shiny pencil box with a sweet-scented eraser and a satchel bought by Martha from her nursing wages. Daniel was making money and the whole family felt a sudden surge of affluence. At the end of the week there was money to go to the huge, jostling markets, there to buy food and clothes. Anna believed everything was possible in America.

Father O'Brian's stories on a Sunday were full of love and admiration for his parishioners. The change in the man was noticeable. Warmth and sincerity shone like a lamp from his face, despite his disfigurement. They looked forward to his visits. His present for Anna's first day at school was a spelling book. Anna took the book to bed with her and learned ten new words every day. She had been taught to read and write by her parents. Books were hard to come by in Ireland, but they had a big family Bible which had a well-worn front cover. Inside was a long list of deceased members of the Kearney family, and in more sombre moments, they wondered if Raymond and Sean would have to be added to the list.

'Hurry up, Anna. We don't want to be late for your first day at school,' Mary said.

Anna brushed her hair carefully and put on her shiny black shoes. She wore one of the dresses donated by Mary Rose. 'You look lovely, acushla,' said Kitty.

Kitty sat at the table in her voluminous nightdress, wrapped in a big silk shawl. One of her admirers was a sea captain. 'I always said I'd stay away from sea captains, but he gives me silks and pearls, so he's an exception.' Often Kitty did not come home at night. Nothing was said, but Anna could tell by Biddy's tightened lips and her mother's face in the morning that they did not approve. When Kitty did roll in, she always had something for Anna who loved her aunt and felt protective of her. This morning Kitty had stayed in to be with Anna before she went off to school.

The sausages were sizzling. The little flat had been beautifully restored by Daniel, and Anna felt at peace with the world.

There were several new arrivals at the school which was three blocks away from the house. Anna danced impatiently as Mary darted in and out of shops. 'I can't get used to all these shops,' Mary said. 'And I have money. It's all like a miracle, Anna.'

'We're going to be late,' Anna said impatiently.

'No, we won't, darling. Let me see. I need three ribbons for your hair.'

'No, you don't, Mommy.' Anna answered the American way.

Mary laughed. 'I'll have to get used to that word,' she said.

Waiting by the school gate was a little clot of newcomers with their parents. The school was old and dark, but the walls were brightly alive with children's paintings. How grown up the older children were! They walked and talked in earnest groups, their arms full of books.

Anna stood beside her mother in the headmaster's room. Beside her was a skinny Jewish boy. She had seen him in the streets near her home. When she asked Biddy why he wore a pancake on his head, Biddy said it was because Jews ate Christian babies on a Friday night and drank their blood. Anna was aghast. 'Don't they get arrested?' she inquired.

'They do it at the dead of night,' Biddy said. 'And they steal babies from prams outside the shops.'

Now Anna was standing right next to a Jewish child who had eaten Christian babies and had sipped Christian blood. Well, obviously eating Christian babies doesn't make you fat, she thought, moving closer to her mother.

'America is the land of opportunity for everyone,' the headmaster explained. 'Here at St Crispin's we expect the children to work hard and to play hard. In my school there is no corporal punishment. A good teacher never needs to hit a child. If a class is restless it is because the teacher is not able to interest the children.' He smiled at Anna. What a pretty child. Rarely did the children of the immigrant Irish look clean and well-fed. In her navy blue frock with a wide sailor collar, Anna knew she looked good. Her shoes glinted after a last minute polish by Martha. She ached to get her hands on her school books.

As they followed the teacher to the classroom, various children kissed or clung to their mothers. But the little

Christian-eating boy walked forlornly beside a tall, matronly figure that must have been his mother. When they came to the door of Anna's classroom, the mother suddenly erupted in a frenzy of ear-popping kisses. Anna winced for him, he looked so bedraggled. He reminded her of a kitten left out in a storm. 'My name is Steven,' he whispered as his mother stormed off. 'May I sit next to you?' He had a lunchbox with him.

Anna looked at the lunchbox. 'What's in there?' she asked.

'Kasha varnishkes,' he said. 'And milk.'

'Milk?' Anna said. 'I thought you drank Christian blood.'

Steven shook his head and looked even sadder. 'No, we don't do that at all.'

'Anna,' Mary interrupted. 'Please say hello to your teacher.'

Anna put out her hand and curtsied. 'Good morning, ma'am,' she said.

The teacher smiled, her glasses glinting in the sunlight. 'You can call me Mrs James. Anna, is this your little friend?'

Anna took Steven's hand. 'Yes,' she said. 'This is Steven.' Anna made a mental note to tell Biddy she had got it all wrong.

They made their way to two empty desks at the back of the class. Simultaneously they opened their desks and exchanged delighted smiles. Sitting in both desks were a pile of brand new books and six fat, shiny, blue-covered exercise books. 'Ahh,' Anna said. She picked up the first book, a beginner's reader. She opened it in the middle. She felt the thickness of the volume and then she bent her head to smell the true smell of all good books. The clean, sweet smell of paper, and behind that smell one of horse-glue in the spine. She wanted to lick the words off the pages. Books made her feel soft and melting.

Steven glanced at her. He was looking at the arithmetic book. 'I like arithmetic,' he said. 'I'm very good at it.'

'I like English,' Anna replied.

'Settle down, Anna and Steven, and pay attention. Turn your English books to page thirteen. We are looking at the work of the great Florentine painter Leonardo da Vinci.'

Anna panicked. The words in front of her were unfamiliar. She looked at Steven. He was smiling. 'It's Latin,' he said. He put his hand up.

'All right, Steven. You translate the first two lines.'

Twelve

The days at school went swiftly. Happy and exhilarated, Anna became an omnivorous reader. Most evenings she sat at the table in the kitchen and dragooned the family into helping her with her homework. Maths she did with Steven. She did not like his cold, hygienic house, neither did she like his overbearing mother and short-tempered bully of a father. 'Who's the shiksa you bring home?' she heard Steven's father bellow at him in the kitchen while she sat primly on the overstuffed Ottoman wondering if all Jewish houses were decorated in gold and ivory and crammed with useless objets d'art. At home Steven looked even more shrunken and wizened.

Now he came to her house where the cheerful, friendly family made him welcome. Mary was always pushing plates of food in front of him. 'Eat, Steven. You need to grow. A wee stick of a thing you are. What does your mother feed you?'

Steven hung his head. 'She doesn't like to cook, Mrs Kearney.'

64

'Doesn't like to cook?' Kitty's voice was full of surprise. 'Well, if she can't cook, she can't be doing any of the other.' Kitty giggled.

'Be quiet now, Kitty. And give the children some of your apple crumble.'

Kitty rolled across the kitchen. 'Men have died for my apple crumble. And for the other thing as well.'

'What other thing, Aunt Kitty?'

'Never you mind, Anna. You'll know soon enough,' Biddy interrupted. 'You two get on with your homework.'

When the room was clear of adults, Anna leaned forward and whispered to Steven. 'Do you know what "the other thing" is, Steven?'

He blushed. 'Yes, I do,' he said. 'And I think it's disgusting.'

'What is disgusting?'

'Doing *it*.' Steven was frowning.

'What's *it*?' Anna was mystified.

'Well, a man puts his thing into a woman's hole and then he goes up and down and makes babies.'

'Oh no. How awful. I'll never do that.'

'Neither will I,' Steven agreed. 'Let's get on with our maths.'

'How do you know that's what happens?'

'I saw my father and mother once when I went into their bedroom with an earache.'

'Did he make a baby with her?'

'Come to think of it, no. He didn't.'

Anna got bored with the subject and they finished their homework.

The next day a much-awaited letter arrived. It was delivered by a chauffeur-driven Rolls-Royce. The whole street turned out to watch the elegant car come to a smooth halt outside Anna's house. Anna was with Steven in the kitchen as usual. Biddy came running into the kitchen breathlessly. 'Anna, there's a man wanting to give you a letter, darlin'! He won't give it to me. It's from Mary Rose, and she has given him orders to put the letter in your hand only.'

Anna was out of the kitchen and she flew on to the front doorstep. Mary was behind her. Kitty and Martha leaned out of the bedroom windows. Kitty graciously waved to the astounded people on the pavement. 'See, Martha? This is how the Queen of England waves. I saw it in the papers.'

Mary was grateful she had just polished the front doorstep. The chauffeur bowed low over Anna's hand. 'Miss Mary Rose would like to ask you to tea this Saturday afternoon.'

'Do you think I could bring my friend Steven?' Anna asked.

'I am sure that can be arranged.' The chauffeur climbed back into the grey car and Anna noticed his uniform was exactly the same colour as the car.

'One day, Mommy, I'm going to buy a car for you just like that.'

Mary hugged her daughter. 'I don't want expensive presents from you, darlin'. I just want you to be happy and healthy. That's what I pray for.'

'Steven!' Anna rushed back into the kitchen. She tore open the letter. A thick, buttermilk-coloured piece of paper fell onto the kitchen floor. Under a crown was an impressive address. Mary Rose had written:

I really do miss you and can't wait to see you again.

'You're invited, too, Steven. Isn't that marvellous? We will both get to ride in that wonderful car.'

But on Saturday afternoon Anna had to go by herself. She left a forlorn Steven on his own doorstep on Friday after school. 'My mother won't let me go. She says it's because it's the sabbath, but they don't even light the candles. I don't dare argue in case they stop me going to your house. I couldn't bear that.'

Anna thought of his little white face and wondered how anyone could have such awful parents. His mother alternately ignored him or pawed at him, and his father just yelled.

Still, she was wearing a brand new dress from a proper dress shop, not the market, and she felt marvellous. Her thick blonde hair now hung to her waist and she wore a black velvet beret which matched the black velvet collar on her bright red velvet dress. Her socks were made of soft silk and they wiggled deliciously inside a pair of soft leather boots made for her by her father. And then she pulled her sky-blue cape aside and sat back in the big, plush, grey leather seats, drinking in the smell of well-tooled leather and running her gloved fingers over the mahogany fittings. She stared out the window and was amazed to notice how the pushing crowds and other cars fell back as the Rolls purred its sinister purr all the way up Fifth Avenue.

The car drew up beside a pair of very ornate gates. The driver got out of the car and spoke down what looked like a tube, and a man came hurrying down the drive. The man wore a green uniform and a leather pinafore with a pocket. 'This is Peter Jenkison, the head gardener, Miss Kearney.'

'The head gardener?' Anna said. 'How many gardeners are there?'

'Oh, twelve, I think, at the moment. In the summer we take on more. Mrs Portney is the housekeeper, and Perry the butler. No one knows Perry's real name, so we all just call him Perry.'

'What is your name?' Anna asked.

'My name is James Stephens.'

'Where are you from?'

'I'm from Dorset in the south of England. I miss the English countryside sometimes.'

'I know how you feel,' Anna said, watching the garden slide by. 'I miss my pigs and my cows, but,' she sighed, 'here life is wonderfully exciting. We passed such tall buildings, they nearly reached up to God's eye.'

James looked at Anna's shiny face in his driving mirror. What a change from that spoiled brat Mary Rose, he thought. Nothing much pleases her. I hope the girl has some effect on the little madam. Still, Mary Rose is a lonely child. This one is surrounded by her family who so obviously love her very much indeed. James felt a sudden urge to get married. Good heavens, he scolded himself. Whatever next? Who needs a ball and chain?

They drew up in front of an imposing flight of white marble stairs. Perry walked slowly and disdainfully down the stairs to greet the car. 'Miss Mary Rose is waiting for you in the nursery,' he said. He stood aside while Anna just stared at him.

She had never seen a real live butler before, and he looked very impressive in a green cut-away frock-coat, a lace cravat and white gloves. 'What do I do now?' Anna asked, unsure of herself and overwhelmed by the grandeur of it all.

'Just follow me, Miss Kearney.'

He even knows my name and I didn't tell him. She followed Perry's elegant slim back up the stairs, feeling the size of the head of a pin.

'You look wonderful, Mary Rose.'

Mary Rose rushed across the floor of a large, square, stark room. The floor was thickly carpeted. There was a big black-leaded grate with a padded leather fireguard, and in the window a very big, arch-necked rocking horse. Mary Rose hugged Anna. There were tears in her eyes. 'I've been so lonely, Anna. I just have my nanny and a tutor, and never go out except if James takes me shopping. Mummy and Daddy are always out at some party or other. The other day Daddy gave me this.' She thrust her arms into Anna's face.

Anna blinked. Stars winked and flashed in front of her eyes. 'What is it?' she said, half-dazzled by the stones. 'Oh, I see, Mary Rose. It's a watch.'

Mary Rose lifted the little cap that covered the face of the watch. 'Here,' Mary Rose said. 'I don't want the beastly thing. You have it.'

'Oh no, Mary Rose. I couldn't. My mother wouldn't let me keep it.'

'You keep it. Tell her I said so.' Mary Rose shook her long hair emphatically. 'Anyway, I'll come with you and explain. I missed you, Anna.'

'I missed you.' Anna smiled at Mary Rose. 'Now we've found each other again, we'll never lose touch.'

A raven flew past the window, croaking, '*Yes, you will. Yes, you will.*'

Anna shivered. She saw a dark cowl around Mary Rose's head. She said nothing.

At the sound of cups clinking, Mary Rose said, 'Let's go to my sitting room.'

'Do you live up here all alone?'

'Yes,' Mary Rose said simply. 'My nanny has a bedroom up here. Daddy is having an affair with my mother's best friend, so he's hardly ever home.'

'What's an affair?'

'Oh, you know. Putting his long dangling thing into my mother's best friend. Her name is Frieda. She's awful, and Mummy hates her now. She says she's a bitch.'

Anna's head began to swim. 'Does your father want babies?'

'No, you idiot. Of course not. It feels nice.'

'How do you know?'

'Because Mummy told me. It feels all swoony and sort of flashy. I can't wait.'

'Oh, Mary Rose. You have to wait until you're married.'

'Oh no, I don't. Mummy first did it when she was sixteen with her groom. He was the best, she says. Daddy's very bad at it. I think she should have her own lover. Mummy cries a lot and goes out all day to play bridge with her friends.'

She led the way down a long corridor, then opened a door. Anna stood on the threshold, speechless. 'This is the most beautiful room I've ever seen,' she said. She felt her feet full of music. 'I must dance,' she said. Her whole body spun like a top.

Mary Rose was laughing and clapping her hands.

Mrs Portney interrupted the dancing with a silver tea-tray. She puffed into the room, her short plump legs moving like railway pistons, her busy bottom encased in her green uniform, her billowing bust covered in a fine linen pinafore. She beamed at Anna. 'From the old country?' she said.

'Yes. County Mayo. The best place on earth.' Anna stood still, her feet in the third position.

'I come from Killarney. You remember the song. "Where the Mountains of Mourne Go Down to the Sea . . ." ' she sang in a crystal clear soprano. 'Ah, I miss it all terribly,' she said with a sob more than a sigh. 'I'll go back, if they'll let me, once again before I die. These New York people . . .' She shook her head. 'The Italians are good, but the English! What cold, rude, hard people. The Scots and the Welsh, they're Celts like us.' She put the tray down and lit the little spirit lamp under the tea kettle. 'Come and sit, girls. May I take a cup of tea with you? It's nanny's day off, and we usually have tea together.'

'Do join us, Mrs Portney. I'm going to drive back with Anna. I want to see her mother and father and her Aunt

Kitty and Aunt Martha. Oh yes, and your grandmother. And where is Father O'Brian?'

'Oh, he's got his own parish and he's very happy. They all love him, and he comes to have Sunday dinner with us.'

'You mean lunch, don't you? I remember your family having lunch on a Sunday. Could I come to lunch tomorrow as well?'

'Mary Rose,' said Mrs Portney, 'you don't invite yourself to other people's houses. That's very rude.'

'Mrs Portney, I consider Anna's family my own. I love them all. At least Anna is never lonely.'

'I have a new friend called Steven, and I will ask him to have lunch with us tomorrow.'

Both girls beamed at each other.

When the car took them back to Anna's house, Mary Rose insisted that Anna wear the watch. Anna held her breath as the glittering watch was put on her slim wrist. 'Oh, Mary Rose! It's so beautiful.'

'So are you. Let me do the talking.'

Anna remembered to let James open the door. She pulled her cloak around her arms and hid the watch. She felt guilty, a familiar feeling when Mary Rose was around.

Mary came to the door and embraced Mary Rose. 'How lovely to see you,' she said in her soft, lilting Irish voice. Her mother's voice always reminded Anna of a little bubbling stream she knew by the cottage in Ireland. The water was so pure that she used to drink from the stream whenever she passed by. The energy of the little spring leaping from a hole in the ground was so like Mary, who sang and danced as she kept Anna's world as fine and as beautiful as it really was.

Anna sent several Hail Marys and a quick St Jude that Mary would let her keep the watch. Daniel she would wheedle, but the final law in the family rested with Mary.

Mary brought the two girls into the kitchen. 'Please stay for supper,' she offered. James, looking at Mary, was once again filled with an uncomfortable longing for a wife to come home to. But where would he find a wife like Mary? Not in New York, he reminded himself. New York women were hard and selfish. 'I'll collect you at eight, miss,' he said to Mary Rose.

As he pulled away he saw Martha coming down the street. Now there's a lovely woman, he thought. He pulled across to the kerb and rolled down the window. 'Want a ride in a Rolls?' he said cheerfully.

Martha was startled out of her reverie. Then she recognized the chauffeur that had taken Anna off to tea with Mary Rose. 'I don't mind if I do,' she said.

James hopped out of the car and opened the back door. 'In you get,' he said, 'and we'll go around the block.'

'Streets, not block. That's awful American.'

'I'm almost American,' James said, expertly weaving through the traffic.

'Well, I'm Irish and shall be until the day I die, even though Mary is trying to clean up our talk. What a day I've had! We lost poor old Mrs Welcome. So sad, she was a lovely old woman. Still, she made old bones. She was eighty-four and it was time to go. I laid her out myself as a last mark of respect for her. I didn't want a stranger touching her. She looked so beautiful. It was as if she were sleeping.'

James listened to Martha's gentle, low voice. She had melancholy dark eyes. Her hair was as thick as Anna's but it hung straight and was not as long. She did not have the radiance of Anna, but she gave off a gentle glow-worm warmth. She would be a peaceful soul. James knew that.

All too soon they were back at the front door. 'Miss Kearney . . .'

'Do call me Martha.' She leaned into the driving window and smiled.

'Would you like to go to the pictures next week? There's a very good Charlie Chaplin on in Times Square.'

'If you promise to ask me to see a film, I will,' she said, laughing.

'OK. Er, all right. Will you come to a film with me on Monday night?'

'Indeed I will,' she said. 'Good-night.' And she opened the front door of the apartment and was gone.

Martha waltzed into the kitchen. 'I've got a date on Monday night,' she sang in her deep contralto.

'Who?' Kitty said. She was sprawled next to Mary Rose. 'Mary Rose is staying for dinner. We can't let her go back now we have found her. James is coming back to get her at eight o'clock.'

'And it's James who is going to take me to a film on Monday,' Martha announced.

'Good for him,' Mary Rose said. 'I'll tease him all the way home.'

'No, you will not, little madam. Good men are hard to find, and James may be the best there is. What is that on your arm, Anna?'

Anna pulled the sleeve of her dress over the watch.

Kitty was the first to pounce. 'And where did you get that thing, Anna? Have you been robbing a bank?'

Anna was bright red.

'I gave it to her,' Mary Rose said quickly. 'I've got several and I don't like it. Diamonds suit Anna because she's fair.'

At this point Daniel arrived home. In the ensuing

73

hubbub, the subject was put aside, but when he sat down, Mary addressed him seriously. 'Anna, show your father the watch.'

Anna uncovered her wrists and wished the thing would stop blazing with light. Daniel looked at Mary Rose. He saw a desperately lonely child with little to give, and he understood her.

'Let Anna keep the watch,' he said to Mary. 'After all, a gift from a friend is precious and to be respected.'

'Thank you, Da.' Anna breathed again. 'Oh, Mary Rose! I can't believe it.'

'Well, put it away in my chest, Anna,' her mother said, 'and you can wear it on special occasions.'

Anna smiled.

Thirteen

JL

For Anna's fifteenth birthday party she and Steven were taken by Daniel and Mary to the theatre on Broadway. Aunt Kitty had married a wealthy theatre impresario, Joe Rapillano, and was now a Broadway star, belting out old cockney and Irish songs. Joe had already been married four times, much to Mary's horror, but Aunt Kitty just winked at her niece. 'I can take care of him,' she said. 'Feed him and water him regularly, he'll behave himself.'

'Really, Kitty. Not in front of the child.'

Now Anna, dressed in white ermine, was getting ready to climb into their car. A lot had happened in the eleven years that had gone by so quickly. America had changed Daniel, more than any member of his family. Like a chestnut tree whose roots finally break rock to free, rich soil, he had quickly bloomed. His boyhood dream had materialized and there were no delusions. He devoured every available opportunity, and there were many. His manual dexterity, intellect and boundless enthusiasm melded to create a quickly thriving business as a shoemaker and repairer. It was a classic migrant's story of the day: a business that began on the kitchen table and which within a few short years developed into a small industry of a factory and several retail outlets. Boosted by this natural success, his country shyness turned to a warm, infectious gregariousness, which induced trust and confidence in his friends and business acquaintances. And, almost unwillingly, his business grew on the strength of his character. From shoes he branched into real estate and property development. The time and the market of New York was ready for someone like Daniel. His aims remained realistic and modest: his County Mayo upbringing had instilled an inherent caution against greed. This caution brought him relatively unscathed through the Wall Street crash of 1929 and, by the beginning of the new decade, he was well on the way to earning the mythical title of millionaire.

Mary often playfully chided her husband for having sold his humility for 'bucks'. She called him 'Mister Daniel, sir' like his affectionate, loyal workers. But she was openly proud of his achievements and rarely stopped telling him so. She was a willing support in his new life: he called her 'the real chairman of the board'. But Mary chose a passive role as far as his business affairs were concerned, quietly listening to his ideas and offering acute opinions when she felt they were necessary. She saw her major role as his wife, not his business partner. If there were to be defined roles in the Kearney family, his was worked out in the office and hers in the home. Despite the open invitations to break with tradition, they chose trodden ground. She became the gentle hostess whose quiet confidence won her universal respect. Her natural inner strength became stronger and she, too, flowered in harmony with her husband, but at the same time apart.

They had moved away from their cramped district. Now Father O'Brian had his new parish nearby and still came for Sunday dinner. Martha was happily married to James Stephens, Mary Rose's chauffeur and, through her, Mary Rose spent much time with Anna. Steven was aware that the richer the Kearney household became, the more his mother and father encouraged him to see Anna. However, Steven thought of Anna as a sister. He had little to do with any other girls and now, since Anna had moved away from the school, he saw less of her.

Today on her birthday he stood waiting for her car to arrive, nervously clutching a book of poems by Wordsworth. The nineteenth of February 1932 was a cold day. He stamped his feet to keep himself warm, and wished his mother let him pick his own clothes. He felt ridiculous in a formal suit and a Homburg hat. He felt like a small imitation of his father. In the last years he had rejected all attempts from his father to be his father's best buddy. Steven was a gentle, shy, dreamer of a boy. This was what Anna so loved about him. His ambition was to be a botanist or, if not that, a restaurant chef. He immersed himself in imagining a dish of roast beef and potatoes.

He saw the car approaching and smiled happily. Anna looked amazing, her wide azure eyes shining from the halo of white fur around her face, her long blonde hair escaping in curled tendrils from the hood. She smiled. Her generous mouth revealed a row of straight white teeth and the grin wrinkled her nose and exposed a small pink tongue.

Daniel swung open the door. 'Get in, Steven,' he said, wishing the boy didn't flinch so.

Steven scrambled into the car and pressed the book, beautifully wrapped in red paper, into Anna's hands. 'I don't know if you'll like it,' he said, 'but it has your favourite poem.'

Anna beamed. Mary took the book and put it beside her. 'We'll open it when we get home for dinner,' she said. 'Mary Rose and Martha should be waiting for us. Kitty and Joe have booked a box. Imagine, Anna, how much has happened in the eleven years we've been in this country. It really is the land of opportunity, you know.'

'Yes,' Anna said, looking out of the window. 'It's all been wonderful for us. Look out there, Steven, at those cars and all the street-lights.' Then she frowned. Now the car had left Steven's house and was moving through streets where she had grown up. It always gave her a jolt to remember how those streets had really seemed like a paradise to her. How slowly, as the years went by, little bits of the once large family had come together again. Raymond was in Texas. He had survived the English massacres. Sean was a priest in Albuquerque, New Mexico. And Donald was in Boston doing very well with his own construction company.

Biddy was very frail now. She was at home, sitting by the fire in the little drawing room, tended by Mary's parlourmaid. Mostly blind, Biddy knew her time was close and was content to enjoy her granddaughter's fifteenth birthday party. Now she saw her husband in her dreams and he was smiling at her. It had been 1921 when they had left Ireland. Biddy swayed gently by the coal fire. She could see the glow in the grate. She heard Bridget, the maid, laying the table next door for the party. She imagined the various members of the family drawing near to the great theatre where *The Painted Forest* was being performed. They had done well, she muttered to herself.

Meanwhile, Anna looked at her mother and said, quietly leaning back against the black leather upholstery, 'Those people out there don't look as if they're very happy.'

'No,' Steven agreed. 'The neighbourhood's changed so much. People move in and out now all the time. I can't leave the house after dark. Remember when I could walk from your place after supper? I always felt safe. It's not like that now. Boys stop me and ask if I'm a Jew. I don't go out now, except to visit you or with my parents. Our neighbours are all Jews and we live in fear of the new waves of immigrants. It's not that we want to live all huddled together, but we have to. Otherwise our lives are in danger. Look.' He pointed to the walls. 'See? See "Kike" written there?'

Anna nodded. 'I can see it.'

'Let's talk about something else,' Mary interrupted. 'We'll soon be out of this area, and today's your birthday, Anna.'

Anna lifted the sleeve of her right hand. She laughed. 'Look, Steven: Mary Rose's watch. I always wear it for special occasions.'

Mary relaxed. With Daniel she had faced so many years of terrible hardship back in the early days of their marriage that she wanted to keep her beloved daughter away from any of the grim shadows that hung over those memories. Yes, times were changing fast.

News from Ireland spoke of feeble attempts at peace. Civil war between the opposing factions of Sinn Fein had lost its initial ferocity, according to the news reports which reached the Kearney family, always hungry for information from the country they still called 'home'. And the latest news was that a new constitution had been drawn which would establish the sovereign country of Ireland, or Eire as the nationalists wanted it known. But Daniel, particularly, had grown cynical about the prospect of lasting peace and of the capacity of politicians to achieve it. And he believed the English would find it difficult after countless decades of domination to stop bullying Ireland. At no time in the past, nor now, had he doubted his decision to flee to America, although the Prohibition Laws, he had to admit, placed some stress on his conviction. But lately there had been talk of repealing the Twenty-first Amendment which would free the bottles of silken Irish whiskey.

Mary gazed at the two young faces before her. Theirs was the first generation to be raised in peace. She crossed herself.

Fourteen

Anna sat in the theatre. The walls were covered with thick, velvet-flocked wallpaper. Anna's handkerchief box by her bed was also padded with the same red velvet. She closed her eyes for a moment and imagined the scene before her taking place inside the handkerchief box: she was sitting on one of her grandmother's beautifully sewn lawn handkerchiefs, watching the story unfold before her. She would much prefer it if all her family and friends were there with her. The softly padded top neatly closed and there was utter silence, except for the actors and actresses. Around her she could feel the audience moving and coughing. People blew their noses and shuffled their feet.

Below her a man sat, his back rigid with anger. Beside him two small stunted children stared at the stage. They were not smiling. When the audience laughed or clapped, the children gazed sideways to gauge the mood on their father's face. He did not smile. Pressed against him a small, thin woman with a flattened nose also gazed at the stage. Their box must have been expensive. They were well dressed. Anna sighed. She could feel the clouds of anger emanating from the man and impregnating the mother and children with fear. Why was he so angry? Anna wondered. She nodded. Everyone's having a good time, she realized, yet he was incapable of it. Other people's bad times were his good times.

Mary Rose heard Anna sigh. 'Are you bored?' she whispered.

'No,' Anna said, surprised.

'Well, I am.' Mary Rose was truculent. 'We're much too old to go to this baby stuff.'

Anna turned back to the stage. A child was standing alone, lost in a painted forest. The green of the trees and the browns and the burnt umbers of the forest floor melded the colours into the song that the child sang. Anna forgot Mary Rose for a moment and flew to the child's side. Singing always compelled her to join in. The sound of the human voice crying in a lost wilderness spoke to Anna of those distant, difficult years when she was a girl in Ireland, reminded her of the stream by her first home, of the smell of the peat-fire and the lovely, dew-lit evenings that stretched for miles over the Mayo hills. Such a longing crept over her that she could feel her eyes filling with tears.

'What are you crying for, you?' Mary Rose pinched the back of Anna's hand.

Anna pulled out one of Biddy's handkerchiefs. 'You wouldn't understand,' she said. She looked at Kitty and Martha. She knew they would understand. And her mother and father. Around their box she could see a warm yellow glow of happiness that included Joe Rapillano and James. But there, next to her, a black hole engulfed the beautiful, torn face of Mary Rose.

Mary Rose's lips were pursed with displeasure. 'There's no kissing,' she said with disgust.

Anna smiled gently. 'What do you know about kissing?' she asked.

Mary Rose grinned and the black hole shifted to allow a flash of red light shot through with purple. 'I've been kissing Evan, my groom,' she said with a giggle.

Anna made a face. 'Does your mother know?'

'Shh, children!' Mary leaned over.

There was an obedient silence and then Mary Rose leaned forward, her gloved hand hiding her mouth. 'Mother says it's best to practise on grooms.'

Anna sat back in her seat and was glad that Steven was so engrossed that he failed to hear anything Mary Rose had said. Anna was aware that she had never kissed anyone. Even though from when she was tiny she had always been alert to the feelings of love, she had still been oblivious to the significance of this great event, drastically explained by Mary Rose. And her romantic vision of herself lying in her husband's arms was too precious a dream ever to share with Mary Rose. Anna often felt splashed and muddied by Mary Rose's revelations. She was, however, aware of moments with Steven when there was almost a hint of electricity between them, a faint prickle in the air, as they stood beside each other. A moment of hesitation. A few words left unsaid in their burbling, familiar conversation. They who both knew each other so well. A moment when Steven arrived at the door. A sudden shyness. It's because we are growing up, Anna comforted herself, because she never wanted her friendship with Steven to change. Steven was her light and her guide, while Mary Rose was her darkness. Where Mary Rose led, Anna often reluctantly followed. Resist it as she might, Anna was still fascinated by Mary Rose.

She knew Mary Rose was bored: not much interested

her except money, which she had; sex, which she talked about all the time; and power. Mary Rose once confided in Anna that her father was a direct descendant from the kings of Ireland, and her ambition was always to kick out the English and go back and rule Ireland.

Anna looked at Mary Rose sitting in her plush, golden seat, her long dark hair pulled back into a chignon criss-crossed with pearls and amethysts. The pose was regal, the brow noble, and for a moment, Anna was thrown back in time; and she saw Mary Rose, centuries ago, sitting on a carved wooden throne in a mighty hall. Anna sat beside her. Before her a knight of the court, his sword on the ground, bowed before her feet. She watched intently as Mary Rose bade the man rise, and for a moment, Anna's eyes were locked into the hot, naked lust in the man's eyes. Anna's hand flew to her throat. She glanced at Mary Rose who smiled a wicked, inviting smile. A pact that would take them through eternity together was made at that moment. Who was the man? Anna did not have an answer, but she felt a warm sensation of liquid drip between her fingers and then she looked down. It was blood. Not her blood, she knew that . . .

The audience clapped and there was a heavy swish of the curtain. Anna lost the vision but not the fear. She came to, deeply shaken. She had thought that the dreams and visions that had haunted her in childhood were a thing of the past. She looked across at Martha and realized that her aunt had been watching her.

The others in the box were putting on their coats. Daniel's face was alive with excitement. Anna went quietly over to where Martha was standing with James. 'I just had an awful vision, Martha.'

'I could see that,' Martha said gently. 'You were in an altered state, darling.'

Anna knew she must not reveal the vision. Martha had

taught her well. What was to happen to Mary Rose must belong to Mary Rose. The events in her life must be of her own choosing, but Anna, with foreknowledge, could act as a guide. She had been born a wise child and now, after long years of abuse, the wisdom was making itself felt again. Anna was both exhilarated with the energy it brought, but also sad at the separation it created. To know but not to tell was a hard discipline for one so young.

Anna was quiet on the drive back to the house.

Biddy was waiting for her family. She could hear Anna's feet coming across the sitting-room floor. She smiled.

Anna bent to kiss her grandmother. She could see the milk-white cataracts that clouded Biddy's eyes. She could smell the gentle aroma of the rosewater her grandmother always used. The sharp sting in her nose of the witch-hazel Biddy used to clean her face. Now, crouched by her grandmother's chair, she felt Biddy's bird-clawed hand stroke her long, fair hair. She readied herself for the day that would come so soon when Biddy's soul would escape her infirmities and soar to meet her Maker, leaving behind her grieving family. And no one would grieve more deeply than Anna. Between grandmother and granddaughter there lived the once-in-a-lifetime relationship where youth and age were combined in a love that had no tension. As a daughter, Anna realized very young, the struggles for her selfhood were against her mother. Her grandmother, having once fulfilled that role, was free to love her unconditionally. And Biddy had offered that love to Anna from the moment she had been born.

With that blessing upon her head, Anna now stood up and shook herself. Enough, she said to her inner world. I'm going to close the door and enjoy my birthday party.

The inner door swung quietly shut and Anna danced across the sitting-room carpet to join the rest of the family and guests in the dining room.

Fifteen

By the time Anna was eighteen, Daniel had made his first million. And it showed. He had proved as astute in real estate as he had been in shoe manufacturing and had developed a keen eye for both beauty and business. The best, an elegant, spacious brownstone in Manhattan, overlooking the trees and greenery of Central Park, he had chosen for himself and his family. Like Daniel, the three-storey building was not ostentatious, but warm and subtle. Inside there was space for all, and Mary had redecorated and furnished it with her unpretentious, genuine touch, creating a welcoming atmosphere that immediately put all who entered at ease. It became the natural focal point for the entire Kearney tribe.

Biddy was now confined to her bed. In the evenings Daniel carried his mother down the stairs of their grand mansion and sat her by the fire in the little drawing room. Usually Anna sat with her. Mary worried that her beautiful daughter made no friends other than Steven, and Mary Rose tried without success to get her friend to attend the balls and parties given by the matrons of New York. 'I'd much rather be here with Grandma,' she said, beaming her bewitching smile at her mother. 'Grandma is much more interesting than all those boring people. Mary Rose does all that stuff and then comes back and tells me the interesting bits. That way I don't have to put up with the dullness of it all.' What she did not tell her mother was that

Mary Rose also gave her vivid descriptions of her lovemaking.

Mary Rose had progressed very rapidly from the strong arms of her groom and was now taking all of New York by storm. The extravagant social climate of the city of the mid-Thirties was designed for her, and she took to it with all the boundless enthusiasm and adolescent verve that her champagne-bubbles character could generate. Newspapers constantly showed pictures of Mary Rose with her latest beau, her dark hair a waving mass of invitation. Even Daniel felt a guilty surge of lust and a hardening between his legs as Mary Rose bounded up to him and kissed him pertly on his mouth with her swollen, bee-stung lips. Only his wife had ever kissed his mouth, and Daniel realized that he felt not only guilty but also flattered. The push of her small, rounded breasts against his suit jacket made the veins in his neck throb. With Mary in their deep contented bed he could restore the harmony within himself. Mary was his lodestone. His life was enharboured by her. Other women, even Mary Rose, could titillate, but Daniel realized he had something unique and precious in this quiet, unpretentious woman. Above all, she was mother to his child. It was through her wisdom and influence that Anna still retained a joyful innocence. Daniel dreaded the day when that innocence would be gone from Anna's eyes. He prayed that the boy who would take Anna's heart would be gentle, would be able to offer his daughter a lifestyle to which she was accustomed. The bitter poverty he had experienced in Ireland was now a trace memory for Daniel. Only in the streets of New York, the sudden reek of stewed cabbage wafting out of a Salvation Army canteen, made him pause for a second and the memories flood back. He knew that it would not be long now before some swain became smitten by Anna. She had had enough offers, and when she could be persuaded to attend a party, photographers flocked to her, blinding her with their flashes.

Mary Rose and Anna were considered the two most beautiful girls of the season. They were sensuous foils for each other. In Anna's face and figure was the promise of great delight for the man who would finally win her. There was an openness in her smile and uncomplicated love and exuberance, a feeling of swiftness and a glimpse into a blue infinity. Her presence brought with her a vitality and an air of perpetual celebration. By contrast, Mary Rose created a dull longing in men. She carried in the slow sway of her hips and the demure droop of her eyelids another promise: that a man would be hard put to wish for an unspoken desire not to be serviced by Mary Rose. The need, if shameful, should never say its name; Mary Rose would know and finish the experience with a new depravity. Lost in Mary Rose's arms, men rarely struggled free. If they did, it was to wander and to wonder, like the ancient mariner, why they had ever been ejected from her erotically tangled paradise. Would the smell of burning poppies ever leave their nostrils? Would the blighted swain ever find the ecstasy so tinged with pain in another woman's arms? It was said that men killed themselves over Mary Rose, and Daniel could well believe it.

Still, it was time to carry his mother down the stairs for her dinner by the fireplace in the second drawing room. He was taking Mary out to a concert. He hummed the first aria from *La Bohème* and chuckled as he bounded up the steps. Here was Daniel Kearney taking his wife to the opera. Who would have thought it, all those years ago?

Anna heard the front door slam and knew that her parents had gone for the evening. The house was empty.

The servants were in their own quarters and Anna made a chicken soup for her grandmother, followed by a salmon trout steeped in a white wine sauce, served over a bed of wild rice and fresh asparagus tips. Biddy loved Anna's light-handed cooking, so tonight was their treat together. Daniel had left a bottle of young white wine open in the pantry.

Anna wrapped a silk scarf around her head and pulled on a long warm house-robe. She slipped her feet into velvet slippers and walked down the hall. As she came down the stairs, she could hear the clear, hard crackle of the fire from her grandmother's drawing room. The wood was dry and sent out an inviting smell of pine. A sudden fusillade of shots made her pause. And then she looked up and her eyes widened with fear.

Upon the wall above the main door a shadow flitted. It was as if the shots had taken matter and form, and a small bird appeared to tumble out of the sky. One wing stretched out in supplication. Anna was startled. She blinked and the apparition was gone.

She shook herself, but unease was her instant companion. In the kitchen it tapped at her elbow as she carried the fish to a tray. It knocked on her heart, causing it to pound. It whispered chilling nothings in her ears. 'Something bad is going to happen,' she whispered. 'I hope Mother and Father are safe in their car.'

She collected the bottle of wine from the pantry and she jumped as the pantry door banged loudly as if shut by unseen hands.

She carried the tray to the drawing room and then smiled. Biddy was sitting quite upright in her chair. Her eyes were shining in the glow of the fire. Anna put the tray down on a low Chinese redwood table. Anna loved that table. As a child she would run her fingers all around the great wood carvings. 'You look marvellous tonight, Grandma,' she said. 'Do you feel like a glass of wine?'

'I don't mind if I do.' Biddy smiled at her grand-daughter. 'You know, child, tonight I feel as if I am going to have a great adventure.'

Anna paused and looked seriously at her grand-mother. 'What d'you mean, Grandma? There's just the two of us here. What kind of adventure?'

'I don't know, darlin'. All day I've felt as if I've had a little bird plucking in my chest. It feels as if it's trapped.' Anna watched her grandmother's bony fingers imitate the bird's struggle against her narrow breast. 'I feel excited. I feel something is happening. You know how Martha knows those things, and so do you. Martha and Kitty came for tea this afternoon and, as I kissed them goodbye, I felt as if I was never going to see them again. You don't think this is what dying is like, do you, Anna?'

Anna lifted the lid off the fish. She felt a well in her heart beginning to drain. 'I don't know, Grandma. I really can't say.' Her hand was shaking. 'You won't die, though, will you, Grandma?'

Biddy smiled. 'I have to one day, my darling.'

'I know.' Anna's voice was hesitant. 'I don't know if I could bear life without you.' Anna put the silver lid on the floor beside her. The fish lay in its sauce with the pale green asparagus shrouded around it. The fish, Anna realized, looked as if it were supported by a bier of rice. 'Would you like a piece of fish, Grandma?' she said, breaking her thought with an everyday offer.

'Of course, Anna. I've been looking forward to this dish all day.'

The room, the fish, and her grandmother came sharply into focus. I'm just being silly, Anna scolded herself.

'What will you do tomorrow, Grandma?' Anna settled firmly into her chair and served herself a portion of fish. The white wine in a deeply etched blue Bulgarian wine glass tasted delicious. Her heavy damask napkin lay on her knee.

'I don't know, Anna. At my age you live each day as it comes. There may never be a tomorrow, so I make each day the best day I can. I say my prayers every night and I thank God that He filled my life with so many good things. But you know . . .' She paused and carefully finished her mouthful of fish. 'I sometimes think it helps if at some time in your life you have faced suffering and death of your loved ones. I know how to suffer and how to survive. Father O'Brian heard my confession yesterday. He told me then that losing his nose deepened and strengthened his faith. I, too, in all those early days in Ireland, and here when we first arrived, knew suffering. So now I can really rejoice in what we all have. And above all, I have you. After dinner will you sing me some of the old songs?'

'Of course I will.' Anna leaned back and finished her wine. 'In honour of the evening,' she said, 'I'll have another glass of wine. Would you like some more?'

Biddy shook her head. 'I can't get used to the stuff,' she said. 'Once you've been weaned on the fresh-milk taste of Guinness from the barrel, this stuff has no flavour. Ah, Anna! We had a man who rolled the barrels down the main street to the tavern. And when your grandfather had a penny – and that wasn't often – I'd carry the pitcher to the tavern with a clean cloth to guard the beer from the flies. I'd carry it carefully home and all of us, all ten of the children . . . Well . . .' She paused. 'Not all ten, of course, because a few had left us, but to me we were always there together. Their bodies may have been in their graves, but their souls attended the table with us.' She cleared her throat and Anna, looking at her, envisioned the scene her grandmother was describing.

There, in a bar-room, was a young girl with a kerchief around her head, holding a white zinc jug. At a long table she could see a very big man roaring with laughter. Seven children sat at the table, and three forever shimmered between the two rows of children. At the end of the table was a pretty woman who was smiling, her head turned to Anna as if she was having her photograph taken.

'. . . And we would pass the jug around,' Biddy continued, 'until it was finished. And then we would move the table back and how we would sing, Anna!'

'I can imagine,' Anna said, grinning. 'Come on. Let's leave the table for tomorrow, and I'll carry you to the piano room.' Anna lifted her grandmother in her strong young arms and, as she carried her gently to the music room, she willed some of the strength of her youth into the old woman she carried.

The music room was her favourite room in the house. A stately ebony Steinway grand sat magisterially in the centre of the parquet floor. The smell of beeswax polish perfumed the air. A small coal fire burned in a Nash fireplace. The walls were flocked with gold and silver scenes of gondolas on the canals in Venice. When she was young and practising for her daily lessons, Anna would watch the gondolas glide up the canals and hope that one day she, too, would lie in the arms of the man she married and let the gondolier canticle their love to the big, shining Venetian stars. She put her grandmother into a green plush library chair, aware that the big wings would protect Biddy from any draught. 'What shall I play?' she said.

' "I'll Take You Home Again, Kathleen",' Biddy answered, her fingers plucking at her chest again.

Anna went to the piano with a worried frown. She began to sing. ' "I'll take you home again, Kathleen, to where your heart will feel no pain . . ." ' Her big, pure voice filled the room. Anna understood at the moment just how homesick her grandmother must have felt and probably still did. She, of all of them, had spent most of her life in her village and now, far away, she could hear the voice of her dead husband and her children all buried in the churchyard next to their house. To be sure, the family and Father O'Brian held a fishing line of communication out to Biddy. Now, in the last few years, most of the talk with her grandmother was of the past. For some time now, Anna was aware that the present and the future were receding in Biddy's life. The past, lit up like a film-set, was now the future. Today's events were of no interest. Biddy was preparing herself for a journey.

The melancholic song finished. Anna played the opening bars of 'Danny Boy'. Her grandmother's hands lay silent on her lap. Her head nodded forward. She's tired. I'll take her to bed. Anna finished the piece. The farewell words hung in the air and Anna moved towards her grandmother.

She stopped, stayed by an invisible icy barrier. 'Grandma?' she said sharply. The body fell forward into her arms. Anna gently pushed her grandmother back upright in the chair and then looked down at the sweet, childlike face, now reposed in death. She sat like a large doll before her. For a moment Anna was terrified, but then she felt a growing feeling of peace. Biddy was gone. Her great adventure had begun.

Tears fell down Anna's face. 'It's all right, Grandma,' she cried, hugging the old lady. 'It's all right. I'll take you to bed as always. Then I'll call Father O'Brian. Don't you worry about a thing. I'll take care of you until Mummy and Daddy get back. And then Kitty and Martha will come. We'll all be together again. Just one big happy family. I'll ask Steven and Mary Rose, and we'll all dance and sing for you and be happy for you wherever you are.'

She carried her grandmother up the stairs into her bedroom. She carefully laid her on her bed and covered her with the thick sheets and woollen blanket. 'I don't want you to be cold,' she said, picking up Biddy's Bible. She put it between her grandmother's beloved fingers. As she slipped the green jade rosary around Biddy's hands clasping the Bible, she remembered the years that those hands had stroked her hair, cooked her food, and plied a needle. She kissed each hand and said, 'I'm just going to telephone Kitty and Martha, and then Father O'Brian. He'll know what to do. He always does.'

After the phone calls, the pain struck her. It was not the death that caused her so much anguish. That was expected. It was the awful thought that her grandmother must now lie alone in the cold grave. Biddy, who loved the light and the sun, would feel neither again. Anna knew the body was only an envelope for the soul, but her grandmother's body was such a beloved body. Not to see her smile or hear her voice on the stairs was unbearable.

Anna went back up to her grandmother's room and pulled a chair to the bed. She began to pray.

Sixteen

It was a long time before Anna could smile again. The evenings were no longer filled with the sound of her grandmother's laughter. The small, eager body no longer leaned from her chair, her face to one side, her mouth letting loose those words – big words, little words – which fell from her lips. Anna used to drink them all up, so much more satisfying than the food and drink served by the cook. Her grandmother's words were exotic and filled her to a bursting brim with excitement. Now the voice was silent for ever. The little hands, crossed at the wrist, with their neat, hard nails, were rotting in the soil of the graveyard.

The funeral was a private family affair, and Anna bore all of it in a stoic silence. She stood between her mother and her father, her throat blocked with sorrow. The workers at her father's shoe factory had all sent flowers, so there was a huge pile of her grandmother's favourite roses. Anna held a single purple rose in her hand, and when the dreadful moment came and the sexton lifted his spade, she leaned forward to drop the flower. 'Goodbye, Grandma,' she said quietly.

Now, in the months that followed, Anna kept very much to herself. Daniel lost weight and was also preoccupied. Mary tried to rally the family. Kitty and Martha were frequent visitors. Not even Kitty singing her Victorian vaudeville songs could make Anna smile. Anna joined the family gardener, Phillip, in the rose garden. Phillip, understanding her distress, kept his own counsel. 'Death comes to us all,' he observed gently. 'The trick is to make death a friend, like your grandmother did. Remember, Miss Anna, you are born alone and you die alone. You have no choice over your birth, but your death is your final performance. Your grandmother knew that.'

Anna remembered his words as she worked beside him. Quietly he showed her how to prune the roses. Spring was coming and everything was beginning its tumescent swell. 'Wait for the plant to throw its third leaf before you move it to a bigger pot.' 'Grow chrysanthemums between your vegetable rows. Bugs don't like the smell, and they hate garlic.'

As the summer threw her shimmering ballgown across the garden, Anna's lacerated heart began to mend. She was thrilled on the first day she found her parsley plants had grown a third leaf, and even more pleased when her French parsley not only threw a third leaf, but when she could see a distinctive pattern forming around the delicate little foliage. 'Phillip,' she said, 'it looks as if it has been stamped out by a cookie-cutter.'

'So it does,' Phillip said, amused by the girl's excitement.

Mary Rose became bored with Anna. 'Look,' she said, marching into the house one day. 'You've got to quit feeling sorry for yourself. Do something interesting. Lose your virginity or something. I'm getting embarrassed having a friend who hasn't done it – ever. You can't go on being a virgin, Anna. It's indecent.'

Anna hesitated for a moment. Normally she would brush Mary Rose off, but today she felt raw and vulnerable. 'Mary Rose, I really can't imagine handing myself over to a man like a cup to a teapot so that he can pour himself into me and then he's gone.'

'Oh, fiddle-faddle, Anna. Affairs are fun. Besides, I always do the leaving.'

Anna looked at Mary Rose. 'I know you do, but loving someone shouldn't be about hurting someone. My mother and father love each other far too much to quarrel. If my father is upset, my mother talks to him gently and he calms down. I come from a warm, loving family, and I want a marriage like my parents'. What's wrong with that?'

'Nothing, I suppose. You hang out with a loner, Steven. You immerse yourself in books.'

Anna smiled. 'You make me sound lonely, Mary Rose. You know I'm not lonely. I have a big family, and Father O'Brian. Steven and I have a wonderful time together. I wouldn't spoil it by sleeping with him for all the world. The right man will come along, and I'll marry him and live happily after. You'll see.'

'You probably will, Anna, but it will be boring.'

'No, it won't, Mary Rose. My parents are never bored,

94

and neither am I. I'm either in the garden or in the kitchen. I'm designing a ball-dress for my mother, and we are going to make it together. I found some really beautiful black velvet and white lace. The lace is from Holland. It really is gorgeous.'

'Oh really, Anna! Sometimes you're too good to be true.'

'Oh, come on, Mary Rose, you're just in a bad mood. Who can't you have now?'

Mary Rose's pink mouth dropped. The corners of her eyes turned down. Tears welled and trickled down her face.

'Very pretty, Mary Rose, but remember, it doesn't work on me.'

Mary Rose flashed a wicked grin, the tears still pouring down her face. 'I know, but I'm just keeping in practice. I learned to do this when my father came home smelling of other women. My, how he'd squirm with guilt! Nah, it's not that I'm in a bad mood. I always feel fine when I leave here. You cheer me up. It's just that Justin Villias is being a bit difficult to snare. Do you know him? I've seen his pictures in the newspapers, but my mother won't let him dance with me. She says the family are no good. But he is really handsome. I know Virginia Arbuthnot, the English bitch, has him at the moment; I want him.'

'Want, as in sleeping with him?'

'Yeah. Why not?'

'You make him sound like a boiled sweet you pass around.'

'Really, Anna, you have a dirty mind.'

'I do not have a dirty mind. I have a great imagination,' Anna said demurely.

Mary Rose looked at Anna's miraculous smile and realized for the first time that when Anna gave herself to this mythical man, it would be completely. There would be no thickets, no woods, no trespassing signs. Just a full heart and a warm hearth to welcome the tired man home. Mary Rose envied Anna. 'If you were me, Anna, how do you think I should get him away from Virginia?'

Anna thought for a moment. 'I think I'd ask your mother to invite him to dinner and cook the meal yourself.'

'But I can't cook, Anna. You know that.'

'Well, send your parents out and give the staff the night off. I'll come around early and help you. But I'll have to bring Aunt Martha, because my parents won't let me go anywhere without a chaperon. But you know she's great fun. And I also suggest that you wear something that makes you look romantic. Lay off the white powder and the rouge. And, Mary Rose, try not to flirt and be smart. Just be yourself. You're lovely as you are.'

'Do I have to ask Virginia? She's so stuck up. She looks down her nose at everybody. It's a hell of a nose. D'you know, Anna, she told me that the rule that applies to men's noses also applies to women's, but that you want men's noses to be big and women's you-know-whats to be small.'

Anna giggled. 'How silly,' she said. 'It's the quality that counts, not the quantity. Anyway, you're in luck with Justin. He's well-endowed.' She giggled and Mary Rose blushed.

'Where do you learn all this from, Anna?'

'Aunt Kitty. She's had trillions of lovers, but she's reformed now and prefers the peace and quiet of her own bed. She exhausts Joe, though.' Anna laughed.

Mary Rose was pleased to hear her laugh. It had been a while since her grandmother died, and Mary Rose was relieved to see the colour rising back to Anna's cheeks and the glow in her blue eyes.

Mary, hearing the laughter, came into the room.

'Mummy, if you were to seduce a boy — not that I think you would,' Anna said hurriedly, ' — what would you cook for him?'

Mary looked at Mary Rose. 'In love again, Mary Rose?'

'More like in lust,' Anna said.

'Well, let me see. I think I'd start with lobster poached in a good champagne. It need not be one of the great years, but fine all the same, with plenty of depth to capture the flavour of the lobster meat. How many of you will there be?' She looked at Mary Rose.

'Let me see. Do I have a partner?'

'Of course,' Anna said. 'It's like playing poker.'

'You play poker, Anna?' Mary Rose looked surprised.

'Of course I do.'

'Oh yes,' Mary Rose interrupted. 'Aunt Kitty. I'll have to talk to her. All right. I'll ask Martin Lowel. At least his blood is so blue, Virginia can't sneer at him.'

'My dear Mary Rose,' Mary smiled, 'you have nothing to apologize for. Both our families are descended from the kings of Ireland. We were civilized when the British were running about dabbed in blue woad. Anyway, for the second course, I'd serve chicken breasts layered with white truffles and *foie gras*. Around the breasts I'd put stuffed grilled mushrooms with black pepper and lemon juice. For the meat course, you can't do better than a good piece of rare beef with brussels sprouts and roast potatoes. Remember, the secret to a man's heart lies in the gravy-boat. Never be without a gravy-boat. The things a woman needs in her kitchen are a wooden spoon and a gravy-boat. Make sure that you use an excellent bottle of burgundy for the gravy, and thicken it slowly with flour and butter. For pudding, I think I'd make a chocolate mousse and then dip your meringues into the mousse and let them sit one night in the pantry.

Choose a good pudding wine and then follow that with coffee, brandy and *petits-fours*.'

'That sounds excellent.'

'When you leave the two men for their port, go to the bedroom above the drawing room and listen to their conversation down the servants' tube.'

'Mrs Kearney, how could you?'

Mary grinned. 'Kearney blood,' she said. 'I come from a long line of criminals and alcoholics. There's not much I don't know and haven't suffered.' *And have suffered*, she said silently to herself. She was pleased to see Anna looking more alive than she had for a long while. 'Your father has just received a letter from long-lost cousins in England, Anna. They live in Devon. I must say, it sounds wonderful. They ask if we will visit. As it happens, your father was thinking of expanding the business to England. Why should we always buy English goods when our shoes are even better and half the price?'

'Quite right. I'd love to go to England.' Anna put her arm around Mary Rose's shoulders. 'I love the idea of England. All that history. All the architecture. If only it didn't have the English living there.'

'Ach, Anna,' her mother said. 'The people of England are fine. It's the rich. They're barbarians. You see, the Irish don't have a class system like the English. We all live together and muck in. The English are quite different. Still, we'll think about going, shall we?'

'If you go to England, I've got to come too,' Mary Rose said.

'You'll do that. I promise. Now I must get back to the church. I've promised Father O'Brian that I'll help with the flowers.'

Seventeen

'Virginia Arbuthnot will arrive at least a quarter of an hour early,' Martha announced. She was standing in Mary Rose's kitchen, surrounded by plates and wrapped in Cook's thick white linen pinafore. She had her hair tucked into a white cooking hat which, being several sizes too large, slipped rakishly to one side. Both girls were in fits of giggles. 'I think both of you should take yourselves off and get ready. I'll just finish up here and you can entertain your guests in the drawing room. There are two sorts of sherry, and I've made some Savoy biscuits. Do concentrate, Mary Rose. That's a bowl of devils-on-horseback. With any luck, it'll be Mary Rose on horseback with Justin.'

Mary Rose cuddled Anna. 'Can you imagine, Anna? Justin sweeps out into the night and wafts me away.'

'He can't waft you, Mary Rose, you idiot. You've put on too much weight. He'd have to hire a crane.'

'Oh, Anna! What a dreadful thing to say! I must go and find a mirror immediately. How could you, you beast?' Mary Rose took off for her bedroom, and Anna winked at Martha and followed her.

Mary Rose's bedroom was big and square. It was at the end of the mansion. Now that Mary Rose no longer used the nursery, Mrs Portney had long been pensioned off. 'Funny,' Anna said as she watched Mary Rose pirouetting in front of a cheval mirror. 'I often think of your Mrs Portney.'

'I don't. D'you really think I'm fat? Oh damn! Look at my chin. I can just feel a spot coming. Look, Anna!'

Anna sauntered over to Mary Rose and took her chin

in her hand. 'I can't see anything. Don't you ever think of Mrs Portney, Mary Rose?'

'No. She was just one of the servants. They come and go all the time. They're like dinner plates. Each one has a pattern, and they pass around my life and then they go. I learned when I was a very little girl not to attach myself to any of them.'

Anna looked deeply into Mary Rose's cavernous eyes. Down in the well behind those eyes, unwept tears were frozen in time. Anna could see the face set in the solidified amber. The face became clear. 'Mary Rose,' she said.

'What is it? Can you see a sight?'

'No.' Anna shook her head. 'I can see a woman's face. It is very white. She has lots of black ringlets. Masses of hair, and she is looking for you.'

A stillness fell over Mary Rose. She pulled her chin away from Anna's hand. 'How do you know her?'

'I saw her in your eyes. You know I can see things.'

'Yeah, I know. Well, that was Victoria. She was my first nanny. She was sacked by my mother. She said she stole things. I know that isn't true. Victoria would never steal anything. My mother was jealous because I loved Victoria, so she got rid of her. She got rid of all the good ones and only kept the ones that were cruel and unkind.' There was a bitter, polar desolation in Mary Rose's voice.

Anna had heard that voice before. She knew it came from a very dark region of Mary Rose's soul, and she feared for her friend. 'Are you really interested in Justin Villias, Mary Rose? Or do you just want to teach Virginia a lesson?'

'A bit of both,' Mary Rose said, pulling her dress over her head. 'I haven't met my match in any man yet. Justin's just practice.' She grinned. 'I'm off to have my bath. You can use the yellow suite.'

Anna picked up her suitcase and walked along the long, silent corridor. Lord and Lady Roswell were in Paris. All the servants were in their quarters. Anna shivered. I'd be so lonely, she whispered to herself.

She found the yellow door leading to her suite. She and Martha were staying the night. James was in his cottage on the grounds, but Martha insisted on chaperoning Anna. 'I don't trust Justin further than I can throw him,' Martha said when James protested. 'Martin is a nice enough boy. I've put them both together in the green room. Hopefully Martin won't let Justin out of his sight, and Virginia is next to Mary Rose's bedroom, so she'll play watchdog. That way I get to go to sleep.'

'Come on, Mary Rose. They'll be here in ten minutes. Aunt Martha's right. Virginia will turn up early, just to catch us off guard.'

'You go down first, Anna, and open the front door. I want to make an entrance. You get them to the bottom of the stairs and then I'll flounce down the stairs so that Justin can see my knees. I've got the most delightful red garter on, and this dress lifts up beautifully when I flounce. Come on. You stand at the bottom of the stairs and I'll do a practice.'

Anna stood obediently at the bottom of the stairs, gazing up at her friend. 'You look really marvellous,' Anna said.

Mary Rose stood at the top of the sweeping marble staircase. Her long, dark hair was plaited with seed pearls. She wore a long, deep velvet purple dress, cut dangerously low. Her full, milk-white breasts rose and fell as she breathed. Anna envied her, demure in an Irish green taffeta dress. She was still forced to wear Peter Pan collars. 'Ready?' Mary Rose called down.

'OK. Shoot.'

Mary Rose wafted down the first dozen steps.

'Oh no, Mary Rose. You can't do that. I can see your knickers.'

'Good,' Mary Rose continued imperturbably. 'Someone's got to see them besides me. They're a present from my father, made of the very best silk, and the lace is from Italy.' She pulled up her dress. 'See?' she said.

'Mary Rose Buchanan! What do you think you're doing?' Martha came into the hall. 'You keep your dress down, young lady. Well, I never!' she said, mounting the stairs beside Mary Rose. 'You both look wonderful,' she said. 'I'm off to change my clothes.' She ran up the stairs just as the doorbell sounded.

Mary Rose backed to the top of the stairs and took up her position.

'What a ham,' Anna muttered. She opened the door and blinked at the strong porch light. 'I'm Anna Kearney.' Virginia managed to look as though there was a foul smell under her nose.

'Hello, Anna.' Martin smiled and took her hand. 'Nice to see you again.'

Anna felt herself blush, and looked at Justin Villias, the man for whom this dinner party was intended. Justin took Anna's hand in his and smiled a deeply practised smile.

Anna instinctively felt all the hairs on her body rise with distaste. How could Mary Rose be interested in this creep, she thought. Ugh. Justin was fair with blue eyes. He had the Villias family look about him. He certainly smelled of family money.

In fact Justin Villias was a by-product of his times, a faithful reflection of the social froth that was America. He had been born with the destructive benefits of luck and wealth, and in his nineteen years had never needed to exert himself for any reason. It wasn't his fault, rather the handicap of an over-confident and over-rich society. Basically, he was an intelligent, humane individual, capable of charity and sensitivity. But these were characteristics no one asked him to deliver. Superficiality was the baseline, and Justin wore it well. He was confident and socially aggressive, using all the tricks of the game. He was an impressive dancer with dextrous feet and flair, and he dressed in the fashions of the day almost before they hit the store windows. He had tried all the cocktails invented by New York's club barmen, and was working on savouring the sexual delights of all the eligible society women: his tall, footballer's physique scored well. Justin Villias had become a highly entertaining social puppet, the Punch to Mary Rose's Judy. But he was capable of, and deserved, much more. The trouble was neither the society, nor those who thought they knew him, asked for more, and he himself had stopped offering it long ago.

Once inside he looked upwards to the top of the stairs. 'Ah, my dear Mary Rose!' he said, walking to the bottom of the stairs. 'What a perfectly marvellous sight you are, darling.' He took Virginia's arm. 'Do we get a drink in this house?'

'Of course.' Anna took charge. 'Do come this way. Martin, will you pour?' Poor Martin, she thought. He's much too slow for all this. She led the way to the drawing room. Mary Rose, upstaged, slouched down the steps.

They assembled self-consciously in front of a big fire. Even though it was early summer, the nights were still cold. Martin poured the sherry and Anna handed round the fluted Kerry crystal. Justin sipped and nodded. 'Hm,' he said. 'Portuguese. A very good sherry. Your father has good taste, Mary Rose.'

Mary Rose gazed at Martin. 'Tell us, darling. What have you been doing since I last saw you?'

Martin beamed. When his Mary Rose smiled at him, the world was a different place. He'd never been in love before. Love, he discovered, was always wanting to take your coat off to cover puddles that could possibly cause

Mary Rose's dainty feet to suffer. Love was forgetting to chew your food forty times because you were talking too much to eat. Love was laughing insanely over nothing anybody else would find remotely funny. Love was dancing on his own in the moonlight from the sheer joy of it all.

Love was all those things for Martin. And babies. Sons with Mary Rose's wild eyes and a daughter with her pouty, kissable mouth. Martin, forever sheathed in the warmth of her body, caressed by her small, supple hands, blissfully asleep on her breasts, the two nipples erect like pink sentinels. How could a woman have skin that soft and white, or a waist so beautifully turned? God must have thrown away the mould after he'd made Mary Rose.

There was something bothering Martin about this dinner party. The hunter-gatherer, dormant male intuition told him that Mary Rose was about to attempt to seduce Justin, but by now Martin knew that the hunter side of Justin had been triggered not by Mary Rose but by Anna. Martin was worried. He was very fond of Anna and he knew she was an innocent to be protected at all costs. As much as he loved Mary Rose, she could take care of herself.

He watched Justin carefully. Justin caught his eye and grinned at him. Martin found himself in a dilemma. If he warned Mary Rose that Justin might make a pass at Anna, it would hurt Mary Rose's feelings and the resulting explosion would shake the roof for several days. He dared not say anything to Anna because he had no proof at all. He liked the look of Martha, but he'd never met her before.

Martha also watched Justin closely. She was so glad she had married loving, uncomplicated James. Men like Justin needed to be attached to girls like Virginia Arbuthnot who was content with a gigolo. Virginia's patrician English nose was long and wet. She looked as if she had a permanent cold. Her voice was high and nasal, and she had a vast behind which had been trained to an English saddle at a very early age. A procession of men had ridden her like they'd ridden their hunters to hound. Virginia was now using the end of her nose to size up Anna. 'I hear you're thinking of going to England,' she said, her witch-like voice hissing through her teeth. 'Well, you'd better dress warmly then.' She gazed at Anna, her metal-blue eyes filled with envy. 'D'you hunt?'

'No,' Anna said. 'I'm afraid I don't. The idea of killing such a beautiful thing as a fox horrifies me.'

'Oh, don't be silly. You Americans are all the same. Neurotic as poodles.'

'I'm Irish, actually,' said Anna, finishing her sherry. 'And now, if you don't mind, I'm going off to the kitchen to help with the food. Brighten up, Mary Rose.' She grinned at her. 'Come on, Aunt Martha. I think it's time for the servants to go downstairs.' She laughed a forced, hurt laugh.

'What a bitch,' Martha said when they both got to the safety of the kitchen.

'Yeah,' Anna agreed. 'But you know, she can never have children. Did you see that, too?'

'Yes, she had a shadow over her ovaries.'

'Not much of a life, being beaten and abused by men.'

'No,' Martha agreed, 'but those are her choices. She is very rich, owns her own house, so she has none of the excuses of women who are poor and trapped. I'm afraid Mary Rose will go the same way.'

Anna smiled. 'Don't worry, Aunt Martha.' She picked up a fresh bowl of double cream and began gently to mix in the pink coral red lobster roe. The colour flooded the cream like a sunset after a beautiful blue day. 'Look at that!' Anna exclaimed.

'Beautiful,' said Martha, lost in the wonder of it all.

When Anna left the room with her aunt, Justin blinked. Something was now missing. Never before had Justin felt like this. It was as though his heart, which was an empty, well-scrubbed grate, had suddenly felt the first kiss of a fire. He certainly had seen small fireflies in Greece, where he had a house. Also huge fireflies pulsating across the plains in Africa. He had been naked in the warm Caribbean Sea, his body outlined by the glow of the phosphorus in the water. He had made love countless times to enthusiastic girls on beaches all over the world, and even a few elderly matrons. But this feeling was new to him. He realized that he felt vulnerable and very raw. Deep down inside a small boy was struggling to get out. Justin was used to the Mary Roses of this world. She was into complicated, exhausting headgames, and Justin at times quite enjoyed the tears and tantrums. But in Anna he felt a terrific sense of surging energy. It was as if Anna took life eclectically, collecting everything around her and making it move and roll and sway. He knew that many people would find Anna dull, but he was quickened by her energy. He loved the feel of an electric current barrelling through the blood in his veins. It was like an intravenous injection of champagne. It was a better high than heroin. He had only known her for a few minutes, and he wanted to catch her like a trout, pull her out of the water of her everyday life, watch her twist and turn in the clear Highland Scottish light. The mountains shadowed in mist. Scotland, the bleak promise of loving. See her eyes widen when she felt the kiss of penetration and then watch the innocence ebb and flow away. Anna was the sort of person that could die for love. Mary Rose was a woman who would be killed for it. There lay the difference.

The common link was that they were both soul-sisters

and protected each other as they met and parted and met again. Down through the centuries they sought each other. Their lives and destinies designed by God before the world began. When He called Anna's name He gave her a life of service and the free will to choose it or not. So far Anna had always submitted happily to her path. To Mary Rose He gave the power to lead, for good or for ill. So far, consistently, Mary Rose chose the left-hand path. Fated to be torn away from Anna and to hurtle into Samsara, never to learn that the true nature of the soul is peace.

Mary Rose, feeling isolated and unappreciated by Justin, rang the bell. 'Let's go in to dinner,' she said. 'I gave the servants the night off. I've been cooking all day. Martha and Anna are just putting the final touches to the food.' Mary Rose led the way to the long dining room. The massive table had now been disassembled and only two leaves were spread out. The gold-plate glittered and the Irish crystal glasses shone from the firelight in the grate. 'How awfully vulgar!' Virginia stood in the doorway. 'Very American. Don't you think, Justin?'

'Sure.' Justin gave Virginia a small push. 'We are Americans, and we love comfort. At least we have houses that are properly heated and toilets that work.'

'Lavatories, dear. Not toilets. *Toilets* is common.'

'I am common, Virginia. I'm American. Remember?' Virginia sniffed.

'And we wash,' Justin hissed fiercely, remembering with loathing the rather horsy smell between Virginia's legs and her bad habit of letting off loud morning farts.

Mary Rose grinned. This was getting interesting. 'You sit on my right, Justin. I shall make you my guest of honour. Martha will sit on my left. And then, Virginia, you can sit at the end of the table with Martin.'

Martha and Anna arrived with a big silver tray with tiny hen lobsters circled in the shape of a wheel, the pretty pinks and reds speckled with the sauce. Bright green watercress lay curled beside the lobsters, and yellow rounds of lemon dribbled beads of juice. Justin felt his tongue flicker. Martha had a bottle of champagne in her hand.

'Ah!' Mary Rose looked at Martha and tried to remember her well-rehearsed lines.

'*Daddy*,' Martha mouthed at her.

'Oh yes. Daddy,' she said brightly, 'brought several cases of Veuve Clicquot Ponsardin. It's chosen as the wine of the season. He got it to celebrate the Scotch Grand National.'

'Scottish, dear. Scottish. What next? You're all barbarians. You're looting Europe for your faded furs. It's *disgusting*.' Virginia shot this latest broadside across Mary Rose's bows.

Mary Rose looked startled.

'Are you always this awful?' Anna said, putting down the tray of lobster.

'She makes it a habit to insult people,' Justin said gloomily. 'She reckons she's so rich, she needn't be polite to anybody.'

Anna stared at Virginia. 'Virginia,' she said coolly. 'I don't care if you're rich or not. If you open your mouth once more in Mary Rose's house and insult anybody, I'll suggest you leave. Do you understand that?'

Virginia's eyes widened. 'Are you threatening me?' she said, her voice trembling.

'I'm not threatening, Virginia. It's a promise. So shut up, as you British say.'

Martha laughed. 'Quite right, Anna,' she said. 'Martin, you open the champagne. I do love a good bottle of champagne. Don't you, Mary Rose?'

'I'll carry round the lobster.' Mary Rose hopped out of her chair and picked up the tray.

Even with her breasts almost touching Justin's cheek, he felt nothing. 'Lovely Mary Rose,' he said, 'did you make all this by yourself? Wasn't it kind of Anna and her aunt to put the finishing touches to the dish?' He smiled at Mary Rose. Mary Rose, he knew with a rake's instinct, had not made this dish or any other dish. Women cook as they make love. Men make love when they are closely allied to things of the earth. For a woman, it is her home and her hearth that ignites the passionate sense of the body. The smell of the lobster and the bright glistening roe hung between Anna and Justin's vision of her, momentarily naked. Martin would never satisfy a woman like Anna, but he would Mary Rose. Martin was no Sybarite. He had been brought up in the stern Puritanism of his Presbyterian ancestors. For him denial of comfort was his way of life. Sex for Mary Rose was just another appetite to be slaked, like her lust for food. Indiscriminate and uncaring. Food and sex and alcohol, he felt, were just drives in her life, even though, for now, he felt real feelings for her. At the end of the long day, much later on, he would choose a compatible, uncomplicated companion and retire to the country where he would stroll on the lawn with his progeny, his wife, moulded like funeral wax into a shape desired by him. Life could slip by; he was fated to lie entombed in the local church. 'There lies a good man,' the locals would say of him admiringly. 'A good man,' he would groan, 'who died of boredom.'

Martin looked at Mary Rose through his fluted glass of champagne. 'Cheers, Mary Rose,' he said. 'To your very good health.' Boring he might be, but for the moment Mary Rose would always come back to him. For now that was his comfort and his solace.

Eighteen

Martha sat up in bed, spectacles on her nose, reading a book on the Caribbean islands. She had a yearning to wallow in the Caribbean Sea with James. Nobody but James knew she wore spectacles. A woman has to have a few secrets, she comforted herself. Slowly the spectacles slipped down her nose and she fell asleep.

Also Martin, after too much champagne, fell asleep. Justin lay there quietly, his eyes glowing in anticipation of the coming event. He had never deflowered a virgin before. Come to think of it, there were very few around these days, and most of those were heavily chaperoned like Anna. He hurriedly collected himself and slid out of bed.

Panther-like, he stalked the corridor. He knew her suite because he had watched her as she had carried her hot-water bottle to bed. Imagine, he thought, a young girl who washed up after the dinner party with her aunt and carried a hot-water bottle. It was the innocence of her life that caught him off guard. Something about the joyous way she smiled. He put his hand on her door and pushed lightly.

The first Anna knew about Justin's visit was to wake up with a start. She opened her eyes and her hand reached for her bedside light. But it was not *her* bedside light. She was in another room.

For a moment she wondered if she was in a former life, but no. There really was a warm, living, breathing man in bed beside her. She was wearing a white cotton nightdress which reached down to her toes. The hot-water bottle was cold now. 'Don't panic, Anna,' Justin said. 'It's only me.'

'What on earth do you think you're doing?' Anna sat up and fumbled for the light.

'I want to make love to you.'

Anna found the light-switch and turned it on. 'Don't be so silly, Justin.' Anna pulled back the bedclothes and revealed Justin's mounting erection. 'What on earth is that?' she said, pointing between his legs.

'It's an erection,' Justin said, cupping a hand over his genitals sheepishly.

'How awful.' Anna peered closely at his body. 'Do you really have to walk about dangling that in front of you?' she asked, her natural curiosity getting the better of her as usual.

'Well, I can't tuck it up behind, can I?'

'No, I suppose you can't. More's the pity.'

'Is this the first time you've even seen an erection, Anna?' Justin pulled the covers back over his body. His primary mission for the moment was an impossibility. His weapon in life had retired to sulk, and he hoped it wasn't permanent.

'Well, I've seen paintings of men, and statues, but they don't paint erections. And after seeing yours, I'm very glad they don't.'

Justin lay in Anna's bed nonplussed. What on earth am I going to do now, he reasoned with his libidinous nature. Shit. I wish I hadn't thrown my bathrobe off by the door. He really did not want to have to rise from Anna's bed totally naked. He could feel his balls retracting in dismay up his scrotum. The thought of Anna eyeing his testicles with her clear, uncompromising gaze appalled him. One was slightly bigger than the other, and she was bound to giggle.

Anna broke the silence by saying, 'You'll feel

so-o-o-o-o silly when you have to walk across the room to get your dressing-gown. I could give you my cashmere scarf to wind round your buns, but I'm not going to. Serves you right, Justin, for invading a woman's privacy.'

Justin felt himself blushing. A very abnormal experience for him. Damn the girl! How could she make him feel like a schoolboy with his finger in a honeypot? Though, this time, there was no honeypot, just a beautiful girl swathed in white lace, laughing at him. 'I think I'll go now,' Justin said in a strangled voice. 'Would you mind putting out the light?'

'Most certainly not, Justin. I want to see you walk across the carpet so I can have a good giggle. Then I'll tell Aunt Martha and Mary Rose all about how you look without your clothes. You don't have many hairs on your chest, do you?'

Justin looked down at his chest. 'I suppose not,' he said.

'You ought really to do some exercise, you know. You don't have any muscles.'

'I *do*.' Justin flexed his right arm. 'Look,' he said. 'Feel it.'

Anna dug her sharp pink nails into the miserably small lump.

Justin restrained himself from screaming. Oh why, he asked himself, did I have to be born a man? He wanted to cry. Here he was, stripped of his dignity, his physique piteously questioned, and now the final humiliation.

'Pigeon's knees. That's what muscles are.' Anna had that curious fighting tone in her voice that let him know she knew what he was going to say before he said it. 'And I can tell you now, Justin, if you don't stop sleeping around, you're going to get a dreadful disease and it'll drop off.'

'Don't say that, Anna. Oh, please don't say that.'

'I must,' said Anna implacably. 'I have to warn you.'

'Oh no.' Justin could see years of impotence stretching before him. He decided an early retreat was the better part of valour. He leapt out of the bed, clutching a pillow to his stomach, and headed for his dressing-gown. He heard Anna's triumphant gales of laughter follow him out of the room and down the hall.

He lay in his bed sweating. Now he was erect again and he very much wished he could sneak out of the house and lift a car.

Anna did not share with anyone the secret of Justin's late-night visit. The next morning at breakfast, Justin had recovered his equilibrium, but found himself still disconcerted by Anna's twinkling eyes. As she passed him at breakfast, she put a hand on his shoulder and he knew their secret was now safe. He heaved a sigh of relief. He could not have Anna as a lover, but now he was free to have her as a friend.

Long ago Justin had learned to divide his women friends from his lovers. Once sex entered into the relationship, friendship flew out of the window, like a mynah bird's endlessly repeating 'Too bad, how sad.'

Virginia was not in a good mood. She snapped her fingers at the butler who stood guard over the servants. 'Why no kedgeree?'

Perry's aristocratic nostrils flared. 'We left that sort of cooking behind us when we came to Ellis Island, Miss Arbuthnot. The chef can make you kedgeree if you so wish. I shall instruct him now.' Perry left the room.

'I can't abide breakfast without kedgeree, Mary Rose.' Virginia went to the sideboard and ladled out a mound of kidneys.

'Umm,' Justin said. 'Pig's urine, Virginia?'

Virginia shot him a furious look. She'd expected a visit from her lover last night and he hadn't come. She had, though, dreaming of banging her vagina on the saddle-pommel of a thundering stallion. It had always been a fantasy of hers to have a real stallion. Now, sitting next to Justin, she caught a gossamer link between the laughter in Anna's eyes and Justin's smile. He will have to be taken away from this one, she thought.

'Do you have any travel plans this year?' Virginia leaned forward, her full breasts touching the kidneys on her plate. 'Oh shit.' Virginia pulled back her chair and began dabbing at her bosom.

'Actually,' Anna said, 'Mary Rose is coming with us to England.'

'Where?'

'To visit my cousins in Devon.'

'I don't suppose I'd know them if they're Irish.' Virginia's tone was dismissive.

'I don't suppose you would, Virginia. They live just outside a place called Axminster. They own a big farm and a manor house called Charters. Their name is Kearney, of course.'

'Well,' Virginia conceded, 'I *have* heard of them. They breed horses, don't they?'

Anna smiled. 'Yes, they do. They won the Grand National with Bullet. He's out to stud now, but my father is really keen to ride him. Who knows? I might have a go. I'd love to ride a horse that has won the National.'

'Do you have a good saddle?'

Anna laughed. 'Mary Rose is a much better rider than I am. I just stick like a burr and hope for the best.' Virginia's nose twisted with jealousy. How could those two bitches not only have lots of money, but also be so classically beautiful? It was just not fair. She gazed down at the brown mess on the front of her blouse and felt her eyes fill with tears. Life had not been the same since Daddy died. Her daddy totally understood her, and without her fat, fussy little father, she was lost and alone. Her mother rode to hounds, played bridge, and went shopping. Virginia could do nothing with her life, since her class was chained by the social climate that considered it vulgar to work. She did not like to embroider or to arrange flowers. The idea of running a house was abhorrent. All she could do was wait for some man to marry her. She would whelp a son and heir and then her life would be secure, and she could jostle and push her way into the cut-throat business of entertaining London society. For now, though, much of her life was lived in a chilled fear of loneliness. Justin offered no hope of permanence. She knew it was her money.

And Mary Rose, sitting on the other side of the table, was also sullen with disappointment. Where had Justin been last night? Certainly not with her. She pushed the possibility of an affair with Justin aside and said brightly, 'Ah! Here's Perry with your kedgeree.'

Perry wafted in carrying a plate covered by a silver bowl. 'Miss Anna, it's a pleasure to have your company.' Perry bowed obsequiously over Virginia's plate. He took a silver serving spoon and, once having removed the dish, he ladled the yellow, spicy rice on to her plate. Inwardly he was laughing. Ah Ying, the Chinese chef, had made the kedgeree after a blood-curdling series of Chinese oaths and grumbles. As he had handed the plate to Perry, he had spat expertly into the heart of the dish. 'May she give birth to dragon,' the chef had said. 'Ohh, yaryar!' And he had leapt off the ground, kicking the imaginary Virginia around the kitchen. Perry had grinned, covered the dish, and had left Ah Ying executing some brilliant sword thrusts with his butcher's knife. Funny people, these little yellow men. Perry had looked forward to the next few minutes.

When he had finished serving Virginia and straightened up, he slowly closed one eye as he turned to leave. Martha smiled.

Martin took Mary Rose off after breakfast to ride in Central Park. Justin and Virginia left after much confusion. 'Come on, Virginia. I'll be late for coffee with my mother.'

'Fuck your mother,' was Virginia's reply.

Anna went upstairs and tried to corral the dithering Virginia.

'I do hate it when he shouts at me.' Virginia was flushed and trembling.

Anna hung over the banister. 'Don't be such a bully, Justin. Shut up.'

Justin flung himself into a chair and sulked.

Anna was pleased to see the back of both of them.

A golden, hazy silence fell over the house, and Anna breathed deeply. Martha came down the stairs. 'Whew!' she said. 'I can't wait to get back to my own little house and the peace and the quiet.'

Anna nodded. 'Nothing is ever restful around Mary Rose. It's the sort of people she's attracted to. Still, Virginia's impossible, poor girl. But Justin could make something of himself, if he wanted to. The life of a gigolo is strictly limited. There's nothing worse than an ageing Lothario.'

Martha giggled. 'Still, it was fun, and the meal was excellent. I really liked the pink sauce over the lobster. Well done, Anna. I'll wait down here while you get your things.'

Anna wafted up the stairs. Martha's sense of fun meant more to her than all the events of the night before. Now she could allow herself to think about the exciting trip to England.

BOOK THREE

ENGLAND

Nineteen

Daniel got on the boat feeling as if twenty years had just fallen off his shoulders. Beside him Mary glowed quietly. Anna wore a black velvet skirt with a matching jacket, a fall of cream lace at her throat. Steven, standing on the jetty, had a white, pinched look on his face. Anna gazed back at him, her heart sore that he could not come; his mother would never allow him to visit the goys. He was trapped in his ghetto until her return. Anna leaned over the rail as far as she could and screamed, 'I'll buy you a special present, Steven.' She was pleased to see him smile and wave back. Beside him, the rest of the Kearney family were waving and yelling.

Mary Rose, standing alongside Anna at the rails, was sombre and preoccupied. She wondered what Anna would say if she knew she was still sore from screwing Justin. She remembered the night. It was a shame that she didn't really fancy him, but she had made sure Virginia would find out. She had left a tell-tale smear of rouge on his shirt. She knew Virginia would inspect his clothes. Now she had a sour taste in her mouth from too much red wine. She wished the damn ship would stop hooting. And Anna's ill-bred Irish family was making a fool of itself as usual. Her own mother and father were not there, of course. For a moment she really wished they were waving to her from the dock, but with a weary sigh she reminded herself not to expect too much from anyone, particularly her father.

Daniel saw Mary Rose's frail shoulders droop. He put his arm around her protectively. Mary Rose smiled at him gratefully. Not all men are dogs, she reminded herself. He was about the only man she knew who did not guard his wife as if she were a bitch on heat. Mary Rose laughed. 'I'm going to enjoy this trip hugely,' she said. 'Come on, Anna, stop being sloppy about leaving Steven and let's go trawling for men.'

'I don't want to go trawling for men, Mary Rose. Your "seduce Justin" dinner party was enough to put me off for life. I just want to go down to my cabin and read Jane Austen. She's my homework for the holidays. I want to learn to use the sort of English words she uses so exquisitely.'

'Anna, you're so boringly intense,' Mary Rose responded. 'If the women are all like Virginia, then I'm in luck. I shouldn't have any trouble finding men.'

They both followed Mary and Daniel up the long ladders to their suites. There was a connecting door between Anna's and Mary Rose's rooms. Both suites were painted a pale ivory. The mantelpieces were fashioned out of heavily carved green marble, and the tables and chairs were Louis XV-style. Mary Rose immediately took off her silk stockings and stood on the thick pile carpet wriggling her toes. 'How marvellous,' she said. 'Thick carpet is so sexy.'

'It also takes a lot of cleaning.' Anna was getting very bored with Mary Rose's continual harping about sex. 'Go away, Mary Rose. The porter will be here in a minute with the cabin trunks.'

Mary Rose ignored her. 'D'you remember the other boat, Anna? When we were little and your Aunt Kitty had to sing for your supper?'

Anna grinned. 'I do.' She sighed. 'Life was so simple then. My grandmother was still alive. I do still miss her so.' The mood between them changed as it so often did.

'I know you do. I can feel it.' Mary Rose gave Anna a big hug. 'I'm off to my bathroom to wallow around in the bath.' She was gone.

They had both received invitations to the captain's cocktail party. Anna made a face. They were also on the captain's table for the duration of the voyage. How very tedious, she thought. Tedious: such a Jane Austen word. Anna tipped the porter, who heaved the two big cabin trunks through the door. There was no sign of Mary Rose, except for a few loud trills coming from the bathroom.

'Mary Rose, the stuff's arrived.' The trilling stopped and the bathroom door opened. Mary Rose came dripping into the sitting room. Anna quickly pushed the cabin door of her suite closed.

'Mary Rose, you can't stand about naked. What if someone saw you?'

Mary Rose laughed. She stood there, flushed from the bath. Anna noticed the touch of blue veins on her breasts. She envied Mary Rose her exuberance. Mary Rose could, and would, walk into a crowd naked. She would just stand and let them stare in lustful admiration.

Anna sometimes wished she could behave like Mary Rose. 'Go and put something on, Mary Rose,' she said.

'I can't, silly. All my stuff's in the cabin trunk. I'll go and get my bag so I can unlock the trunk and find a negligée to spare your blushes. Goodness, Anna, you've seen me naked often enough.'

Anna smiled. 'You're such an exhibitionist.'

Mary Rose came back into the room, swinging her handbag on a long black silken ribbon. She swirled it around her head and then did a high kick.

'Put some clothes on, Mary Rose, and stop being such an idiot. Here, give me the key, please.' Anna felt like a mother scolding a naughty child. She didn't much like being put in this role. Most of the time she realized that she let Mary Rose take all the risks, and then, underneath a pile of self-explanation, she rather resented the fun she missed. Not the sexual encounters, she told herself firmly, unlocking Mary Rose's trunk, just the teasing and flirting.

'Second drawer down.' Mary Rose continued to dance about the room, examining her body in the big gilt mirror over the fireplace.

Anna pulled out a deep purple lace dressing-gown. 'Where on earth did you get this?'

'Oh, I stole it from my mother. She's got cupboards full of negligées and silk underwear. A different colour for each of the lovers she's had since we came to America. I guess the purple was for the bishop she was balling.'

Anna looked disapproving. 'Your language, Mary Rose!'

Mary Rose shrugged. 'I told you it's from hanging out with stable boys. At least I'm honest about it.'

'Sure you are, and at least you don't swear in front of guests like Virginia. Oh dear, I do hope she's not a sample of all English girls. Anyway, let's get moving.' Anna consulted her watch. 'We have half an hour before we need to go down to the cocktail party.'

'I wonder what the good captain will look like. Bald, old and stout I suspect.'

Anna raised her eyebrows. 'Why, Mary Rose, d'you fancy adding a captain to your list?'

'Nah. I'm looking for something quite different. Someone out of my class. A swabber perhaps.'

'What on earth is a swabber?'

'You know, someone who cleans the decks. I've been doing my homework for this trip.'

With a grand sense of hollow drama, Mary Rose swept out of the room. Anna stood for a moment. Mary Rose did this to her. It was as if her friend took a little bit of Anna away with her. Anna felt a little depleted, a little weary. A hot bath will soon put everything right, she thought. That's what I need, a good, hot bath.

Twenty

On the way up to the dining room, Anna held her father's hand. Daniel was now wearing tails for dinner. Anna marvelled at how handsome he was. Beside her, Mary shimmered in a frost-blue, long silk dress. Anna wore a long cream evening gown. She had a red cashmere and wool shawl around her shoulders. The breeze from the sea was light and it nipped at her nose and her shoulders. Mary Rose walked beside her, also wearing a slim-fitting, full-length black lace dress. The front was cut low but, for once, not so low that Anna was embarrassed for her. Mary Rose's head was held high and she walked with her sexually provocative wiggle. Passengers stopped and stared at the four of them. They did look rather wonderful, Anna thought. There was a radiance about the fact that all four of them loved each other. All had strong electrical field forces. Anna could see tranquil yellow lights streaming from their faces and hands. Even Mary Rose shone pink in the setting sunlight.

The boat rolled gently, her humming Rolls-Royce engines driving the prow of the great ship in lifts and drops over the deep blue waves. 'Look!' Daniel pointed to flashes of silver. 'Flying fish.' Mary clasped her hands and ran to the side of the boat. Daniel joined her and put his arm around her waist. 'It's been a long time, darling,' he whispered gently, 'since you and I have been on a boat together. Do you remember the last trip?'

Mary lifted her head to kiss him. 'I do,' she said. 'My

darling, we've come such a long way since then. Do you remember poor Father O'Brian so sick all the time?'

'I do indeed. But more I remember the hope I had for us all. To get away from Ireland and all the awful things that were happening.' He paused and looked down at his wife. She knew there was always a great sadness in Daniel. She, though, was happy wherever she was. As long as she had Daniel, the rest of the world did not exist. He was her moon and stars.

She glanced at Anna, who was also leaning on the railings a little way away. Both girls were talking quietly and Mary smiled. 'One day,' she said, snuggling into Daniel's arms, 'we'll go back to Ireland.'

'We won't, ever!' Danny's face was set. 'I promised myself when I left, Mary, that I'd never step on Irish soil until the day the English were cleared out. Ireland is England's last colony. They won't leave.'

Mary nodded. 'That's the truth. But now, Danny, it's a lovely evening and we are all going to have cocktails with the captain. Let's enjoy it, shall we?' She put her small hand on his arm and smiled at him, that half seductive smile that Daniel loved so much. The smile told him of the making of love after the dinner to come. He squeezed her hand and his smile said, 'That will be lovely.'

Anna was seated at the bottom end of the long central table. The men rose when the small party arrived. Anna caught fleeting glimpses of faces, mouths, moustaches, earrings and pearls. There must have been about twelve people awaiting their arrival. 'I'm so sorry we're late.' Mary's voice shook a little with nervousness. But her laugh was sincere.

An officer towards the head of the table took her by the hand and said, 'For you, dear lady, you may be late for dinner any time you wish. For you I can see time will always stand still.'

'Why, thank you,' she replied.

The ship's purser, Rupert Evans, introduced himself to Mary and to the rest of the small party. Anna stared at him. In all her wildest dreams of fantasy about the English poet Rupert Brooke, whom she genuinely loved, she had imagined him to look exactly like this. Anna couldn't bear it. A strange feeling passed over her, causing her to flush and to feel faint. The room began to whirl and turn around her. She blinked and tried to will the room still. She put her hand out to her mother who took it.

'Are you all right, darling?'

Anna shook her head. 'No. I think it's the sudden heat. I feel a little faint.' She saw a look of consternation on the purser's face. He came towards her and then Anna knew she was going to make a fool of herself. Just as he reached her she dissolved into the blackness.

She felt herself being deposited very gently on a big leather sofa. She opened her eyes and stared into another pair of eyes, very intense and dark blue. They were rimmed with long, soft feathery lashes. Anna smiled and then she softly laughed. The face lost its look of concern and then a deep masculine voice asked gently, 'Why are you laughing?'

'Because,' Anna explained, 'it's not fair. Men always get the long eyelashes. Look at mine, they're terrible.'

The purser sat down carefully beside her. 'I don't think so at all. We haven't been properly introduced yet, you know.'

Anna looked up at the back of the sofa and she saw her mother and father watching her. 'I'm all right, Mom, really I am. It was just the heat.' She swung her legs down to the floor and then stood up a little shakily. 'Thank you, Mr Evans.'

'Rupert,' he said. 'And your name is?'

'My name is Anna Kearney.' She took the purser's hand in her own, shook it softly, and then looked down at his left hand. He was married. A deep pang of regret shook her heart. He would be, of course, all the best ones were. 'I'm fine now,' she said. But her heart was breaking.

They went back into the dining room next door. Mary Rose was sitting next to a young officer. They took their seats, Anna opposite Mary Rose. Anna was most quiet during dinner, although she did talk a little to the couple next to her. Mrs and Mr Baxter had been in Africa most of their lives. Now they were returning to England for good. Leaving Africa grieved them very deeply. They spent most of the evening telling Anna stories of the bush and the elephants and the tiger shoots. Anna, sickened by the idea of so much killing, still listened thankfully. Thankfully because she so much wanted to take Rupert by the hand and run away. She did not have a plan, she just wanted them to have time to look into each other's eyes again. How old is he? She began her inner dialogue. Oh, I would think about thirty-five. That's awfully young to be the purser of a ship this big. Maybe he's a young forty. His age didn't matter. He could have been a hundred or two: Anna would have loved him anyway. She smiled and nodded her head and said yes and no, always conscious of an emotion that seemed aborted like a foetus before its time.

Later the diners moved to the ballroom. Mary Rose danced with all and sundry. Anna sat quietly, watching her father dancing with her mother. That's what I want, she told herself, some man who is for ever. I want to know the certainty that my mother has, and always had, that my father adores her. She felt a tall figure behind her chair.

'May I have this dance, please?' It was Rupert. He took Anna in his arms. The band played 'The Last Waltz'. She realized it was indeed the last waltz. She could hear a clock striking the notes of midnight. Anna was lost to the world. Rupert's blond hair mingled with hers. She could feel his soft breath as they turned the corners. He was a superb dancer. They both melded as if they had been born to dance together. Anna felt it was as if they had both been two peas in a pod, and that someone with careless hands had popped the shell, causing him to fall out before his time and her to lose her other half. She could feel the delicious colours they left trailing behind them. Other dancers stood with their arms around each other, gazing at the beautiful couple. When they stopped dancing, the audience was quiet for a moment, and then people clapped. A soft sound of pleasure rained down on the shoulders of the two dancers. They stood smiling at each other.

Twenty-One

𝓙𝓵

When Anna got to her stateroom, she said goodnight to her mother and father. Mary Rose was nowhere to be seen, so Daniel went off to look for her. Anna saw a quizzical look in her mother's eye, but she felt if she opened her mouth she would scream and scream. So she kissed her mother again and gently pushed her away. This was something she was going to have to do for herself.

As she walked into the sitting room, she paused and looked at her flushed face in the mirror. She looked beautiful. She looked different. She was different. She was in love for the first time in her life and she was going to lose him. She went through to the bedroom and threw herself down on the bed. Face buried in her pillow, she sobbed.

'How could you do this to me?' she begged God.

'How, after all these years of being a faithful servant, could you send me a man who is married? I love him,' she wailed. Her voice frightened her. She hadn't cried like this since her grandmother had died. The lingering pain of Biddy's death mingled into an agonizing mass of twisted emotions. Both losses piling one on top of the other. Anna writhed and rolled with the pain. She screamed and she yelled. Now completely out of control, she let her body experience all the agony it could take until she was drained and exhausted. Finally she slept.

The early dawn broke into the cabin and the first rays of the sun stroked her kindly. She twisted and groaned in her sleep, but the sun calmed her. The sun had seen it all before.

Anna awoke late. She heard Mary Rose moving about in the sitting room next door.

'Hey, lazy bones, get up.' Mary Rose put her head round the door connecting their two staterooms. She surveyed Anna's bleary-eyed, fully dressed figure. 'Oh dear,' she said. 'You've got it bad, haven't you?'

Anna nodded. 'Yes,' she said, gasping for breath from the pain. 'I didn't know anything could hurt so much.'

'Well, it does, Anna. They say the first time is always the worst. Like virginity.'

Anna winced. Why must Mary Rose always be so crude? 'There's no chance of that, Mary Rose. He's married, and I won't touch married men.'

'You can always change the rules, Anna.'

Anna shook her head. 'No, you can, Mary Rose, but I can't. I know what I can do and what I can't do. If I break any of the laws that govern my life I hate myself. I don't lie and I don't cheat and I won't make love to another woman's husband. I'll just have to wait for the hurt to go away,' she said forlornly. 'How long does it take, Mary Rose?'

'Depends.' Mary Rose sat down on Anna's bed. She

was wearing last night's purple negligée. It was loosely tied at the waist and her white breasts spilled out. One long white leg stayed on the floor while Mary Rose clasped her other knee with her hands. Anna so wished she could be like Mary Rose. She suspected that Mary Rose had been making love. Indeed, on her upper thigh she had a crescent mark where her lover had been biting her.

'Who was it this time, Mary Rose?' Anna asked without much enthusiasm.

'Oh, it was the young man who sat beside me at supper. His name is Neil Renton. He's quite a good lover. Anyway, back to your problem. They say it hurts for ages. You will feel as if you have been torn in half and all of you will be jagged and raw. And then slowly, once you leave the ship and don't see him again, you will begin to heal. Honestly, Anna, you will. I know you will feel as if you never will, but you will, darling.'

Mary Rose's eyes were concerned: she had never seen Anna so upset. She put her arms around her and hugged her. 'I'll tell you what. I'll ring the steward and tell him to order us a good bottle of champagne and some scrambled eggs. They say there is nothing better for grieving than champagne and scrambled eggs.'

Anna looked up. 'Do you still feel that awful pain, Mary Rose? You seem to fall in love so often.'

Mary Rose stood up and stretched. 'Honestly, Anna, I'm a bit cynical. I don't give my heart away, just my body.' She grinned. 'It's better that way, it really is. Men are quite simple really. They want what they can't have. Take my advice and don't give them anything. You'll be amazed at the result. You'll be surrounded by swarms of men who will love you. Give yourself to one and the others will melt away. Men are simple really. Pat them and feed them and occasionally fuck them and they'll eat out of your hand. But just let one of them think he's got you in a corner and he'll turn on you.'

Anna's face dropped. 'Oh, Mary Rose, is it really that bad between men and women?'

Mary Rose nodded. 'Yes, it is, and it always will be. Look at the knights of old. They left their wives chained to their castles and then ran off and hung outside their lady's chamber. None of them were faithful. I don't think men are capable of being faithful. So either you join them, like I do, or you remain the nun that has none.' Mary Rose picked up the internal telephone and ordered the broken-hearted breakfast. Or that is what Anna thought she heard her ordering. Mary Rose made the order sound like a direct sexual invitation to the man on the other end of the telephone.

'I shouldn't be surprised if he arrives stark-naked on a silver platter with a rose between his teeth,' Anna said. 'How can you, Mary Rose, at this hour of the morning? And after you've been making love all night?'

Mary Rose grinned. 'Not all night, dear, just most of it. I'm off to have a bath and then I'll be back. Do you want your breakfast in your stateroom or mine?'

'Yours,' Anna said hurriedly. 'I've got to get out of this evening dress and bathe too.' Mary Rose left and Anna lay for a moment staring at the ceiling. I'll never wear this dress again, she thought. And I'll put away the shoes as well. She got up and inspected her tear-stained face in the mirror. I look just awful, she thought, and made a face at herself. The telephone rang.

'Hello,' she said bleakly.

'Darling?' It was her mother.

'Oh, hello, Mom.' Anna tried to sound bright and cheerful, but she knew she couldn't fool her mother. 'I'm not all right, Mom.'

Mary paused. 'I know you're not, but we both trust you to do the right thing.'

'You can trust me, Mom. You and Dad know I'd never let you down.'

'Sometimes life is very hard, Anna,' her mother said. 'And we are faced with terribly painful choices. Choose well and honourably and in time God will send you your angel.'

'I hope so. Thank you, Mom,' Anna said, unconvinced. 'It's just very painful at the moment.'

Mary was anxious. 'Do you want me to come round?'

'No, thanks. Mary Rose has a sure-fire remedy for pain. It's a sort of say-goodbye-to-your-man breakfast. She's ordered champagne and scrambled eggs. I think she also ordered the waiter.' Anna gave a spasm of a laugh. It didn't relieve the pain, but at least her face didn't fall apart.

'Mary Rose would!' Mary snorted. 'Still, you're in better hands than mine. Mary Rose has broken many hearts in her time; she's the expert. If you need me, darling, I'm here all morning. Otherwise I'll see you at lunch.'

'I don't feel much like eating, Mom. I think I'll skip lunch and see you at dinner. I'm going to curl up with Jane Austen and forget the rest of the world. It's too horrible a place.'

'Things will get better, darling,' her mother responded.

'I hope so, Mom, I hope so.'

Anna put down the telephone and slid the dress over her head. The dress still smelled of the night before. She kissed the silk where his hand had rested, then cradled the dress in her arms. Tears ran down her face. She dropped the dress on the floor and looked at the new shoes lying by her bed. She picked up one and inspected the leather sole. There were scratches from dancing with Rupert the night before. She kissed one shoe, then the other, then put them in their shoe bag. Afterwards, she opened the trunk and hung the dress carefully on the railing. Closing the trunk, she sighed. Slowly she ran the bath and lay back. Now, along with the pain, was a terrible feeling of sexual longing. So far in her life, her sexual urges had been contained in erotic dreams and self-satisfying stroking. Now she had a man she wanted and desired, and knew what it was to want but not to have.

She lay in the bath, observing herself with a sense of surprise. How could sex be such a simple matter of coupling between animals, yet so complex between a man and a woman? Why should she feel this heat and urgent need to orgasm with Rupert? Why Rupert? What was it between them that was so instant that they were drawn into each other's arms as if all time in the world had been waiting for this moment. Had it? Or was she just being ridiculous: somewhere, busy on the boat, had Rupert forgotten all about dancing with her last night, or carrying her to the sofa after she had fainted? Maybe she was making all this up. But she wasn't: the pain was very real, as was the urge to make love. She wanted to laugh with him and tell him everything she had done in the last eighteen years, beginning from the first thing she could remember.

She heard a knock on Mary Rose's door. Must be breakfast, she thought. She climbed out of the bath and pulled on her pink cotton dressing-gown. I even look like a virgin, she muttered, crossing the sitting room and opening the connecting door. She stood in the doorway, looking at the table that had been pushed in by the waiter. On it were two silver serving dishes covering the scrambled eggs, a wine cooler with the bottle of champagne, and a very large bunch of flowers with a neat little card. Probably Neil Renton, Anna thought, and didn't bother to open the card. She sat down and waited for Mary Rose.

Mary Rose came into the room dressed in a pale blue

walking suit. 'Flowers. How nice!' She picked up the little white envelope. She tore it open and then grinned. 'It's for both of us from your Rupert.' She read the inscription: ' "To the beautiful twins. I'll see you both at luncheon. Love Rupert." Imagine that, Anna. He is interested in you after all!'

'So what, I'm not interested in him. He's a married man, remember?'

'Sure, but rules were made to be broken. Don't be such a stick-in-the-mud.'

Anna expertly opened the champagne. She poured a little into her flute and tasted a little. 'A very good bottle, Mary Rose.' She sat down and lifted the lid of her silver serving dish. She smiled. 'I'm not really hungry, but I am going to eat the scrambled eggs and then I'm going to drink most of this bottle of champagne. It's over before it has begun and, as you said, time will heal me.'

Mary Rose sat down and beamed. 'Atta-girl, Anna.'

Twenty-Two

Anna dreaded dinner. She didn't want to see Rupert — but she wanted to see him badly. The thought of him caused her to talk furiously to herself. She spent the day in a trance. That morning she had hung over the rails watching the reassuring waves roll by. If the worst comes to the worst, she told herself, I can always throw myself into the waves and drown like a little tit willow. Now she understood exactly how the poor little bird felt. She also hoped that in London they would stay at the Savoy, where D'Oyly Carte had built a hotel with massive showers especially for Americans. There was a theatre next door which hosted all the Gilbert and

Sullivan productions she so loved. But she would stay there without Rupert, and her eyes again filled with tears. Anna didn't know that her body could house so much water. She watched all the first class passengers flooding through the doors for lunch. She sat on a completely deserted deck looking out to sea. The boat moved on, pulling her willingly and unwillingly to her destination. A deck-hand put his head around the door and, seeing a pretty girl crying, tactfully withdrew. He wondered who had broken her heart. Probably another of the purser's conquests.

Anna was shaking when she dressed for dinner. She wore a pale pink, soft, floor-length dress. The neck was rounded. The bodice fitted tightly and then fell into beautiful folds around her feet. She wore a pair of gold sandals with crossover straps. Tonight, she outlined her lips with pink lipstick, applied with a soft brush and just a hint of rouge. She misted herself with Mitsuko and was then ready to face the world in general, and Rupert in particular.

'You look marvellous.' Mary Rose stood in the ship's corridor gazing at Anna with amazement. 'A bit of suffering obviously agrees with you.' Anna gave Mary Rose a wan smile.

'Mary Rose, suffering like this is a mug's game, and I'm going to bully myself until I get over it – even if I have to have all my meals in my rooms.'

Mary and Daniel joined the girls. Mary put a protective arm around her daughter. 'Darling,' she said gently, 'we all have our hearts broken at one time or another. We just have to learn how to deal with it.'

'You said you never suffered from a broken heart, Mom.'

'Yes, I know I did, and when I'd put the telephone down I thought of Johnny Corona at my graduation. He was the most handsome boy in the school. He was half-Irish and half-Italian. His father was from Rome. I prayed every night that he would ask me to the dance. We didn't call it graduation in those days. They were just end-of-term dances. Well, he did ask me to the dance, and I accepted. Your poor father was broken-hearted. I made the most marvellous dress.' By now Mary and Anna were following Daniel and Mary Rose to the dining room. 'The night of the dance I was so excited I was shaking,' Mary continued. 'He came and collected me, carrying a beautiful corsage of flowers. Then we danced until he saw another girl called Vanessa O'Toole. She was the class prostitute, and all the boys were after her. Johnny Corona was no exception, and I lost him. I remained a wallflower, which was just as well because your father had loved me from the moment he had seen me when I was a very little girl. I learned a big lesson from Johnny Corona.' Mary fell silent.

'What did you learn, Mom?' Anna was careful. She felt as if she stood on a patch of black ice in her mother's heart.

'I learned, darling, not to trust blindly. To respect one's own standards and sense of integrity. Lots of men will come into your life, Anna, and say they can offer all sorts of things.' Mary shook her head. 'But don't believe them. You know what's right and wrong: just stick to that.'

Anna nodded. By now they were moving into the dining room, and Anna could see Rupert's blond head bending over Mrs Baxter, who was talking animatedly to him. She felt another surge of pain, rather like an Arabian knife being plunged slowly into her heart. Mary went on ahead and tucked her hand under her husband's arm. Anna desperately wished she, too, could one day walk with Rupert that way, but it was not to be. She knew that her love for both her parents precluded her from doing anything that would hurt them. As she gazed at Rupert, she very much hoped that she had the strength of will to resist him.

As soon as Rupert saw Anna his eyes lit up. Anna didn't think that a tired old cliché like 'his eyes lit up' actually ever happened, but in Rupert's case his eyes did glow. Anna felt her own eyes beginning to shine too. Oh dear, she thought, love is going to be very banal. Spoon in June and honey and roses. She restrained an urge to rush off to the kitchen to make Rupert something wonderful to eat. Why wasn't Martha, with her broken-mouthed smile, here? She would know what to do. Aunt Kitty would tell her to go ahead and screw him. That's why her mother was always a little wary of Aunt Kitty. Anna wished she had both of them here now. She found herself reacting gracefully to Rupert's extended hand. 'Thank you so much for the flowers,' she said.

'Think nothing of it,' he replied easily. 'The waiter told me you were both having a bottle of champagne for breakfast, and I simply couldn't resist sending you both an expression of my appreciation. It isn't often that an old man like me gets to have two beautiful girls at his table.' He smiled at Mary Rose. 'Darling,' he said, 'you look divine.' Anna felt a pang of a feeling she had never experienced before. This must be what jealousy feels like. She didn't like the feeling at all. She turned to Mary.

'Suddenly I am very hungry, Mom. What are you going to order for dinner?' Although it hurt her, she ignored Rupert for the rest of the meal.

When it came time for the people at the table to leave to go dancing, Anna excused herself. 'I am really tired,' she said apologetically to the table in general. 'And I have a slight headache. Please excuse me.' She got up and fled from the room. The corridors were long and dimly lit. She felt like a bud, destined never to bloom.

When she got to her suite she unlocked the door and slammed it hard, breathing heavily. She stood in the dark of the room, crying gently with her arms wrapped around herself for comfort. The pain was back in full force, but she knew she must not give in to it. She must go on day by day. In three more days they would be in the harbour, and she would leave the boat and Rupert for ever. Maybe every woman has a Rupert in her life. The memory of Johnny Corona still hurt her mother after all these years. Maybe she had to get hurt really badly to teach herself a lesson. No is the answer, she said fiercely, as she moved towards the big heavy lamp beside the armchair. As she pulled the brass chain, she heard a firm knock.

'Who is it?' she said, terrified. She knew who it was.

'It's Rupert, Anna. I was worried about you.'

'Don't be.' She knew her voice sounded rude, but she was in too much of a panic to be polite.

'Let me in, please. I just want to see that you are all right.'

'I am fine, thank you, Rupert. Please go back to your guests.'

'Only if you will just let me see your face, then I promise I'll go.'

Anna sighed. 'All right, I'll just open the door and you stay in the hall.'

Rupert was fascinated. Here was an eighteen-year-old virgin daring to resist his attentions. He was used to women and girls throwing themselves at him. He very much wanted Anna, but there was a part of him that also wanted to protect her. Anna opened the door a little. Rupert, with gentle force, leaned against it. The heavy door swung open and Anna stood in front of him, defenceless. Rupert put his arms around her and drew her to him. Their mouths met in a well-remembered long kiss. How she could remember ever kissing Rupert she

137

had no idea, but their lips met as if they had never been away. Anna's body folded into Rupert's arms like a wood pigeon folding her wings for the night. Behind them the moon now gazed into the window where the sun had watched Anna cry.

The moon rose higher and smiled. Often sister sun was there to see the tears of the morning after the night before; this was going to be one of those nights, she thought, as she sailed gallantly in the sky. The stars shone and the Milky Way cackled with mirth. Orion smote his mighty sword against Jupiter who happened to be passing through his equinox.

'Dirty bastard,' shouted Orion, who was noted in the celestial skies for his temper.

'Lucky bastard, you mean.' Jupiter could not resist gloating. 'I was rather good at that in my time. Come to think of it, I might just get down there myself.'

Anna felt the skies reverberating and she shuddered with passion. She found herself breathless. She could feel Rupert getting ready to lift her. His shoulder muscles tensed and his arms began to slide around her waist.

'No, Rupert,' she said, gently pushing him away. 'I can't let you make love to me. Apart from anything else, you are a married man and I couldn't do that to your wife.'

Rupert drew a breath to steady himself. 'I'll divorce her.' He was shocked to hear himself say those words. 'Honestly, Anna, I'll do anything to have you in my life.' Good God, he observed, I must be out of my tiny mind.

Anna just shook her head. 'Please go now, Rupert. You promised you would, and I'm quite all right.'

'OK.' Rupert dropped his arms, and Anna felt an ice wind of regret blow around her. Rupert spun and left the room. There was a horrible silence. A terrible loneliness filled Anna's heart. So this is what loneliness feels like, she thought as she shut the door behind Rupert. She walked over to the porthole and looked at the moon and the stars. I feel like Juliet, she said to the myriad of twinkling jewels in the night sky.

But you don't have a Romeo, they cried back.

I know I don't; and Anna began to cry again.

Twenty-Three

🖋

The next day Anna put on a pair of dark glasses and walked the deck alone. As she turned on to the foredeck, she found herself directly in the line of Rupert, who was barring her way.

'I've got to talk to you,' he said when their paths met.

'I don't want to talk to you, Rupert. You're a married man. That's enough and you shouldn't be talking to me alone. My mother and father would be furious if they knew.'

'I know.' Rupert sounded so miserable that Anna felt herself softening.

'What's the matter, Rupert? Surely there are several women you can have on this trip. Why me?'

'I don't know why you, Anna. I really wish I did. I feel like a very dirty old man chasing you. Believe me, Anna, I've never felt this way before.'

Looking into Rupert's eyes, Anna did believe him, which just made matters worse. 'Oh, Rupert, please don't make this hard for me. Please! In future I'll have dinner in my cabin so we don't have to share the same table. I can't bear the pain. I've never felt so much pain in my life before. Please let me go. Time will take the pain away. It always does.'

Oblivious to everything, Rupert wrapped his arms around her and held her desperately. 'I can't let you go, Anna. Really I can't.'

Anna gently opened his arms and moved a few feet away. 'Rupert, we are star-crossed lovers and it wouldn't ever work between us. The shadow and the guilt of your wife would forever be a stain on the love we shared. I know I can't let my mother and father down like that. I'm not like Mary Rose and never will be. I want a man of my own. Not somebody else's. Goodbye, Rupert.' With that, Anna swung around and walked down the deck to her cabin where, yet again, she lay prone for the rest of the morning, crying.

At lunch, Mary came to Anna's room. 'Are you not coming for lunch, Anna?' She saw her daughter's swollen eyes and tear-stained cheeks. 'Oh, darling, I know how it hurts, really I do. But it's best that you wash your face and we'll have lunch here together. I'll tell your father that we need mother and daughter time together, and he can go with Mary Rose to lunch.' She left the room.

Anna got up from the bed and gazed at her face in the mirror. She looked and felt awful. Mary returned. 'Your father sends you his love and he will look in on you after lunch. What would you like to order, darling?' Mary took the menu from the coffee-table drawer.

'I don't feel hungry,' Anna said, glancing at the ornate list of dishes. Her mother looked at her.

'Let's have some lobster and I'll order a bottle of Pouilly-Fuissé for both of us.'

Mary telephoned her order and then sat down on the sofa and patted the space beside her. 'Come and sit down, Anna. Let's talk about this situation with Rupert.'

'He says he is really in love with me, Mom.'

'I'm sure he is, Anna.' Mary shook her head and smiled. 'But you must always remember, if a man cheats on his wife, he can always – and probably will – cheat on you.' Mary sighed. 'I wish it weren't true. I've had so many women friends really believing a married man, who then turned and did the dirty on them. That's why you can't trust Rupert.'

Anna leaned up against her mother. 'I just want to die, Mom.'

Mary kissed her. 'You won't die, darling. You'll just suffer from a broken heart for a while and then it will go away. Only two more days and he will be out of your life for ever.'

'Not for ever,' Anna said. 'I'll never forget him or the pain. It's terrible, Mom; it tears at me like a wild animal.'

The waiter arrived with the lobster and the wine. Anna drank most of the bottle, and then Mary helped her get into bed, pulling the heavy brocade bedspread over her grieving child. Mary didn't know whose pain was worse: Anna's grief over Rupert, or her own suffering watching her only child in such agony.

When Daniel's worried face came around the door, Anna was asleep, with Mary sitting beside her holding her hand.

'She's all right, darling,' Mary said quietly.

Daniel came over and touched Anna's cheek. 'She's too young to suffer so.' Both of them stood side by side, looking at their sleeping daughter.

'She'll mend,' Mary said gently. 'Everybody needs to suffer from a broken heart. It will make her more careful the next time.'

'I'll vet any man that comes near her.' Daniel's voice turned angry. 'I feel like horse-whipping the bastard.'

'You don't have to do that, Danny. I do believe he really is in love with Anna, but he had no right to tell her. He's behaved very selfishly, but I do believe he is suffering too. I think we take to our cabins until we arrive in England. Hopefully the excitement of the new country and the English family will take Anna's mind off him.' Mary's voice did not carry much conviction. If only Martha were here, she thought.

Twenty-Four

As Anna walked down the gangplank she looked over her shoulder to the bridge. She could see Rupert looking sadly down at her. A rat entered her soul and tore at it with its giant, long nails. Her heart lay in her chest, open and bleeding. She tried not to breathe. Mary, behind her daughter, saw the gesture, and her face saddened. Some day the light would come back into Anna's eyes, but for now there was a dark cloud around her. Behind her Mary Rose was pouting.

'Really, Anna, this is silly mooning over that man. I've just said goodbye to my boyfriend and I'm delighted to be rid of him.'

Mary looked briefly at Mary Rose and then said: 'Mary Rose, one of these days you are going to fall in love and then you'll know what Anna is suffering.' There was more than a hint of prophecy in Mary's tone.

Mary Rose shivered. 'No I won't,' she said stoutly. 'No man will ever get the better of me.' They walked down the rest of the plank quietly.

On the wharf, a very large Daimler stood parked by a massive iron bollard. Anna looked at the thick rope wound around the metal post. She smelled the sharp smell of the hemp and wished she could hang herself. A brown-uniformed chauffeur jumped out of the car and came running towards Daniel.

'Are you the Kearneys?' he asked.

'How did you guess?' Daniel was smiling.

'James Stephens is an old boyhood friend of mine, and he sent me a picture of your family.'

'Good heavens, what a small world it is!' Mary extended her hand. 'I'm Mrs Kearney, and this is my daughter Anna and her friend Mary Rose.'

Johnson raised his gold-braided hat. 'Pleased to meet you, I'm sure,' he said. He opened the back door and Mary, followed by Anna and Mary Rose, climbed in. Anna took one of the little seats facing her mother, and held the other down for her father. Johnson, aided by a sweating porter, filled the boot of the car with the smaller trunks and then tied the remaining ones to the roof.

Anna, hidden behind her dark glasses, sank back into the seat. Her mind was full of Rupert. His hands, his face, his jaw. The feel of his lips on her mouth. Now it was all in her past, as of an hour ago. She saw the empty look in his eyes as she caught her last glimpse of him. So this is how a broken heart feels, she told herself. Never again. Never, never, never again.

The car pulled away from the wharf. The boat was just another boat tied to the huge jetty in a place called Liverpool. Anna watched the scenery. How ugly, she thought. All those pale white faces. The dirty docks. There was none of the excitement she felt in New York harbour. Here the people were sullen and resentful. In New York harbour there was a multitude of different-coloured faces: black, Italian, Chinese. Here they all looked the same.

'Do all English people have blue eyes?' she asked her father.

Daniel smiled. 'No,' he said. 'But then this is not the land of the free. England is known for its racial intolerance.'

'Then I'm not going to like it very much here.'

'Oh yes you will, Anna,' Mary Rose said. 'You'll meet a swell guy and forget all about old Rupert. You just wait and see.'

Anna shot her a furious look. 'No I won't! I won't ever let myself do anything so stupid again. Once is quite enough. I'm going to die an old maid. Or maybe I'll go into a convent. Yes, that's what I'll do. I'll go into a nunnery and spend all day praying for your soul.'

Mary smiled. Anna's eyes held the hint of a smile. She'll get over him, Mary sighed to herself. She really will.

Twenty-Five

Was there life after love? Anna wasn't sure. Did you ever recover your heart again? All she knew was that Rupert now held her heart firmly in his hands. He did not have an address to which to send it back. Maybe he would trace her through some shipping documents, and one day a small package bound with red sealing wax might arrive. 'Return to owner with love,' the message might say. But then again, Anna rather thought not.

So began the first day of her new life without her heart. She felt strange and amputated. The pain was still fierce. She knew she must go down to breakfast in this big, sprawling house in the Devon countryside. The owners had welcomed them in the dark of the night. Johnson had helped her out of the car and Anna felt he knew of her sadness. He was a little, wizened gnome of a man. Most of the night had been a blur for Anna. She remembered drinking rather a lot of good French wine and then excusing herself after coffee. She badly needed to be alone. By herself. To lie on the big generous window cushions in the bay window of her bedroom and just to wait, like one of those statues in a church, for life to go away.

As she dressed she looked out of the window. Across the lawn was an enormous, spreading pine tree. It reminded her of an old woman wearing green flannel petticoats. The spread was wide and the tree ancient. Anna comforted herself with the fact that the tree would be there long after she and Rupert were dead and buried. There was a certainty and a permanence about the tree. It stood tall in all its dignity and must have seen several hundred years go by. Nothing affected the tree, and Anna smiled for the first time in a long while. I am looking forward to lying under you, she told the tree, with my Jane Austen. Anna felt a longing for time with her favourite author. Jane's sly wit and pungent observations comforted her. Jane Austen might have died a long time ago, but her written words were as alive now as when she had first written them. So really, Anna reminded herself as she brushed on some face powder, time in its way is seamless.

She sighed and opened the door to find Mary Rose, who was across the hall.

'How did you sleep?' Mary Rose asked Anna gently. 'You looked right out of it last night.'

Anna smiled again. 'I was really tired. All this pain is so very exhausting.'

Mary Rose nodded. 'Yeah,' she said briskly. 'That's why you don't do it again.'

'Don't worry, I won't.' Anna was quite surprised at the bitterness in her voice, and at the feeling of abandonment. She had no one to blame for the feeling of abandonment. Rupert would not have abandoned her. But he was not free to love her, nor she him. What a freak thing to happen, she thought, as she followed Mary Rose down the hall.

They both walked into the wide dining room. For a moment they stood looking at the very large English family sitting happily down to breakfast. The scene was not that different to Anna's dining room in New York, but the accents were certainly different. The English Kearney cousins slouched in a way that Anna would never be allowed to do. Amelia Kearney was a large, matronly figure. She had a strangely stuffed bosom, tied rather like a sack of onions around her middle. Her stomach rolled over a pair of baggy corduroy trousers and, as she stood to welcome the girls, Anna could see that she was wearing what looked like a man's thick socks and leather brogues. Under the table there seemed to be a continual growling. Anna wondered if Mrs Kearney kept an insane relative under the table. But no, she could see the ends of tails and muzzles of rather a large number of scruffy terriers.

'Jack Russells,' Mrs Kearney said, answering Anna's unspoken question. 'Bloody beasts.' She aimed a kick at the snarling ball of dogs, and Anna winced. 'Do sit down, girls. Let me see. There's Crispin, Charlie and Shane.' The three men nodded and grinned.

Crispin waved a very languid hand. 'Hello there. Sorry I wasn't around last night to greet you, but we were at the Fanshaws' do. Glad you missed it. Dreadful, absolutely dreadful.' Mary Rose sat down at the table.

'And this is Theresa, and Catherine, both called after saints by their hopeful father.'

Colonel Kearney looked up from his plate of bacon and eggs. He had a weak, watery smile and pale blue eyes with albino lashes. He seemed permanently bent over, as if perpetually looking for something missing on the ground. He waved his fork and got on with mouthing his food.

Crispin turned to them. 'Don't expect Shane to say

much, girls. Cat got your tongue again, Shane? Can't you say something to our new guests?'

Shane looked shyly at Anna. 'Hello,' he offered.

Daniel and Mary walked in, arm in arm. 'Great place you've got here, Amelia, really great,' Daniel said. 'Sorry we are late, but we got lost in the corridor and then I just had to go out and stand on the grass.' Anna heard the difference between her father's accent and the English cousins. His voice sounded so loud and flat. She felt defensive because she enjoyed the enthusiasm in his face, as well as in that of her mother. So far, in the interaction between both families, the English contingent seemed so colourless.

She knew Mary Rose was sizing up the three sons in the family. Crispin, Mary Rose thought, watching him with a level stare, was gay. Well, if not gay, sufficiently feminine to have all sorts of sexual difficulties with women. Better left alone. She could warn Anna, who was such a fool in these matters. Charlie was far too horsy. He was sitting in a pair of dirty jodhpurs and muddy riding boots. Definitely not! Mary Rose's nose wrinkled. That left Shane. He looked like a possibility, but Mary Rose felt she would have to groom him before she could possibly share a bed with him. The two girls in the family looked like pregnant llamas. Under the table, Mary Rose surreptitiously pinched Anna. Anna kicked her ankle.

Amelia Kearney slapped two enormous plates of grey, lumpy matter on to the table in front of Anna and Mary Rose. Mary Rose peered down at her plate.

'Scott's porridge oats,' Mrs Kearney said fiercely. 'Excellent for you. Make all my children eat it every morning. Makes you go first thing. Awfully important to go first thing in the morning, isn't it, Shane? I have to soak a prune in hot water for Shane every night. He has trouble going, d'you see. Such a shame. All those hot curries in India, you know. Terrible. Terrible. I kept telling him, but would he listen? No, he would not.'

Daniel and Mary were sitting opposite each other. Anna could tell her mother wanted to laugh, yet hid her smile behind her hand. 'I think, Amelia, I would rather like to skip the porridge and have a plate of that delicious-looking bacon and eggs,' she said.

'Well, you can do anything you like, of course,' Amelia replied. 'But Cook will be furious. She can't bear it when guests don't eat her food. Still, I'll explain that you are foreigners. That'll probably do the trick. She can't abide foreigners.'

At this Anna found herself genuinely laughing. 'Mrs Kearney,' she said, 'we're all foreigners in this room. We're all Irish, aren't we?'

'Do call me Amelia, dear. We don't stand on ceremony in this family.'

Theresa leaned forward and gazed soulfully at Anna. Her long upper lip trembled with sincerity. 'Catherine and I have been so excited to have you visit us. We want to show you off to all our friends. Tomorrow night we have organized a cocktail party so you can meet them all.'

Crispin grinned. 'I can assure you that Theresa and Catherine's friends are perfectly frightful. I invited some of mine. Much more interesting and very decadent.' He looked meaningfully at Mary Rose. 'I know you will find them all very interesting, Mary Rose.' He gazed at Anna. 'They are very decadent, and not for a pretty, nice little girl like you.'

Anna was rather taken aback by such honesty. She wondered if all English people talked as if their souls were bared like the open pages of a book. She rather hoped not.

Charlie nodded vigorously. 'I can promise you that Crispin's friends are as ghastly and decadent as he says they are. It's all Mum's fault for calling him after her first lover.'

Mary made a little surprised noise and looked at Daniel. He smiled. His English cousins were going to be fun, if a little eccentric. But he didn't mind. It made a change from the bluff heartiness of his friends. The summer in England was going to be different.

Twenty-Six

Well, Anna thought, surveying the scene before her. This certainly is different.

Crispin strolled over to Mary Rose who was standing just behind Anna. He took her hand and pulled her forward. 'Come and meet my friends, Mary Rose, before the girls roll on their elephantine chums.' He smiled at Anna. 'You, too, my sweet, but you're off limits to the lot of them.'

Mary Rose frowned. 'What makes you think I'd want to know any of your so-called decadent friends?'

Crispin grinned. 'You're like me, sweetheart, perverse and neurotic. Without people like me around, you easily become bored and start manipulating everybody within reach. Am I right?'

Anna found herself convulsed with laughter. 'I have never,' she said, still shaking with giggles, 'seen anybody second-guess Mary Rose in my life.'

Crispin shrugged. 'It's not difficult. We are all rather boring and juvenile. None of us plans to grow up, do we, Mary Rose?'

Mary Rose's face was set in a cast-iron sulk. 'Really, Crispin, you are just too silly to argue with. Where are these people?'

Crispin turned and began walking. 'They're in the gunroom cleaning the guns. Come along, follow me.' His tall, emaciated figure led the girls down a long, rather sparse hall. The walls were painted a very depressing green. It was very cold and bleak, but then much of the house was cold and bleak. The house spoke to Anna of the great days when it had stood resplendent in its summer finery. Much love and care must have gone into the huge gardens and belvedere, but now they were shabby and sad. The twenty gardeners had been reduced to two and a garden boy. Johnson the chauffeur, and Mrs Dobbs, the irascible cook, completed the household staff.

'Here we are.' Crispin pushed open an old oak door. Anna blinked at the sudden flood of light. She could count five men in a semi-circle. They all stood up when the girls walked in. 'May I present to you the lovely Misses Mary Rose Buchanan and Anna Kearney, who, for her sins, is a long-lost cousin of mine and lives in New York,' Crispin announced with ceremony. The men seemed very tall. All were blond and blue-eyed except for Ralph. Anna decided she liked Ralph because he did not resemble Rupert at all. She watched Mary Rose's face as she, too, sought and picked her way through the silent men, smiling so amiably at them.

'Hello.' Anna put her hand out to Ralph. He turned her hand over and gently kissed it. Anna flushed. Ralph looked at her, one black eyebrow raised. Anna realized that here was a man who understood and liked women. The thought rather frightened her. She smiled in acknowledgement.

'My name is Ralph Fanshaw.' He took Mary Rose's hand but did not kiss it. There was a babble as the other men introduced themselves, and Anna became lost. It sounded as if the fat one was called Podge, which didn't seem very kind, and then there was a Kit, a Bunny, and an Oliphant.

'I'll tell you what, Crispin,' Ralph suggested. 'Why don't we escort the ladies back to the library, where I am sure Theresa and Catherine will be panting for their presence. I've finished my gun. I've greased it and I only have to wrap it now.' He nimbly put his double-barrelled shotgun into its thick leather carrying case and then said, 'OK, my American friends, let's go.'

Twenty-Seven

Anna felt a great curiosity about Crispin. He was sexually ambiguous, there was no doubt about that. But maybe that was just what she needed for the moment. He had the face of a collie dog, long, pointed and fine. His features were almost exaggerated, that fine balance between almost ugly and exotically beautiful. Overall it was a serene face, made even more so by the fine, slightly curly blond hair which fell from his scalp wherever it wished, framing his face and draping over his lily-white ears. His complexion was also white, almost pallid apart from the splotches of red on his cheeks. But any inspection of Crispin's face invariably led to his eyes, icy orbs which cancelled any previous impression of tenderness. His face seemed to exist just for them. His gaze was disarming, penetrating, commanding, not in any benignly authoritative way, but sinister and cruel. Anna immediately thought of a wolf. His body, too, had a canine aspect to it, thin and wiry and slightly hunched as if continually on the prowl. His movements suggested he was on the hunt, distrusting all but those he considered his potential victims.

Anna shivered. Crispin's eyes were cool towards her, as was his kiss on her wrist. The kiss was not an innocent kiss. Anna felt an air of command and control in his lips. For the moment she didn't mind. The best thing to keep the pain at bay was to be as busy as possible. A whole load of new people to meet and to analyse was a wonderful opportunity to keep her memories of Rupert buried.

The library was a long, low room with two big French doors leading on to the lawn where Anna's special tree sat awaiting her. She smiled at the tree and nodded. Soon, she thought, very soon, Jane Austen and I will be with you. For the moment she was quite content to stand in the background and watch Theresa and Catherine, in filmy yellow and pink cocktail dresses, flutter about the room. Six of their friends were waiting there already. The gentle, filmy dresses looked like the wings of a hawk moth as they flitted and darted about the rather dark room. Anna liked the big brass chandeliers hanging from the ceiling and the wide, wing-tipped reading chairs by the fire. It was summer now, and the doors were open to the garden. The crickets and the frogs were loudly wishing each other good-night. The bees and the buzzing hornets had stamped off to their hives. A slight silence was descending, disturbed only by the call of an irritating cuckoo. For the moment the world was a beautiful place; but why must the cuckoo spoil it all? Anna sighed. Somehow, when she encountered something nice, like a pretty scene, the fact that Rupert wasn't there to share it with her hurt more deeply. Sometimes she wondered if she had ever truly been in love with the real Rupert, or in love with the idea of being in love; perhaps Rupert had just happened to step into her world at the right moment. What a confusing thought.

'Come on, darling.' She felt Mary's arm link gently in hers. 'Let's go out and have a stroll on the lawn. This is such a lovely time of night.' Anna felt herself relax as she always did when she was close to her mother. I'm so lucky to have good, loving parents, she thought. She walked past Mary Rose who was flirting with Oliphant. As she stepped out of the French doors, the wind raised the hem of her long skirt and teasingly wrapped it around her slim form. She saw Crispin's eyes follow her and she shivered. She very much hoped that Mary Rose would stay away from him.

Once out on the lawn she could see the tall, elegant figure of her father bending his head to listen to the stream of words that poured from Amelia's mouth. She smiled. 'Dad seems to be enjoying this holiday.' Mary hugged her daughter's arm.

'He really is having a wonderful time.' Mary felt quite guilty that she and Daniel were so much in love, while their only daughter seemed to be suffering. 'Are you feeling any better, Anna?'

'At times, Mom. I think it will take me a long time to get over the whole nightmare. I never, ever thought I'd fall in love with a married man. I keep telling myself it was just an infatuation, but in my heart I know it wasn't. It was an enormous sense of belonging. When you feel you belong to someone like that it seems as if you've known them all your life, that you will always know them until you die, and even after that. What hurts is to have to go away leaving all that loving in tatters and in shreds. Still, I comfort myself with the fact that, however much it hurts, I do know what real love is. Millions of people probably will never suffer as I have. But I do know what to look for next time. If there is a next time!'

Tears were running down her cheeks. Mary put her arms around her. 'Darling, there will be a next time, I promise you. You'll know the man when you find him. He'll be a good man and faithful. It hurts dreadfully to grow up, but I'm proud of you, and in time this pain will fade. Rupert will be a memory. You'll look back on this with your beloved husband and my grandchildren.'

Anna smiled and brushed away the tears. 'How many do you want, Mom?'

'Scads, Anna; as many as you can have.'

'It's a deal. Now let's go in and get on with this party. Ralph looks OK. I think I'll talk to him.'

Ralph was nice and reassuringly normal. He, too, had suffered a recent heartbreak, and Anna found great comfort in comparing notes. By the end of the evening, she realized that she had quite enjoyed herself. She looked around the busy room and saw that, now, Mary Rose was sitting next to Crispin. Her huge eyes were fixed in her well-known seductive pose. Well-known to Anna, that is. Gee, she's going to get caught up with him! Anna saw that Ralph was also watching Mary Rose.

'She is beautiful, isn't she?' he remarked. Anna felt a wistful tug at her heart. She knew she too was beautiful, but in a more quiet, understated way. Mary Rose's looks were so dramatic.

'But then, Anna, don't underestimate how lovely you are,' he added.

Anna blushed and looked down at the glass in her hand. 'Well, I'm not in Mary Rose's league.'

'I'm glad you're not. Mary Rose is a tart, in my opinion.'

'She's not a tart — she's my friend.'

'Well, if she's your friend, Anna, warn her to stay away from Crispin. He's my friend, too, but I wouldn't offer him to my worst enemy. He's a very dangerous man and he plays awful headgames. I should know — he nearly crucified my sister.'

'What do you mean, Ralph? How can Crispin crucify somebody?'

'He can, and he will. Underneath all that warm act is a man who will go to any length to punish women. All women. Tell your friend to stay away.'

Anna could see that Ralph was upset. 'I'll try, but Mary Rose is not easily warned. She, too, can play a lot of games.'

The evening came to a close and the guests slowly made their way out of the house. The last tyres crunched into the silence of the night and Anna went to bed. She was too tired to talk to Mary Rose. Tomorrow would have to do. Still, as she climbed into bed, she comforted herself that there were men like Ralph around who were kind and good fun. The world was not as dark as it had looked.

Twenty-Eight

Mary Rose and Crispin left for a swim at Lyme Regis in Crispin's green Morgan. With a long face, Anna watched them go. Before breakfast she had tried to argue with Mary Rose, but to no avail.

'I don't care what you say, Anna, this is my summer holiday and I'll spend it how I want. I can handle Crispin. I've dealt with men like him before. If he thinks he can outsmart me he's got another think coming.' Anna gave up. Mary Rose's mouth was set in a pout and she knew when she pouted like that her friend would do whatever she wanted to do.

'OK, have it your way, Mary Rose, but don't expect me to waste my time listening to your wailing when he hurts you.'

'I won't. Although I listened to you enough, Anna.' Those were Mary Rose's last, guilt-inducing words.

Ralph was waiting for Anna in the study. He wanted to take her for a ride.

'I did try to warn her.' Anna greeted Ralph with a smile. He looked wonderful and very English. His eyes were deep brown, very different from Rupert's. And he was taller, with broader shoulders. Today he was dressed in cavalry twill jodhpurs. He wore a blue cashmere roll-necked pullover, and carried a riding crop in his hand.

Anna was wearing American blue jeans with a thick fleece-lined waistcoat. She felt underdressed. She quietly promised herself a trip with her mother to a local store to buy decent English riding equipment.

'Come along, it's a super day for a canter,' he said. 'I've brought my spare polo pony Nabob for you to ride. She's a good mare and has a wonderful gait.' Ralph strode down the hall, with Anna running after him.

The morning flew by. They cantered and galloped on the downs. Anna loved the feel of the horse under her legs. The mare was lightly built with wonderful large eyes. She followed Anna's knee instructions superbly. Anna found herself laughing into the wind. As they rounded a corner her horse shied. Anna looked down and saw a grey snake with a black diamond pattern on its back. She turned white.

'Stay still,' Ralph said quietly. 'Nabob knows what to do.' The horse backed slowly away from the snake, which was curled on its coils waiting to strike.

'What is that?' Anna's voice was shaking.

'It's an adder. Our only poisonous snake. We get them on the downs. They like hot stones. Nabob was raised in India so she's used to snakes.'

'You know, Ralph,' Anna said. 'When I looked at the snake for the first time, I swear it looked a little like Crispin does when he's about to make a point. There is something reptilian about him.'

'You're right. I saw Mary Rose go off with him this morning. I passed them both in his car. She was laughing at something he said. Two perverse people together spell trouble.'

'Mmm, better Mary Rose and Crispin, who are used to hurting other people, than the two of us. We're like the walking wounded.' Anna felt a flash of pain again. 'Time will heal us. It always does.' That phrase was like a prayer now.

Ralph smiled. 'Come on, I'll race you home. Just give her her head. She knows the way back blindfolded.' The pounding of the hoofs comforted Anna. At least this part of her life was under control.

That afternoon, after lunch, Anna prepared to go with her mother into Exeter to buy formal English riding clothes. There had been no sign of Crispin and Mary Rose.

'He's probably taken her off to the Douglases' house.' Ralph's voice was weary. 'They're a bloody awful lot of people, yet he likes their company.'

'Well, if it's trouble Mary Rose wants, she sure is going to find it. Anyway, it's none of our business. Thanks to you, I'm off with Mom to spend a lot of cash on a whole new riding wardrobe. I think your riding clothes are beautiful.' Anna looked thoughtful. 'Do you think I could learn to ride side-saddle? I saw a very elegant side-saddle in the barn when we took the horses back.'

'Certainly.' Ralph grinned. 'Women look magnificent out hunting side-saddle. I'll come over tomorrow and give you a lesson.'

'OK.' Anna ran off to find her mother. She waved wildly at him as she ran. Ralph watched her long hair streaming behind her. He sighed. He wished he could love a girl like Anna. But he couldn't. He kept prostrating himself in front of women who used him.

How odd life is, he murmured to a passing cat. Here I am with a beautiful girl, about to give her riding lessons, and I don't fancy her at all. He shook his head and squatted down to stroke the cat who was nuzzling his ankles. I'd best stick to animals and leave the woman business alone. Both Anna and I have had our hearts broken. Still, he stood up and gave a boyish whistle. Both of us can have a lot of fun getting them mended.

Exeter, with its great cathedral, excited Anna. She walked around the thick walls and gazed at the big stained windows inside. She had always read about cobbled streets, and now she was walking with her own feet over history itself. It was a strange feeling. She and Mary walked with a lilt in their limbs. 'I feel light, as though I could fly, Mom.'

'I know, it's all very exciting.' Daniel had told Mary to be generous, but then he always was where Anna was concerned. Mary was pleased to see Anna's face relax. Ralph was just what she needed this summer. An unspoiled young man to squire her to all the local events.

Now, standing in the clothes shop drinking in the delicious smell of the tweeds on display, Anna felt the first jigsaw piece of her heart falling back into place. She fingered the long black riding skirt.

'Fustian, Miss. The very best.' The old man smiled at Anna's delight. He was used to bored and badly behaved American tourists with no manners. Thank goodness there were exceptions, like these two ladies. 'See this, madam, cut on the bias and then lined. All the seams are oversewn for strength. You won't find a finer skirt in all of England.'

'I believe you.' Anna pulled the skirt into her arms. 'I hope it fits.'

'We can always alter it for you.'

'I really want to take it home tonight.' She disappeared into a little square fitting room. The skirt fitted her perfectly. Anna twirled in front of a long mirror.

'Now I need the jacket and a stock of lace for my throat.'

'My,' Mary teased, 'you've done your homework.'

Anna studied the different riding stocks intently. She picked a thrilling fall of lace and then reached for a small, round riding hat. She plonked it on top of her head and grinned at her mother. 'How do I look?'

'Wonderful,' her mother replied. Indeed she did look lovely, and Mary felt her heart swell with pride. As a final gift, Mary bought her a riding crop with an ivory handle.

Anna chatted all the way home. When they reached the front door, they saw Crispin's car parked in the drive.

'Oh good, they're back.' Anna was genuinely excited. 'I can't wait to show Mary Rose my new stuff.'

They swept into the library, where they heard the voices of many people laughing and arguing. It was the same crowd as before. Anna stood by the library table with her new parcels in her hands.

'Go on, Anna,' Mary prompted. 'Show them your new stuff.'

'No, Mom,' Anna whispered under the noise and the chatter. 'They don't want to see my stuff.' She could see Mary Rose in the centre of the crowd. A lump came to her throat; yet again she felt excluded. Her enthusiasm for her new clothes evaporated. She felt silly and childish. She turned and ran, followed by Mary.

As they walked up the stairs towards their rooms, Mary said: 'You know, darling, you aren't any more of a misfit with those people than your father and I are. Don't think we don't notice them stop talking when we come into the room. Our cousins are nice enough people, but they don't live the moral way we live. Because of the way you have been brought up, you will only be really comfortable around our sort of people. Mary Rose will find her level.' Fearful of hurting her daughter's feelings, she resisted mentioning that the level would be pretty low. 'Just think how much Ralph will enjoy seeing you all dressed up tomorrow.'

Anna gave a quick smile. 'I tell you what . . .' The old enthusiasm was evident in her voice. 'I'll go to my room and get dressed up and then make an appearance in your bedroom. Warn Dad I'm coming.'

She left, and Mary smiled. You couldn't keep Anna down for long.

'Wow!' Daniel gave a low whistle of astonishment. 'You look fabulous, honey.' Anna spun round, her cheeks red with excitement.

'Don't I, though!' She caught sight of herself in the bedroom mirror. Her hair was up in a bun under the small riding hat; the long skirt with the tightly fitting jacket cutting into her waist; black riding boots and the crop in her hand. As she twirled, the unspoken wish hung between the three of them: they all knew she was wishing that Rupert could see her now. But Rupert was somewhere on the high seas. The wish would never be fulfilled. That was the ever-present sadness.

Twenty-Nine

The weeks passed by. Anna loved her English cousins. Daniel and Mary enjoyed most of their stay. They made no attempt to understand the strange and eccentric way of life shared by their relatives. They just blissfully visited all the local historic houses and churches, and then toured Wales and Scotland. Both girls were enjoying themselves so much that they preferred to stay within the confines of the circle of their new friends and acquaintances.

Ralph proved to be a true friend. Anna found solace in his arms. He hugged her and kissed her so gently. They were even able to talk about their need for each other as friends. All that long, golden summer Ralph helped to bring back the laughter in Anna's voice and the colour to her cheeks.

Anna loved swimming and walking on the great stretches of beach at Charmouth Bay. All of Devon and Dorset was there to be explored. For now, Anna didn't want big tourist experiences, just floral delights. The English flowers were so delicate and dainty compared to the much bigger and coarser flowers of America. She fell in love with the tiny, shy violets and the pretty blue grape-hyacinths. She spent long afternoons under her favourite tree in the garden reading, as she had promised herself, Jane Austen. She now realized she understood so much better the irony of this great writer. You almost have to live with cousins like mine, she thought, to grasp what it's all about. Everything they say, or do, has a double meaning.

'Why,' she asked Ralph, 'should Crispin get cross with me if I say couch instead of sofa?'

He looked at her gently. 'Well, first of all, it is very rude and not done to tell you off. You're an American now, and you speak a very different language. Actually, I think it's because the great English establishment likes to have a public school code which allows it to talk in a way that excludes most of the country. It's terribly snobby actually. I always annoy Crispin by referring to the fact that I experience a great deal of "*ennui*" in his presence. It's not OK to use French words in his book. So he gets cross.'

Anna nodded. 'He has Mary Rose so well trained she is running around saying things like "looking-glass" instead of mirror, and "scent" instead of perfume.' Anna put her head on one side. 'I don't think she's terribly happy, Ralph.'

'Well, we did warn her, and I don't think there's much we can do. I asked her to play tennis with me yesterday, but she preferred to mope about waiting for Crispin to turn up. It's a hell of a shame that a brain like Crispin's is wasted playing silly little paranoid games with women. As usual he turned up fashionably late, and Mary Rose shouted at him. I could hear him screaming back at her from the tennis court. Podge was playing with me. He said that a girl he took out after Crispin said he was like a greedy child in bed, and got his real sexual kicks from screaming at women.'

Anna winced. 'Ugh, how horrible. Poor Mary Rose. She looks awfully miserable.'

Later that day, Anna tried to talk to Mary Rose. They were sitting in the garden room. It was a beautiful Edwardian conservatory and, unlike the rest of the house, it was meticulously kept. This is where Amelia spent most of her time. She usually wore a brimless old gardening hat and shapeless thick skirt, even in the height of summer, and her husband's old tennis shoes, and an English Aertex shirt. Today she was absent. Mary Rose sat sullenly in a wicker armchair. She wore a white summer dress with cap sleeves, silk stockings and very high-heeled white summer shoes. By her side on a coffee table her pretty broad-brimmed hat sat awaiting the moment when she would pick it up and run down the corridor to join Crispin.

'He's an hour late, Anna.'

'Mary Rose, he's always hours late. Can't you see that it's his game?'

'I don't care. I love him and I'm going to marry him.'

'Has he asked you yet?' Anna tried not to let the horror in her voice show.

'No, but he talks of our future together a lot, so I expect he will. He needs my money. He hasn't any of his own.'

'Really? I thought he was loaded.'

'Nah, that's all stuff other women have given him. Even the car was bought for him by one of his many mistresses.'

'You're not seriously thinking of marrying a man who only wants you for your money, Mary Rose?'

Mary Rose nodded. 'Only Crispin. He's fun and we understand each other very well.'

'Sounds like madness to me, but it's your choice.'

'I think I can hear his car now,' she said hopefully. 'I'll wait for him in the drive.'

Anna watched her go. Suddenly she felt depressed, a hollow lump of futility forming in her chest. Mary Rose had been singled out by Crispin as his prey and, like a lone wolf, he was circling in on her friend. For the first time she had lost the initiative. Anna could not see Mary Rose as a partner to Crispin, only a victim. What enhanced Anna's exasperation was that she realized Mary Rose was on a track from which no one, not even her closest friends, could deviate her. She thought of Justin Villias and the way Mary Rose had played him like a cat with a mouse. Although Justin repelled Anna, he was at least a harmless, playful individual, and far more a match for Mary Rose than Crispin. Justin loved life, that was obvious, and he lived it to the full. Crispin had a grudge against his maker and was out for revenge. The lump in her chest hardened. How sad, she thought.

* * *

A week later, ten days before Anna and her family were ready to go to London for a final night of theatre and a stay at the Savoy, the twins finally arrived from Italy. Before they had left New York, Daniel had spoken briefly of their plight, a story which had shaken Anna. Up until then the brewing poison in Europe, mentioned in newspaper articles and vague table talk, had concerned people she had never known in countries she had never seen. But her father's emotional recounting of a family wrenched apart by the partial politics of self-interest had rudely brought the reality home. Daniel had met the twins' father on a business trip to Italy, and had learned to his dismay that the man's life was so threatened by the emerging Fascist thuggery that he feared not only for his own life, but for that of his family. In tears, the man had told Daniel of his only option – to send his children in exile abroad until they were safe to return. Overcome by the horrifying yet courageous choice, Daniel had offered to help; apart from his natural compassion, in the back of his mind was the memory of his early days in America, a refugee from Ireland, and how much the help of others had contributed to the ultimate well-being of him and his family. He had agreed to meet the twins in England, and had warned Anna that they might even take them back to New York for safe-keeping until the situation in Italy improved.

Mario and Fosca Biancharini, who were about Anna's age, both looked as if they had been through a terrible ordeal. They spoke little English, but Anna could talk to them in her halting French, resorting to English to fill the inevitable gaps. But their arrival was no time for prolonged conversation; they were exhausted, confused, and shy in their strange surroundings.

After dinner that night, Anna took them upstairs. Even though they had already been shown their rooms, Anna was aware that, for them, it was a very big house and completely unfamiliar. Once in Mario's room, Fosca asked Anna shyly if they ate pasta in England. Obviously the fare that night had shaken her, as it had Anna and her family.

Anna laughed sympathetically. 'Yes, I think so. But we have lots of pasta in New York because of the big Italian section there.'

Mario looked around his shabby room curiously. 'Are your cousins poor?' he asked Anna.

'No, I don't think so. It's just that the English don't spend much on themselves. They spend most of their money on horses and killing things. At least that's what I have worked out.' She paused for a moment. 'It must be awful to have to leave your mother and your father and everybody you know to come here.'

A tear welled in Fosca's eye. 'It is. But my mother and father were in a great deal of danger. There are Fascists everywhere. Mussolini has big white-painted notices everywhere encouraging people to spy on each other. In our town, Asciano, I am happy to say there are very few Fascists. Still, my mother and father had to go into hiding. Many of their resistance friends are working in the Crete getting caves ready in case the Germans do go to war and involve Italy.'

Mario put his arm protectively around Fosca. 'I wanted to stay and fight but my father said my duty is to look after my sister.'

What a nice-looking boy, Anna thought. She smiled at them. 'Both of you, I can promise, will just love America,' she said reassuringly. 'When we get to the Savoy we can all have a blow-out. I must say I am getting really tired of rice pudding and Mrs Dobbs' foul temper. "Foul" is an English word. I've been studying Jane Austen all this summer. Now I understand her

165

perfectly. Do you like Jane Austen?' She saw the blank look on their faces and curbed her enthusiasm. 'Are you happy to stay here or would you like to come downstairs? We are all going to play charades in the library. Ralph is rather good at it, especially when he's had a whisky or two.'

Mario shook his head. 'I think we will stay. We are both tired.'

'OK.' Anna kissed them both good-night. Mario had smooth, pale golden skin and his mouth was wide and mobile. Anna liked his mouth.

Thirty

Anna hated saying goodbye to Ralph. She hugged him to her hard and whispered into his ear. 'I'm really going to miss you. Thank you for all you did for me this summer.'

Ralph looked down at her upturned face. 'The help is mutual. I'm glad to know that you are my friend. Yours is the best friendship I've ever had with a woman.'

Anna blushed. 'Promise me,' she said, 'that if you ever come to America you'll look me up.'

Ralph smiled and kissed her gently on her lips one more time. 'I promise.'

Mary Rose came into Anna's bedroom that night. It was past midnight and Anna was asleep. 'Anna! Anna! Wake up.'

Anna sat up groggily. 'For heaven's sake, Mary Rose, what on earth is the matter?'

Mary Rose switched on the light beside Anna's bed. 'Look,' she said, holding out her hand. There, on her wedding finger, was a large diamond ring.

'Golly.' Anna had to admit she was impressed. 'Crispin, I assume?'

'Sure thing. I'm engaged to be married.'

Anna leaned back against her pillows, her brow creased in thought. She could not tell Mary Rose what she knew about Crispin. If she did she would risk antagonizing her. Far better to wait this one out and hope that Crispin, once out of sight, would be out of mind. 'That's wonderful.'

Mary Rose's face was alight. 'He loves me so much. He's not going to sleep with me until we are married. Can you imagine that? He says I'm different to other women he's known. I'm much finer. And now he's found me he won't look at another woman again.'

Anna tried to smile. 'That's great, Mary Rose, that you have so much faith in him.'

Mary Rose's eyes shone. 'You know, Anna, this is the first time I've ever been in love. Real love. It feels so blissful. You are quite right, you know. I do feel clammy and all tingly. I don't feel that terrible passion and "*Sturm und Drang*".' She drifted away for a moment and then continued. 'Talking about "*Sturm und Drang*", how are the Italians doing?'

'Just fine,' Anna replied. 'I think they will both be glad to get out of here.' Anna was wide awake now. 'I played tennis with Fosca and Mario yesterday.' She grinned. 'I'm going to learn Italian. Mario said he'd help me.'

'Why don't you fall for Mario? He's such a good-looking guy.'

'Please, Mary Rose, don't you even suggest it! It's taken me all summer to get over Rupert and I'm not falling in love ever again. It's a disastrous state to be in.' She ran her fingers through her hair. 'I'm looking forward to seeing Steven very much. I got a letter from him yesterday and he says he's got a girlfriend. I'm so pleased for him. He sent a photo. She looks really nice.

He says his mother is furious because the girl is not a Jew. A goy, no less, she says.' Anna laughed. 'Now go away, Mary Rose, and let me go back to sleep. We all have to get up very early in the morning and drive up to London.'

Mary Rose leaned over Anna and kissed her. 'Goodnight, Anna. I'm going back to my room to look at my ring. I want to see the fire in it when the sun rises.'

'You're an incurable romantic, Mary Rose.'

'I know, Anna. For me it's always the moon in June, and roses and chocolates and diamonds.' She stood by the doorway. 'You do think I'm doing the right thing, don't you, Anna?'

Anna tried to sound objective. 'Mary Rose, what I think doesn't matter. It has to be between you and Crispin. You must know that he wants to marry you for your money and that's OK by you. So, as long as you remember that and don't get hurt when he spends it, it should be all right.'

Mary Rose let out a sigh of relief. 'Well, there's lots of money and we can both enjoy spending it together, I guess.' She left the room. The 'I guess' hung in the air like a little lost lamb. It's not OK, Anna thought as she tried to sleep. It's not a bit OK. When she finally did fall asleep she had an awful nightmare that Mary Rose was falling down a cliff, and she saw Crispin's face at the top, grinning.

Thirty-One

Both Fosca and Mario smiled at Anna as the car pulled up in front of the Savoy.

'We are going to see *Trial by Jury* tonight,' Mary told the twins. 'It's a little gem of an opera.'

Fosca nodded enthusiastically. 'I am glad for the music, but I am more glad for a comfortable hotel.' She was dressed in a navy blue sailor dress with a big wide lace collar. Her little hands were folded on her lap, and Anna watched how the fingers twisted themselves into knots. Both Italians obviously tried not to show their feelings. Anna knew well enough that they were really suffering, not only from the loss of their parents, but also from the worry. Around the hotel, and in and out of the revolving doors, men in uniform moved quietly and efficiently about their business. Driving up from Trafalgar Square there had been a crowd waiting outside the Foreign Office.

'Somebody arriving with more news from Germany.' Daniel strained to read the banner headlines on the evening newspapers: PEACE IN OUR TIME. 'Dear Lord, I hope so,' he said gravely.

The ensuing disembarkation of the Kearney family and guests took quite some time, but soon the porters, led by the genial general manager, had escorted everyone into adjoining suites. 'For you, our valued visitor, and your lovely wife, the best.' The general manager opened the door to the River Suite with a flourish.

Mary's eyes glistened with surprise. 'What a beautiful place, Danny.' She touched her husband's arm. 'You've

169

always told me about this hotel, but I never really imagined such magnificence.'

He laughed. 'That time when I first came to England on business, I couldn't believe the cold, the discomfort and the lack of bathrooms in the other hotels I tried. This is a home away from home for Americans, and it's the only place where I could find a decent steak to get my teeth into!'

The general manager discreetly withdrew. He could tell a couple that was madly in love, and he envied Daniel his beautiful wife. Daniel put his hand in the small of Mary's back. He guided her to the big picture window that spanned the whole of the drawing room. Before them lay the bridges over the River Thames. The lights had just been turned on and they glowed softly in the grey haze.

'What a beautiful sight,' Mary whispered. Daniel drew his wife close to his chest and kissed her gently on the mouth. Mary laughed and reluctantly pushed him away. 'Not now, Danny, the children will be here in a moment. Wait until after supper. We can retire early and leave them in their suite.'

Daniel's eyes sparkled. 'In that case I will order several bottles of Chambolle-Musigny and I'll see that Mary Rose doesn't drink most of it. It's for us, darling. A special night that I have waited so long to spend with you here.'

Mary hugged him. 'Ah, Danny, will there ever come a time when we will be too old for love-making?'

Daniel, still with his arms around her shoulders, shook his head. 'Never,' he said fervently. 'I promise you, never.'

He drew back at a knock on the door. Anna came into the room. 'Well, the twins are changing for dinner. I'm changed, and Mary Rose is on the phone to Crispin, so she's not ready.'

Daniel circled his daughter. 'You look lovely. We have reservations in the River Room tonight. Usually I eat in the American Grill with the other businessmen. But tonight we celebrate our last moments of a wonderful holiday. Why don't you take the kids down to the cocktail lounge and order yourselves drinks? We'll change and then join you.'

Anna agreed, but was pulled by the sight of the great river. 'Can you imagine the history of that river?' She stood mesmerized. The evening had now fallen like a black silk nightdress over the body of a beautiful woman. The river that had glinted in the pale autumn sun had been guileless. Now Anna felt it had changed. It brooded on deep secrets in its depths. As she stood there, for the first time she felt she was able to completely let go of her relationship with Rupert. She moved to the window, watched by her parents. They both stood helplessly, feeling all that their daughter was feeling. Mary leant lightly against Daniel.

Anna gazed impassively down at the bridges. Dear God, she prayed for the last time, I hope this feeling really has gone. She knew she must recover herself. The golden summer was over. Her broken heart had been much mended by the busy English country life. Still, now she was returning to her country and her home. Tomorrow, she vowed, is going to be the first new day of a new life in America. She turned and smiled to her parents. 'OK, I'll take the twins down and wait for you.'

Mary kissed her daughter and saw her to the door of the suite. 'It still hurts her,' she said when she had returned.

'Yeah,' Daniel agreed, 'it does. Time will help, it always does. We seem to have been saying that sentence all summer long.'

Mary smiled ruefully. 'Well, one day we won't ever have to say it again.'

Joe Loss and his orchestra were playing that night outside the River Room. The music reminded Daniel that he was quite homesick and ready to go back to America. He missed the genial enthusiasms of his adopted compatriots, the unassuming cheerful manners. Daniel often felt constrained in England. The people, he thought, looked upon all Americans as barbarians and foreigners. He hated the way the English casually made anti-Semitic and other racist comments. Even the Kearneys in Devon were guilty of that. Colonel Kearney called Italians 'wops', and the Irish 'Paddies'. Daniel had pointed out a little heatedly that the Kearneys were 'Paddies' themselves. 'Indubitably,' the colonel had replied, and Daniel had cursed his own lack of education. His colonel cousin made him feel so illiterate and ignorant. Daniel knew that the education standards in America could not, and would not, provide great scholars. Perhaps, he surmised, it was something to do with the fact that the children were educated among the ancient stones and bones of his country, in sharp contrast to the newness and rawness of a country that was still very much in its infancy. Maybe, he mused as they were escorted to their seats in the River Room, this explains why Americans were so good at futuristic sciences. They were in the process of inventing themselves a future culture. He sat down. All this musing could wait for those wonderful hours with Mary when they were home in their own big bed. The dissecting of every minute detail would be a shared joy.

The *maître d'* came quickly to the table. He was pleased to see Daniel. Word had circulated around the hotel that Daniel had brought with him three beautiful girls, but none more beautiful than his wife. The *maître d'* was Italian and had the well-known fondness for older women shared by all his countrymen. He looked at Mary and his eyes sparkled. 'How nice to have you here,' he said, his voice emphasizing the 'c' in the word 'nice'.

Mary smiled: she knew from Daniel that he had spent many years in England, but he still had a beautiful, lilting Italian accent.

'Pietro,' Daniel gestured towards Anna. 'This is my daughter, Anna, and her companion Mary Rose.' Pietro bowed and shook the proffered hands. 'And these two young people are coming back to America with us. They are Italians. Meet Mario and Fosca Biancharini. Hey kids, give Pietro a smile.'

Pietro turned serious. 'Maybe they do not have much to smile about.' He spoke a hurried stream of words in Italian. Mario nodded eagerly. His eyes lit up and Fosca smiled. Anna could sense the relief in both of them in being able to talk to another Italian soul about their fears and frustrations. The three Italians were quite lost in their conversation.

Anna looked around the big, square room. The tables were full of people who all looked rather like the Kearney cousins and their friends en masse. A few yards away, a long table held about a dozen people, all in their thirties, Anna guessed. The men were in black tie and the women in long evening dresses. There was an impressive display of the great British bosom, proudly presented and beruffled. Anna thought that, together, they all looked like a massive waterfall about to spill out of the silks and satins. If the six breasts on the left of the table all happened to fall out at once, the sight, she presumed, would be like a dam breaking. For once Mary Rose was quite outclassed. She leaned forward and passed that fact on to Mary Rose, who tossed her jet black hair and sniffed.

'Yeah, they have big tits,' she huffed. 'But English girls don't know what to do with them.'

'How do you know that?'

'Crispin told me. He says they just lie on their backs waiting for their men to finish.'

'Maybe Crispin knows Virginia?' Anna was laughing.

'He does. You have to get used to the idea that they all know each other, so if you cough in Gloucester you can be heard and reported in Dorset.' Mary Rose shrugged. She was bored and likely to remain so until she could get back to Crispin.

After the meal they moved back to the cocktail lounge to watch the dancing. Soon Daniel was on the dance floor with Mary. They waltzed well together, and Anna flushed. Mario, seeing her cheeks redden, pulled her to her feet and took her to join the other dancers.

'I don't know,' he said in French, 'if you dance the waltz the same way we do, but let me show you how we do it.' He put a surprisingly firm hand in the small of her back and lightly bore her around the floor. As they moved, Mario could feel the tension in Anna.

'You have unhappy memories, Anna?'

Anna nodded, a lump in her throat. 'Yup, I guess you could say that.'

'I too had to leave someone I loved in Asciano. We had to say goodbye for good. She will probably marry someone else because I shall be away for so long a time. She is so very beautiful.'

Anna could see the sorrow in his face. They danced closely, each involved in their own memories, and each a comfort to the other.

Thirty-Two

🙞

It was the lees of the summer when the Kearney family got back to its home in New York. The first evening back they went to Kitty's house where the rest of the family had gathered to welcome them. There, too, was Steven, who eagerly awaited the arrival of Anna.

'I did miss you so much, Anna.' His eyes were shining with happiness. He looked closely at her. 'Are you all right? I mean about what happened on the boat.'

'I did write you a long letter,' Anna replied, 'but then I tore it up. What happened to your girlfriend?' Both really wanted to leave the assembled family gathering and go away somewhere quiet. For Anna, seeing Steven again made her realize just how much of herself she had had to contain. Steven was so embedded into her life that, without him, she felt as if a large chunk of herself was missing. Such a different feeling from that she had for Rupert.

Now, standing beside Steven in the noisy, busy room, Anna managed to give his hand a squeeze before finding herself swept up into Aunt Kitty's performance, which was laughingly called 'high tea'. They all crowded around the big mahogany table. Aunt Kitty sat at one end and Joe, her husband, played host at the other. Joe was delighted with Daniel's acquisition of two fellow Italians. He burst into impassioned speech.

'I speak to them in Italian,' he said, beaming. 'See, they understand.' Both Fosca and Mario nodded and laughed delightedly. 'For you,' he said, answering a question from Mario, 'I'll go into the kitchen myself, tell the cook to go, and cook the pasta myself. I have not cooked pasta for anybody for years. Pah, these lousy ignoramus Americans, they can't tell good pasta when they eat it. "No olive oil, honey",' he mimicked. ' "Remember it gives you the shits. No garlic, honey, remember it makes your breath smell." ' Joe was off and happy. 'Come along *ragazzi*, you can help me.'

'But Joe, we have a huge meal already cooked,' Kitty protested, knowing it was a waste of time.

'I'll be back, so don't get too full.' Joe was off down the stairs whistling Puccini.

Mary smiled at Daniel. She had been worried about the twins. It was one thing to get rail-roaded into an act of charity to save two children's lives. It was quite another then to realize that these eighteen-year-old people were not really children. Indeed, Mary had already observed that they were a great deal older than Anna in many ways. Mary looked around the table carefully. Being away for so many months from her sisters-in-law made her realize how elastic time was. During those months life had continued quite uneventfully for both Kitty and Martha.

'I am afraid we have some bad news about Father O'Brian,' Martha said. 'He had a stroke just before you arrived back.'

Anna leaned forward, concerned. 'He is going to be all right, isn't he, Aunt Martha?'

'I hope so, Anna. He is paralysed down his left side. But he can recognize people and can talk a little.' Martha smiled at Anna. She's changed such a lot, she thought. My golden child has lost some of her lustre. Well, the world does that as one gets older. Verdigris begins to coat the soul and the pure light gets dimmed. But not for long. She was pleased Anna had made the right decision about the purser on the boat. Mary's worried letters were upstairs. 'I'll go and see Father O'Brian tomorrow. Would you like to come with me?'

'Thanks, Aunt Martha.' Anna felt comforted.

Anna was aware of the general conversation washing backwards and forwards across the table. Mary Rose was telling Steven about Crispin and showing him her engagement ring. James was discussing the merits of English gardening with Daniel. Anna still wondered what had happened to Steven's girlfriend. The cook arrived with yet another plate of cake. The teapot passed from hand to hand and then was replenished with copious amounts of hot water from the kitchen. The little kitchen maid scampered up and down the stairs.

'Thanks, Kathy,' Kitty said. 'You can go off now. I'll do the rest myself. I know Joe is down there making a terrible mess.'

Kathy grinned. 'Great, Mrs Rapillano.'

'You going out with your young man tonight?'

'Yeah, he's taking me to see Fred Astaire and Ginger Rogers in *Top Hat*. I've already seen it so many times.'

'You can never see *Top Hat* too many times,. dear. Mind you, you must only see it when you are in love.' Kitty's bosom heaved dramatically, but her wistful musings were interrupted as Joe strode into the room with a steaming platter of spaghetti. Behind him Mario carried a bowl of sauce and Fosca a cheese-grater and a hunk of Parmesan cheese. 'Now for real food!' Joe announced, sitting down at the table. Mary watched the Italian twins' faces. She was delighted to see them both looking more relaxed than at any time they had been with the family. Joe Rapillano, bless his heart, would be the link with their Italian roots they both needed. Mary heaved a sigh of relief and held out her plate.

Thirty-Three

Anna was shocked when she visited the local hospital that served Father O'Brian's area. 'Why on earth is he in a poor people's hospital?' she asked Martha. 'I know Dad would pay for him to go privately to a good clinic where he could be looked after properly.'

'Father O'Brian would never agree to leave his people. After all, he has devoted himself to a life of poverty. Don't think both Kitty and I haven't tried.' They were walking up a long, dark, urine-smelling corridor. Anna tried not to look into the rooms where rows and rows of barely human figures cried and groaned in unison. For Anna it was a glance into hell. It reawoke her deeply-hidden memories of the English atrocities in Ireland. But here, nurses and doctors did their best to cope with the impossible. A naked man was tottering towards them down the hall. He had his flaccid penis in one hand. His tongue lolled out of his mouth and he bore down on Martha. He was drooling and trying to talk to her. Anna watched nervously as Martha put a steadying hand on the man's arm. Then, it was as if the calm and the confidence that flowed through Martha towards the troubled man now reached Anna. She felt for the first time in a long time a warm feeling. The temperature in her hands rose, and they began to itch, especially her palms. She looked wonderingly at Martha.

'We both have healing hands, Anna. Don't be afraid of such a gift.' The man moved on down the corridor. 'I have been waiting for the moment when you first felt that strange healing feeling. You see, everyone has the gift of healing, but very few know how to use it. I think the gift manifests itself in people who are capable of feeling intense compassion.' She smiled at Anna's expression of surprise. 'Alas, my dear, those of us who are capable of feeling intense compassion also suffer more than others.'

'Is that why you never had children, Aunt Martha?'

'Maybe. I guess children weren't in my fate line. I was sad about that for a while, but then I have always had you in my life. I feel more like a second mother to you than an aunt.' She stretched out her right hand. 'See that line that runs up the middle of my palm?' Anna nodded. 'Well, that is my line of destiny. It's pretty straight and very strong.' She stopped still, took Anna's hand in hers and both gazed at the palm.

Anna looked up at her aunt. 'Look, I've got the same line on my hand. It's just like yours.'

Martha nodded and then she looked at Anna with a worried frown. 'Anna, for a long time, much later on, life isn't going to be very easy for you. I can see it in your hand. I want you always to remember that, whatever happens, nothing can harm you. You have been specially chosen for a task. I don't know what it is, but it does involve protecting people.'

Martha shook her head and slowly resumed walking. They came to a wide, shallow flight of stairs. 'One day you will remember this conversation.' Martha laughed. 'You know, it's so ridiculous. Why do all these prophecies happen at the most inconvenient time? Why couldn't we be sitting in my house having a cup of tea? You know, sometimes I get the most intense understanding of what's going on when I'm in the bath, and then I have to leap out and rush to the bedroom to write it all down!'

They climbed the stairs. 'Turn right and then left. Anna, don't be too upset. Father O'Brian really doesn't look well. Say goodbye gently to him. This may be the last time you will see him. Your father and mother are coming in tonight. I can see a dark shadow over him and he is beginning to pluck at his chest. That is always a sign that the soul is ready to leave the body and go to its Maker.'

Anna felt her eyes fill with tears. She still grieved for Biddy, her grandmother, and she had known Father O'Brian all her life.

Martha led the way down another long ward. This one was for men. They lay mostly flat, staring at the ceiling. A nurse bustled about, straightening covers and plumping pillows. Nothing, however, could quell the stench of sour bodies and that dreadful smell of urine. Anna tried not to wrinkle her nose in disgust. Martha serenely sailed on. At the far end of the row of beds, Anna recognized Father O'Brian. He lay very flat in the bed. He was never a fat man, but now he was spare and gaunt. The veins in his neck stood out like ships' ropes. His huge hands plucked at the blue striped pyjama top. Anna noticed that the pyjama top was buttoned incorrectly. She leaned over the old priest and gently rectified the situation. Feeling her touch, Father O'Brian opened his eyes and then tried to smile. It was a crooked, heartbreaking smile. The two holes that were his nostrils quivered. 'Anna?' he managed. Anna smiled down at him with such love in her heart. Father O'Brian was her dearest and oldest friend. Now he was dying. She felt Martha slip her arm around her shoulders and hug her. 'He's fine, Anna, really,' she whispered.

'You've come back, Anna?' His voice was very faint.

Anna leaned down and put her mouth close to his ear. 'I'm back, Father. I'm back for good. I'll come and see you every day now until you're better.' She knew her words were hollow. Father O'Brian was not going to be here for long. She could see that his eyes had already taken leave of absence from this world and that they were staring into the next. She kissed the side of his cold, cold face. She picked up those great hands that had carried her as a child and put them under the sheet. He was asleep, or unconscious, she couldn't tell which.

Martha pulled her away. 'Come on now, Anna, let's go home to my house and have a cup of tea. He'll be at peace now that he's seen you and he'll wait for Danny and Mary.'

'Is he going to die tonight, Aunt Martha?'

'I think so, darling. He's ready to go. He's had a wonderful life devoted to God. He'll die peacefully in his sleep.'

Tears were rolling down Anna's face. She knew people

were staring, but she didn't care. 'Oh, why does life have to be so painful, Aunt Martha?'

'So that we learn, Anna. Without pain and suffering we don't learn. Most people run away from the responsibility of suffering. But you must learn to meet it head on. You're hurting now. Just sit with the pain. Talk to it . . . make it a friend. Let it roll over you in waves and then, slowly, you will heal, and Father O'Brian will be a lovely, happy memory.'

'I know that, but I'll miss him so. He and Grandma were such an important part of my life. I still miss her dreadfully and now I am going to lose him.'

'You'll never lose him, Anna. He will always be with you. His soul is eternal. Both your grandmother and Father O'Brian will be with you all the time, if you so wish. But it is better in time to let them go and get on with the rest of their destiny. We are only on this earth for such a short time.'

They were at the front door of the hospital. Ambulances screeched up and down the road. It seemed to Anna that a horde of people were streaming into the hospital. A river of bodies. Some broken, some on stretchers, bleeding. Again, memories surfaced of other broken and bleeding people. She had a horrid vision of the first time she saw Father O'Brian in her father's arms. His terribly mutilated face gazed at her. She pushed the memory away. Martha called a cab. They sat in silence all the way back to Martha's house.

Much later that night, Mary and Daniel returned from the hospital. Mary's eyes were puffed from crying. Daniel was ashen. He went straight into the drawing room and poured a glass of brandy for Mary. 'Anna,' he called.

Anna was standing on the stairs. She lingered there, not wishing to hear the news. Finally she walked across the hall into the drawing room. 'He's dead, isn't he?' she said quietly.

'Yes, he died in my arms.' Daniel's voice was trembling. Anna went up to her father and put her arms around him. 'I'm so sorry, Dad. I know how you feel. He was such a good friend to us all.'

Mary joined them and the three stood in a small circle. Father O'Brian had come a long way, both in time and distance, and now his journey had ended. From the medieval charm and social poverty of County Mayo in 1866, to the confusing cosmopolitan whirl and dollar-driven life of the New York of the 1930s. For a simple man with a simple faith, he had travelled well, maintaining his strong links with his past, yet marvelling at the new. For Anna, and for the entire Kearney family, he was their cultural bridge, their link with a past which always risked being overwhelmed by the present.

Anna bitterly wished she was a small child again. That the sun could always shine. That she and Steven could go to school together with not a care in the world. This business of being a grown up is just too difficult, she thought, as she took comfort in her parents' arms.

At least though, unlike Fosca and Mario in bed upstairs, she had access to her parents' arms for comfort.

Thirty-Four

The next morning, Anna hurried to Mario's room to tell him of Father O'Brian's death. In the short time since their return from the summer in England, Anna increasingly turned to Mario for consolation. He had a deep understanding of life. It almost seemed that

Mario had never been a child. Maybe living on his father's estate, surrounded by huge peasant families, animals and vast tracts of beautiful, unspoiled land, Mario and his sister had been encouraged to mature at a very early age. Anna pushed open his door after knocking and saw him lying propped up on his pillows, reading.

'Father O'Brian died last night.' She heard her voice wobble.

Mario looked up from his book, preoccupied. She could imagine him translating the English into Italian. Then a look of comprehension cleared his brow. 'I am so sorry, Anna. You all loved him so very much.' Mario's understanding comment caused Anna to cry again. She walked over to the bed and he opened his arms to her. Without a second thought, Anna flung herself into the waiting, comforting arms that crossed over her back like a blessing. Softly, he held her, and lightly caressed her hair.

Mary, walking past the door on her way to the garden, saw them both together. She flitted by and was glad that she had not disturbed the moment. She really liked the Italian twins, and in her maternal heart hoped that, if not Mario, Anna would at least find a suitable suitor who contained many of his qualities. There was a smile on her face as she found Daniel poking a long stick into the fish pond.

'You know, darling, I wouldn't be at all surprised if Anna and Mario don't get involved with each other. I've watched his face when she's around, and he does look as if he's mooning after her. What do you think?'

'I think,' Daniel said, pulling Mary into his arms, 'you should stop match-making and pay attention to your handsome husband who loves you very much.' He kissed her passionately until Mary pushed him away, breathing heavily.

'Danny Kearney, we will have none of your randy Irish behaviour here! And just after a full breakfast.'

Daniel sighed. 'I am trying to keep cheerful, but it's a hell of a blow to lose the Father. He's my last spiritual link with Ireland. I know how much he wanted to go back, and how homesick he was. But he promised, as did I, that he'd never set foot on the soil of Ireland until the English have gone. Well, it wasn't in his lifetime, and I don't doubt that it won't be in mine.'

Mary put an arm around him. 'Come, let's go in. I need to ring the nuns about the funeral. We will miss him dreadfully, but he was full of years and he died peacefully. What more can a man want?' Daniel looked at his dear, pragmatic wife, and hoped that some of her quiet patience would be translated to his sensitive daughter. He rather doubted it.

Comforted by Mario, Anna felt settled enough to deal with Mary Rose, who was coming over to have tea. She had Crispin with her, and Anna found Crispin an enigma.

Usually Anna could read a person like she could read a book. Seeing the energy and colours flowing from a human body had always been natural to her. In fact, she took these things so much for granted that she rarely talked about it, except to Martha who could see and sense these things as well. Anna was very afraid to tell other people, because she was afraid that they might think her mad. Even Aunt Kitty had shooed her away when she was smaller and had tried to tell her aunt that she had seen yellow flames of energy coming from her throat when she opened her mouth. 'Off with you, you silly one. You're as daft as a brush.'

Crispin was the one person who stumped Anna. Mary Rose had parts of her nature that were crystal clear. To be sure there were large, deep black holes. Those holes were well known to Anna. Mary Rose's rages and manipulations dwelt in those holes, but Anna loved Mary Rose anyway. She loved the warmth of her passion and the waywardness that made her such fun to be with. Today, however, with Crispin in tow, Anna doubted if lunch would be anything other than the two of them provoking each other. Still, she thought as she went off to organize the menu with her mother, maybe Crispin without his horde of friends might be better behaved.

Most of the discussion at tea revolved around the arrangements for the funeral. Father O'Brian had no relatives, but hundreds of parishioners wanted to attend. Martha, looking tired and emotional, had been with his nuns all morning. 'It is so sad for them all,' she said, pouring a cup of tea. 'He was so much loved in the Irish community. We'll miss his sense of humour and his great love of the people.' She smiled at Mary Rose and Crispin. 'Sorry,' she said. 'I was so busy with the arrangements I didn't see the two of you at the end of the table. You must be Crispin . . .'

Anna glanced at Crispin's face. It was white and tense. Opposite him, Mary Rose sat sullen and staring. Anna tried to see into Crispin, but he had a firm shield across his body. Mary Rose's aura was black and spiky. They must have been quarrelling again. Mary Rose tried to smile at Martha but failed miserably.

'Crispin doesn't like New York. I told him he's only been here for a few days and that he'll get to like it once he gets used to the noise. I can't imagine anyone not liking New York.'

Crispin protested. 'Mary Rose, you took me to Times Square. Honestly, Mrs Kearney.'

'Do call me Mary. I must say I agree with you, Crispin. I came here all those years ago from Ireland and I thought I'd die of the shock. After a while, New York grows on you. Or maybe it doesn't. I've known people come here and fall in love with the place and others who hate it. It's a funny city, New York. Everyone is on the make. Here you get the feeling that ninety per cent of the energy goes nowhere, but the other ten per cent takes people to the top. Here, all Americans expect their sons to be president and their daughters to be Bette Davis. There's no in-between. I often think that's what makes America such a desperate place to live. Everyone wants to be famous. Such a pity.' Crispin's face had softened now.

Fosca passed him a plate of cakes. 'Mario and I were afraid to go out on the streets for days.'

Mario nodded. 'For me it was the homeless people. Even young children begging on the streets. We have never seen anything like that in Asciano where we come from. The family is responsible and each in it takes care of the other. If a brother dies, then the other brothers take in the wife and the children. Here I find out that old people go into homes for the elderly. That's a terrible idea. I cannot imagine an Italian doing that to his parents.'

Through Joe, the twins had managed to get news of their father. Mario's face became leaden. 'But it seems everything's changing now . . .'

'Unfortunately it looks like it,' Daniel said. He turned to Crispin. 'Their father is finding the situation in Europe at present extremely difficult and dangerous. If war breaks out, then God forbid.' He shrugged his shoulders and spread his hands. 'There will be families decimated all over Europe. If England joins in, she too will feel the brunt of the Germans' hatred. These are early days, and I don't foresee war for several years yet. But men with foresight, like Mario's father, know that it is better to be ready and to know your enemies than to get caught at the last moment. This man Hitler is now only considered a house painter and a rabble-rouser, but he is a symptom of the people of Germany. He symbolizes the feelings of a people who lost the First World War and do not intend to lose a second. Unfortunately, we in America have helped rearm the Germans. He is an evil, obsessed little man. Unfortunately, he is very characteristic. He says the things frightened people want to hear. He feeds their ignorance and paranoia. The Germans are now afraid of everything. They have a country overrun by refugees from the last war. There is great destitution still in wide parts of the country. A huge black market. Much of the American money has gone into the hands of corrupt, high-ranking German bureaucrats. Now Hitler only has to promise to restore law and order, persecute anybody who doesn't follow him, and make an example of the Jews. Listening to him last night made me very afraid for Europe. Your father and mother were right to send you both away for the time being.'

'I would much rather have stayed behind with them, sir,' Mario responded. 'I don't mean that I am not grateful to you, but it is hard to hear of these things and not be there to help.'

'Actually, I think that the fact that you are here and safe gives both your parents peace of mind. They can do whatever they have to, knowing that no one can denounce you or take you away. Though, so far, the Fascists have very little power. But it is growing. Anyway, let's get off the subject – it's depressing. Mary, would you pass me some of that lovely chocolate cake? What's Ralph's news, Anna?'

The tense atmosphere began to loosen as Anna replied, 'Nothing much. He says he's hoping to visit before Christmas, which would be nice. But if Crispin doesn't like New York, Ralph, who is such a country boy, won't either. I tell you what, Mary Rose, after the funeral, why don't we take the twins and Crispin and spend a few days with Aunt Kitty's friend, Ross Williams, in Boston? Is that OK, Mom?'

'Of course. I think it would do you all good to have a break. I find funerals so difficult.'

'Do you?' Crispin's voice was light. 'I have terrible trouble controlling my giggles.'

Anna felt an immediate anger. 'I hope you will be able to contain yourself at Father O'Brian's funeral, Crispin. He was much loved by everyone around here. If you find you can't control yourself, please don't come.' Anna found she couldn't bring herself to smile at him in an attempt to soften her stinging retort. For a split second she saw the head of a serpent form in his eyes. The serpent was silver and its black tongue flickered back and forth between its jaws. The eyes were a lacklustre black. It opened its jaws and spat poison at her.

'I'll be on my best behaviour, Anna, I promise,' Crispin said demurely.

'I'll keep him to that promise, Anna, really I will.' Mary Rose knew that Crispin had gone too far.

Martha stood up. 'I must go and get on with the arrangements. I'll see you all at the church tomorrow afternoon at two o'clock.' She brushed her skirt with the back of her hand. 'Oh, dear me, I'm so messy. Cake crumbs everywhere.' She bent and kissed Daniel and Mary and waved her hand at the others. 'Goodbye,' she said, and left the room.

There was a moment of uncomfortable silence. 'We must go.' Mary Rose nodded to Crispin. 'We are having dinner with friends. My friends!' She almost hissed at Crispin. He stood up and followed Mary Rose to the door. 'Goodbye everyone. We'll see you at the church tomorrow.'

When they left, Anna felt the tension easing.

'I really don't know what Mary Rose sees in that young man.' Mary turned to Anna. 'They always seem so unhappy when they are together. What on earth is the point of a relationship when all they seem to do is to bicker and fight?'

'I wish I knew, Mom. She's miserable without him, and now he's here, she's even worse. I don't even get a hug from her any more.'

'That's because Crispin is a very jealous man,' Mario observed. 'He does not want Mary Rose to have friends. He wants her for himself. This is not good.' He gazed earnestly at Anna. 'To love somebody they must be free. Love is not possession.'

Anna knew he was thinking of his beautiful Italian girlfriend he left behind in Asciano. Fosca also felt his sadness and she put her hand on his arm. Anna remembered his warm, comforting hug that morning, and she was amazed to find herself blushing. Mario saw her redden and, for a moment, they were back in each other's arms.

'I must get on with some studying,' he said, pushing back his chair.

Fosca stood up. 'I also,' she said.

Anna sat for a moment with her parents. The sadness of the day was all around the room, but for Anna, the sadness at Father O'Brian's death was natural. It would eventually clear away, like storm clouds, leaving behind it clear and happy memories. It was the sadness around Mary Rose and Crispin that worried her.

Thirty-Five

The funeral was held in Father O'Brian's church. The nuns filled the front pews. Behind them sat rows and rows of his parishioners. Anna was acutely aware that the good father had been instrumental in enhancing the lives of so many of those now kneeling before him. His body lay in a long, narrow coffin.

'How small he appears in death,' Anna whispered to Mario, who was kneeling beside her. She was glad that he, too, was a Catholic. On the other side of him knelt Fosca. She was praying hard; Anna could tell from the tense whiteness of her knuckles. Towards the end of the pew, Mary Rose sat next to Mary, with Crispin beside her. Crispin looked so out of place in this quiet little urban church. His fair hair shone. He wore a long, double-breasted camel-hair coat and a big red flowing tie. Anna felt embarrassed for him, but she knew she needn't bother. Crispin was quite unaware of anybody else's feelings but his own.

The nuns had swathed the altar in a deep mourning purple. The stations of the cross were also muffled in the same funereal colour. Somehow, even though the church was darkened by the colour, it looked magnificent. In dying, the humble Father O'Brian finally had the homage paid to him that he had been denied all his life.

Anna bowed her head and felt tears fall down her cheeks. She looked up as Mario handed her a clean white handkerchief.

'Thank you,' she said gratefully. She took the handkerchief and sniffed it appreciatively. She liked the smell of the cologne Mario wore. It was not an English smell. She resolved to ask him what it was after the funeral.

Little children with such reverence came up the aisles, herded by their parents. No doubt most of them would have been christened by Father O'Brian. The mothers took the flowers and put them on top of the casket. Then Anna watched the wondering little eyes as they struggled to interpret the events that were occurring. The older ones realized that, for some reason, their priest was lying in this box, and their eyes contained a hint of fear. But the younger ones' eyes were guileless.

So lucky not to have known pain and sorrow, Anna thought. She remembered the days when she and Steven were that age. Today Steven could not be with her: his mother would have had a screaming fit if she thought that he had even considered entering the goys' church. She still believed that Mary and Daniel were after his little Jewish soul. So, Steven said, he'd say Kaddish for the Father and stay away.

Recently, Anna had felt her relationship with Steven slip away. He spent more and more time in his Hebrew school. His friends were now almost all Jewish, except for her. As she knelt next to Mario, she wondered if perhaps Steven were jealous of him. Lately, since she'd been back from England, she and Mario had been getting much closer. And Fosca was now like the sister she had never had. Mary Rose was so immersed in Crispin that she was not around much. So Anna's constant companions were the two Italians.

At times Anna found herself looking carefully at Mario's mouth. It was a slender mouth. Beautifully chiselled. He had big, soft brown eyes with large curling eyelashes. His very high cheekbones gave his face a slightly oriental slant. In fact, Anna realized, looking at him surreptitiously, he looked very much like a drawing of a young courtier by Michelangelo which she kept in a folder by her bed. Imagine, she thought, I cut that drawing out all those years ago and here he is kneeling right next to me. The thought gave her a little frisson of pleasure. Come on, Anna, you have to concentrate, she reproved herself. Mentally she apologized to Father O'Brian.

Now the senior priest came into the back of the chapel. He, too, wore purple, as did the other two junior priests who were to accompany him. Ahead of him strode a young boy carrying the tall cross. Behind them came the choir, a wide range of boys wearing white lace over their purple habits. They filed up the church aisle, the senior priest shaking the swinging incense burners. He put the burners on each side of the altar and then opened the door carefully to where the living body of Christ resided. He took the monstrance out and then briefly held it up in the direction of the casket. Every head bowed low and felt that familiar feeling of adoration for this miraculous moment. Here, lying in the coffin, was a man who had given his life and everything he had to serve this mighty God. He had forsaken the love of a wife and family. He had devoted his days and his nights to the cause of others, and now he was to receive his final reward. Anna contemplated what that reward would be. For her, all she asked was to see God's face. At school, in Bible study, her favourite moment was when Moses turned his head so that he would not be destroyed by the light shining from God's face. Sometimes, Anna thought, she could get a glimpse of that light in the brilliant blue of an early summer morning. Mostly she just hoped that she would live a life that would entitle her to be a happy and contented woman. Giving up Rupert was the hardest thing she had ever done in her life. But she had done it. In part, the man lying in front of her was responsible for her decision. He had played such a big role in forming her conscience. Now she was free to love again, but her heart was still sore from the bruising. She felt it would be a long time before she would trust herself again, let alone another man.

The High Mass for the dead progressed. Shrill voices sang the Te Deum. 'Out of the depths have I cried unto thee, O Lord.' Anna quivered to the words and the music. She remembered those depths of anguish in herself not that long ago. Mario felt her tremble beside him and put a gentle hand in hers. She held it gratefully. The hand spoke of friendship and understanding, both of which she needed now. Her world was changing.

She was changing. She was frightened of the change. The world no longer seemed to be safe. She still had the love and devotion of her parents, but she was aware of the look in other men's eyes, a look not of love or affection. They had eyes like Crispin's. Dead and full of lust. Anna did not want to deal with male lust. What she felt for Rupert had indeed been lust, but it had been clean and honest. There was nothing twisted in what she had to offer. Unlike Mary Rose. She peeked towards the end pews. She could see Mary Rose's mouth whispering in Crispin's ear. From the expression on Crispin's face, Mary Rose was up to her usual perverse tricks. Trust Mary Rose to enjoy talking dirty in church. A faint feeling of disgust flickered in Anna's heart, but then Mary Rose had never bothered much with Father O'Brian. Anna banished the thought, and the congregation stood up to receive the last blessing. As the coffin was carried past her, Anna reached out and touched it for a last goodbye.

Later, standing in the rain beside the grave, Mario put his arm around her as she sobbed. She watched the long brown casket, lowered by ropes, slip into the deep hole. Several people threw earth into the grave, but Anna just stood and shook with grief. Finally, with Mario still holding her, she turned and followed her parents back to the car.

'Hi, Anna, we're off to have dinner with my mother. What time d'you want us to come to your house on the way to Boston?' Mary Rose's face was untouched by sadness.

Crispin was stifling a yawn. 'Jesus Christ! You Catholics take for ever to bury somebody.' Crispin put his hand to his mouth.

Anna felt her blood rise. 'He's not somebody — he's our priest! And don't say Jesus Christ, it's blasphemy and you will go to hell.'

'My, my. Aren't we a virtuous little virgin today?' Crispin winked and Anna shot a furious glance at Mary Rose, who gazed back innocently.

'Leave him alone, Anna.' Mario pulled her back. 'He's not worth talking to, that one.' Mario said it loud enough for all to hear. Crispin flushed slightly, then walked away with Mary Rose.

'Thank you for that, Mario.' Anna was surprised at how pleased she was by Mario's defence of her. Steven would never have said anything. He was always much too frightened. Mario was no wimp. The thought heartened her.

Thirty-Six

Mario drove Daniel's big new Lagonda to Boston. The car gave an air of excitement to the journey. Anna sat in the front next to Mario and Fosca, Mary Rose and Crispin sat in the back.

As they left the teeming city of New York, Crispin seemed to revive. 'Thank goodness we're away from your bloody awful city, Mary Rose.'

'It's not my bloody awful city, Crispin. It's just that you're too much of an English boor to enjoy the things that we could have done together. You don't like art galleries, you don't like films, you don't like concerts. All you want to do is hang out in Harlem in the jazz clubs and get drunk.'

'Mary Rose,' Anna said firmly, 'you both can't bicker all the way to Boston. I really can't see why, on a lovely day like this, we can't all just be happy.'

'There goes Pollyanna again.' Crispin sighed loudly.

Mario touched his head slightly in Crispin's direction.

'She's not being a Pollyanna, Crispin. She is just saying what the three of us really feel. We are bored to death with the two of you either bickering or pawing each other. We are all hoping to have a holiday with a man we don't even know. Anna particularly needs a break. I, for one, am not going to let you ruin it for her. Fosca is really looking forward to seeing Boston. And so, if you both persist, we will leave you on the side of the road.'

'Since when did you become so bossy, Mario? Just remember, it was my parents that put both of you up when you were in England. I think you should at least be properly grateful. And while you're at it, learn some manners.'

Mario pulled the car over to the side of the road, and with a speed of movement that caught everyone unawares, he pulled Crispin out of the car by his overcoat and punched him soundly in the face.

Mary Rose gave a loud scream. She grabbed Crispin and pulled him back into the car. Crispin, visibly white and shaken, sat in a crumpled heap, nursing his wounded eye. Mario climbed back into the car and continued the drive in tense silence to Boston. Anna looked at him sideways. His face was composed. He behaved as if nothing had happened. Fosca leaned across and patted his shoulder. Anna could sense the approval in the hand. She too, though frightened by the violence, found herself wholeheartedly approving of Mario's action.

'You bastard, Mario,' Mary Rose said finally, her voice shaking. 'I'll get even with you one of these days. Who the fuck do you think you are? You're just a silly little refugee living off Anna's parents.'

'Mary Rose, you stop right now or I'll get out of the car and take a swing at you myself.' Anna was furious. She could see the barb had gone deep into Mario. She knew how badly both brother and sister felt because it was not possible to send money through from Italy where their parents were in hiding. 'Our family business is nothing to do with you, so shut up.'

The car ride continued in a disagreeable silence. They passed through some lovely countryside, but all five of them were deep in their own thoughts.

Mary Rose lay dramatically in Crispin's arms. His eye was now swollen and beginning to turn blue. After stopping for a final tank of petrol, they were soon enveloped in the city traffic.

Anna had been to Boston on several occasions, but she had never met Ross Williams.

Just before they had left New York, her mother had expressed her usual caution. 'Kitty, you are sure that this Ross Williams is a respectable person to chaperon these young people around the city?'

'My dear Mary, do I know any other people except respectable people? Ross is a little eccentric, but an absolute darling. They will have a lovely time with him. He is a party kind of guy. It will do Anna good to have a bit of a laugh and a giggle.'

Mary's face had been dubious, but under pressure she had agreed. Her old friend in Boston did not have room for five guests. Apparently Ross had a huge apartment overlooking the river. In the end, Anna had persuaded her mother that they would be well chaperoned by the two men, the other being Mario. Now, having watched him deal with Crispin, she felt even safer. Mario knew what he was doing and was not afraid of enforcing his views when he knew he was right. Hopefully, Mary Rose and Crispin would behave themselves for a while.

Anna navigated for Mario and presently they pulled up in front of a very large, art deco-style house. It had a sweeping front lawn and a pair of elegant, ornately designed gates, beautifully geometric.

'How marvellous,' Anna exclaimed. She could feel Crispin's disapproval.

Mario got out of the car and put his finger on the electric bell. They could hear it faintly ringing in the house.

The front door opened and a slim, brown-eyed man came running down the steps and to the car. 'Hello,' he said. 'I'm Ross Williams. Your Aunt Kitty told me all about you, Anna. I assume you're Anna.' He put his head into the car window. 'You look quite like your Aunt Kitty; I hope you're just as much fun.'

Anna laughed. 'I don't know about that, Mr Williams.'

'Do call me Ross, darlings. Come along, let's get your things inside the apartment. We're all just changing for cocktails.'

Anna perked up. In the awkward silence of the drive she was thrust back into the sorrow she felt at the loss of Father O'Brian. The idea of changing for cocktails amused her. Driving through Boston, she had been struck by the order and the cleanliness of the place. The people on the streets were mainly white. There was a smattering of black people, but they looked lost and out of place. Somehow Anna missed the diversity of people, but not the noise and the dirt. Here the traffic took its stately time. Polite policemen directed the cars and waved happily at the Lagonda. Anna felt safe in this city in a way she never felt safe in New York. The danger and the lack of safety was also part of the attraction of New York for many people, but not for Anna. Cocktails seemed a very Boston thing to do.

Ross carried Anna's suitcase into the house. The others followed. Once inside, Anna caught her breath. The staircase leading up to the second landing was open-plan. The stairs were made of white marble and the staircase itself was fashioned out of gleaming bands of brass. All five visitors stood lost in admiration.

Even Crispin was impressed. 'That's absolutely beautiful, Ross,' he said.

'I know it is,' Ross grinned. 'I designed it myself. My friend Harry Collins lives in the apartment upstairs. You'll meet him in a moment. We're both nuts about art deco. Follow me, and I'll take you to your rooms.'

Anna watched wide-eyed as they walked through several elegant drawing rooms and a black and white dining room. She had never seen this form of decoration before. 'I really think it's lovely, Mario.'

Mario nodded. 'It reminds me of some of the architecture you find in Italy, particularly in Siena. The cathedral is designed in black and white stripes. So amazingly original for its time. Yes, I really do like this type of architecture.' He gazed at a magnificent *trompe-l'oeil* painting at the end of the long hall leading to the bedrooms. He grinned at Fosca who was walking beside him. 'I feel as if I could walk straight into that garden, it's so realistic. Who did that painting, Ross?'

'Harry did. He makes his living painting *trompe-l'oeil* for the rich in Boston. He has some commissions in New York now. I do furniture and interior decorating. We both love what we do. And it gives us the freedom to travel. Most of all I like the idea of not having to get up in the morning. I'm a night owl. Harry is an early morning person. He's up at dawn. He says the light is best then for painting for pleasure. We tend to meet now for cocktails and dinner, and then Harry goes off to bed. Here you are, Anna.' He opened a door in the middle of what looked like a lush green jungle. A monkey's head with white fur ears proved to be a door handle. 'In there is a suite of three bedrooms with a shared bathroom for the girls. Across the hall, Mario and Crispin can share the duplex. Off you go. I'll see you all back in the drawing room in a few minutes. I'll introduce you to my absolutely lethal coconut cocktail.'

Mary Rose's eyes lit up. 'What do you mix it with?'

'Ah, never you mind. But I can tell you this. I just scamper past with the gin bottle.'

Washed, refreshed and changed, Anna was pleased to see Mario standing in the elegant drawing room. The overstuffed Victorian architecture so beloved of Aunt Kitty had no place here. The chairs were made of polished leather, stretched over chrome metal bars. Gingerly, Anna sat down on one, and then she relaxed. 'They're really very comfortable,' she said, smiling at Ross.

Just then a tall, willowy man came into the room, followed by several men and women. They were talking furiously with each other. 'I tell you, Harry, that bitch Clarice Cliff won't last. She's only such a success because she's balling the boss.'

'You're quite wrong, Peggy dear, and you're wild with jealousy because I picked up her creamware dinner service for nothing in Philadelphia. Clarice is a brilliant designer. What d'you think, Werner?'

'I tend to agree with you. I collect her stuff. Tex and I found a small potter's cooperative in England called Soho Pottery. I bought an amazing coffee set there. It's black and pink. Adorable.' Werner was a small, compact man with a baby face.

Ross took Harry by the arm. 'Harry dear, meet my friends. This is Anna, Kitty's niece.'

Harry put his hands either side of Anna's face. 'Beautiful,' he said, 'simply beautiful. Kitty told me so, but I never imagined you'd look so fine. I shall have you sit for me before you go back to that hell-hole.'

'There, you see,' Crispin flushed, 'somebody else agrees that New York is a horrid place.'

'What on earth happened to your eye?' Harry raised his brow.

'Nothing. I just ran into a door.'

Ross laughed. He was shaking a silver cocktail shaker. 'Convenient for you, dear boy. Are you sure someone didn't just deck you?'

'Quite sure.'

Anna realized that Crispin felt completely out of place with these artistic, self-assured people. This is the life that Crispin always wished he'd lived. In the English countryside, Crispin and his friends might seem different and exotic, but not here in the real world where people were genuinely gifted and the artistic had no need to pose.

'Here Anna, you go first.' Ross expertly poured a frothy liquid into a small, triangular-shaped glass. 'Just a moment, I need to put the finishing touch to my concoction.' He went to a small black chrome-lined bar at the back of the drawing room and came back with a handful of tiny pink Japanese parasols. 'Aren't they beautiful?'

Anna kept a wary eye on Mary Rose. For the moment she was getting far more attention from her new friends than Mary Rose. She could see Mary Rose's eyes narrowing. She bent her head and took a sip of the drink. She paused a moment to savour it. 'That's wonderful.' She took another sip. 'I can taste the coconut, maybe some pineapple, and a touch of gin. I like the fact that the gin isn't too strong.'

'You're quite right. I told you I'd sprint past the glass. I can't have you telling your Aunt Kitty that you got legless the first night you stayed with me.' He turned to Mary Rose. 'How about you, my dear? Would you like to have a try?'

'No, thank you. I'd much prefer to have a gin and tonic. My mother always said that cocktails were a very vulgar idea.'

Inwardly Anna groaned. She could see the look of horror on Fosca's face. Mario showed no concern.

Crispin was grinning. His tight jaw showed approval for Mary Rose's bad behaviour.

'That's fine, my dear.' Ross's voice didn't betray any emotion. His friends went on talking among themselves, ignoring Mary Rose's remark. Ross poured a gin and tonic for Mary Rose with a twist of lemon. 'I hope you like this, dear. The gin is from London and so is the tonic. American tonic is far too sweet.' He gazed blandly at Mary Rose, who accepted the drink and felt at sea. There had been no seismic reaction from these people at all. It was as if her little outburst had not occurred. She took the drink with bad grace and pulled Crispin down the room to a sofa. There she talked to him earnestly.

Dinner was not served until ten o'clock that night. Harry was cooking and Tex and Ross were aiding and abetting. There was much laughing and joking among Ross and his friends. Finally, just as Anna thought her stomach might become impaled on her spine, Harry called everyone to the dining room table.

'For the first course we have Black Sea blinis. I was taught to make these by my friend the chef at the Savoy. Do you know the Savoy, Anna?'

'That's where we spent our last night in London. It is fabulous.'

'Only hotel in England that understands Americans. This is Sevruga caviare. It is considerably cheaper than Beluga, and if you are going to use it like I do with chopped egg and a little chopped onion, there is no need to use more expensive caviare. If you can't find Sevruga, try Ocietre, it's also excellent.'

Anna looked at the neat little pancakes sitting on her plate. Harry had sculpted a little fan of onions and pale yellow lemon rind. 'No wonder Aunt Kitty is so fond of you both if you always cook like this.'

Ross beamed. 'We both love to cook and we love to eat. I'm only chief bottle-washer and barman, but Harry is one of the best cooks in Boston. Here, try a bottle of white wine from San Gimignano. It's a very famous wine. I got it for my two Italian guests.'

Fosca's eyes were shining. 'Thank you,' she said shyly.

She looks so lovely when she smiles, Anna thought. I wish she'd do it more often.

The meal progressed and so did Mary Rose's consumption of wine. Anna watched uneasily. She knew Mary Rose was intending to get drunk and would probably pass out. She was quite comforted when Ross winked at her. The gesture let her know that he and his friends did not hold her responsible for Mary Rose's behaviour, or Crispin's. He, too, was drinking heavily, and his voice rose as he talked at Werner Lowe.

'I'm going for a job in the City.' Crispin's words slurred. 'Lloyd's you know. Daddy is arranging for me to be a "Name". Costs a bomb but he thinks I'm worth it.'

'Only the English could use a word like "Daddy". So infantile!' Anna caught Harry's muttered comment to Ross. 'Just wait until he's drunk enough to start calling his parents "Mater and Pater".'

Anna sat back and waited for the inevitable. You ain't seen nothing yet, brother, she thought, imitating Aunt Kitty.

The second course was a curry from Somalia. The lamb was a yellowish colour and tasted quite muddy. But Anna enjoyed the flavour: it wasn't exactly hot, but muted and spicy.

'You see, I like that kind of gentle heat and the perfume,' Harry explained to Peggy, who was picking at her food with a fork. 'Come on, Peggy, you can't be dieting again.'

'Of course I am, idiot. A woman can never be too rich or too thin.'

'Peggy, you're practically a skeleton!' Tex's voice was raised in mock horror. 'I can see right through you. One day you simply won't be there. Why do you do it?'

'Because I want to find me a rich, handsome young lover. Someone who will sweep me off my feet. Anyway, these days starving is all the rage. My mother swallowed a tapeworm in a pill. That's what they did in those days.'

Mary Rose heard the last remark, went purple, then grabbed her mouth and ran out of the dining room.

'Very cool,' Werner remarked as she left the room.

'Hey, did you hear that word in Harlem?' Crispin asked.

Werner raised his eyebrows mockingly. 'No, darling. I first used the word in Harlem. I make the fashion in this town.' He flipped back his beautifully fashioned silk cuffs, exposing a gold watch in the shape of a clown, and laughed animatedly. 'And now, child, don't you think you should go and take care of your little playmate? After all, if we are old enough to have supper with the grown ups we should be able to hold our drink, shouldn't we?' Even Crispin realized that he was being made to look a fool. He got to his feet and left the room.

Once he had gone, the whole table relaxed. The conversation ranged through discussions on the theatre to the Museum of Modern Art. Ross's friends all seemed to know everyone in the field of music and art. Anna enjoyed herself immensely and was glad to see that both Mario and Fosca were joining in. She realized that both of them knew an enormous amount about those worlds as well. She also realized that they must so miss all the history and the architecture they had left behind. She resolved to see that the three of them went to the theatre more often.

Later, after she and Fosca had crept into their bedrooms, Anna looked at herself in the bathroom mirror. Her face was gently flushed and her eyes were shining. Maybe I am quite beautiful, she thought. She went to bed and slept happily.

Thirty-Seven
♫

After the first few days sightseeing in one of the most beautiful cities in the world, Anna was ready to sit by herself for a morning and just take stock of her life.

Christmas was around the corner, and all the shops in Boston were overflowing with exquisite things. She had been wondering what to give Fosca and Mario. Mary Rose was an easy bet – some erotic silk underwear, as usual. While Anna, Mario and Fosca toured the art museums, Mary Rose took off with Crispin to restaurants and, after dark, to night clubs. Anna declined their offer to join them. The night clubs that they frequented seemed to Anna to be filled with 'abnormals', as she privately called them. As she sat in the drawing room looking out over a panoramic view of Chestnut Hill, she watched the leafless trees imploring the winter sky for a gentle wind this winter. It was cold outside, but a brisk, healthy cold. Not the bone-chilling, chilblain-making cold of New York. Tonight, she remembered, they were all going out with Ross and Harry to a club partly owned by Werner Lowe. Anna was excited about that, and had already picked out a long, pale blue evening dress with matching kid gloves.

She knew that Ross and Harry were lovers, but she also respected the fact that it was nobody's business but their own. When Mary Rose attempted to gossip about them, Anna cut her off with a cold stare. 'They are my aunt's friends, and now they are my friends as well. Please, Mary Rose, don't say anything unpleasant about them.'

'My, you are getting boring these days, Anna. Crispin is probably quite right. It's because you fancy that little prig Mario.' At the time Anna had been very shocked at the suggestion and had protested indignantly, but now, sitting in this lovely room, she realized that her thoughts were much taken up with Mario. The twins had been in the Kearney household now for several months, and so far Anna had not even looked at another man. Among this Boston crowd, several of Ross's friends had tried to initiate conversations with her, but she had been far too shy to respond. She wondered if her relationship with Mario was comfortable; he now knew her very well and always came to her aid when she was approached by an amorous male. She gave the matter some thought and then wandered down to the kitchen to make herself a cup of coffee and root about the capacious American refrigerator. Her summer in England made her grateful to be an American. She really was appalled at the lack of kitchen equipment in England. The English seemed to have no inclination to wash at all – and, given their plumbing, no wonder. She found a tub of Italian ice-cream in the freezer and resolved to tell Mario of her find.

Later, after a hot bath, she slipped out of the house, telling Fosca and Mario that she had some shopping to do. She walked up the road and, feeling very adventurous, flagged a taxi.

'Where you from, doll?' The taxi driver was unwelcomely familiar.

'I'm from New York.' Anna folded her black-gloved hands primly on her lap and crossed her legs at the ankles.

'Whatcha doin' here?'

'Visiting some friends.' Anna was beginning to think her trip into the centre of Boston was perhaps not a good idea. She looked at the back of the man's neck and then at his face in the driving mirror. She saw his sad eyes, the disillusioned droop of his mouth, and she felt his sadness invade her. She only had to endure this depressing feeling for the trip into the city, but this man, she knew, was bound to live with it all his life. She smiled into the driving mirror, willing him to feel some joy. He caught her eye and then, after a moment, he tried to smile. It had been a long time since he had smiled. He remembered the time when his shrew of a wife smiled at him like that. The girl in the cab lit up the car with her golden face. He felt a warmth in her presence and then a feeling of intense calm.

'Well, I hope you're having a good time.'

'I am, I really am,' she replied, relieved at his change in tone. 'Could you tell me where I can get good Christmas presents?'

'I guess the best place is probably the Oriental Emporium in the centre of the city. They have stuff from all over the world.'

'OK, take me there, please.'

Just the fact that she bothered to say 'please' touched him. He turned down his radio and carefully drove his now precious passenger to her destination.

Anna realized that, here in Boston, even the busy Christmas present-buying public did not push and shove as they did in New York. She entered the big black swing doors of the shop and was amazed to see tier upon tier of floors reaching to a high glass ceiling. The shop was built in a massive circle, and in front of her was a bank of lifts staffed by men in crimson uniforms. 'Going up,' one announced loudly. 'Going up.'

Anna guessed that she'd find what she was looking for

on the seventh floor. She had always liked the number seven. It stood for seventh heaven, a place that Anna was firmly resolved to inhabit most of her life. She left the lift and started to browse around the floor. Her intuition about the seventh floor was right. Here they sold silken robes, underwear and kimonos from Japan. That's what I'll get Mario, she thought, a kimono. She let the silk run through her fingers. Finally she chose a purple silk kimono with a small yin and yang design. She loved the ever-revolving symbols with the one eye staring out of the circle impassively, viewing the antics of the rest of the irrelevant, so-called real world.

'I'll take that,' she told the assistant, and then she wandered over to another counter. The assistant fluttered beside her. She was a much older woman with a cheerful face. She looked as if she attended a Baptist church regularly and made excellent apple pie. Anna felt herself blushing; was she really going to have to choose sexy underclothes for Mary Rose in front of this woman? The assistant would automatically think Anna was buying the clothes for herself and be shocked.

'I want to buy some ... er ... underclothes for a friend of mine ...' she said haltingly.

'Certainly, honey.' The shop assistant pulled out a tray of pretty vests. Anna lifted one and looked at it. Mary Rose, she knew, would never wear that.

'Ah well, of course, it's very beautiful, but I'm afraid my friend is a very fashionable woman.' Anna gazed pleadingly at the shop assistant. 'I mean she likes ... well ... she likes sexy clothes.' Anna felt a complete fool.

The woman's face hardened. 'Come this way,' she said stiffly. Anna followed her disapproving bottom down the aisle. 'Here we have the sort of thing you require, Miss.'

Anna rummaged around several drawers and tried to

find the least sexually exotic item of clothing. Most of the panties were crutchless and the bras had holes for nipples to protrude. Anna had not actually envisaged such erotic clothing, but she was far too intimidated by the shop assistant even to try and discuss the matter. She grabbed a couple of pairs of crutchless panties and two peek-a-boo bras, paid the woman and fled to another floor. Goodness, she thought as she exited the shop, Mary Rose will think I have gone mad or perverted.

Later that evening while she was wrapping the presents, she decided to keep one pair of the crutchless knickers. She giggled as she tucked them into a side pocket in her suitcase. This was something she was not going to share with her mother, or even Aunt Kitty. She enjoyed the perverse tingle the secret gave her.

The club was set back in a private garden. The road was unpaved and ran through a dense forest of pine trees. Ross was driving his black Bentley. It was large and luxurious. Anna sat snuggled in the cashmere blanket. Beside her, Mary Rose lay back in Crispin's ever-ready arms. She was wearing a lime green halter-neck dress. She looked stunning. The green of the dress matched her eyes. Mario sat on the little bucket seat in front of her, wearing a black dinner jacket and a red cummerbund.

'You look marvellous, Mario,' Anna commented. 'And so do you, Fosca.' Fosca smiled. She was wearing a cream silk evening gown and gloves. In fact, it was Fosca's love of hats and gloves that influenced Anna away from Mary Rose's careless concept of fashion. Mary Rose's idea of fashion had only really been to flaunt her sexuality. Fosca's was simply to present herself as a woman.

Several of Peggy's men friends were Italian, and Anna loved the way they kissed Peggy's hand. As she was still unmarried she could not have her hand kissed, but she looked forward to the day when it would be her turn. 'I can see why Italian women spend so much time on their nails,' she said, laughing with pleasure at the night to come. 'If all those lovely sexy Italian men kiss my hand when I'm married, I'd spend most evenings repairing my nails too.'

'Who says Italian men are going to kiss your hand?' Mary Rose was not in a good mood. So far Harry had largely ignored her and Ross was implacably polite.

Mario smiled at Anna. 'I'll kiss your hand for practice for that wonderful day when you marry a very lucky man.' He pulled off Anna's glove and lifted her hand to his lips. At that moment something broke inside Anna. After her erotic dreams of making love to Rupert, the nights fantasizing about the man she would marry, tossing and turning and crying, this simple and tender gesture captured her scarred heart. She looked at Mario. A shyness enveloped her. She realized that she was looking at him and seeing him in a new way. It was as if she had always seen him through a pair of dark glasses, and now the glasses were off and she felt vulnerable and naked. Mario, too, seemed to feel the change. He gently put the glove back on her unresisting hand. The only person who noticed the interchange was Fosca, and she was smiling with approval. Anna smiled back.

The car drew up in front of an imposing mock colonial mansion. It was the sort of great house Anna would have expected to see in the deep south. 'Where's Scarlett O'Hara?' she joked.

'Right next to you,' Crispin replied.

Mary Rose preened. 'Ah guess ah always did see mahself as Miss Scarlett.' She shot a languorous glance at Mario. He got out of the car and held the door open with a flourish.

'Come, Miss Scarlett,' he said deliberately to Anna, 'your audience awaits you.' Anna got out of the car holding the short train of her dress carefully in one hand. She admired her white pearly shoes and stockings.

Together they all made an impressive sight. Harry's waistcoat was made of embroidered yellow satin and it matched his cummerbund. Anna was glad she was going to sit for him tomorrow; but tonight she was going to dance with Mario, and the thought thrilled her.

Thirty-Eight

Posing quietly for Harry in his studio, Anna thought over the events of the night before. Dancing with Mario was not the heady, physically erotic dancing that she had shared with Rupert. No, she thought, watching the rays of sunlight dance through the dusty Boston morning air. It was more like a certainty that they would be together for ever. It was almost as if they took vows that night. Silent and unheard by those dancing figures around them, but they each understood. They danced together all night. Mario danced quite differently from Rupert. Rupert had a well-practised way of dancing that involved moving Anna's body between his legs, causing them both to feel the maximum physical feelings. Dancing with Rupert had been the closest they had come to making love. With Mario it was very different. They danced intensely, but to music. The music was all important to Mario, and with him living in her house she knew just how much music meant to him. Holding her closely in his arms he led her through all the graceful notes and the complicated timing that was required of a quickstep. Dancing with him she was aware of music in a way that she never really had been before. She realized as they moved to an old English waltz that they became the music. She, a graceful, swaying oboe, and he a deep and passionate cello.

The evening had been wonderful. Mary Rose had forgotten her sulks and had danced with both Ross and Harry. Peggy's Italian cohorts turned up and delighted everyone with their high spirits. Werner Lowe had bowed low over Anna's hand and had declared that she was the most beautiful woman at the party. Mary Rose had been miffed after this remark as well as by Giorgio, one of the Italians, who had called Anna '*bellissima*' all evening. Mary Rose had abandoned Crispin to dance with Giorgio for the rest of the evening which had caused a quarrel on the way home. But Anna had been too happy to care.

'A penny for your thoughts, Anna.' Harry broke her train of thought. 'You really are the best sitter I've had in years. You don't move a muscle.'

Anna felt her face go red. She wrinkled her nose. 'Actually, I was thinking about relationships. I find them very hard to understand.'

'So does everybody, Anna. Ross and I have been together for twenty years. We are lucky. Both of us are faithful to each other, which is quite unusual in our gay crowd.'

'I think it's unusual in any crowd. I'm amazed at how women sleep around so casually.'

'I really don't think that sex has much to do with it. I think it's more to do with trying to discover a sense of self-esteem. Before I met Ross I was miserably and unhappily married and I played about endlessly. You could say I lived on the end of my dick. I wasn't so interested in the act of sex. What thrilled me more was to watch a woman take her clothes off and to know that she did it for me. I felt validated. Then, often, I was stuck with the rest of the routine! Now I put so much of my sexual and sensual energy into what I do creatively and

I am so much happier. Ross and I are not only lovers but really good friends. I can trust him with my life and I know he lives for me, as I do for him.' He smiled at Anna. 'There is a contentment in a happy relationship that is heaven on earth. Anything can happen to us. We could go broke, and we have in the past. But we have each other and we just rise above it all. Ross keeps a bottle of good champagne in the fridge and a jar of Beluga caviare, so if anything gets us down we repair to bed with both items, and the rest of the world can go by.'

'That's a marvellous idea. You also keep Italian ice-cream in the fridge. I took some yesterday,' Anna confessed, laughing.

'You are in love with Mario, Anna, I can see it written all over you. And last night I watched you dancing with him.'

'I don't know if it is love, Harry. I know I care for him very deeply, but I was very badly hurt in the summer. I very stupidly fell in love with a married man and I suffered dreadfully. I never thought anything could hurt so much. But I'm over it now. At least I think so. Sometimes it all comes back and the pain is intense. Mary Rose says it all takes time and I guess what she says is right. But I have such happy memories of that time we had together, even though it was very little. What bothers me is that with Mario it is all very different. With Rupert everything was so intense, so highly coloured. The world looked like a different place. But now, with Mario, it is gentler and kinder. I'm not sure what that means.'

'It means that your love is more mature this time, Anna. You were a child last summer, and all that pain and grief has forced you to become a woman – and a very beautiful one at that. Come over here and look at your portrait.' Anna got up and stretched. Her muscles were sore from the stillness.

'Wow, that really does look like me. You're a great painter, Harry.'

'Thanks. That's it for now. Off you go. You can sit again tomorrow if you have the time.'

'OK. I'm off to find Mario and raid the fridge.' Anna ran off happily, glad to have been able to share her feelings with Harry.

Thirty-Nine

As soon as they got back to New York, Crispin left to take up his new job on London's Stock Exchange. Anna was glad to see him go. The day he left she invited Mary Rose for dinner. She decided that it would be best if they dined alone because she knew Mary Rose would want to talk privately ·about her relationship with Crispin. 'Do you both mind if Mary Rose and I have dinner by ourselves?' she asked the twins anxiously.

'Not at all.' Mario put his hand on Anna's shoulder. 'I'll take Fosca out for a pizza.'

'OK. Mom and Dad are going out to the movies so we can both have time alone. I know Mary Rose is miserable and it will be just great for us to have time to put our feet up and just talk girl-talk.'

Mario grinned. 'Then I'm really glad that I shan't be here. You women are incestuous when you get together.'

'Thanks for being so understanding.' Anna kissed him lightly on the cheek. She went off to the kitchen to ask the cook to make veal scaloppine, Mary Rose's favourite dish. That done, she wandered upstairs to her bedroom and pulled out a volume of Jane Austen. She sighed as she read her book. Life seemed to be complicated again.

Here she sat, really wanting to be with Mario. She had to admit she would really like to be in Fosca's place tonight. She loved going out to eat with Mario. He was always so delighted with his food, and pizza was his favourite. He had explained to her when he first arrived that some food had been in short supply in Italy. The burgeoning Fascist movement had kept food stocks low in his town to encourage people to tattle about each other in return for flour and sugar.

Anna stopped reading when she heard the front door close and the sound of Mario revving the engine of one of her father's cars. Why, oh why, does it have to be Mario, she thought desperately. Why do I have to get involved with anybody at all? I'm much better on my own. I feel safe. Now, with all these confused feelings about Mario, I feel very unsafe. She promised herself that she would not go through the agony she had experienced with Rupert. She envied her mother, but then she also recognized that her mother could not help her. Mary could sympathize and feel sorry for her, but her mother had had only one real relationship. And so Anna really had to rely on Mary Rose, who was in a worse mess with Crispin than Anna was with her feelings about Mario. Now that Crispin was gone, maybe Anna could risk discussing Mario with Mary Rose.

There was no point in trying to continue reading Jane Austen's magic prose. Today it did not soothe her at all. Maybe, she told herself as she dressed for dinner, it's because today is a Thursday; never a good day for her. The thought cheered her up.

Mary Rose arrived swathed in a blue silk and a cashmere shawl. 'A present from Crispin,' she said, throwing it on the sofa in the drawing room. She stood examining her face in the mirror over the mantelpiece. 'I've lost an awful lot of weight.'

'You have.' Anna stood looking at Mary Rose's slender back. 'Are you eating properly, Mary Rose?'

'Not really.' Mary Rose sounded evasive.

'What do you mean by that?' Anna was anxious. Mary Rose's face was hollow and her wrists were thin. During their time in Boston, Anna had noticed that Mary Rose seemed to pick at her food. They were all having such a good time that she forgot her misgivings and just put it down to Mary Rose's quarrelsome relationship with Crispin.

Looking straight at Anna, Mary Rose tried to smile. But the smile was troubled. 'Anna, Crispin can only get it up if I am thin like I am now. Or even thinner.'

Anna frowned. 'That's ridiculous, Mary Rose.'

'You might think it's ridiculous, Anna, but it's true. I'm afraid if I don't try and get thinner he'll lose interest in me. I love him, Anna, I really do.'

Anna felt the panic in Mary Rose's voice. She heard the fear and the pain. 'Mary Rose, you'll just have to try and talk to him.'

'I have, but he says he can't help it. All his girlfriends are the same. They're all skinny models with figures like bean poles. My tits are much too big, he says. I wondered if I ought to have plastic surgery and have them made smaller.' She looked down at her breasts. She had lost so much weight that she really did look top heavy. Her breasts seemed to rise from her thin shoulders. 'I can't lose him, Anna, he's the only man I've ever loved.' Normally Anna would have smiled at this statement. She had heard it so many times before. But this time she knew Mary Rose was telling the truth. 'I'm so out of control on this one.' Mary Rose was talking to herself in the mirror. 'I have always known what was going on, even in bad relationships. I have always known that I could pull out if I wanted to, but now I am stuck. Does that make any kind of sense, Anna?'

'Sure it does.' Anna's words seemed to hit the mirrored glass all around Mary Rose's head. They splattered with emotion and fell to the floor. Anna imagined she saw little crimson stains of blood. 'I know exactly what you mean. I will never forget what I went through with Rupert. Maybe Crispin just needs time and confidence. Maybe when you get married and he feels secure he will not need you to be so thin.'

'Maybe.' Mary Rose's voice was bleak. 'I'll have to wait and see.'

'Look, I have ordered veal scaloppine for you tonight. It's your favourite. Also, Dad put out a very fine bottle of white wine. It's on ice. Let's go and eat. After all, Crispin is not here and won't be coming back for a while. So let's enjoy the evening together.'

Anna noticed as they sat at the dinner table that Mary Rose was pushing her food around her plate. 'Can't you eat it?'

'It's lovely, Anna. I'm just not hungry. I seem to have lost my appetite.' She ate a few more mouthfuls of veal and drank a glass of wine. 'You know, I'm beginning to think Crispin is far more complicated than any other man I've ever met. Most men are no problem if you fuck them and feed them. But he seems to have so many different parts that I can't even reach.'

'I think you're right, Mary Rose.' Both women fell into their own silence. 'I'm just plucking up courage to admit to myself that I am falling rather heavily for Mario.' Anna made a face. 'I really don't want to admit it because I am still so bruised by Rupert. What do you think, Mary Rose? Am I just being silly?'

Mary Rose smiled. 'I wondered how long it would take you to come to your senses. I've noticed the two of you for weeks now. He's in love with you, Anna. When you're together you seem so happy. And when he leaves the room you look like a puppy who has lost its bone. You're so obvious, Anna.' Mary Rose gave a short laugh. 'You're also lucky. Mario is a nice man and he will never hurt you. He's the sort of man who will always be faithful.' The maid changed the dishes and left fruit and coffee on the table.

'Let's take the coffee and fruit into the drawing room,' Anna suggested. 'Then we can sit by the fire.' Mary Rose followed her, carrying the fruit. They sat in front of the fire on the two familiar leather armchairs. 'Goodness, how many years ago was it that we sat here talking about our futures, Mary Rose?'

'Yonks, Anna. It all seemed so simple then. I was going to be a famous actress. You were going to be a married woman with six children. Now look at us, two spinsters. Well, I'm engaged to be married, and it won't be long before you are too. So things aren't too bad, are they?'

'No,' Anna sighed. 'Not really. But I must tell you I'm scared, really scared. I sometimes think it would be much easier to be a nun and not have to bother with men at all.'

'Ah yes, but think of all that sex nuns miss!'

Anna smiled. 'There are other things in life, but I'm beginning to think you might be right.' She laughed. 'I'll put off applying to the convent for now!'

After Mary Rose left, Anna joined her parents in the library. 'Mary Rose is looking awfully thin,' Mary remarked.

'Yes, she is. But maybe if she marries Crispin, things will get better. They are both so highly strung.' Anna was straining her ears to hear the front door. Fosca and Mario should be back any minute. They both had the Italian habit of walking immediately after meals. At first Anna had found this very strange, but now she delighted in walking with them, exploring the streets. Other American families in their local pizzeria came and went. They barely sat down. When they got the food – after an impatient snapping of fingers – they bolted it down, hurriedly paid, and left. Now, knowing Mario and Fosca, Anna realized that their pace of life was quite different from that of normal Americans. Even Daniel, with his huge enthusiasms and dynamic work energy, seemed brutal beside the two quiet, calm Italians. Some of their peaceful way of living now seemed to permeate the house.

Anna heard the front door slam. 'Mario is back,' she said immediately. Mary's eyes met Daniel's and she gave him a slight nod. The nod said: 'There, see, I was right all along.' Daniel grinned, amused. 'Right again,' he signalled.

Forty

Mario proposed to Anna on her twenty-first birthday. The two years leading up to that day had been spent getting to know each other. 'I need to learn to trust,' Anna had explained. 'I never, ever want to go through all that pain again. In fact, I don't think I could. I've read all about tragic love affairs like Anna Karenina's. My favourite book was always *Gone with the Wind*; now I don't believe Scarlett O'Hara finished her relationship with Rhett Butler by saying "tomorrow is another day". When you have a broken heart there is no tomorrow, only endless yesterdays.'

Even then Mario had realized Anna was not over the hurt. 'I promise it won't be like that for us, Anna. I'll never hurt you. I love you far too much; you are so precious to me. I can't believe my luck that you really can say that you love me.'

'I do, Mario. But it will take a long time for me to

trust you and to have for you those feelings I had for Rupert. Maybe those intense feelings never come again. I sometimes even wonder if I ever want to feel like that again. It was like holding a hot iron close to my face. I got burned, Mario, badly burned.'

He looked at her with compassion. 'I know. My girl got married and I thought my world would fall apart. But then I had you close to my side and you comforted me. You didn't have the safety net I did. I wondered if I was falling in love with you because you were my safety net: that would not have been good. Now I know that isn't so. *Cara*, I love you because you are beautiful and wise.'

'Ah yes, Mario, but will you love me for ever? So few people seem to be able to do that. My parents are really the exception.'

'Come here, Anna, and let me stop your mouth with kisses. You analyse things far too much.' He pulled her into his arms and Anna was washed away in the warmth of his mouth. Though she was frightened of letting herself go, she found tremendous comfort in simply being held. Mario was gentle with her. He realized it would take a lot of time before she would dare risk responding to his love-making. The wounds were still there. Anna, gentled by his calm touch, radiated happiness.

Mary and Daniel watched indulgently as the two young lovers spent their time together. Mario was now working in Daniel's factory as his assistant. He was pleased to be learning the business. He knew that this training would be invaluable for him when he went back to Asciano. All his plans now included marrying Anna. Fosca was in on his secret. She watched and waited for the moment when Mario would feel he could ask Anna to marry him.

The subject of marriage first arose when Anna was

twenty. Before this they had only talked of matrimony and children in general terms. On a bright, sunny day in May they had been on the tennis court playing tennis. Anna was two sets up on Mario and very pleased with herself. 'I'll win all three sets for the first time, Mario. It's all that sitting in the office. You're out of shape.'

'Just you see. I'll catch up.' But Anna realized that he was distracted. When she beat him she was jubilant. They had shaken hands over the net and the wind had fluttered the frills of her tennis dress. 'Come on, let's go and lie down under the shade of the oak. I'm hot and sweaty.'

'Ladies don't sweat, Anna, at least not Italian ladies.'

'I'm not an Italian lady, I'm American, and we do sweat.' Anna had run under the tree and had thrown herself on the ground. 'Boy, that grass feels wonderful.'

Mario had knelt down beside her and had put his arms around her, completely enveloping her with his body. 'Would you ever like to be an Italian lady?' he had asked.

Anna had gazed up at him, her eyes widening. 'Oh, Mario.' They had then kissed. Neither of them ever understood how they could have been caught up in such a moment of passion. Mario had found himself gently helping Anna to take off her underpants. Anna had found herself shivering and whimpering, but she could not stop. She had reached for Mario's now bare shoulders, and helped him undo the buttons of her tennis dress. He lay her back on the grass as she lifted her arms for him to remove her lace bra. Lying naked in front of him, she realized she felt no shame, only a searing need for him to be inside her body. Mario gently eased her knees apart with his legs and then began to burrow. Gently and easily he entered her. She put her hands on his shoulders and lifted her hips to accommodate him. For a few split seconds she saw them both from above, lying in each other's arms. She felt Mario shake uncontrollably and responded by locking her feet over his back to bring him even closer. A rhythm in the union of their bodies overtook them there. There was a momentary shaft of pain for Anna. Then she lost control and her body hummed and vibrated. Mario gave a great muffled cry and then lay still, lying slightly on one side of her body yet still inside her.

'Did anything happen for you, Anna?' he whispered.

'I don't know, Mario. I don't really know what is supposed to happen.'

'Here, let me show you.' He withdrew from her body and then put his fingers between her legs. Slowly, he ran them in and around her vagina. Anna felt a burning sensation in the soles of her feet that began to travel up her legs. She could hear herself groaning.

'Don't stop, Mario, please don't stop.' She was half embarrassed, but the wanton in her had found its lover. She arched her back and tried not to scream. 'Put your hand over my mouth,' she gasped. Mario covered her mouth with his lips. Then he tasted her hot, shuddering breasts with his tongue. He licked her gently under her arms. Then it happened. A great gust of passion shook her. She descended into a gorge, and as she fell deeper and deeper, she was alone in this night of flashing sensations with a man. At the end of the descent a sweet peace stole over her. She held Mario in her arms, his head on her breast. They lay together without speaking for a moment.

'I'll love you till the moment I die, Mario,' she said.

A feeling of boundless gratitude had come over her. Now she felt she could trust him. Now she knew what it was that cemented a relationship between a man and a woman. It was not the kind of sex that Mary Rose sought. It was not dark, or difficult, or dangerous. It was a communion of two souls, and for Anna that would be the only way she could ever share herself. Now the sharing had been done and there was no mystery. There would be many more ways of making love, and she and Mario had the rest of their lives to explore and to initiate each other into new realms of the erotic.

'I'm sorry, Anna.' Mario broke the silence. 'I really didn't mean to get carried away like that. Are you all right? I didn't hurt you, did I?'

Anna rolled over on her stomach. Mario, lying propped up on his elbow, smiled down at her and ran his hand down her back. Anna could feel liquid running between her legs. She put her fingers down to find out what it was. 'I'm not bleeding. I thought you were supposed to bleed the first time.'

'Not all women bleed.'

'How do you know that?' Anna looked at Mario in amazement. 'I thought you were a virgin like me?'

'Italian men don't stay virgins for long. Only the women. We have a double standard.'

'That's not fair. Mary Rose would be furious if she heard you say that.'

'I don't care. I'm your first man and I want it that way.'

Anna sat up. 'Hey, we'd better get some clothes on. What would happen if the gardeners found us?'

Back in the real world, embarrassment had caught up with her. She scrambled hastily into her bra and knickers and then pulled on her dress. 'I won't get pregnant, will I?'

'I hope not. But if you do we will just get married immediately.'

'I don't want to get married because I'm pregnant. That would be a bad thing to do.'

'Anna, you won't get pregnant. I promise you.'

'How many women have you slept with?' She

hadn't wanted to ask the question, yet it had come spontaneously from her mouth. Anna realized she was jealous of them all.

'That is my past, and we will leave my past alone. From today onwards we live our future together.' He kissed the back of her neck.

They walked across the lawn holding hands. Anna looked at the house and said sadly, 'My parents would be awfully hurt if they knew.'

'Then they won't know. Anna, it's time you had a life that is separate from your parents. I didn't mean for us to make love at all, but it has happened and it is our business alone.'

'You're right, Mario.' Anna realized that she could never discuss this momentous event with anybody but Mario. That's what made it all so special. They were a man and woman in the universal cosmos, united together in a shared bond of loving. That was their secret, and that was what made them different to any other lovers anywhere else in the world. Anna beamed at Mario. All her questions were answered. She now knew peace, the peace that comes after the fusion of two bodies.

Forty-One

Ji

Anna knew that Mario was going to propose to her officially on her birthday. She had pushed him out of her bedroom door when he had dropped by to tell her he was nervous. 'You've nothing to be nervous about, darling,' she had laughed. They had never made love in her bedroom, or in the house. For both of them the disloyalty to her parents made it impossible. All of their love-making had been in the open air. During the winter, Anna had worn her mink coat and they had lain wrapped in its huge folds and made love in the snow. Anna remembered the day that they had washed their bodies with snow after making love, and the delicious feel of the cold snow between her hot legs.

'Go on, you wimp. Daddy is going to say yes, and you know it.'

'I am not a wimp, Anna.' Mario frowned. 'I'm supposed to be nervous at a time like this. Anyway, when I'm back I'll show you what a wimp I am.'

'Where, just tell me where, and I'll be there.'

'Where we first made love.'

Anna's eyes shone. 'OK. I'll wait for you under the tree.'

Mario went off to find Daniel. 'What a wonderful, wanton woman she is,' he told himself aloud. In his pocket he had a little aquamarine ring that belonged to Fosca. When he told his sister of his intentions it was she who had insisted that he take the ring. He smiled happily as he made his way towards Daniel's study. Fosca really loved Anna. The three of them would soon return to Italy. He was so looking forward to showing Anna the family farmhouse, the *fattoria*. It was beautiful, spacious and tranquil.

Mario knocked on the study door and heard Daniel give him permission to enter.

'Danny?' Mario cursed himself because he was shaking with nerves. 'May I marry your daughter, I mean Anna . . . ?'

Daniel stood up. 'Well, I never thought you'd get round to asking. Of course you can. Both Mary and I would be delighted to have you in the family. Not that you aren't already.'

'Great!' Mario beamed at Daniel. 'Will you excuse me? I'll go off and tell Anna. She's waiting for me.' He hoped that Daniel would not pick up on his guilty blush.

The thought of Anna waiting for him to make love to her fired his imagination. She had such beautiful, soft, silky skin.

'Off you go, and I'll find Mary. We'll open a bottle of champagne tonight at dinner to celebrate.'

Mario ran into the garden. He rounded up a dozen red roses from the rose garden and continued to run to the tree. Anna was waiting for him, lying on the grass under the tree.

'Your father said yes.' He took her in his arms and hugged her. 'You're mine, all mine. For ever and ever.' He laid her gently on the grass. 'Here,' he said breathlessly, 'it's Fosca's ring, but she wants you to have it. I'll get you a proper one when we go to Italy. My mother has a family diamond ring that belongs to my future bride, and, oh Anna, that's you.' He turned her hand over and kissed her palm. Anna took him in her arms and they made love on the grass under the tree just as they had a year ago. As her arms moved around his body she caught the blue flash of the aquamarine ring. She remembered the ring Biddy had given her as a child. Blue is my lucky colour, she thought. Then she abandoned all thinking.

Forty-Two

🥢

The wedding took place in Father O'Brian's old church. Mary Rose was the senior bridesmaid. Fosca was also a bridesmaid and carefully shepherded three of Joe Rapillano's nieces, all dressed in pale blue. Anna wore a white, pure silk gown that whispered encouragement as she wafted up the aisle on her father's arm. Daniel knew he should be bursting with pride, but what he actually felt was a pang of loss and regret. So much of his life had been centred around Anna. She was, and always had been, a living flame in his existence, so much so that he couldn't imagine life without her.

The young couple were going to the Caribbean for their honeymoon, and on their return to the States they would live in a small house near her parents.

As the mother of the bride, Mary stood in the place of honour. Tears of emotion and joy were trickling down her cheeks. She watched Mario carefully as he tenderly removed the veil from Anna's face and carefully kissed her. Then the radiant bride came floating down the aisle, trailing her procession of bridesmaids. Mary sighed as she watched, transfixed. This was to be the happiest moment of Anna's life. It should also be for her mother. But Mary felt torn. The past now lay so far behind her that she had almost forgotten the beginnings of Anna's life. Father O'Brian was now dead, and Biddy.

Kitty and Martha stood nearby with their husbands. So much good had come from so much fear and horror, Mary thought. The English still ruled Ireland, and so they were still in exile from their homeland. But today their beloved daughter was getting married.

Mary collected herself as Anna came down the aisle and stood beside her. Anna leaned forward and kissed her mother, then smiled. Mary had never seen her looking more radiant. Beside her, Mario stood still and tall. He too kissed Mary and then the couple moved on. The organ swelled with the triumphant Wedding March.

Mary recalled her hurried marriage to Daniel in Father O'Brian's small church in Ireland all those years ago. Only Kitty and Martha had been in attendance. The dreadful Kearney family had been barred from Father O'Brian's church because of their wild, drunken behaviour. She smiled at the memory of her wedding night and hoped that Mario would be as gentle and kind with Anna as Daniel had been with her. She and Daniel had both been virgins. She doubted if Mario was still a virgin, but she was sure her daughter was. But then Mary paused: she had noticed a marked change in Anna over the past year. A sort of calm maturity, a sense of awareness. None of Anna's behaviour ever resembled the sexual delinquency that so obviously lay in Mary Rose's face and eyes. No, it was more than just a certainty of her place in the universe. Anna no longer blushed and squirmed with embarrassment. It was as if she knew herself and her body at a very deep level and was comfortable with herself. It was as if she had left behind her childhood and was now a fully formed woman. Sometimes she had caught Anna looking at Mario with such an intense, knowing gaze. Maybe her daughter was no longer a virgin? But she wasn't worried. She loved Mario like a son, and whatever had happened in the past between him and her daughter, she knew he would love Anna for ever. With that her soul was content.

Daniel put a ticket for their honeymoon into an envelope. He ruefully contemplated the fact that he was paying for a young man to deflower his daughter. It was an uncomfortable thought, but he entertained the emotion for only a short while. If it had to be anybody, he was glad it was Mario. He really loved both Mario and Fosca, but he also felt quite sure that now Mario was married, he would want to go back to Italy and begin his life as an independent man. Here, working for Daniel, he was dependent, and Daniel knew it irked the young man not to have his own money. Over the years, Mario had learned the shoe business well, and back in Italy he could pursue his own business life. On the other hand, Daniel felt that Mario might well run his father's estate. Mario was wedded to the country.

He worked alongside Phillip in the formal gardens surrounding Daniel's massive mansion; the excellence of the vegetables he grew was the talk of the family.

After the wedding service, with eyes dried and lumps removed from their throats, Daniel and Mary supervised the wedding feast. Mario and Anna cut the wedding cake with a gold knife. Anna felt Mario's warm, competent hand on hers as it firmly guided the knife through the thick layer of icing. She smiled as the gilt slid through the cake and hit the bottom of the silver platter. She so much wanted to avoid anything going wrong on her special day. Nothing did and, dressed in her pale blue going-away suit, she kissed Martha and Kitty goodbye and then waved from the car window. The boat hooted and Anna leant over the railing and watched the vessel tear away from the jetty. People lined the dock, some crying, others cheering. For a moment she felt a tremendous sense of isolation. So far her life had been peopled principally with her family. Now she was alone with Mario. Her married life stretched ahead of her, and it was for the rest of her days. Would their love sustain them? Would she find that the intimacy of a one-to-one relationship was too cloying? She didn't know, but as the boat pulled away, and the dark, dirty water swirled around the hull, she walked back to her cabin where Mario was already stretched out on the bed.

'I have a headache,' he said. 'All those people. Very nice and kind. But the noise.'

'I know what you mean,' Anna said, beside him on the bed. 'I tell you what, let's just order dinner in the cabin and forget there is a boatload of people with us.'

Mario smiled, his dark eyes glowing. 'That's a very good idea, *amore*. What shall we order for dinner?'

'Oh, the usual,' Anna teased. 'I'll have lobster, caviare and a salad. Followed by coffee and cream.'

'That sounds fine. I'll ring down and order. I think we

should drink some champagne, or maybe I'll order a bottle of Chambolle-Musigny. I know it's a red but I think it's a bottle we should share on our wedding night.'

Anna looked at him lying stretched out on the bed. 'OK,' she grinned. 'Do you have any specific plans for tonight?'

'Wait and see,' Mario replied.

'In that case I'm going off to the bathroom to soak in oil and generally make myself available to my lord and master.'

She strolled across the thick carpet. The unpacking had all been done by a maid. She chose a plain silk singlet and matching underpants. She smiled at herself in the mirror. The silk sent an erotic wave of lust through her whole body. She and Mario were going to enjoy this trip. She doubted if they would ever see the light of day. Now they could legitimately make love all day and all night: she couldn't think of anything she'd rather do.

After the excellent dinner, Mario changed into his black silk kimono. Anna sat across the room in a big armchair. She rose to her feet and crossed the room. Mario watched her carefully. She dropped to her knees beside his chair and looked fixedly up at him. Carefully she folded back the silk robe. She removed her flowered evening wrap, revealing her silken underwear, and knelt beside him. Mario put his right hand on her shoulder and ran his fingers down to her breasts. He could feel the tight knobs of her nipples and could see the slight dew of sexual desire on her upper lip. They were both breathing heavily. Anna took Mario's erection into her hands and gently ran her tongue over the tip of his penis.

'How wonderful,' she said between her gentle nibbles, 'to be able to do this in the comfort of a warm room.'

Mario answered with a comfortable sigh. 'We can do this for ever.' He lay back in the chair with his eyes closed. Anna was a wonderfully inventive lover for someone who had had no experience other than with her new husband. The night ahead stretched before them with promises of endless delight.

He knew from his other experiences with women that he was lucky to have married the one woman whose lust and passion matched his own. She had a strong will, but he had a strength and an understanding of her that held her in check. They both recognized that sexual passion needed a pavane of willing submission on both sides. Anna was sexually aggressive, but Mario was male enough not to let that deter him from making love to her. In the white heat of their moments of climax they met each other on several different planes. This was the basis of their marriage, and everything else paled in significance. Mario was sufficiently experienced to recognize that they were blessed to have each other. He felt her mouth engulf him and he groaned the pure sound of a man sexually possessed.

Forty-Three

When Anna left on her honeymoon, Mary Rose was surprised to find herself bereft. She had not given much thought to Anna's absence from her life as her best friend. Now she could see that Mario would replace her in Anna's affections and that she would have to take second place. She had tried to discuss her feelings with Crispin, who had now moved in with her.

'Really, Mary Rose, I don't want to discuss such things. Messy human emotions aren't English at all. You Americans blether on about feelings all the time. So very boring.' With that comment he had stalked out of the bedroom.

She was lying in the bed, surrounded by the smell and the disorder of their lust for each other. She found her eyes filling with tears. Often Crispin hurt her this way. He had developed a convenient sense of giving, but underneath there was a curious sub-text. Other people marvelled at how kind and gentle he now was with Mary Rose, but she knew better. Why did she love him? She wished she knew the answer. Maybe it was because Crispin had a certainty about him that she lacked. Underneath all the tears and the tantrums, Mary Rose knew she was a very frightened woman. Now that Anna had taken the big step of getting married, Mary Rose felt that they had both left their childhood behind. Now she felt she must really put her own life in order, and Crispin seemed able to give order to her chaos. Still, the tears came, and she struggled with an urge to bawl. Hearing the front door slam, she finally gave in. She sobbed and sobbed. She cried for Anna's happiness and for her own misery. She knew she should not continue with her plans to marry Crispin, but he was now firmly dedicated to the idea. After half an hour Mary Rose got out of the bed and rang for one of the servants to tidy her room. She picked out a tight pair of black silk trousers, an Italian purple silk blouse and very high, dangerous-looking black stiletto heels. She took the clothes with her to her spacious, marbled bathroom. There was a cream marble bathtub sunk into the floor. She filled it and poured in a stream of bath oil. A smell of roses filled the room. She immersed herself in the oil and lay back thinking of what she would get Crispin for Christmas. Maybe he might like six beautifully cut jewel-coloured shirts from Fortnum and Mason's in London. Mary Rose loved ordering clothes for both of them. But Crispin was difficult; he usually sent anything she bought him back. She considered also buying him a Gucci watch, the one with the gold face she had seen a few days ago in Bonwits. Maybe she should get dressed and go out and have another look at it. Anna would not be here for Christmas. She and Mario would be in Jamaica, so she would buy their presents and hold them until they returned.

Mary Rose realized that buying other people presents was her way of making time go away. She had no qualifications and no wish to work. She rather pitied her girlfriends who played at having jobs. Still, there were many hours when time hung heavily on her hands. Often she reached for the gin bottle and her world became cloudy and a little clogged with alcohol. Recently, she had been getting worried about how much she was drinking. But then Crispin was a heavy drinker too. His drinking really worried Mary Rose. Her father had always warned her against getting involved with a mean drunk. 'You can always tell a man by the way he drinks.' This was one of his maxims in life. Crispin was a mean drunk and became abusive and cruel after two or three glasses of alcohol. 'Fucking little whore,' was one of his favourite epithets. He was always sorry afterwards, but each time he did it, it tore her apart. Maybe I deserve Crispin, she thought as she stepped out of the bath. I've broken enough hearts in my time. She looked at herself in the mirror. Perhaps it behoves me to have a broken heart, she mused. She smiled a wan smile in the mirror and then turned and left the bathroom.

The bedroom had been restored to order. The bed lay neatly and primly, refusing to give up the secrets of their activities the night before. Crispin's love-making was of the fast and furious kind. He was slow to come and this made Mary Rose impatient. Sometimes she wondered if Crispin really liked sex with women at all, or if it was something he did only because he felt he had to. Usually Crispin seemed to be happiest in the company of a close male friend. Then he was witty and amusing. On his own, with only Mary Rose to witness his behaviour, he usually sulked or slept for hours. Mary Rose never knew anybody who could sleep like Crispin. Often she would wake in the morning and slip out of the bedroom. She found all the lying in bed, waiting for Crispin to get up, very boring. Even making love in the early morning was boring. She put on her coat and realized with a jolt that she was bored with being bored. Today she would drive her car into New York and spend what was left of the day shopping. Having filled the car with her purchases she would return home and spend the evening admiring and wrapping them. It didn't look as if Crispin was in a good mood, and taking him out to dinner just to stare at his handsome, vacant face did not turn her on. Maybe she should ring an old boyfriend and get him to take her out. At least he could pay for her meal. There was something curiously demeaning about always paying for your lover's meals.

She telephoned Justin Villias from Bonwits. 'Long time no see,' she said smiling.

He responded quickly. 'Have you got rid of that gigolo yet?'

Mary Rose made a face at the telephone. 'Not yet. Anyway, I'm engaged to be married.'

'Mary Rose, you surprise me. I've never seen you as the kind to accept a leash around your neck.'

'I'm not. Anyway, I want you to take me out to dinner tonight. I haven't seen you for ages and it would be fun.'

'I agree, but on one condition.'

'You know I don't go for conditions, Justin. Haven't you worked that one out yet? Anyway, what is it?'

'That you accept a nightcap at my place afterwards.'

'Mmmm . . . a girl might even be swayed.'

Justin remembered with a blinding force the feelings he'd had for Anna. Why, oh why, could he not love a

233

woman like Anna? Here he was propositioning Mary Rose and he knew they would both end up in bed together. He also knew that Mary Rose was not just ringing him up for old times' sake. She was probably angry with her English lover and out to teach him a lesson. Still, he'd seen the man around at parties and he didn't look the sort who'd resort to a gun. Justin grinned. Maybe a night out with Mary Rose would be a good idea after all.

'Catch you later, Justin. I'm off to find something sexy for you to discover tonight.' Mary Rose rang off.

Justin stood up from the phone and stretched. The 'after-dinner' would have to be at his place. He rang the bell for his English valet. 'Change the sheets, Edward,' he commanded.

Edward, seeing the look on his master's face, said, 'Might I suggest the silk sheets?'

'You've got it right on the nose. Edward, you're a marvel. I'll just telephone the restaurant. I will be back at about eleven. Just leave the lights on in the study, make a small fire, and see that the drinks cabinet is in order. We will have a nightcap before we retire.' Edward wondered who the lady would be and, as he took out the silk sheets, he mused on whether his employer was ever going to grow up. Probably not, he decided.

The shops glittered and twinkled. Mary Rose, now curiously elated for the first time in months, realized that part of the problem with being with Crispin was that she was bored. Perverse he might be, but he was also too neurotic to be much fun in bed. Justin was very good in bed. She would have to keep him on the side. Even having strenuously summoned her sense of loyalty, she couldn't really see any conflict between her coming marriage to Crispin and what she hoped could be a continuing affair with Justin. The two men were so wildly different. She had always believed that no single man could ever supply her with all her various needs: it was too much to expect of one person. The solution as she saw it was to create a whole from several parts. She would not ask from Crispin that which he obviously was unable to give, and the same applied to Justin. But together, the two men seemed a satisfying combination. Quite apart from Justin's undeniable sexual skills, he attracted her physically, causing involuntary excretions which sent electric tingles throughout her entire body. He had the physique of a Johnny Weissmüller, a V-shaped torso moulded from smooth muscles, and small, tight hips from which grew long, beautifully sculpted hairless legs. He was well aware of his beauty, and carried his body like a standard, tall and proud. The only similarity between him and Crispin was that they were both blond, although Justin's hair was close-cropped in the modern, crew-cut style of a college footballer. Crispin . . . ? Yes, Crispin. He was her fatal attraction, a curious, powerful magnet which drew her psychologically, helplessly. She was drawn to him not only by what she could see and comprehend, but by his hidden perplexity. She needed someone like Justin who exposed himself for all to see. This time she would not tell Crispin. It seemed a pity to lose an opportunity to make him jealous, but if Justin would play ball and they could run off together occasionally, perhaps she would be less depressed.

The rest of the day she shopped for Christmas presents and carefully chose herself some sensational underwear. The little vest was made of cream silk and the pants were matching with a soft edging of lace. She smiled as she ran her hands over the silk. I'll wear my crimson sheath with my new mink coat, she thought. The mink coat had been one of her father's 'guilty' presents the year before. She remembered the look of fury on her mother's face when she saw Mary Rose unwrapping the present. 'Really, darling,' her mother had drawled in her fake English accent, 'you treat your daughter like you treat your whores.'

That sort of remark had blistered Mary Rose in the old days, but no longer. Once she discovered the power she had over men, she slowly cut off her feelings for her hard, cold, remote mother. She found solace in the men she slept with. Some were bad experiences, but most were genuine and developed into friendships. Whatever else, Justin was good fun. She drove home and came bouncing into the sitting room.

'I'm out with a girlfriend this evening,' she said as casually as she could.

'Good.' Crispin was truculent. 'I could do with a quiet evening at home without you rushing about the place.'

Mary Rose eyed him thoughtfully. 'Crispin, I've been meaning to ask you . . .' She used her hurt, little girl voice. She walked over to him and put her packages on the floor. She sat surrounded by beautifully wrapped Christmas presents that bulged out of carrier bags displaying scenes of Father Christmas and little gnomes hard at work preparing for Christmas. 'When do you think we are going to get married?'

Crispin looked down at her wild black hair and her cheeks flushed with the wind. She looked lovely and, sod it, she was so rich. Crispin couldn't decide which attracted him more, women or money. He guessed it was probably the money. Women he could have any time, but money was harder to find. 'Soon,' he said, sounding bored. 'Very soon.'

'I'm glad.' Mary Rose got to her feet, picked up her packages, and kissed him on the forehead. As she walked to the bedroom, she wondered why she really did feel pleased. Marrying Crispin wasn't going to make him any less boring. She put the carrier bags down on the big double bed and she pulled out the silk underwear. Impatiently she removed her coat and threw it on the floor. She took off her clothes and slipped into the bodice and the panties. 'Lovely,' she mouthed at herself in the mirror, 'quite lovely.'

Sitting on her bed she took out her packages. She wrapped Crispin's three silk shirts, the Gucci watch, and a small velvet mouse. Crispin liked to tell her that her cunt resembled a mouse, and this was to be their joke together. She was grinning as she wrapped it. For Anna and Mario she wrapped a big book on Italian art, and earrings for Anna. Fosca got a silk blouse and six pretty coffee spoons. Fosca seemed to have taken Anna's marriage to Mario far better than Mary Rose had. In fact, Fosca was still beaming every time she ran into Mary Rose. She had given Mary Rose details of the wonderful honeymoon that Anna and her brother were sharing.

Sitting on the bed, Mary Rose enjoyed the wonderful feel of the silk against her skin. Slowly her hand crept between her legs and, with her fingers pushing the silk between her legs, she came quickly. She rolled over and fell asleep among the presents. Crispin came in a bit later and smiled. Mary Rose has been wanking again, he thought. He wished he could keep up with her sexual needs. Maybe marriage would settle her down a bit. He went back to the sitting room and telephoned his mother in Dorset.

'Mother, I'm thinking of setting a marriage date to Mary Rose. Could we marry in our chapel?'

'Of course, darling. How marvellous. We'd all be thrilled. She's such a dear girl.' Crispin grinned. His mother wouldn't have been nearly so thrilled had she seen Mary Rose lying on her bed with her hand between her legs and a beatific smile on her face. Crispin left the room. Now the decision was made he felt pleased. Although he was ambivalent about the marriage, he needed to secure his income. Once he was properly married to Mary Rose, he had thousands and thousands of dollars at his disposal. Crispin smiled. His mother and father would also be thrilled because they needed money badly to refurnish their family home. Crispin rather fancied being the prodigal son bringing home the fatted calf. He very much hoped Mary Rose would not become a fatted calf though: he couldn't get an erection with a woman unless she was rail-thin, and Mary Rose tended to put on weight.

Forty-Four

Anna, lying beside Mario on a long white padded deckchair on a pink coral beach, couldn't imagine that life could be so wonderful. She loved looking at Mario's beautiful, big, brown eyes, alight with love and sexual desire. Neither of them had bothered to leave the bedroom for the first two days of their honeymoon.

'I'm glad I still feel sexy, even now that we're married,' she confessed shyly to her husband. 'I was quite worried about it.'

'It will never change between us, darling. I promise you that.' Mario pulled her back into his arms and covered her with long, luxurious kisses. 'You're far the most beautiful thing in my life.'

'Even more beautiful than the girl you left in Asciano?'

'Far more beautiful.' Anna was pleased to see that there were no shadows in his eyes any more. They were clear and deep. She loved his eyes and his long, slender hands. When he buried his head on her breasts and sucked gently on her nipples, she felt a corresponding need to arch her back. The soles of her feet tingled. She was so glad that now they could legally make love whenever they wished. So far they had made love on the beaches, with the sun beating down on them, and in the night time, their bodies lit by the fireflies. In the sea they floated lazily around, touching each other's bodies gently. Of course, Anna realized that she knew Mario very well. But in the first week of their honeymoon she also realized that she didn't know him at all. Now they were together all the time. Nobody else was allowed into their hallowed space. Other guests at the hotel bobbed around in their consciousness, but they alone floated gently and serenely above everyone. The guests, almost awestruck by the beauty of the young couple, glowing with health and sexual happiness, did not invade them.

Now, lying with postcards strewn across her lap, she wrote to Steven. 'Am having a wonderful time.' How awfully trite, she thought, and tried again. 'Miss you and hope you will be wildly jealous of my tan.' In fact she did miss him and his intensity. She hoped that he was happy and well, but she didn't express that on the postcard. She resolved that she would get in touch with him when she got back to New York. She just hoped that his horrible mother had removed her claws from his back.

Next she wrote a postcard to Fosca. 'Dear sister-in-law,' she wrote, chuckling. 'Here I am with your brother having a wonderful time. We think of you often and look forward to seeing you soon.'

She stretched her arms above her head and thought about Mary Rose. Oddly enough she did not miss her friend nearly as much as she missed Fosca. Fosca was gentle and sweet, and respected Anna's boundaries. Mary Rose would sulk as soon as Anna got back because Anna was not prepared to discuss her sex life with Mario with her. She found it very awkward when Mary Rose had just given her a detailed description of her latest lover's penis. 'Like a droopy watering spout, darling,' was one of Mary Rose's more vivid descriptions. When

Anna had had to sit next to the man with 'the droopy watering spout' she found she couldn't enjoy her dinner. No, Mary Rose was lovely, but Anna needed some time away from her perverse world. Anna's world was now just as full of sex, but for her it was a time of loving sexual communion.

'We don't have to use that awful thing any more,' she told Mario. 'If I get pregnant that's fine. I want your baby more than anything in my whole life.'

Mario gave a sigh of contentment. 'I never thought I'd be thrilled to hear a woman say that,' he grinned. 'Usually when I hear that I know it's time to run to the hills. But with you it is different. Making babies is going to be a whole lot of fun.'

But in the second week Anna felt as if Mario had drifted far away. It was not that he was less attentive or that he was less loving. In bed he was as passionate as ever. But something was missing. She knew not to push him. She just held him patiently in her arms. She knew he would tell her what was bothering him in his own good time. And soon after he did.

'Anna, I've been thinking.'

'I know you have, darling. And whatever it is it's been bothering you, hasn't it?'

'I've been wondering if it is not possible for us to go back to Italy. The war seems to be always with us, so why not just get on with life. I've been trained by your father and maybe we could open a shoe factory in Asciano. I know Fosca is as homesick as I am. I do love America, but it is so different from Italy. Americans are nice, kind people, but they have this terrible streak of puritanism that is so boring. Your people are different because they are Irish, but the men and women I work with drive me insane. Sometimes I think if I hear "have a nice day" again, I'll hit somebody. I'm afraid I am getting as violent as they are. All they do is talk about baseball and sex. The sex they know about is nothing to do with love. All they know how to do is to screw.'

Anna smiled. Mario's pronunciation always got muddled up when he was really upset.

'I've been wondering when you would get round to wanting to go back,' she said. 'I know how much you miss your family and friends. I have been thinking hard myself. I'd miss my mother and father, but I do see that you need to go back. And I'd love to live in Italy. I've always read books about the place and we could see all the great works of art rather than just reading about them. Yes, darling, if you wish to go back I'm quite willing to go with you. Mom and Dad can always visit.'

They were sitting on the terrace of their Caribbean hotel at dinner. The huge palm trees swept their trailing arms on the sand. The new green coconuts nestled in the branches. Mario got up from the table, picked up a machete from under the tree, cut down one of the small coconuts and expertly chopped off the top. He came back to the table and put a drinking straw into the coconut. Anna could see he had been crying. She said nothing but smiled at him and accepted the nut.

'That's lovely, darling,' she said, raising the coconut high. 'Here's to our new future in Italy.' She laughed lightly.

'*Salute!*' Mario bent his head and kissed her fiercely. 'You'll never regret your decision,' he said. A large black cloud covered the moon. For a moment neither of them could see in the darkness.

Arina blinked. 'Wow!' she said. 'What was that? I'm all covered in goose bumps.'

'Just a cloud. It will be over soon. The wind is getting up.'

Anna had a restless night. She turned and tossed as the wind moaned and howled around the little cabana.

They would be boarding ship at the end of the week. This most perfect time in her life was coming to an end. She padded into the sitting room and sat down under the lamp. She picked up her book of poems by Judith Lamont, her favourite American poet. She read aloud:

> 'Nothing is forever I hear you say,
> I didn't think you meant
> That you would go away
> If nothing is forever
> How can I say
> Hello instead of goodbye?'

She stopped reading the poem because she found her throat filled with an aching lump. Now she had this great love in her life she was afraid that she had something to lose. Life had been so easy when she had been with her mother and father. Yes, the pain of Rupert had torn her apart, but then Rupert had never been a possibility. But Mario was hers now for ever, and as the poet reminded her, nothing is for ever. She read on:

> 'Through tears and pain and laughter
> I'll remember you forever
> I'll hear your voice in moonlight
> I'll see your face in starlight
> I'll cry for you in autumn
> I'll hold you in the winter
> Because if nothing is forever
> How can I say hello only goodbye?'

Anna was crying again, not just for Judy Lamont who had committed suicide, but for herself; she must leave her mother and her father and follow her husband to a foreign country without complaint. She was also confused by all the differing emotions. Why, she wondered, must life be so hurtful?

Forty-Five

🖋

Dinner with Justin Villias turned out to be a fascinating affair. Mary Rose had forgotten quite how much she missed Justin; he knew her so very well. He understood her, which was so comforting. They both shared the same devils. Supping together gave her time out from her life with Crispin to really think about what she was doing.

'Aren't you bored with your weedy boyfriend yet, Mary Rose?'

'No.' Mary Rose knew that Justin did not believe her. He could see the answer in her eyes. Not only was she bored with Crispin, but she was beginning to be quite afraid of him. Justin was not twisted like Crispin. Underneath that charming manner, Crispin was tortured. Whatever had gone on between him and his mother must have been very strange. Amelia Kearney looked like a shaggy labrador, but underneath all that flab and woolly cardigan, there lurked a very powerful woman. A woman who ruled her family by fear. Never a cross word escaped her lips. All the manipulating was done with a look in the eye, a shake of her head. She rode her children and her husband as if she were training horses. Mary Rose, looking at Justin, realized that she too knew how to manipulate. But for now she was tired of headgames between Crispin and herself and was just enjoying sitting in a lovely restaurant with a handsome man smiling at her.

Justin ordered his surprise dish for her. 'I discovered this last time I was here,' he said proudly.

'Did she enjoy it?' Mary Rose asked sweetly.

Justin grinned. 'Not as much as you will. She knows nothing about food.'

'Then she can't be any good in bed.'

'True. But she is a funny little thing and she makes me laugh. I'm off all this bed stuff for a while. It all gets too confusing. I came in the other evening and there were ten messages, all from women.' He heaved a hurt sigh. 'I just want to be loved for myself, Mary Rose.'

'Pull the other one, Justin. You'll never be faithful to any woman.'

As the waiter approached the table, Justin looked bleakly at Mary Rose. And neither will you, he thought.

Mary Rose realized they were going to end up in bed together and she felt a slight thrill. Justin was a good lover. 'Ummmmmm.' She sniffed the steaming sauce that covered her pasta entrée. 'What is it?'

'It's Italian sausage with prunes cooked in vodka, all wrapped in a parcel. The dish is called "Italian Parcels". It is covered in a white vermouth sauce with lemon juice and nutmeg.'

'Absolutely heavenly, Justin.'

Which is what Mary Rose said later that evening before she drifted off to sleep. 'Wake me up at one o'clock,' she whispered before her eyes completely closed.

Crispin was asleep and snoring loudly when she slipped into bed beside him. She had taken a bath and had very carefully oiled herself to remove the smell of Justin. Men's semen all smelled different inside her. She often felt, when she was seeing three or four men, that she was a walking silver cocktail-shaker. Now she lay clean and serene next to her husband-to-be. And she realized that she was bored with only one man in her life. Justin had given her back a sense of purpose. Yes, she would go ahead and marry Crispin. She wanted to be a wife. She didn't like the idea of being on her own and the thought of being called a spinster terrified her. She fell asleep planning her wedding.

At breakfast the next morning she watched Crispin eating his toast. The way he ate his toast always annoyed her. Why must he look like a mouse? He wrinkled his nose, put both hands on the morsel and pushed it into his mouth. His slightly protruding front teeth opened and shut very quickly. The butter caused his lips to shine unpleasantly. Was she really going to marry him, she wondered? She knew the answer was yes. She would marry him in spite of his mousy toast eating, his tendency to sinus trouble and foot rot. After all, she consoled herself, most men would be boorish if they didn't have foot rot or if their breath didn't smell. And if their breath didn't smell they had piles. Men, she thought, don't last as well as women. Pity she didn't fancy women instead. She had considered it, but at the end of the day men were so much fun to tease and so easily fooled. She beamed at Crispin.

'Darling, I think we ought to seriously consider getting married. What do you think?'

'I don't know, Mary Rose. I wonder if we'd make each other happy?'

'Of course we would. We get on, don't we?'

Crispin sat in his chair, finishing the last piece of toast. He watched Mary Rose watching him. He knew he would marry her, but largely for her money. He also knew that he had cracked Mary Rose's sexuality. While he wasn't particularly sexually attracted to her, he enjoyed the hold he had over her. When she climaxed she lost control. He felt omnipotent and it was that sense of power, combined with the money, that held him. Truly, in Mary Rose, sex, power and money all resided. She was generous with money, and so far had never tried to control his spending. Once married he would be free to do as he pleased for the rest of his life, and that meant he would not have even to think about getting a job.

'Well, Mary Rose, I'll go out and get you a bunch of roses and a box of chocolates and then I'll propose to you in the good old-fashioned way. I'll ask my mother if we can use the chapel. Would you like that?'

'Oh, darling, that would be marvellous. I'd love it. Do you think she'll say yes?'

'I don't see why not. After all, I'm the son and heir.' He was pleased that he had already cleared the matter with his mother. He kissed Mary Rose on the top of her head and went off to get the flowers and the chocolates. He decided he would take her out to dinner at the Caprice. It was suitably expensive and he didn't owe them any money, which is more than he could say for most other restaurants.

He whistled happily as he walked the crowded pavements. Christmas was only three weeks away. He thought he'd buy Mary Rose a really tarty little silk negligée. After dinner he'd get her to put it on and take her over his knee and spank her. He loved to do that to her, and she now enjoyed being spanked. That's the one thing he could thank Amelia for. Spanking him had always been an erotic experience for both of them. She used to make him lie across her knees with his pyjama bottoms trailing around his ankles and she spanked him briskly and in silence. When he got to the age of twelve it would give him erections, and she was well aware of that. Finally, when he was fifteen, he came all over her knees. He was purple with embarrassment, but he saw a strange look in her eyes. She never spanked him again. Nowadays, with Mary Rose's provocative bottom on his knees, something tarty and slinky around her delicate ankles, he relived those intimate moments with his mother and came strongly.

He hurried into the flower shop.

Forty-Six

On the journey home, Anna felt she had stored enough
beautiful memories in her mind to last her a lifetime.
Though they had the rest of their lives together, she
wondered if those molten days in the hot Caribbean sun
could ever be matched. The thing that enthralled her
was the light on the island. Around evening the hot blue
changed into a dazzling Van Gogh sunflower yellow,
and then almost imperceptibly the palest pink fell upon
the island, giving the whitewashed houses the blush of
early spring roses. Anna was enchanted. Now, lying on
a deckchair on the boat back, she hoped that when she
got to New York she would not find the world she had
left behind to be too grey. Somehow, the knowledge that
there were all these marvellous colours in the Caribbean
basin delighted her. That the skies could turn from the
brightest blue to a thundering black enchanted her. Now
would the New York skies disappoint her?

As the boat pulled into the dock she leaned over the
rail, looking for her father's face. Christmas had been
and gone. She had Christmas presents from the island
wrapped up for all her family. For Steven she bought a
hand-made plaited rush hat. He would look good in its
broad brim. She particularly liked the black coral neck-
lace that she had chosen for Mary Rose. It was a sophisticated, daring design and she knew it would suit her.
Aunt Kitty and Martha got rush place-mats with delicate
designs of birds and fishes. For her mother and father
she chose two locally made, brightly coloured T-shirts.

Mario put his arms around her and hugged her. 'Glad
to be back, darling?' he whispered in her ear.

'Yes I am, but I know I'm going to miss all those wonderful colours.'

'When we go to Italy you will see them all again, don't worry. We are only an hour and a half away from the sea so we can swim and snorkel. Italy is very beautiful, Anna.'

Anna watched his eyes shining with happy memories. He had been away for far too long and now she must prepare herself to make the journey with him. Mario was a man who needed to go home. America was not the place for either him or Fosca. They both shared the spirit of being totally European, and Americans generally simply could not live with that depth of history or tradition. She knew Mario was constantly irritated by American behaviour. Fortunately Joe Rapillano and Daniel reassured him that not all Americans were total morons, but they were few and far between.

After the kissing and the hugging, Anna was glad to get home. The whole family had gathered at her parents' house to greet the returning honeymoon couple. Even Crispin was gracious enough to acknowledge his presence with a bow. Anna was surprised to see a beaming Mary Rose.

'Crispin and I are going to get married in June. I've always wanted to be a blushing June bride!' Mary Rose was ecstatic.

'You'll have to practise the blushing, Mary Rose,' Anna teased her friend. She was really glad to be back and to see Mary Rose. Now, after all those weeks of carefree love-making with Mario, Mary Rose's lifestyle seemed silly and immature. Anna hoped that now Mary Rose had decided to make an honest woman of herself, she and Crispin would be very happy together. Today they both looked radiant. Their love for each other and their contentment in each other's company seemed to create an aura of light around them. Anna could see the light and there was nothing in it to frighten her.

She smiled happily at both of them as she made her way into the dining room to find Mario. He was at the end of the room talking to Fosca. They were talking a torrent of Italian. As Kitty and Martha pulled in their chairs and the big family table was now full, Anna felt she ought to get on with breaking the news about their departure, despite the fact it was what might be considered an inopportune moment. She felt sure that was what Mario had been talking about with his sister. She had never before seen such a look of happiness on Fosca's face.

'Dad and Mom,' she said hesitantly. 'Mario and I have decided that we should go back to Mario's house and settle down there and have a family. Mario wants to build a shoe business there and work directly with you, Dad. I know that there is still a chance that Italy may have to go to war. But we spoke to English people on holiday, and they all said that Prime Minister Chamberlain says there will be peace. So really we would like to go as soon as possible.' Anna could feel her face setting into a frozen mould of misery. She knew how much she would miss her family, but she was a married woman now and she must make her own way with her husband. She also remembered how Mary and Daniel had had to leave Ireland all those years ago, along with everybody else and everything they loved so much. They were in exile in America, even if they had built a wonderful world for themselves.

Daniel spoke first. 'I guess it's come as a bit of a shock to us, Anna, but I can't say we're all that surprised. But we'll worry about you. I don't believe that little Englishman when he says there will be no war. I must admit, though, the threat seems to have receded. And so, I do accept, and so does your mother, that you will want to go back with Mario to Italy.' He smiled a strained smile. 'I suppose I accepted that I would lose you when I stood beside you in the church on your wedding day.'

Mary was almost smiling. 'Of course you must go with Mario. And I know how much Fosca misses her parents. From all her descriptions I also know how beautiful Italy is, and the farm that belongs to Mario sounds wonderful. A married woman needs a home of her own.'

'We'll come and visit you,' Kitty said.

Joe beamed. 'That's a promise!'

Only Martha seemed uncertain. She saw phantoms and shapes moving about behind the young couple. She screwed up her eyes to ward off the unpleasant sensation, and then she decided to say nothing. Why, after all these years, should she let her superstitious Irish imagination spoil a perfectly happy evening?

Watching her aunt's kind, loving face, Anna felt a peculiar frisson of doubt touch her heart. Like her aunt she shook her head. She would keep her misgivings to herself. Mario looked so deliriously happy that she too was not going to spoil the day.

Mary Rose turned up a few days later, grinning with delight. 'I like the idea of being married,' she burbled in a sing-song voice.

Anna smiled. 'And I'm going to Italy.'

'You can't go until you've been my matron of honour. I was your chief bridesmaid, and now it's your turn.'

'Mary Rose, you know I wouldn't miss your wedding for all the tea in Jamaica. I'd love to see you happily married, and when we have kids I want you to be their godmother. You can teach them all your bad habits! I always thought godmothers should be utterly bad and dangerous.' She looked quizzically at Mary Rose. 'I am right in assuming that you are going to be happily married?'

'Your guess is as good as mine, Anna. My parents have made a hell of a mess of their marriage, so I can't do much worse.' She hoped Anna could not see the bruises under her arms where Crispin had held her down roughly and raped her. The memory of that event half horrified her and half excited her.

'I guess you can say that we have reached an understanding with each other. He bores me sometimes, but then I go off and find another lover. Then I go back and I'm OK for a while, until I get bored again. The trouble is,' Mary Rose heaved a sigh, 'I don't think any man could keep me satisfied for the rest of my life.'

'Oh yes, a man could, Mary Rose. But you won't ever choose a good man. You always choose such bastards.'

'I know.' Mary Rose made a face at Anna. 'Bad men, white truffles and champagne, my most favourite things in the world.'

Anna laughed, but she laughed uneasily. There were pale purple rings under Mary Rose's eyes, but her mouth was happy and she seemed to be content.

'I suppose I can't ask much more than that.'

Anna felt a sudden surge of need for Mario in her heart. When he was beside her, the world seemed to be such a safe place. Mary Rose made her feel unsafe. She made her feel that there were deep, dark shadows in relationships that she didn't want to know or understand. The dark pools that were Mary Rose had always frightened Anna. She knew that strange, deep-sea creatures lurked down there.

'Darling,' she whispered, as she put her arms around her friend. 'I love you very much and I'd be delighted to be your matron of honour. Have you decided yet on the exact date?'

'On 21 June, in his family's private chapel. Apparently Amelia, the old bat, is thrilled to have it there. She's banking on me restoring the family fortunes. So I will

251

have a great time doing up the dower house and hunting with the local hunt. Hunting men make great lovers. It's all that beating the horses and killing things.' Mary Rose gave an exaggerated shudder.

Anna laughed. 'Hang on, Mary Rose. You can't talk about lovers, you're not even married yet.'

'Oh yes I can, believe you me. I'll be faithful for a few months and then I'm off into the field.'

Anna saw her friend off with a sigh and then went off to join her husband. 'She hasn't changed much, Mario; in fact, not at all.'

Mario pulled Anna into his arms. '*Cara*, when will you stop trying to reform Mary Rose?'

'Never,' was the muffled reply.

Forty-Seven

Mary Rose gazed at the gathering of people before her. She had her veil drawn back and she was aware that her eyes were blazing in triumph. Directly in front of her she watched her father's face closely. On it she could see a hint of amusement at his promiscuous only daughter now dressed in white with a legal husband on her arm. She knew her father doubted that she intended to keep any of the vows she so prettily recited. But as she swept past him he couldn't help muttering: 'You've come a long way, baby!'

She knew he was impressed. Her mother was even more impressed that her little baby had been married in a chapel belonging to an old Irish family in the English countryside. Mary Rose knew her father had handed over a large amount of dollars to her trustees to see that she and her husband could satisfy their every whim. She also knew, as she put her arms around her father at the reception, that in his own perverse way he was very fond of her, and that possibly she was the only person in his life that he really loved in his own tortured way. Her mother was just a dark flame. Nothing shone in those eyes. She dabbed them very faintly during the ceremony, but she was probably replaying a bridge move in her head.

Crispin, she knew, had a hangover from the night before. In fact, it had been touch and go as to whether there would be a wedding at all. 'You fucking bitch,' he had screamed at about midnight.

Mary Rose, lying on the bed, had grinned at him. 'All right, lover boy, I can't help it if you can't come. I'm bored and I'm probably going to be bored with you for the rest of my life.' She had rolled over on the bed, exposing her naked behind.

Crispin, livid with emotion, had slapped her hard. He had watched the red mark of his hand rise on her white skin. She had rolled over on her back. Her bottom lip had quivered with the pain of the blow, but she had still been laughing.

'I see, a little S. and M. before I go up the aisle with all those little virginal bridesmaids. Now can you come?' Despairingly, Crispin had fallen on top of her and had tried to enter her. He had been torn between the need to prove himself a man to his bride-to-be, and the knowledge that he could never cope with Mary Rose's sexuality. Lying between their bodies were the US dollar notes now deposited in Mary Rose's bank. Crispin also knew that Mary Rose's father had given instructions that no money could ever be drawn out of Mary Rose's account except by her. The magnificent house in New York was to be in her name only and there would never be a joint account. Oh yes, Buchanan Senior knew Crispin's type well. Finally, feeling like the last horse in the race, Crispin had come and then fallen asleep, but not before he had heard Mary Rose say, 'There's a good boy.'

Now he felt wretched, even if he knew he looked wonderful in his new morning suit. He smiled at his brothers, who were wearing similar suits that had graced their bodies through many a wedding and hunt ball. He promised himself that Charlie and Shane would not have green moss growing across their shoulders; that soon they, and Theresa and Catherine, would wear whatever they wished. Crispin was tired of the Kearneys looking dowdy. He straightened his shoulders and went off to find Bunny and Podge.

Ralph found Anna in the conservatory. He sighed when he saw her radiant face. The glow in her eyes would never be for him. Yet, as much as he had always tried to convince himself that she was not for him, looking at her now after so long a time he felt he had been wrong. But it was too late, his chance had long passed. His emotions for Anna must be choked, both for his sake and for hers. His respect and admiration for her was such that he would never allow himself even to tarnish her joy, let alone place himself in desperation between her and Mario. Ralph quickly realized that he had only one real choice, and that was emotionally and geographically to distance himself from Anna. To do otherwise would be to abuse their natural affection for each other and risk cancelling it altogether. He must never indicate to her, or anyone else, that his feelings for her were anything other than just socially friendly and platonic. It was going to be hard, he knew.

'Ralph, it's really you. I've been looking for you everywhere.' The sun shone on Anna's wheat-coloured hair. Today her eyes were a deep aquamarine. Ralph had never seen a pair of eyes like Anna's. They were all the colours of the sea. He put his arms about her slight

254

frame. He smelled the familiar smell of her hair. He was sure she smelt of butterscotch. He felt her familiar snuggle as she burrowed into his body and his heart.

'Hey! That's my wife you're holding.' Mario came round the corner with Fosca.

'I know, I got there too late, Mario. Still, she looks very happy. And see she always looks that way, or I'll come on my horse and steal her away, even if I have to cross the ocean.'

'You will have to cross an ocean.' Anna's eyes were shining. 'We are going to live in Italy, near Siena. Mario and Fosca want to go home to their farm near a place called Asciano. I'm so excited, Ralph.'

'I'm happy for you, Anna. I love Italy. I was there just a few weeks ago.'

'You will promise to visit us, won't you?' Anna's face was imploring. 'I'll need visits from handsome Englishmen. I guess it will be quite lonely at first, until I learn to speak Italian. I am trying, but it's not easy for an Irish-American.'

'I'd love to come and see you, Anna.' Ralph felt he had to get away. There was a longing in his heart that he had not experienced before. Somehow Anna had remained such a pure light in his life. The women he now pursued seemed so shallow and artificial. Anna had not changed, and probably never would. She seemed to live calmly and sweetly in the moment that she experienced. She never seemed to wallow in the past: he remembered the trembling, hurt little girl that had survived the ship's purser. Nor did she fuss and fret about the future. Now she was going to Italy. No dark clouds hung over her. Ralph wished his life was like hers. He went in search of his current lover, Alice, and he made a face. Alice's life was one long drama between tense sexual encounters. He searched the room for her slender figure. Finally, he saw her leaning against a wall talking to Oliphant, who was nervously backing away. Alice was far too intense for any of his boyish crowd of friends. They all wanted women who could hunt and fuck, not fuck and fight. Ralph felt the familiar feelings of lust for Alice, but now he knew the signs within himself. Fucking his way out of a relationship was often the most exciting sex he could get, and he could see the leaving signs written all over Alice.

'Hello there,' he said, sliding an expert hand down her back. She arched like a cat on heat and he smelled her pungent odour.

'Come on,' he said, pulling her away from a nervous Oliphant. 'We have to get back to London in time for dinner with my folks. Sorry, Ollie, but we have to go.'

'OK by me. I've got to go and kiss the bride. Now she's an honest woman, we won't be able to do that too often.'

'Don't you believe that.' Ralph was quite surprised by his own vehemence. The last few years had made him more cynical than he cared to admit. Still, as he left the house and the glittering wedding party, he knew he had an open invitation to visit Anna whenever he wished. He tucked the invitation next to his heart.

Mary Rose threw her bouquet at the posse of bridesmaids. She was miffed to see it fall into Theresa's hands. She had meant it to go to Catherine, who at least pretended to like her. Theresa, once she had discovered that Mary Rose was going to marry her beloved brother, made no attempt to hide her dislike. Mary Rose went upstairs to change her clothes. Outside, the white Rolls waited for them. Another present from her father. The plates read MR 1. She grinned as she ran up the stairs. MR 1. Then 2, 3, and 4. Good old Dad, he was a brick.

Under a shower of rice from well-wishers, Mary Rose kissed her father and said stiffly to her mother, 'I'll telephone you from Paris.'

'If you have the time, dear. I hear the bridal suite at the George V is quite riveting.'

Mary Rose was repelled by her mother's knowing smile. 'Don't worry, Mom,' she said coldly. 'We've been screwing all night so we're both tired.' She stormed off feeling tears in her eyes. Why couldn't her mother say something soft and gentle? But then she never had, so why did she expect her to now? Mary Rose leaned out of the car window and waved her black-gloved hand. She had a moment's flash and wondered why she had chosen all black for her going-away outfit. More fit for a funeral than a wedding, she told herself as she settled down beside Crispin. He looked marvellous surrounded by the buttercup-yellow leather seats. She touched the side of his face with her gloved finger.

'Darling,' she said, 'd'you think we'll live happily ever after?'

'I do hope so, Mary Rose, I really do hope so.' Crispin accelerated the car down the road and the engine roared its approval.

Forty-Eight

Anna and Mario made their plans for leaving. Fosca flitted about, thrilled to be leaving America but sad to say goodbye to Anna's parents. So far, she had found no man who interested her. She was fastidious and, try as the young American college men might, she found them too lumpen and crude. Steven was the only American man she found attractive. When Anna invited him for dinner, or for the weekend, he spent time with Fosca.

'I'm going to miss you, Fosca,' he said on one of the final times that he saw her.

'I will miss you too, Steven, but you have your girlfriend that you are going to marry, no?'

Steven nodded his head. 'Actually, Fosca, I might as well marry her. It will make my mother happy since they are virtually family anyway. Anything else is far too difficult. My mother would have a fit if I married outside the faith. I had enough problems befriending Anna. In the end, my mother made such a fuss we sort of lost touch with each other. I'm glad she contacted me. You know she sent me a postcard on her honeymoon.' He paused and there was a painful crease on his brow.

'I used to think ages ago that maybe I could marry Anna but . . .' He shook his head. 'My mother would have made her life a misery. It is better this way.' He raised his head shyly. 'But Fosca, you have been a special friend and I don't want to lose touch with you. Can I write to you?'

Fosca nodded. There was a lump in her throat. Tears squeezed at the corners of her eyes. 'Oh, Steven, why must saying goodbye be so sad? Why do we have to make these friendships and then leave them behind? You'll always be with me in my mind. I will always remember your beautiful brown eyes and your long, gentle fingers.'

She reached out and lifted his right hand to her lips. Gently, she kissed his hand goodbye. He put his hand tentatively on her right shoulder and hesitantly pulled her to him. For a moment their lips touched. Butterflies and nightingales with jewelled wings hovered between the hollow spaces left between their shy bodies. Steven very much wanted to pull her into a full embrace, but he was unable to take that step. He had a fiancée now and his love belonged to her. Yet he knew after today that, above all else, he was losing Fosca. She, amazed and a little frightened, held her mouth to his a second longer than necessary. She felt and saw a slight flush in

Steven's face. A melting of his body towards hers. She, too, remembered that he was not free to love and pulled gently away.

'We can't, Steven, we can't.' Her voice was weeping with regret. 'It's too late for us.'

'It's always too late for me.' He gazed soberly at her. 'I always leave those things that I ought to say unsaid. I lost Anna because of this, and now I have lost you.'

'You loved Anna?'

Steven nodded. 'I did very much. Anna had such blonde hair and blue eyes as a little girl. She looked like those Christian angels my mother was always threatening would take me away for ever. I always used to look at Anna and think what a good idea it would be to be taken away by her.' While laughing at the memory, his whole face lit up. How very handsome he is, Fosca thought as she smiled at his recollections. 'Yeah, Anna was my first girlfriend. We sort of slipped into girlfriend-boyfriend, and then we drifted apart. I to my Hebrew school, and Torah school in the summer, and she off to live with Mary Rose.'

There was a moment's silence, broken by Anna's footsteps. 'Ah, Steven, I have come to say goodbye.' She paused and looked at her two friends. 'I know it is sad,' she said quietly. 'Sometimes we see things too late and the opportunity is lost.' She could see torn tentacles wrapped around Fosca and Steven's hearts. They were tiny baby octopus tentacles, so the wounds would heal very quickly, although not the memories. Steven's emotional triptych would for ever hold Anna in the first gold frame, his fiancée Sophie in the second, and then Fosca. In front of Anna's image, try as he might, he would never be able to extinguish her flame.

* * *

Fosca was very quiet as she packed her suitcases. 'I arrived with you, Mario, and one suitcase. And look what we have now.'

'I know, Daniel and Mary have been marvellous to us,' Mario said. 'And Mary's given me lots of coffee, sugar and flour for our parents. It's odd to think of Asciano short of all those things, but then I remember it was getting difficult when we left. I often wonder if I'm doing the right thing for Anna. I know that not much is happening now, but war could break out and then life could get very dangerous again.'

'Anna wouldn't want to be left behind, Mario. And anyway, the whole of life is dangerous. She could get run over by a bus on Fifth Avenue. Try telling Anna she can't come!' Fosca snorted with laughter.

'Who's talking about me?' Anna bounced into the room. 'Look at this, darling. I bought a lovely evening dress for when we get to your house.'

'It's not a house, darling, it's a *fattoria* – a big farm with lots of houses. There's the main house where we'll be, and other smaller houses scattered around the property where the farm-workers used to live. Most have gone now, though, run out by the Fascists because of their political views.'

He grinned at Anna, who was holding the dark blue silk dress against her waist and twirling around the room. 'I promise, darling, even if you have to traverse the duck pond, I'll take you into Siena and you can show off your fine dress.'

'Thank you, my darling.' Anna hurled herself into his arms. 'I am so looking forward to getting there. *Parleremo italiano, ma molto lento,*' she said and then grinned, proud of herself.

As Mario pulled down another suitcase a bleak shadow covered his eyes. Dear God, he prayed silently, don't let anything happen to my beloved wife. He knew how much that prayer was also being prayed by both Daniel and Mary. The burden on his shoulders included the weight of the knowledge that, to her family as well as to him, Anna was a priceless treasure.

The final goodbyes were as painful and sorrowful as any Mario had ever experienced. He felt the guilt of separating Anna from her parents, from Kitty and Martha who were both openly crying, and from Mary Rose, whose down-turned mouth made her seem like a small lost child. Since her honeymoon, Mary Rose seemed to have lost much of her belligerence. Crispin's eyes carried an odd look of certainty. Mario wondered if Crispin now knew that he had a hold on Mary Rose that no one could shake. Still, that was their affair: he had things of his own to do.

Putting his arm around Anna he pulled her away from Mary. 'We must go, darling. The boat is waiting and we have a long drive.'

'Oh, Mom and Dad, promise you will come just as soon as we've settled in?'

'Sure we will, honey. We'll be with you in no time at all.'

Daniel's heart was breaking. He felt the way he felt the day he saw his beloved Ireland sliding out of sight, hoping with all his heart that, before too long, he would set foot on her soil again, but with a dreadful foreboding that this might never happen. Still, he comforted himself, Italy is not yet at war and maybe never will be. He and Mary could go for a great vacation. He pulled Mary to him. 'We'll go and visit Anna and Mario and then I'll take you to Venice and we'll stay in a big palazzo for a whole week.'

Through her tears, Mary smiled up at Daniel. 'Do I get time to go on a gondola?'

'Sure, honey, you do anything you want.' Daniel was so aware that, had he not had Mary in his life, losing Anna would be unbearable. He gave Anna a last, desperate hug and then walked away, his arm around Mary, without looking back. Kitty and Martha headed with their husbands towards their cars. They were going to the dock. Daniel knew he could not afford to make a spectacle of himself at the dock, and he knew Anna understood. For now he was off to his library to nurse a large glass of whisky and drink until he hit oblivion.

Forty-Nine

On the trip to Italy, Mario and Fosca talked in Italian until Anna thought she would tear her hair out. Many other Italians were on the boat, all lulled into a sense of security that the war was not going to happen. The women wore elegant padded American jackets over pencil-thin skirts.

Regina d'Albro, who befriended Anna when they first climbed on board, had obviously modelled herself on Joan Crawford. She had square shoulders, a slim waist, long black hair, and even longer legs. Anna thought she was gorgeous.

'I am taking my new lover back to Palermo to see my family. My mother says he is no good, but I say, Mamma, I do not like good men. I like bad men like my Tony.'

Anna laughed. 'You sound like my best friend Mary Rose. She says just the same thing and, actually, she got married a few weeks ago.'

'To a bad man?' Regina lifted a heavy black silk eyebrow.

'I hope not. Well, actually, now you ask, I suppose he is not what your mother would think is a fine match. But then if he keeps Mary Rose busy with his badness she'll be happy enough. I hope.' She muttered the last words under her breath.

During the day, Regina and Anna sauntered around the deck. In Anna's suite, Mario and Fosca made endless plans for their future in Asciano. In Regina's cabin, Tony slept off his hangovers and the night's sexual athletics.

'Tony is good for the fuck,' Regina explained with refreshing honesty. 'No good for money, no good for anything but for bed.' She grinned. 'So what I am good for is the money and for the life, so I keep him.'

'Don't you love Tony, Regina?'

'Phew, I love nobody, only my father. He is very special man. He is a big cheese in Palermo. Everybody's frightened of my father. Especially Tony.' She chuckled. 'My father will not be pleased to see Tony. He does not like a man who is kept.'

'Regina, Tony is not a kept man, he's a trucker. They work hard for their living.'

'He cannot be a trucker and live with me. He is always on the road. I went with him once, but the bed is too small for the fucking. Anyway, he had his buddy there and they drink beer together and talk all the time. Terrible. We stop at this truck hotel. I get out. I am his girl, no? Everywhere we go there are women that Tony has fucked. All the time he fucks these women so I decide no more trucks. We go to Italy, he meets the family. If they say yes we get married *e basta*. He fucks me, I work, and we will be happy.'

'You just said yourself that he is boring, Regina. How do you think you can be married to a man who bores you?'

'Most men are boring. Italian women know that, so they find a man who is nice to look at. A man who does not get fat but keeps fine. They dress them properly and then they get on with their lives. Italian women's lives are much better than American women's. American women guard their men. They work, they cook, they clean the house, but they do not have girlfriends like Italian women. When I get back to Palermo we have a flat. If Tony bores me I go off to stay with my girlfriends. No problems. No argument. I stay away until Tony is sorry, then I come back if I feel like it. This way Italian women do not have a problem with their men. Only their waistline. But me, I never get fat, too much fucking. And it's good for the face. Look, no wrinkles.'

In spite of herself, Anna had to laugh. Regina had a rare ability to frame what might normally be considered base crudity in a way that rendered it entertainingly inoffensive. Anna, still shaking with laughter, agreed. 'You're right. Fucking is good for the face. And for the soul.'

In the bright moonlight, Regina laughed. It was such a wild and free laugh that it gladdened Anna. Somehow Regina didn't seem to suffer as much as Mary Rose. This Italian beauty reminded Anna of a fine diamond. Whatever was going to happen in Regina's life, she would survive it. Anna wished she could say the same about Mary Rose.

'Come on, Anna, you go and wake Mario and I'll take Tony to bed – if he is not too drunk. Silly boy, I'll have to make him wake up if he is.'

Anna returned to the cabin and slinked theatrically to her husband's dozing side. 'Regina said I had to wake you up and make love to you.' She breathed gently into Mario's ears. She curled behind him and gently began to play with him. She felt his erection growing, and then, almost in his sleep, she slithered over him and guided him into her body. She loved watching herself watching him making love to her. Regina's right, she thought to herself as the rhythm took hold of her, it is good for the wrinkles. And I'm right, it is good for the soul.

'You know, Mario,' Anna said later. 'Maybe I got

it wrong and I should keep you for the fuck like Regina says.'

'Don't be so silly, Anna. You get me for the fuck. But I make money and take care of you. What more do you want?'

Anna sighed contentedly. 'You're right, darling. After listening to Mary Rose and Regina I get my head messed up.'

'Anna, you are listening to two frightened women whistling in the dark. A good marriage, I have always believed, is like heaven on earth. We both have parents who love each other very much. I have never wanted anything for myself, and now I have you my happiness is complete.' He pulled her down on to their bed and gently kissed her pink nipples until they stood erect like two raspberries.

Later on, Anna awoke and couldn't sleep. She wandered out on to the deck. The moon was merciless that night. She shone so brightly that the ship seemed to be illuminated by an unseen hand that painted the rigging and the deck in silver. A harsh metallic glare caused her eyes to strain. Over in the corner of the railings she could see two figures who seemed to be making love. But as she drew closer, averting her face so as not to embarrass them, she realized that the woman was sobbing wildly and struggling to get away. As she drew near she saw the man swing back his hand and hit the woman hard in the face. The woman's neck jerked sharply. Anna heard a gasp and then a high-pitched scream that was quickly lost in the wind. The sound of the scream reminded Anna of the thin cry of a rabbit caught in a trap. She froze and then watched in icy horror as the man raised his hand to hit the woman a second time. She leapt forward and then, as her hand reached out to grasp the man's wrist, she realized that the man was Tony and the woman who now stared at her with terrified eyes was Regina.

'Go away, Anna,' Regina pleaded with her. 'Go away, please.'

'I can't let him hit you, Regina.' Anna turned to Tony. 'Who do you think you are, hitting a woman – you disgusting coward!' She found herself shaking with rage.

Tony's shoulders sagged. Both hands hung by his side. He shook his head. 'I'm sorry, Regina, but I can't cope with you flirting with every man we meet. You know I can't bear it, but you do it always.' He turned to Anna, his big blue eyes glazed with beer. 'I'm just a trucker's mate and I don't know why I'm going to Italy. I don't like drinking wine. It gives me a headache. But she says real men don't drink beer. I miss my truck and my buddy. Now I'm going off to the bar to get me a real drink. Good ol' American beer. I'm not a coward, Anna, I'm just confused. She told me she loved me. She told me it was OK to be a truck driver. I dunno. I just dunno.'

Tony rolled off into the night and Anna took Regina's chin and anxiously inspected her face. 'You look all right, Regina, but he sure walloped you.'

'He's had too much to drink, poor Tony. He is so good in bed, but boring. He talks about trucks and roads he drives with his buddy, and baseball and football. I am not interested in baseball or football. I talk to the man at dinner. He is nice, not so good-looking as Tony, but intelligent. Sometimes I think I need a man for the night time and the fucking, and then another for the talking and intelligence. Why I cannot find one man for both things?'

Anna bade Regina good-night. She knew she was lucky.

Fifty

🐦

Mary Rose was amazed at how little she missed her life in New York. The Manhattan apartment given to her by her father stood empty as she and Crispin moved into the dower house that stood behind huge gates at the beginning of Amelia's drive.

'Really, we ought to put your mother in the dower house and we should live in the manor house, Crispin. After all, dower houses were built for widows or mothers-in-law to get them out of the way when the son and heir brought back his bride. That's me, isn't it?'

'Oh yes, I can just see me giving my mother her marching orders. Death would be preferable. You don't know Mum, darling. She might look like the gardener's wife, but inside she's tougher than a general. We're all terrified of her.'

'Well I'm not. Anyway, I don't really want that rotting pile. I guess I can fix this up beautifully. I'm off to London to go shopping.'

'Can I come?' Crispin looked hopefully at his young, beautiful, rich wife.

'Nah, Crispin, you just get bored and irritable. I need to shop for curtains and pelmets. I need to look up Dad's friend who runs an interior decorating agency. He's really good and has done lots of English homes. There's nobody more dedicated to an English way of life than an ex-pat American. I should know.'

'Does that mean we're going to have bags of chintz and cabbage roses stalking about the house? Come on, Mary Rose, you always said you were into art nouveau before we married.'

Mary Rose looked coolly at her new husband. 'That was before we were married, dear. Now we are married, things are going to change. Remember . . . in sickness, in health, and all that stuff about until death us do part . . . ? Well, until death us do part I'm doing what I want to do. It's my money and I'll spend it how I wish to spend it, Crispin. Your days of telling me what to do are over.' She swung her body out of the room, leaving Crispin wondering why he felt such a surge of murderous rage.

Once in London, Mary Rose went straight to the Savoy. Even if she gave Crispin the impression that she was perfectly capable of running her own life in a strange country, she was, in fact, very frightened.

'Shit,' she whispered, as she gave the keys of her car to the doorman, 'what the hell am I scared of?'

'Does madam intend to pay by cheque?' The assistant manager had not recognized her from all those years ago. He smiled in open admiration at the well-dressed woman who stood before him. Well-dressed and obviously well-heeled women were not usually on their own in the Savoy.

'Coutts Bank.' Mary Rose stood looking at the assistant manager through her very dark glasses. He was tall and blond with broad shoulders. A definite improvement on Crispin, who was much thinner. Mary Rose wondered playfully if it was the done thing to seduce assistant managers of the Savoy, and then decided it probably wasn't worth it anyway. If the Savoy was to be her headquarters, she would have to keep her carpet clean. Pity, she thought. The bell boy came up and removed her two suitcases.

'I'll be here for several days.' Mary Rose tried to introduce a plummy sound into her voice. She realized rather miserably that she failed utterly to sound the least bit English.

'This way, madam.' The assistant manager decided to take Mary Rose up to her suite himself. She was in one of the biggest.

Mary Rose breathed a sigh of relief as she got in the door. There was a bottle of champagne and a bunch of roses waiting on a centre table. 'That's really great,' she said, dancing to the big picture windows overlooking the Thames. The assistant manager smiled. She looked so much prettier when she dropped her pretentious manner. Such a pity she was a guest of the hotel. He would so much have liked to get to know her better. But rules are rules, he told himself forlornly as he left her standing by the windows.

Once he had gone, Mary Rose wandered into the bedroom and bounced upon the big, wide bed. The cupboards were lined with mirrors and the carpet on the floor was luxurious. She finished bouncing on the bed and wandered into the bathroom. Gleaming marble, a huge bath, and lots of lovely oils and lotions. She switched on the bath water and watched the steam mist the mirrors. She heard a knock on the door and realized that it was the bell boy. She tipped him and opened both her suitcases. 'I'll hang my clothes myself,' she told the boy, anxious to be alone. She stripped off and lit a cigarette. She gazed at her naked body. Why did being in a luxurious hotel fill her with rampant lust? The idea of anonymous sex, she supposed as she walked back to the bathroom. She turned off the gushing taps and poured in the oil. She lay back and fantasized about the assistant manager. She imagined him lying in the bath with her. Herself on top of him with the water dripping from her long hair. She rubbed a little soap on to her fingers and slid her hand between her legs. She heard the water swish as her fingers voluptuously caressed her clitoris. When she came she found herself crying. Surprised, she sat up, the water falling off her oiled shoulders. She gazed across the room at the mirror over the basin. She saw the tears falling down her face and thought how beautiful she looked. What a bloody waste of a wonderful room, she thought. Maybe Dad's interior decorator will be a bunch of fun. She leapt out of the bath and went to the telephone. Standing naked by the phone she ran her hands up and down her long, lean thighs.

'Hi, this is Travis speaking.'

At the sound of an American voice, Mary Rose felt very close to tears again. 'Hi,' Mary Rose said. 'I'm in London to organize doing up my house, and my father, Lord Roswell, suggested I gave you a ring. I thought I'd like to meet with you to see if you would be interested in helping me.'

'Of course I'd be interested. Where are you calling from?'

'The Savoy.' She liked the sound of his voice.

'OK, let's get together. Your place or mine?'

Mary Rose giggled. 'Now I'm here, why don't you come round for dinner tonight if you're free?'

'I'm always free for dinner at the Savoy.'

'OK, shall I book for eight o'clock?' That would give her time to have her hair done at the hairdresser's downstairs.

'Sure thing. I'll be in the foyer at eight o'clock sharp.'

'By the way, my name is Mary Rose Buchanan.'

'Great name, Mary Rose. I'll see you then.'

Mary Rose put down the telephone and grinned. Things were definitely looking up.

At eight o'clock there was a discreet ring of her telephone.

'A Mr Travis Mainwaring asking for you, madam.' The voice sounded a little wary. I do hope he hasn't arrived in jeans and no tie, she thought. Mary Rose had already noticed the loud Americans in the foyer when she arrived.

'Do send him up,' she said, offering a little prayer that she might not be embarrassed by her visitor. After a few minutes nervously puffing her cigarette, she heard a loud knock on the door. She opened it and stared in amazement. In front of her stood the most delicious man she had ever seen. He was brandishing a cane with a big polished brass knob on the end, which explained the loud knock on the door. He smiled, and then he offered her a very large hand.

'Travis Mainwaring. You must be the lovely Mary Rose Buchanan.'

Mary Rose found herself blushing. For a start she had not imagined that she would ever meet an American who looked so much like her idea of a Left Bank French bohemian. Travis was wearing a long blue velvet coat which matched his eyes. His long hair was tucked behind his ears. Instead of a tie he wore a floppy red velvet bow. He was wearing a dinner jacket and his cummerbund was red to match his bow tie. Mary Rose inspected his shoes. Her mother had always told her that you knew a man by the kind of shoes he wore. Well, enough said: his were soft black leather.

'Am I going to be allowed in?' There was a light of amusement in his eyes.

I could curtain my bedroom windows with the colour of his eyes, Mary Rose thought. She had always read florid descriptions of eyes that looked like velvet pansies and had dismissed the comparison as ridiculous. But now she realized that it was no exaggeration and that Travis's eyes really did look like those big tiger pansies she saw in the Botanical Gardens in New York. His irises were yellow, the outer rim violet with a hint of black. The face itself was soft and gentle. Mary Rose stood back and motioned for Travis to enter the suite.

'I'm sorry if I seem rude,' she said a little hesitantly, 'but I wasn't expecting you to look like that. I mean . . .' She was now sounding very silly and she felt it. 'Most Americans in London, at least the ones I've seen . . .'

'. . . Are loud, and brash and vulgar. Those are only the tourists and you get them in any country. Those of us that come here and love the place tend to disappear into the Tudor woodwork and get on with our lives. Darling,' he said with an endearing smile, 'I just have to have a drink. The Savoy is the one place that will have my favourite American whisky. There's not much of it around at the moment due to all the scare about the war in Europe.'

They entered the lounge room of Mary Rose's suite.

'Do you think there will be war in Europe? My best friend, Anna, is going to Italy with her new husband, Mario. I am very worried about them, but her father says not much is going to happen. People in America seem to feel it is all a little storm in a teacup. I hope so, I really do hope so.'

Travis shrugged. 'I don't know much about politics, but I'd be careful if I were Anna. When things happen in Europe they happen real fast.'

Anna rang the bell and waited for the bar boy to come in. 'You order your whisky . . . better still, ask that he leaves a bottle in the suite. Then as we come and go you can help yourself.'

'Thanks.' Travis took off his cloak and stood looking about the room. 'Where can I dump this? I'll put it on the hanger in the hall if you don't mind.' He left the room and headed into the hall. She couldn't think why he made her so nervous. Maybe it was because she had never met anyone quite like him. She wished Anna were here. Anna could read people like a book. She had always trusted Anna's Celtic assessments of the men she met. Travis definitely was a man that interested her, but she could not decide in which way. Yes, she was physically attracted to him, but she could detect no fire in him that responded to her. It was all very odd, but she was prepared to bide her time.

'Hell of a nice room you have here, Mary Rose. Where is your husband?' She twisted her wedding ring around her finger and looked at Travis through her lashes.

'Crispin is a pain in the ass when it comes to remodelling a house, so I left him with all his male English friends to get drunk and talk about the good old days when they were all at school together. That's all English men seem to do, talk about the "good old days". Though what's good about those barbaric schools they attend I shall never understand.' She laughed and called out for the bar boy to enter. After he left, she and Travis had a rather desultory conversation about her new house. Mary Rose felt it was desultory because neither of them had the measure of the other yet. They were forging a relationship that would last over many months and which would involve great amounts of time spent together. Mary Rose's interior decorators in New York were all gay and she was happy and comfortable in their company. She did not feel Travis was gay, but there were question marks in the air as if they were both tiptoeing around a large black hole. Still, she reasoned, pouring herself a large gin and tonic, I'll be a couple of drinks up on him if he keeps sipping his whisky so shyly.

Four gin and tonics later, to Travis's two glasses of whisky, Mary Rose was ready to go down to dinner. Travis opened the door of the suite and Mary Rose noticed the height and breadth of him as he held the door open. He strode beside her as if he owned the hotel, and guests walking past turned to stare at him. He seemed not to notice. They left the fourth floor in a small, highly decorated lift.

'I do love this lift, Mary Rose. It must be one of the prettiest in London.'

'Do you come to the Savoy often?' she asked.

'Sure, most Americans come here because they make it so very comfortable. It has all the charm of the old colonial English style, but with all the luxury that we spoiled Americans equate with good living. I'm here all the time.'

That became very obvious as they swept into the dining room and a raft of waiters left their tables and came over to shake Travis's hand. Mary Rose was speechless. She felt as if she were with a film star. Some of the reflected glory fell upon her.

'And who is this lovely young woman we are having the pleasure of serving here tonight?' The Italian *maître d'* took her hand and lightly brushed her fingers with his lips.

'A new client of mine, Mary Rose Buchanan. Her father is an old friend of mine. We're going to do up her house together.' Mary Rose noticed that quite a few people at the other tables must have known Travis. They were leaning forward, whispering to each other. A light hum of gossip, dipped in honeyed words and vinegar malice, flew about the beautiful room. Mary Rose sat on her chair and lit a cigarette. Whatever the people were saying was something she would find out later. She was good at deciphering atmospheres and, whatever Travis was, or had been, people in this restaurant knew it.

She could wait. The view was fabulous and the room was bathed in the gentle lights of candles on all the tables. Around her, trolleys of gigantic sides of roast beef trundled up to tables already groaning with food. She received the menu and then asked Travis to help her choose. She did not want him to know that her French was rudimentary.

'I'd have the oysters if you like oysters. They're in season and, unlike everybody else, I like the little Portuguese oysters because they are small, sweet, and the shells are very deep so they hold a lot of liquid. Their lobster thermidor is excellent and also their guinea-fowl. Much tastier than chicken.'

'OK, I'd like to try both those dishes.'

'I'll order some good white wine, and then a red. How about a Pouilly-Fuissé for the oysters, and then maybe an Italian Brunello?'

Mary Rose smiled. 'An Italian Brunello would be fine: then we could drink a toast to Anna and Mario.' She began to tell Travis all about Mario's mother and father. She was glad that he seemed to be really interested. They ate their way through what seemed to be a huge meal. Then she relaxed with a big balloon of brandy and a small cup of very strong coffee.

Going up in the lift, Mary Rose felt very peculiar. She was not drunk, but rather light-headed. Her body seemed to float along the corridor beside Travis. He walked slowly. They had managed to drink two full bottles of wine and several brandies.

Once inside the suite she found that the lights had been left on by the fireplace and the room was now clean and the table free of the used glasses.

'Do you want a nightcap?' she inquired, feeling so wide-awake after the coffee that she hoped Travis would say yes.

'Sure I will. Tomorrow we'll talk business, but tonight, after such a marvellous meal, let's just talk about ourselves.'

He settled himself down on the sofa and stretched out his large frame. Mary Rose poured out a whisky for him and a gin and tonic for herself. She picked up a silver boat filled with truffled chocolates.

'Hmmmmm . . .' Travis took the floury round ball in

his long, delicate fingers. He nibbled at the chocolate and left a large tooth mark when he paused to take a sip of his drink. Mary Rose sat at his feet on the carpet. She felt she needed the ground beneath her. Never before had she felt so out of control in a situation with a man. She was used to calling the shots, to being in charge of the moment. But this time she had no idea of what the shots were, or where the moment had gone. So she resolved just to let him talk.

Travis told her all about his childhood on an island in Alaska. How he had loved the icebergs and the lights and the life when he was a small boy. Then how his life had changed as he had grown older, and how much he had not wanted to be a home-steader like his Dad, or watch his mother slave to keep food in his mouth and a fire alight in their little log cabin.

'Am I boring you?' he asked anxiously at one point.

'No.' Mary Rose shook her head. 'You're not boring me at all. I just think it is so wonderful that you had such a happy childhood. Were there any other brothers and sisters?'

'I had a sister, but she drowned.' Mary Rose heard a 'no trespassing' tone in his voice and decided not to push the question.

'I'm sorry,' she said, and let the matter drop.

Travis was now drinking quite quickly and Mary Rose became aware that she had stepped on a land-mine. She went back to the sideboard to pour herself another drink and realized that she was now quite drunk. She swayed so much on the way back that she spilled some of the drink on to the floor.

'Ooops,' Travis giggled.

She attempted to sink gracefully to the floor, but succeeded in ending up half on and half off the end of the sofa beside Travis's feet. He leaned forward and pulled her on to the sofa.

'You were going to fall on to the floor, and we can't have that, can we?'

'No, we can't,' Mary Rose whispered, her face now close to his. She felt his muscles throbbing in his arms. His body seemed to want her urgently, but his face remained untouched. Usually, when a man was blind with passion for her, she could see it in his eyes and in the veins in his forehead.

'What's the matter, Travis?' she said gently. 'Don't you want me?'

'I do, oh I do. And I did from the very moment I set eyes on you. But I'm afraid I can't.'

'Can't what? Are you married, or are you with a woman?'

'No, it's not that, Mary Rose. You see, I'm impotent.'

Mary Rose stared into his beautiful face. 'You can't be impotent, Travis. It's just not possible.'

'It is all too possible, Mary Rose,' he said quietly. 'I've tried everything and nothing works. The doctors tell me it's psychological and the psychologists tell me it's medical. I suppose Freud would say I hated my mother, but I didn't hate either of my parents. In fact, I loved them very much.'

'Can you have any kind of sex at all?' Mary Rose was now very curious.

'Not the kind of sex you would understand,' Travis mumbled.

Mary Rose reached down and pulled the zip of his trousers gently. Travis put a hand to attempt to stop her. 'Don't be such an appalling prude, Travis. Oral sex is great fun.' She slipped to a kneeling position on the floor, pulled his legs either side of her and began to run her tongue gently over his exposed pubic hair. She inhaled and was pleased with the smell of him. She covered him with feathery kisses. Travis buried his hands in her long black hair. Slowly she gained mastery of him and began to nibble and tickle.

'Are you really enjoying this?' Travis asked, looking down at her enraptured face.

'I love anything to do with sex, Travis. It's all such fun. Are you enjoying it too?'

'Immensely.' He groaned with pleasure. 'How did you get so good at this?'

'Lots and lots of practice.' Mary Rose smiled. She enjoyed watching him come. Here was a big, strong, sophisticated man like putty in her hands.

Mary Rose was well pleased with the night's events. When she put herself to bed later that night, she grinned. Crispin would never guess. He thought all interior decorators were fruits, as he called her friends. So, now she had a nice rehabilitation job on her hands with Travis, and under her own roof too. She gave a little sigh of perverse pleasure and fell asleep.

Fifty-One

There was nobody to meet them when the boat docked in Genoa. Mario was puzzled at first, but then they realized, looking at the muddle of uniforms on the dock, that movement in Italy was restricted by the possibility of war. The road out of the dock was clogged with large transport lorries.

'Everybody seems to be in uniforms,' Anna remarked as she leaned out of the taxi.

'Italians love uniforms anyway, but the chance of war gives everyone an excuse.' Mario winced visibly as a group of young men passed by wearing brown shirts.

One of them peered into the car and shouted something in Italian.

'What did he say?' Anna inquired nervously.

'He just asked which side we were on.' Mario smiled at Anna. 'Don't worry, darling. We can cope with all this. After all, we are used to it. These are our own people.' He sounded so happy and so confident that Anna realized that what seemed like aggression to her was just another way of life.

The taxi took them to the main train station in Genoa. The place was teeming with men, women and children. Anna noticed the elderly being helped tenderly from the trains. The children, looking white and bewildered, were being bustled here and there.

'Mothers taking their parents and their children into the countryside,' Fosca remarked. Even with all the congestion and the shouting, the people seemed remarkably cheerful and resilient.

They found their train bound for Florence, and then Siena. They were travelling first class, and Anna thanked her father silently for his forethought. She sank into her seat and looked at the passing countryside. To begin with it was brown and flat. The sun beat down on the train and she felt the scorching heat from the arid plains. Hours later they began to climb, and then it grew cooler until she fell asleep. She awoke with a start, her mouth dry and her head aching. Mario took her hand.

'Darling, you slept for ages. We are coming into Florence. We will spend the night here and then go on to Siena and Asciano tomorrow.'

Anna smiled weakly. She glanced out of the window and saw long, thin trees standing in lines like guardians on the hill tops. 'Those,' Mario said, pointing with his chin, 'are cypresses. Oh, how homesick I have been for cypress trees. My two wishes are for Tuscan bean soup and for cypress trees. I do hope our mother and father will be at home to welcome us. The situation is so muddled and unclear I think we just have to get there and then see if things sort themselves out. So far, Anna, I don't feel there is much danger. I feel a lot of people are scared and I've seen quite a lot of Italian soldiers. Maybe if I go out into the corridor and find a conductor I can catch up on some news. Would you like something to eat, Anna? You missed lunch.'

Anna shook her head. 'I don't feel much like eating at the moment. I think I'll just sit here quietly and watch the scenery.'

When Mario left the carriage, Fosca shook her head. 'He's much more worried than he lets us know. I think he expected some news of our parents before we left America. Still, he'll take care of us both.' She grinned. 'Do you have Regina's address? I saw her just before I went to pack and she said she was on her way to see you. She had an awful bruise on her face.'

'I know. Tony did it.' Anna paused. 'Actually, she did come and see me, and she gave me her mother's address in Genoa. I really like her. I hope she gets rid of Tony, but I very much doubt it. Even if she does, she'll probably pick up an Italian version of Tony. I thought only Mary Rose needed lousy relationships, but Regina is just as bad. Thank God I don't have those needs. My life seems so uncomplicated by comparison.'

Fosca smiled. 'Actually, Anna, you have been very lucky and very protected by your parents. For me suffering is something I understand better now. I too was very protected until we were sent away. I shall never forget the pain of being parted from my parents and all those people and things I loved. I really thought I might die from it. For you, if and when suffering comes, it will hit you hard. I hope it never will happen to you. But you have nothing to measure pain, except of course that experience you had on the boat. That hit you hard.'

'It did, but in a funny way it made it easier for me to understand some of the stuff that Mary Rose did, and also the other night when I saw Tony hit Regina. I think before Rupert I would just have dropped Regina and never spoken to her again. I could not have imagined making a fool of myself over a man before I met Rupert. It was a lesson well learned.'

'What are you two in deep conversation about?' Mario squeezed back into his compartment seat.

'Women's talk,' Fosca replied. 'You look pleased with yourself.'

'I am. The guard tells me that, though there is trouble between the Communists and the Fascists, the Germans are pulling back for the moment and so, in the foreseeable future at least, there is no danger of war. Hopefully our parents will be down from the mountains. The guard says that most of the resistance was up in Mount Amiata, and that's not far from our house.'

Anna was too tired to make love. So Mario held her while she fell asleep. Looking down at her face, he wondered if he had done the right thing. Would an American girl like Anna, used to all the modern comforts of an American way of life, translate to a big farmhouse in Tuscany? Sure there were bathrooms in the farmhouse, but certainly no showers. Siena was a beautiful city, but the Sienese did not welcome strangers, and certainly not American women. But then Mario relied on the fact that Anna had a loving and warm nature and most Italians responded to that. Also, and he grinned ruefully, she was blonde and blue-eyed in a country where most women were dark with brown eyes. She would be called Madonna by the men. She was certainly no Madonna, he had seen to that. But now, as he lay beside her, gazing at her face drowned in sleep, he hoped very much that she would love him for the rest of her life, and that they would always make love with such verve and enthusiasm. She had proven to be an apt pupil. As he watched her he felt such a surge of love roll over his body that he began to tingle. Little ripples of sexual energy caused him to slip his hand under Anna's soft back. 'Anna,' he whispered. She turned towards him, mostly asleep, and opened her legs. He stroked her flat stomach and then reached down further. She arched her back and sighed happily. He watched the smile grow on her lips.

'Come into me,' she whispered back. Now fully awake, they made love.

'My first time in Italy,' she said with much satisfaction. 'Now you have to get me something to eat. I'm starving after all that exercise.' She sat up and put on the light. The room was ornate and vulgar, but cheerful. The armchairs in the big bedroom were overstuffed. They reminded Anna of the black-clad widows she had seen in the train station in Genoa.

'What would you like to eat?' Mario lay beside her looking at her perfect left breast. The nipple trembled as Anna laughed.

'I think this calls for a celebration. Let's have some champagne. And what do you suggest would go well with champagne in Italy at, let me see – ' she consulted her watch – 'at two o'clock in the morning?'

'I think a plate of cold roast guinea-fowl and two bowls of Italian ice-cream. How does that sound?'

'Marvellous, darling.' Anna leaned over him. 'You may kiss me,' she said laughing. Mario kissed her nipples first and then her mouth.

'I'll order the food first,' he said firmly. 'Otherwise you'll never get fed!'

Fifty-Two

Day-time with Travis proved to be much more fun than Mary Rose had had in a long time. Though he was quiet among strangers, when they were alone he kept her vastly amused with his imitations and observations. He took her to Harrods food hall, which was still an amazing sight. They bought lemon marmalade in Fortnum's, and after a particularly busy morning choosing furniture for the master bedroom in the dower house, he took her to Simpson's for a big plate of rare roast beef and fluffy light Yorkshire pudding.

'English food can be so good.' Mary Rose was smiling at Travis.

'Yeah, the English can be so good at many things, but unfortunately they are beginning to lean towards all things American. I don't mind if they adopt our standards of comfort, but if they adopt the great American lifestyle they'll be finished as a nation.'

'Do you really dislike America that much?' Mary Rose was troubled.

'Yeah, I do. Not those Americans who have kept their own cultures, like the Italians and the Jews, but the vast mass of American first- and second-generation immigrants who have lost everything and now just live for the great American idea of money and bigger and better cars. I'm not the only American who feels that way.' He sighed. 'But I do miss San Francisco. I miss driving for hundreds of empty miles. I miss the deserts and the high forests. Oh boy, did you ever do that drive from LA to Colorado? It must be one of the most beautiful in the world.'

'I know very little about America,' Mary Rose admitted.

'Well, some day we'll do that drive together.'

'With Crispin in the back seat complaining,' Mary Rose laughed. 'Come to think of it, I'd better give the old dear a ring tonight. He'll be wondering what's been happening – if he isn't worn out with hunting, shooting, and murdering things.'

Later that night, when Travis left Mary Rose in the suite, she lay back on her pillow and thought about him. He never stayed the night. He seemed really grateful that she could make him come with her mouth, and she enjoyed making love to him very much indeed. She realized that it left her randy and unsatiated, but there was a very definite unselfish pleasure in pleasuring him. She liked the way his normally rather sad eyes filled with pleasure before he finally let go of himself. She liked the moments when he held her gently and tentatively in his arms. She knew enough about men to realize that she must not pry into his past life. She did wonder if all his experiences had been homosexual. Or perhaps he was one of those men who had no relationships at all with men or women. They remained a kind of neuter in a sea of copulating bodies. Sex seemed to be the central hub of everything that happened between people. Mary Rose had long ago realized that you did not know a man until you had shared a sexual experience with him. But with Travis she shared very little. Still, for now she was content to wait. They had many months together. Somehow they were forming a friendship and that meant a lot to Mary Rose. She was aware that she had lost a big, central part of her life when she said goodbye to Anna. Even now, married to Crispin, she had a big English family behind her. But in the exclusive, restrained, ironic world of the English (and the Kearneys had become very English), she felt out of place. She felt brash, and both Crispin's sisters made sure she looked that way.

When she awoke to the knock of the floor waiter, she stumbled out of bed, threw the lock, and immediately returned to the warm bedclothes. She yelled for him to push open the door and bring in her breakfast. Lying propped on her pillows, she surveyed the new day. It was now Wednesday. The days had slid by so quickly. Beside her the pink-rimmed plates with a little gold gondola made the morning seem brighter than ever. She did not order the coffee. Even the Savoy's coffee tasted nothing like good American coffee from home. It must be the water, she thought, stretching out for the pot of tea. Her grapefruit was big and lemon yellow on the outside and ice-cream pink on the inside. She picked up the telephone.

'Darling, did I wake you?' There was a muffled curse on the other end.

Crispin spluttered. 'You know I hate being woken up by the fucking telephone. Where have you been, anyway?'

'Here in the Savoy,' Mary Rose answered innocently. 'I've been working very hard with Travis Mainwaring. He's very nice and efficient. We've been doing an awful lot of work together.'

'I take it you mean interior decorating.' Crispin was not convinced.

'Sure I mean decorating. Travis is not interested in anything else,' Mary Rose lied fluently, thinking of the moments he was very interested in doing something else.

'Good.' Crispin opened one bleary eye. He saw a brassière hanging off the end of an armchair and winced. Shit, he thought, who was in his bed? He couldn't remember getting to bed last night, let alone screwing anyone. He lifted up the blanket covering a small lump beside him. Holy mackerel, it was Philippa, Theresa's best friend. Theresa was sure to find out.

'When are you coming back?' he asked quickly. He'd have to sort out this little complication before Mary Rose came back or she'd rumble him like a shot. Mary Rose had a nose for illicit sex that put his best bird-dog to shame.

'How about on Sunday? Would you like to come up for the day and we could perhaps drive down to the country on Monday. I can get Travis to fill your car and mine. That way I can bring all the stuff at once.'

'OK, I'll be up for lunch on Sunday. See you then, darling. Miss you.' Crispin made a face. He did miss her. Mary Rose was so practical about sex. Now he had to get this woman out of his bed and out of his life. He was not going to mess up his chance of a lifetime's playing – supported by Mary Rose's money – for a quick roll in the hay with Philippa. She wasn't even that good in bed; but at least she wasn't sexually demanding. He felt good about himself as the events of the night flooded into his brain. Philippa was just frightened enough of his advances to make him feel very male and potent. He shook Philippa awake. She lay staring at him blearily.

'Do you want to make love again?' she lisped hopefully.

Crispin shook his head. 'Darling, that was Mary Rose on the telephone.' Philippa sat bolt upright in bed.

'She's not coming home now, is she?' Philippa pulled the top sheet up to her armpits. She was such a skinny little thing. She had deep armpits and big flat nipples like brown bathplugs. Crispin felt a pang of sexual regret. She was such a contrast to Mary Rose. Philippa exuded the need to be bullied; Mary Rose fought back.

'Philippa.' Crispin lay back on his pillow and began his much practised, world-weary man-about-the-bedroom speech. 'There is no need to hurt Mary Rose. This was a lovely night of passion between both of us, wasn't it?'

'Yes, it was lovely,' Philippa began hesitantly. 'Was it lovely for you too? You seemed to be a little drunk.'

'It was marvellous for me, darling, absolutely marvellous. You have such a wonderful body and you don't giggle and laugh all the time. Making love to Mary Rose is rather like trying to catch the Edinburgh Express on horseback.' He put a comforting hand on her shoulder. 'I know we can keep this little episode just between the two of us, can't we?' Implied in the question was that she should not unburden herself to Theresa, who was a wicked gossip.

'I won't tell anybody, Crispin. When is Mary Rose coming back?'

'I'm going up to London to help her bring stuff back in my car on Sunday.'

'Well, we can go on making love until Sunday, can't we?' There was an edge in Philippa's voice that Crispin recognized from other sexual escapades.

'Well . . . if you are sure that is what you want to do.'

'I'm sure. And you don't have to worry. I won't get pregnant.'

'That's good then.'

Philippa was gazing at him expectantly. It was that awful look on a woman's face when she insisted on hanging on to what was really only meant to be a one-night stand. It totally turned him off. He reached for her with a nagging sense of dread. He pinched her bottom fiercely while she was labouring away solicitously trying to please him. The pain startled her and she burst into tears. With a thin smile of contempt, Crispin came and then apologized.

'I don't know what came over me,' he whispered. 'It was such a moment of passion.' He watched as Philippa's eyes cleared of the tears.

'Oh Crispin,' she said.

Fifty-Three

Mario stood with his arm around Anna's waist. They had been met at Asciano Station by Tommaso, the farm foreman. He had a big, blazing grin. His wide tombstone teeth glistened in the sunshine.

'Ahh, Mario!' He greeted Mario with a fierce, rib-cracking hug and then he pulled Fosca to him. 'Your parents will be with us this evening. D'you remember Lisa? She will be making the meal tonight. The cook is away in Genoa getting her grandchildren out of there. Such a mess in Italy now. Everybody running everywhere like chickens without heads.'

Anna walked from the tiny platform, through the square ticket office and down the stairs to the car. Will I ever learn this strange language, she wondered? All the way to the farmhouse, Mario translated Tommaso's sibilant stream of conversation. Anna was stunned by the great beauty of the countryside.

'Now we are cutting through the *crete*,' Mario explained to her. 'Look, can you see the mountain over there? That is Mount Amiata. There have been chestnut woods up there since the fifth century. The wood from there was used to fashion the Roman galleys.'

'Mario loves the history of this part of the world,' Fosca said.

'How I missed such ancient things when I was in America,' Mario continued. 'Here I feel as though I have always belonged. My roots in the clay of the *crete*. My heart always at the top of Mount Amiata. In the winter we will go up there and ski, Anna. You can fly like the ice bird down the mountain. In the summer we can go down to the Maremma, and in the remote mountains we can see the grey *chianini*, those oxen bred in ancient times. And we can swim in the sea there.' He heaved a huge sigh. 'In Tuscany there is something for everybody. But most of all there is Siena. The most beautiful city in the world.'

Now standing in front of a big, sprawling house, Anna was puzzled. 'This is not a farmhouse, Mario.'

'No, I know. It's really a villa, not a farmhouse. Tommaso lives in the actual farmhouse with his relatives. I don't like to think of us as land-owners, so I call this villa the farmhouse just to convince myself that I am going to be a working farmer. My parents are quite happy to be capitalist land-owners. But I always found it very difficult to be with my friends in the village and to know that I had a future and they didn't.'

Fosca nodded. 'I felt the same way. So many of my friends are either working from dawn to dusk, or married with more children than they would want. Life is hard for the worker in Italy. Here we have great wealth for the few and very little for the poor. The young go to the cities to find work, leaving behind the old and the children. This happens everywhere, not just in Italy. But America is so big and so uncrowded.' She smiled at Anna. 'There people can just get up and move on and make a living. Here we are stuck with our old ways. People have been farming here since the year one thousand. They don't want to change their ways. So when I was in America I loved the way Americans were willing to experiment and try new things. Now I have got used to the idea that I must conform to our Italian ways. I cannot wear jeans in my village of Asciano. I must cover my head to go into a church. I must learn to lower my eyes in the presence of men or I will be called bad names. Still, I am happy to be back. Come now.' She took Anna's hand. 'We will show you inside the villa.'

On one side of the villa was the old farmhouse. It formed an L-shape with the main house. The square was completed by a bricked hay barn, and the courtyard was closed off by an ornate wrought-iron gate. In the centre of the courtyard stood a well.

Anna stood on the upstairs porch, gazing over the courtyard. Somehow she felt as if she had been here before. 'D'you ever get that feeling you've been in a place before, Mario? I feel as if I've always known this house. I bet our bedroom is at the end of this corridor and to the left. It has two big four-poster beds. Two big windows with pale blue shutters, and the floor is not tiled like this.' She squinted. '. . . It is more like a herring-bone tile.'

Mario hugged her to him. 'You are my little witch,' he smiled. 'You certainly have been here before. I don't know how you do these things. You can read my thoughts, know what I want to order for dinner, guess what our room looks like . . . Are you sure you're not a witch?'

Fosca had gone off with Tommaso, chattering loudly. Anna and Mario were alone on the upstairs terrace. 'For a long while I seemed to have lost all my Celtic gifts. It used to worry me because I liked to live with that kind of intuition. I think I got very bogged down in day-to-day living. I didn't have time enough to just be by myself. Here, I think I will find it all again.'

She drank in the smell of the wild thyme from the courtyard. She could hear birds singing and chickens and roosters celebrating the hot Tuscan sun. Even in the heat of the morning, Mount Amiata stood cool and imposing. The wind sent gusts of fleshy smells into the house.

'Come.' Mario tenderly took her arm and began to

lead her inside the house. 'Tommaso will have taken our suitcases into our room by now. I want to make love to you the first time in this house. I don't want to wait until my mother and my father arrive. The night will be late and we shall be tired.'

'Quick!' Anna giggled. They both dashed up the corridor and turned left. As Mario opened the door of the bedroom, Anna caught her breath. Sure enough, the room was exactly as she had described it. She gazed at the floor. The tiles lay like the spine of a fish. Laughing and whooping with joy, she threw herself on the bed. 'Take me, I'm all yours,' she declaimed in a loud, Victorian voice.

Mario pounced on her, and they began to roll around until passion overcame their sense of fun with each other. The silence was only broken by the sounds of heavy breathing and then a slight moan from Anna.

'Now,' she said as she lay spent. 'We have all the time in the world to make babies.'

'This is my mother Elisabetta and my father Francesco.' Mario's eyes were dancing as he formally introduced his parents to their new daughter-in-law.

Elisabetta took Anna in her arms and kissed her gently on both cheeks. 'My darling child. Now I have somebody to talk to and try and speak my English with.'

Francesco kissed her hand and then hugged her. They were all standing in the big loggia which ran down the side of the villa. Through the arches in the thick wall there was a breathtaking view over the valley.

'It's lovely to have you back, darlings.' Elisabetta put her arms around her son and daughter. 'We both missed you so much. But then, had we not sent you away, Mario would not be here with his beautiful bride.'

Anna blushed. 'They missed you. And they both missed Italy, especially Tuscany. And I can see why.'

She was conscious of how inelegant she looked. Her clothes were expensively designed, but they lacked the cut and the quality of those worn by Elisabetta and her husband.

'I must go into Siena and do some shopping,' Anna said nervously. 'I don't think American clothes fit in Italy.'

'I'll come with you,' Fosca offered. 'And we'll take Mother. She knows all the shopkeepers. And we can use her dressmaker. She's been going there for years. I know what you mean, though. I feel the same way. In those few years in America I caught the American way of life and I now realize that what suits that country doesn't look good here. But you know, Anna, I'll miss the casual American way of life. Not all of it, though, such as its awful bad manners. But just the fact that you don't have to spend your life wondering what the neighbours are saying about you.'

'*Ouffa*, Fosca,' her mother intervened. 'I shouldn't worry too much about the neighbours of Asciano. If the present situation deteriorates again, they will be far too busy trying to survive rather than living on a diet of gossip and innuendo.' Lisa put her head around the door. '*Tutti a tavola, signori.*'

Elisabetta took Anna's arm. '*Grazie*, Lisa. *Andiamo!* Dinner is served. Come, Anna. This is your first real Tuscan meal, is it not?'

Anna shot an amused look at Mario. She remembered the plate of roast guinea-fowl and the ice-cream of last night. Mario winked at her quickly. Both very much in love, Elisabetta thought to herself. She was well pleased with her new daughter-in-law.

Fifty-Four

Mary Rose nervously waited for Crispin to arrive. She sat on the long window-seat in her suite looking down at the tugs and the police boats as they fussed up and down the river. It was late summer, and the pleasure boats on the Thames were few, partly, Mary Rose assumed, because the threat of war had considerably reduced the number of visitors coming to England. Indeed, as she and Travis wandered in and out of shops looking for treasures for her house, they both remarked on how empty it all was. Sometimes a uniformed figure could be seen crossing St James's Square. Around Victoria Station, there were mobs of brown-jacketed soldiers, all seemingly on their way to somewhere else. The paper-sellers screamed themselves hoarse nightly with news of various events in troubled spots of the world. Austria seemed to be the most quoted. Mary Rose pressed her nose against the window and wished she could be really happy to see Crispin. Maybe he might be in one of his really good, incandescent moods, she thought, where he was able to light up the room and make her roar with laughter. At those moments she knew she really loved him and that marrying him had not been a mistake. At other moments she just wanted him out of her life. She waited tensely for the phone call announcing his arrival.

'Mr Kearney is waiting for you in the lobby,' a voice said discreetly on the phone.

'Send him up, please,' she replied.

Crispin was grinning from ear to ear. 'I like seeing you all set up in your finery. Which knickers are you wearing? I bet they're the black silk ones you got from Harrods.'

'Actually they're not. I'm wearing something you haven't seen at all yet, and you'll have to wait until tonight to see it. I've booked lunch in five minutes, so we have to get going.'

'OK.' Crispin shrugged. He'd had a hell of a few days satisfying Philippa who, amid tears and tantrums, had threatened to tell. So he was in no hurry to perform. But he had to admit Mary Rose was looking marvellous. 'You've lost some weight, old thing. How did you do that here?'

'I just ate very little.' Mary Rose smiled demurely, thinking of Travis. Crispin's eyes narrowed. When Mary Rose struck her demure poses he knew to watch out. He didn't want anybody threatening his territory.

'Who've you been seeing while you've been up here all alone? Any of the old crowd?'

'No, the only people I know in England are all friends of yours. I've just been really busy collecting stuff with Travis.'

They walked into the River Room and the *maître d'*, who'd known Crispin for years, smiled. To himself he wished wholeheartedly that the radiant American can woman had not thrown herself away on such a wastrel.

'Welcome, madam,' he said, leading Mary Rose to the best table in the dining room. 'I kept this specially for you, and of course for your charming husband.' He nodded at Crispin, who smiled back blandly. Crispin knew that the *maître d'* had seen him many times in this restaurant with girls of all kinds. One thing they all had in common was the ability to pay the bill, both for the food and also for the rooms upstairs. Oh well, he thought, he couldn't care less, and he employed his new-found American slang. 'Good to see you again.'

Now he was safely married to a bank full of money, he could afford to be patronizing.

That's what Crispin liked about the Americans. There was a certain cut-throat ruthlessness that created the exciting frisson in New York. He looked about the restaurant. At the American business tables he could hear the gunshot sounds of deals being forged. Names of markets. Huge amounts of money. The smell of serious negotiation. Blood-letting. How unlike the English tables, where the men muttered deprecatory remarks and the women talked of their Labradors and rose gardens. Crispin felt the familiar threat of boredom steal over him.

'I'll have a bottle of the Dom,' he told the wine waiter without even looking at him. 'Choose a good year for me, will you?'

The waiter nodded and hurried off to get the ice-bucket. 'What a smart little bastard that man is,' he muttered to the *maître d'*, who nodded and wondered how long it would be before Mary Rose lost the blush on her cheeks and the lights dancing in her eyes. Not long, he thought.

After a long and very liquid lunch, Crispin tried to seduce Mary Rose in her suite. She fended him off. Even if the sex with Travis was unsatisfactory for her, it was a kinder and gentler way of making love than being mugged yet again by Crispin. Anyway, Mary Rose knew that Crispin just wanted to feel that he had made love to his wife in a suite at the Savoy. His other women were not wealthy enough to afford to stay in this particular suite.

'No, Crispin, I'm just beginning my period.' Fortunately for her, Crispin was repelled by anything like that. She rang the bell and waited for the floor manager to see them out of the suite. He arrived with a large bunch of purple irises. She smiled at him, thinking how like a continental man to remember that she had arrived in a purple outfit.

'Thank you so much,' she said simply.

As they left the hotel, the floor manager kissed her hand, then handed her the keys to her car. She could feel Crispin's angry disapproval as an army of Savoy staff came crowding around the car to wish her goodbye.

'You Americans throw your money about. No wonder they all hang round you. So very vulgar,' he hissed at her as he pretended to peck her cheek goodbye.

'Jealousy, darling, jealousy,' she said sweetly. But as she took her car out into the busy traffic that roared past the oasis that was the front of the hotel, tears dripped down the side of her face. It won't be long and I'll be back, she promised herself. She so much missed the quiet efficiency of her own home in New York, and this had been a real respite. Even if her mother was a bitch and her father a philanderer, at least they were both civilized and well read. Conversations with Crispin tended to get nowhere. Still, if war were declared, she might be able to get rid of him. But then Travis might have to go back to America. She decided not to think about that uncomfortable fact. Just remembering that Travis would be coming down during the week to look around the house and to measure up made her smile again. She passed Chiswick House and promised herself a visit the next time she came up. The house came very highly recommended by Travis.

Once back in the dower house, Mary Rose found a letter from Anna. It was full of marvellous descriptions of Tuscany. 'I am really happy,' Anna assured her. 'Mario's mother and father are wonderful, but I do really miss you dreadfully. I thought I'd never find anybody like you, but on the boat I met a woman called Regina d'Albro. She is an Italian version of you. I hope to go up to Genoa to see her in a month's time.

But I'd so much rather see you. Any chance of coming down here for a visit? I know visas are difficult, but the man from Thomas Cook could probably fix something up for you both.'

Mary Rose meant to write back. But the weeks went by so fast that, having put the letter away in a drawer of her writing desk, she forgot about it. Slowly the house took shape under Mary Rose's excellent eye. She found a new confidence in herself, partially encouraged by Travis. During the rest of the year he came and went regularly. She followed him up to London when she could get away. Crispin grumbled and moaned, but left her alone. He was very taken with the amount of reflected praise he received for Mary Rose's ability to entertain in great style. From being considered a local arriviste, he was now taken far more seriously. He began to gamble with Podge in a gambling house belonging to Jimmy Leadbetter. The first few times when he couldn't pay his debts, he went to Mary Rose, who was sympathetic.

'Couldn't you just take out your original stake when you win and then gamble with the profits?' she had asked.

'I know I should.' Crispin felt miserable. Not because he had asked her for money, but because he felt as if he had played into a huge trap that he couldn't avoid. Winning didn't excite him any more. No, the moment that excited him was that moment when he knew he might lose but that all was not lost. It was only a split second, but that moment when everything hung in the balance was his adrenalin high. He needed that shot more than he needed sex. In fact, his need for sex was low during those months. Mary Rose didn't mind. She recognized Crispin's insecure sexuality and preferred to pleasure Travis, or to party in London with his friends.

Finally, when they had run out of excuses for renovating the dower house, Mary Rose took her suite in the Savoy for a final meeting.

Travis arrived on the Friday night with a sheaf of bills. He seemed unusually quiet.

'What's the matter, Travis?' Mary Rose was wearing a black silk negligée. She no longer tried to flirt with Travis, or to impose on him sexually. They had become very good friends and each knew the other extremely well.

'I'm sad,' Travis said simply. 'I knew we would have to say goodbye at some time, but now that the time is here I find I really don't want to let you go. It's not just that. You make love to me, and nobody's ever done that for me before.'

'You really mean to tell me that you were a virgin?' Mary Rose was astonished.

'Yeah. I sort of played around with myself sometimes, but I guess I was a virgin until I met you.'

'Well I'll be darned, Travis. How on earth did you miss all that messing around with sex that we all did as kids?'

'I don't know.' Travis twined his fingers. They had been having dinner in her suite. The table was spread out in front of the open windows. The distant sounds of cars and buses rushing along the road below came floating through the windows. The tall branches of the trees on the Embankment were now deep yellow with the approaching autumn. It was the loveliest time of the year. Mary Rose picked up a glass of red wine.

'Here's to us,' she said falteringly. 'I'll miss you too, Travis.' She decided to leave the question of sex open-ended.

'I've been thinking, Mary Rose.' He put his hand across the table and took hers. 'What about you joining my firm as a director? I know you don't need the money, but you're one hell of a good interior decorator, and I could do with a woman in my firm. Sometimes the rich foreigners are far more comfortable with a woman. Especially Arab women and others from the Far East. They find it uncomfortable to be only in the company of men.'

'Travis, do you really mean that?'

'Sure I do. I've given it a lot of thought, and the boys all agree they'd like to have a Yank like you around.'

'You're not just saying that to make me feel better, are you?'

'You know I wouldn't do that, Mary Rose. My business is much too important to me. Look,' he said, taking out a pencil. He pulled a sketching pad from his briefcase. 'This is the design for Jack Yen's house in South Kensington. His wife wants her own suite of rooms, and that could be your first job.'

Later, Mary Rose floated about the bath, thinking about Travis's offer. When she had gently made love to him in her big bed after dinner, she had decided that she must try and get through the block that made it impossible for him to trust any woman. Before she got into bed, she reached for the drawings of Jack Yen's house. Looking at the brilliantly pencilled lines, she thought again about Travis. Just before she put the light out, she idly flipped the drawing over. There was a much smaller drawing of a little girl. The figure was drawn with such intensity that Mary Rose gasped. That must be his little sister that drowned, she thought. Now she knew that Travis had left her a big piece of the puzzle. It was as though he'd been drowning off the shore, and had seen her standing by a beach and recognized that she could help him. She switched off the light and blessed the fact that she did not have to share her bed with anybody, especially Crispin. Certainly she could help Travis, but could she help herself? She very much doubted that she could.

Fifty-Five

Anna found the change in her lifestyle exciting, yet puzzling and upsetting too. The upset was in the complete change of timing. Here, in the depths of Tuscany, she had to adjust to the slowness of time. It was as if a hand had reached out and stayed the arms of her watch. Often she would habitually check the time as she had done in New York, and then, looking again, find that only a few minutes had elapsed. At first, the slow pace of the days as they faded one into the other bothered her and made her impatient. But slowly, as the months turned into winter, she began to settle and her own internal clock adjusted.

The puzzling part was the shock of feeling so alien. She understood how Fosca and Mario must have felt when they came to live with her family in New York. Now, looking back with hindsight, she also understood that her well-meaning attempts at encouraging them to join in with her family must have felt as intrusive as Fosca's attempts with her mother to get Anna to join them in their social obligations.

One of the jobs that Elisabetta and Fosca had was to visit all the women on the estate, which could often be a delightful surprise. Fosca and Anna would walk behind Elisabetta carrying a bowl of broth, or medicines should anyone be ill. Yet Anna found the whole business faintly embarrassing. She could not understand why the women, with their wide-eyed children, looked up to the three of them as if they were oracles. She stood often in the shadow of the little cottages wishing she was elsewhere. She remembered the stench and the smell of urine in Father O'Brian's hospital and how she had vowed never to allow that smell to enter her life again. Now it was back, and under her nose almost daily. Of course, there were well-scrubbed cottages with happy, cheerful children. But then they did not visit those cottages that often. Elisabetta's life was taken up with the cottages where there were troubles. Women who met them at the door with missing teeth and black eyes. This reminded Anna of Regina and it disturbed her.

'Can't you do anything about Cato's wife?' she asked Mario. 'She's always bruised. Can't you tell him if he beats her again you'll get rid of him?'

'No, *cara*, it's not my business. Those two have always fought like cat and dog. If I tell him to leave she'll just pack her bags and go with him. Then what will happen to the children? We pay good wages and treat our peasants well. Anyway, I wouldn't want to lose a good shepherd.'

Anna took her troubles to Fosca. 'Mario is right, Anna. In America you all interfere with each other. You talk and talk and talk about the ideas of the Viennese doctor Freud. But for us in Europe, you have the talking disease. Life is not something you can explain with words. Cato and his wife live the way they do because they want to live that way. If Cato's wife wanted to leave him, she could always go back to her family. But she does not want to leave and that is her business.'

'But you do interfere in other ways. Your mother is expected to be a doctor, have the knowledge of a midwife, give advice on everything under the sun, isn't she?'

'Yes, but only when she is asked. You see, here life is very much more sensitive than it is in America, or indeed in England.' Fosca winced at the memories of meals at the Kearneys' house in Devon. 'It is very difficult for *stranieri* to follow our ways. There are layers and layers of understanding that go down deep in our culture. There is not only the matter of running a large farm, but also of the role required in checking everything, from Lisa's job as the housekeeper down to the school houses and seeing that the children get a good education.'

'I feel as if I will always be a foreigner here.' Anna was crying in Fosca's arms.

'No you won't, Anna. The people love you and they are always telling me how beautiful you are. Give it time.'

And then, Anna was pregnant. When she told Mario he was thrilled. She placed a trunk call to her parents and heard her father roar with delight.

'We're coming over to see you,' he bellowed. Anna was worried following the rumours pouring out of the radio every night. She had been reticent to ask her parents to make the journey. The man called Hitler filled the night air with his screams, and the Fascists were on the move again. Yet the people of Asciano did not believe there would be war. Il Duce would never allow it, they convinced themselves. Walking down the narrow cobbled streets to the little marketplace behind the square, Anna, too, felt very cut off from all that was happening in Germany. She was pregnant, and for now that took up all her time.

One day, as she was loitering on the way back to the house, she paused to gaze at a little hut that nestled in the forest behind a big pine tree. Smoke was coming out of the chimney. For the first time in a very long time, Anna felt drawn to the little hut. She tried to resist the feeling, but it was as if whoever was in there was willing her to come in. Anna reluctantly began to walk towards the front door. She could see no one but, as she moved forward, she felt a gentle sense of encouragement from the house. For a moment she panicked and felt disapproval wash over her. She took a deep breath, squinting into the sun so that she could see if there was an aura around the house. She was pleased to see a light yellow colour. It was not threatening, so she moved forward again.

'*Buon giorno*.' She heard a very old, crackly voice address her.

'*Mi scusi*,' she said, wishing she'd tried harder at her Italian. A very firm, wrinkled hand took her by the wrist and drew her into the darkness. For a moment Anna could see nothing at all and then, dimly, as her eyes adjusted to the shadows, she saw a very bent old woman. She had a hideously deformed hump on her back. Her nose was long and as bent as her back. It nearly touched her lower lip. She was bewhiskered and obviously suffered from some kind of unsightly disease. Large clumps of cysts clung to her face and her arms. Her legs, mercifully, were covered by a long black skirt. The old woman pulled her down into a chair by the fire. She took a long metal spoon and dipped it into a pot on the grate. She tipped the liquid into a cup and gave it to Anna.

'*Grazie*.' Anna smiled at the woman sitting so upright in her chair.

'My name is Pilar.' Anna was grateful she was able to translate that much at least.

'Thank you, Pilar.' Anna's normal sense of caution seemed to disappear in the old woman's presence. She felt strangely secure, immediately at ease. She unhesitatingly sipped the liquid and found that it was a very pleasant combination of herbs she recognized.

'For the baby,' Pilar cackled. 'You have two babies there, you know.'

Anna's eyes widened. 'Is that true?'

The old lady nodded. '*Due*.'

After finishing the drink, Anna almost ran up the track through the forest to the house. She found Mario in the barn and threw herself into his arms. 'This very old lady in a hut along the path here told me that I'm going to have twins.'

Mario's arms tightened around her. 'That must be Pilar, the witch,' he said smiling. 'Well, if she says it's twins, darling, it's twins. I've never known her to be wrong yet.'

'Twins!' Anna hugged him. 'I'd love to have twins. Now we have to plan everything in duplicate. Do you want boys or girls, or one of each?'

'Anything, as long as they are both in good health and they look like you,' he said, kissing her soundly. Anna went off to the house to dream about her babies. Now she was pregnant, Italy didn't seem quite so alien. And her mother and father would be arriving in the next few weeks. There was a lilt in her walk and a spring in her step that she realized had been missing for a very long time.

Fifty-Six

Mary Rose heard on the grapevine that Anna was expecting twins.

'She always had to do things properly,' she said with a touch of jealousy in her tone. 'Well, at least Danny and Mary are going to be grandparents.' This exchange took place at one of the usually dreadful Kearney Sunday lunches. This time the whole family happened to be present. The girls were down from London and stared at Mary Rose.

'You don't think you might be sterile do you?' Theresa asked sweetly over her plate of spotted dick. Privately, Mary Rose had dubbed spotted dick disgusting. The pale suet with its turd-like pellets of raisins appalled her.

'No, I am not sterile. Thank you for asking, Theresa. I just don't want children at the moment.' She didn't look at Crispin, who knew that they had never used contraceptives. Mary Rose flushed with anger. Slowly she was beginning to realize that Amelia not only expected her to contribute to the family fortunes, but also to supply her with grandchildren. Now Amelia didn't even hint at what she needed for the estate. After coffee, Amelia stood up and pushed her low-slung belly away from the table. 'Daddy and I have been discussing the tennis courts, and we both feel that we need to build clay surfaces. The upkeep of the grass is really far too expensive. Don't you agree, Daddy?'

Colonel Kearney had the grace to blush and clear his throat. 'Actually, darling, it was you who thought we must have clay courts.'

'Actually,' Crispin drawled, 'I think Mother is right.'

Mother is always right, Mary Rose thought impatiently. Crispin caught her stern look and then backed off. He had another gambling debt that needed paying by the end of the week. Jimmy Leadbetter was charming, but some of his henchmen could get very rough. And Jimmy never took any responsibility for the broken bones, or in one or two cases the so-called suicides, of the people who could not pay their debts. Jimmy understood gamblers, and he also understood fear in a way that made Crispin admire him. Crispin too understood fear and terror. As he grew older, and more accustomed to living with Mary Rose, he knew more about how to keep her frightened and vulnerable. Now he operated with a mixture of tenderness followed by trenchant bullying.

'Perhaps, Mother,' he said placatingly, 'we should wait until next year. We have put an awful lot of money into the dower house and we have yet to finish the swimming pool.'

'I think your swimming pool is a very American, over-the-top exercise in vulgarity.' Amelia left the table and sniffed loudly. Several smelly dogs trailed after her. She took her gardening hat off its peg behind the dining-room door and jammed it on her head. Wisps of stray hair straggled around her face. 'I'm going off to do some work. More than I can say for some of us!'

Mary Rose stood up. 'I have to pack to go to London. I have a client I must see tomorrow morning.'

'I can't see why you have to keep dashing off to London, Mary Rose,' Crispin said. 'After all, there's lots to do here.'

'Crispin, I want to earn a living. I can't lie around doing nothing all day like you can with your friends. I need to feel involved with people who are doing things that interest me. You don't even read books!'

'None of us reads books, Mary Rose. You're unhappy because you're out of your depth with us. Why don't you go back to America? We don't always need to prove we're educated. We're English.'

'I know that.' Mary Rose smiled at Catherine. 'You have some of the best opera in the world, some of the best theatres, and yet you are all Philistines.' She swept out of the room, leaving behind her a dead silence broken only by the colonel.

'What does she mean "Philistines"? Those were the fellows that blinded Samson in the bible, were they not?'

Mary Rose heard Theresa's sigh of impatience. Then she smiled; at least the old man did not pretend that he ever read anything other than *Horse and Hound*.

* * *

'Why do you stay with Crispin when he makes you so unhappy, Mary Rose?' Travis was sitting with her in an Italian restaurant on the King's Road in Chelsea.

Mary Rose shrugged. 'I don't have much option, Travis. What else have I got in my life? Both my parents are totally wrapped up in their lives. When Crispin and I get on we get on, but he is never able just to be happy. He seems always to need to complicate things. It's like living with a terrorist. Just as things are going well between us, I find he's run up another gambling debt, or he's bought another horse that he can't afford. I suppose the thing I find most difficult is that he won't work and that he can't understand why I need to.'

'He does understand, Mary Rose, he's just bone idle. I have found that with a lot of these public school types. Life really never happens to them. They always live in the sixth form. I don't know, they all seem like dodos to me, a sort of doomed species.'

'My mother-in-law is pissed off at me because I'm not pregnant. Anna is expecting twins, so she says. Trust Anna to get it right and in duplicate. Maybe she can give one to me and I'll pretend it's mine.' Mary Rose was laughing, but Travis could tell she was hurt. He stared at her and wondered just how much thinner she was going to get. Her collar bones were sticking out and her wrists were fragile. He was pleased with her work with his difficult clients. She had an excellent way of calming even the most demanding millionaire.

'Tomorrow you have to deal with Mrs Gulbenkian,' he said. 'I'll escort you back to your hotel and then go home. You're going to need all the patience you can muster.'

Why, Mary Rose wondered as she sat alone in her suite, watching the moon shine down on the long snaking river, does Anna get to be happily pregnant and I sit here all alone? Maybe I am sterile. She got up and looked at herself in the mirror over the fireplace.

'Sterile old bitch,' she whispered. She didn't like her face. 'Never mind,' she whispered at her reflection. 'Tomorrow is another day and Mrs Gulbenkian and I will go out on the town and spend an awful lot of money.'

She met Mrs Gulbenkian in the banking hall at Harrods. She knew the woman would be late. The rich – apart from herself – always kept everybody waiting. Her mother was famous for her 'fashionably' late habits. 'I'm sorry, I'm sorry, I'm sorry,' was a litany that Mary Rose grew to despise. Today she had her book of poetry. Since losing Anna she had had no one to talk about books and poetry to. In her earlier days, Anna had read everything, digested it, and then given Mary Rose the gist of the books. Now, with Travis around to take her to the theatre, and to translate what was happening in the art galleries, Mary Rose was beginning to develop a very real love of literature.

An hour passed pleasantly in the big, comfortable leather chairs in the banking hall. Eventually Mary Rose got up and wandered over to a writing desk. I'll drop a line to Anna, she decided; after all, I can get stamps here. She dashed off a letter, mostly congratulating Anna on her pregnancy. 'Life is a bit difficult for me now,' Mary Rose wrote, 'but I'm struggling on. I enjoy my job, which is interior decorating. Funny, Anna, I never thought I'd want a child, but now I do. I don't know if I'd be any good as a mother, but I know I'd like to try. Can I be godmother to the twins? If anything happens to you I'd like to feel that they would be safe with me. Of course, nothing will happen. I'd just like to be a wicked fairy godmother to them both and teach them awful, evil ways. Every child should have a wicked godmother. You had Aunt Kitty. What's happened to Kitty and Martha? I do miss them. Do you hear from Steven sometimes? It all feels so very far away, but also so close.'

She saw a small plump woman come into the hall. That must be Mrs Gulbenkian, she thought. Nobody else could look so Hong Kong. She was wearing a turquoise suit. Thai silk, Mary Rose noted. She had a black blouse with a floppy collar and very, very high-heeled shoes. Large diamond earrings matched the rings on her fingers. The right foot was tapping impatiently as she looked about the hall.

'You must be Mrs Gulbenkian.' Mary Rose approached her quarry warily. She had learned to work out whether or not her customer's bark was worse than her bite.

'Let's go to the executive suite,' the woman commanded. 'I have an appointment with my personal buyer.'

'Do let's,' Mary Rose replied amiably. At least I'll get a decent cup of coffee while she shops until she drops, she thought. 'Let's go, Mrs Gulbenkian.' She followed the little imperious figure out of the hall, dropping Anna's now stamped letter into the postbox.

Fifty-Seven

Anna sat on the stone bench that leaned perilously against the wall of her house. Now that she was pregnant and secure about her new family, she felt very much at home in Tuscany.

She leaned forward and picked a luscious black fig off the tree that shaded her from the hot sun. She sank her teeth into the pink seeded middle and a flood of sweet juice ran down her throat. Far away she could see the claylands. It was a strange and barren land in the hot, dry summer. Nothing grew. Many people denigrated the vast, bleak expanse of moonscape, but Anna loved it. Millions of years ago, Mount Amiata had spewed a fountain of magma into the air which formed the mountains and hills of Tuscany. Here around Asciano, the town had a special blessing. The sheep so beloved of the local shepherds were specially bred to crop on the barren soil. Anna reckoned she could taste the magma in the pecorino cheese made by Tommaso. The cheese had a sharp bite which followed the initial creaminess of its taste.

Now she wandered into the long, low kitchen to find a piece of pecorino to eat with another fig. She heaved a sigh of happiness. It was now late summer and her parents were arriving in a week. The trees were laden with fruit and the fields were erect with corn and wheat. Funny, she thought, I love sweetcorn, but nobody ever seems to grow it here. There's only maize, and all that goes to the pigs and the chickens. She made a note to ask Tommaso to plant some if she could get some seeds from her parents.

Daniel and Mary were originally from the country in Ireland, but she wondered how they would fare in Tuscany where, not only was the fruit larger than anything she had ever seen in America, but so were the bugs. Vipers nested in the long grass, and they were deadly. She remembered the story of how Tommaso lost his toe. Mario had been in a field with him, scything the long grass in preparation for the planting of white and red clover. Suddenly Tommaso had jumped and brought the scythe down hard on the stubble at his feet. But it had been too late, a viper had sunk its long fangs into his boot, penetrating the worn leather. Grimacing with the instant searing pain of the reptile's venom, Tommaso had taken off his boot and had neatly severed his toe.

'I will live without a toe,' he had said, his face red with the intensity of the pain, 'but I won't live to get to hospital.' Mario had taken him by the arm and they had hobbled back to the house leaving a trail of scarlet blood behind them. Now there were several vials of snake serum in the fridge. In May, when the vipers crawled up into the trees, Mario reminded Anna that she would have to wear a hat when she went walking in the woods looking for mushrooms.

Anna sighed contentedly. There was so much to learn about Italy, so much that it would take her a lifetime. For the moment she was chasing the elusive porcini mushrooms. Fat and delicate, these overblown air blimps were considered the fillet steak of the vegetable world, and now she was pregnant she craved them. She wondered if she should take the car and drive to the village of Pienza where her favourite shop sold the best dried porcini mushrooms she had ever tasted. She struggled with her greed for a moment, and then decided that that was just what she would do. Maybe the butcher in Pienza might have some wild boar meat, another of her new addictions.

'I'm going to be fat,' she happily confessed to Mario as they lay close together in bed that night. 'I bought prosciutto, wild boar, and porcini mushrooms, and tomorrow I'm going to tell Lisa that I want to cook my first Italian meal for you, darling. I do want to be a good Italian wife.'

'You don't have to be anything but yourself, Anna. I'll always love you for who you are.' She fell asleep, deeply comforted.

Daniel and Mary arrived at the end of the week and were amazed at how well their daughter looked.

'Italy suits you, Anna.' Daniel smiled at her and realized just how much he had missed her in his life. Yes, he would spend time with her now, but then he must go away and leave her behind again. She now belonged to another man; after all the years of loving her and living with her this still hurt. He tried sometimes to talk it over with Mary but, while sympathetic, she could not quite understand the depth of his feeling. Mary had always devoted her whole life to him, he knew that. He, though devoted to Mary, was also equally devoted to his daughter. As he stood surrounded and a little swamped by the beauty of the Tuscan countryside, he couldn't help wishing that Anna would come home with her husband and the twins. He put his arm across his wife's shoulders and gave her a hug. 'Let's go in and see what Anna has for us for breakfast.'

Lisa had laid large, green-speckled plates on the long dining table on the loggia. Across the valley, the signs of winter were unmistakable. There were gaps like missing teeth among the trees where the leaves had already fallen, and in the distance guns could be heard firing at random.

Mario came in from the fields and joined them. 'Anna should be down in a minute,' he said, smiling at his parents-in-law.

'How well you look, Mario.' Mary sat down beside him on a severely carved armchair. 'Marriage must agree with you.'

'It does.' Mario's eyes shone and Mary, watching him, thought how lucky Anna was to have such a handsome and attentive young husband.

Fosca arrived, frowning. 'I've just been checking the bed linen and we are four sheets short. I do hope that awful family at the bottom of the drive hasn't been stealing again. Mario, what can we do about them? Tommaso says they've been stealing the sheep as well.'

'Not much, Fosca. They're very vicious and will make trouble for us, I think. All we can do is to tie one of the dogs up by the washing line and try and move the sheep to a higher pasture.'

'I'm so sorry,' Fosca apologized. 'I don't mean to sound rude, but it's all so difficult now. Everyone talks as if there will be no war in Italy. But there is a sort of war already, with people taking advantage of the situation, stealing and looting, knowing that the country is in such an uproar nothing will be done to stop them. Pouf!' She sank into a seat beside Mary. 'Where is sleepy-head?'

'Right here.' Anna wandered in, dressed in a long, pale blue dressing-gown. 'I'm afraid I've given myself the licence to be a slob all during my pregnancy. I guess if I'm to have two babies I'm not going to have a moment's peace ever again. So I might as well make up for it now.' She bent down to kiss her mother and her father. 'I'm taking you to San Gimignano for *pranzo* so don't eat too much *colazione*. There . . . that's it: all the Italian I know.'

'That's not true, darling,' Mario said. 'You understand well now, though you never seem to have to speak Italian. You seem to have the knack of speaking in tongues. It's amazing really. When I take her to the markets she asks for whatever she wants. She chats about everything under the sun and they all seem to understand her. Her Aunt Martha always said she was a creature of light, and it is the light around her that draws people to her like a moth to a flame.'

Anna blushed. 'Well I don't feel too much like a light today. More like a blippy toad. You know, Mario, one of those speckly toads we see shouting in the frog pond.'

'Yes, I know what you mean. I wish I could come with you to San Gimignano. It's one of my favourite towns. It was built in the twelfth and thirteenth centuries and now has thirteen surviving towers out of the original seventy. Anna and I have a favourite restaurant there, don't we, darling?'

Anna wrinkled her nose at him. 'Yes, and if I take them there I'll eat lots and lots of pasta. Can't you come, darling?'

'No.' Mario shook his head decisively. 'I really must

313

finish the harvesting, and then I have a hundred sheep to milk. Tommaso is finishing off the top of the hill and then the grape picking starts tomorrow.'

'Grape picking.' Daniel was enthused. 'That sounds wonderful. Can we give you a hand?'

'Sure thing. All the villagers are coming in tomorrow, and we'll pick until it's all harvested. Then we'll take the grapes across to a neighbour. He has the very latest crushing machine, so you won't have to dance on the grapes this year.' Mario grinned. 'I remember when we all climbed into the vats with our trousers rolled up. It took ages for the stain to come off my feet and the smell of the skins to leave my clothes. When people go on about "the good old days", I remind them that there was not much good about those days. Now we have hot water and electric light and, above all, a telephone.'

Lisa interrupted him, carrying a huge platter of cut meats and raw sausages, and a flat rush basket full of bread. Behind her, one of the workers' children brought a flagon of wine.

'Working farmer's breakfast,' Mario explained. 'I get up at five with Tommaso and we go into the fields after a coffee. Then at nine we come back and eat a big meal.' He grinned. 'I tell you, in the cold winter months I need a big meal. I'd forgotten just how cold a Tuscan winter can be.' He slit a sausage and squeezed the meat out on a chunk of bread, snorting with pleasure.

'Is raw sausage all right for you, Mary?'

'I'll give mine to Danny. He can eat any amount of meat even if he's only just gotten out of bed. Can I just have coffee?'

Lisa came back carrying the coffee pot on a tray. Anna went over to the window and brought back to the table a wide bowl of fruit. 'Here, Mom, try the oranges. They're home-grown and taste delicious. No way can I eat meat first thing in the morning. I just take coffee.' She breathed deeply as Lisa poured her a cup. 'This is such wonderful stuff, Mom. I can't even remember what American coffee tastes like.'

'Not as strong as this, Anna. I'll be up all night.'

'No you won't. I found it amazing when I first arrived. For the first few days I awoke at daylight because all the animals were screaming and yelling. Who on earth said that the Italian countryside was peaceful? Then I slept for ages and ages. I thought I had sleeping sickness. Now,' she grinned, 'I sleep like a baby. And when I wake up in the morning I am thrilled to see the sky. I can't imagine living without the blue of a Tuscan sky. Odd, isn't it? I do miss New York and I very much miss Mary Rose. She wants to be godmother to the twins. What do you think? She says if anything happens to us they can go and live with her. That's what godmothers are for. I know nothing will happen to us, but it is sweet of her to offer. She promises to be a really wicked fairy godmother, a little like Aunt Kitty. She asks after both Kitty and Martha.'

'And they both asked after her,' Mary said. 'I hope she's happy, but there is no way of knowing with Mary Rose. Aunt Kitty is getting a little wobbly on her legs, but Joe looks after her so well. And Martha? Well, she misses you terribly. She is working as a volunteer in an old people's home. She seems happy and we all get together regularly and talk about the old times. The times when we first arrived in New York and survived that awful first hovel, with Father O'Brian popping in, and all of us squashed like the cockroaches that scuttled around the floor. Do you remember when you first met Steven?'

'Yes I do. And I was so happy he was my first friend.'

Fosca leaned forward. 'I got a letter from him the other day. He's doing very well. He's working for his father and is engaged to be married to a next-door neighbour's daughter. He sounds happy and content.'

Anna made a face. 'I don't think he's happy or content. I think he's just taking the easy way out.' Anna knew how much that letter had hurt Fosca. For months now there had been a flow of letters between Steven and Fosca, but Anna knew that Steven was far too frightened of his mother to look at anyone not chosen by the family.

She shrugged. 'Pity,' she said. 'He could have done so well for himself.' There was a moment's silence, almost a moment of mourning for a boy, and now man, who had been so much a part of their lives and now was gone. On the hill in Anna's heart was a small cross with Steven's name on it.

Fifty-Eight

Anna stopped the car on the brow of a hill leading into the town of San Gimignano. Ahead of them they could see the slender, majestic towers. 'Looks like a mini Manhattan,' Daniel joked.

Anna grinned. 'I'm glad you're alive to see them. It was diplomatic of you not to say anything about my driving. I've learned Italian style – point and shoot. I noticed your knuckles were a bit white. You must be worn out braking.'

'Yeah, well, I never could stand to be driven. Your mother is now the only person I allow to drive my car, apart from my chauffeurs. Look at that skyline, Mary. I want to pinch myself. I feel like I'm inside an Italian painting.'

'That's how I felt when I first came out here,' Anna

said. 'I know the fall in Boston is beautiful, and I remember the time we went to Long Island to see the trees. But somehow this is all so much more vibrant. I can't really explain it ... it sort of shimmers inside me. Come on, let's go. I'll show you a most beautiful courtyard.'

Daniel sat in a jewel of an arched courtyard with his eyes closed, listening to a flautist playing Mozart. Beside him he could feel Mary drinking in the notes. The three of them were sitting on an ancient, carved stone bench. There were no other people present, just the flautist who seemed to be playing only for himself. Although he had a music book open beside him, his eyes were closed as he played, and he swayed with the lilting notes. To Anna, he and the music were one. The notes embraced the old arches gently, trickling down and around the flagstones. For a moment the courtyard was the music and the music was the courtyard. Mozart's secure and confident expression held them all spellbound.

When he stopped playing, Anna saw his earthly figure re-emerge from the stonework. She smiled at him. Shyly, as if he'd been caught playing truant, he smiled back.

'Who are you to be playing so beautifully?' she found herself asking.

'My name is Claude,' he said simply.

'Do you live here, or are you studying here?' Anna couldn't hold back her curiosity.

'No, I'm just travelling. I come here to play for the tourists, but because the season is over, I must get back to Switzerland. I'm studying there. But I love Tuscany so much, I want to stay as long as I can. I have about a month left ... if I can find a place to live.'

His expression was so full of gentle passion that Anna's heart immediately went out to him. Once again she fell victim to her spontaneous compassion in which calculated reason had no place.

'Come home with us. We have a farm with plenty of room. And if you're prepared to help with some of the chores, I know my husband would be delighted to have you.' She turned to her parents who were standing close by. 'Don't you think?'

Daniel and Mary introduced themselves. Daniel laughed. 'That's just like my daughter. She'd invite the whole world to come and live with her. She's right, though, they have a big place and both of them love music. You'd be welcome, there's no doubt.'

Claude laughed. 'Are you serious? Although I suppose I shouldn't be surprised: Italians are the most hospitable people on earth. Well, if you're sure, I can go and get my few things together and meet you somewhere in half an hour.'

Anna looked pleased. 'Do you know the Bel Soggiorno restaurant half-way down the hill?'

Claude nodded and grinned knowingly. 'Sure I know it, at least from the outside. I've never eaten there. It's somewhat out of my economic range.'

'My treat.' Daniel was in an expansive mood. 'I can drink as much wine as I like because my daughter's doing the driving. Come to think about it, I'll probably need all the wine I can drink to cope with her antics behind the wheel!'

'Offer humbly accepted,' Claude said, waving a long, slim hand as he headed into a small medieval alley.

Anna and her parents lingered a while in the piazza. 'He'll be good company for Fosca,' Anna said, grinning slightly, knowing what her mother's reaction would be.

'You never change, Anna. Matchmaking again.'

'Maybe,' she replied. 'I must admit I do feel a little guilty when Mario and I are so much in love and Fosca is so alone. Claude may be good for her and help her get over the hurt of Steven.' She grinned. 'Besides, I'd like my twins to have their own personal musician and listen to Mozart even before they are born.'

Anna was a little nervous as they approached the house. She knew Mario wouldn't mind her bringing someone home, but she was not so sure about his parents. Elisabetta and Francesco were kind and gentle, but she already realized that in Italy the family and its members could live together in all sorts of combinations. However, they rarely invited *stranieri*, or foreigners, to join them. And Claude, with his willowy walk and rather long blond hair, was definitely a *straniero*. From his right earlobe a gold ring dangled, and on his wrist he wore a flashing topaz ring.

All the way back in the car he had chatted quite happily with Daniel and Mary. In the back of the car was a guitar and a flute; all his other worldly possessions seemed to be crammed into a small leather satchel. Anna looked at his slanting green eyes and was glad Mary Rose was not here; he wouldn't have lasted five minutes. Anyway, she had earmarked him for Fosca. Even if Fosca didn't fall for him, at least he could amuse her with his music.

Now, with the rumours and threats of war abounding, the radio rarely broadcast classical concerts. She was more likely to hear Hitler screaming and ranting or hear Il Duce promising that Italy would never go to war. 'Don't worry, my children, I am as a father to you. I give you my word.' Everybody seemed to believe him, but not Francesco, who often looked meaningfully at his wife. She would shake her dark head in what Anna took to be sorrow. Anna could follow most of the conversations by now if the family and the farm-workers spoke slowly to her. But when the talk rippled around the table like waves on the shore she was lost.

'This is Claude.' Anna, overcome with sudden shyness,

introduced him to Mario. 'We met him playing the flute so beautifully. He needs somewhere to live so I invited him to stay with us and help on the farm.'

Mario made a face, then his eyes twinkled with laughter. 'I see you have been adopted by my wife. Welcome. We could do with some good music about the house. Let's go and introduce you to my parents. They're on the loggia.'

Anna heard the sound of running footsteps. Fosca came bounding down the stairs to the car. 'I'm so glad you're back, Anna. I just took a phone call from Mary Rose. She is booking a trunk call for six o'clock.' She paused and gazed at Claude in astonishment.

'This is Claude. He is going to stay with us for a while. I decided the twins need a resident musician so he can play his flute and his guitar and help Mario in the fields.' Privately, Anna didn't think Claude looked quite the type to sweat it out in the fields. But then at least Fosca would have some company.

'Ciao.' Fosca put out her small hand.

Claude grinned. 'You didn't tell me you had such a pretty sister-in-law, Anna.'

'I was keeping her as a surprise for you.' Claude laughed.

After dinner that night, Francesco asked Claude to play his flute. As he left the room to collect the instrument, Anna relaxed. She knew that once everybody heard him play they would be glad that he was with them. She leaned back against her chair in the drawing room and watched the flames leaping in the grate. She was sure she could feel movement in her womb. When Claude put his flute to his lips she heard a gasp of astonishment as the high, pure notes filled the room. Francesco and Elisabetta leaned slightly towards each other as they listened to Mozart's music. Mario took Anna's hand and then let it fall gently on to her stomach.

While Claude played, he watched every move Fosca made. I made the right choice, Anna thought.

Then she wondered how Mary Rose was really feeling. The telephone call had been a series of crackles and blips, though she had managed to reply to Mary Rose's request to be godmother. 'I'd love that, and so would Mario,' Anna had screamed.

Now, listening to the peace and the quiet in the house, she felt a certain sadness creep over her, as if she could not believe that life could continue to be this happy. Outside, the cold night settled in, and inside the fire warmed her legs. The music came to an end and she stood up to thank Claude. She saw tears in his eyes.

'What's the matter?' she asked.

'I'm so grateful for your hospitality,' he replied, a little embarrassed. 'I feel happy here with all of you and I want you to know how grateful I am.'

'You don't have to be grateful.' Elisabetta stood up and then put her arms around him. 'With a talent like yours you will never be short of friendship, particularly ours.' She kissed him gently on both cheeks.

Something awful has happened to him and he is running away, Anna thought. She was determined to find out what had happened in his life to cause him so much pain.

That night, Anna tossed and turned during a terrible storm. She was not yet used to the frightful howls and shrieks of rage, when the wind bent the trees to the ground and great bolts of lightning split the earth around the house. Usually she held on to Mario and shook with the fear. But this was a dream that refused to let her wake up. She felt as if she were being drawn inexorably into the maw of something evil. Whatever the monster was it had her leg and was pulling her away from all those people who loved her. Behind the feeling of being drawn into a hole which was black and furry with evil, was the sound of men ranting. She half managed to wake up, but was so firmly held by the nightmare that, although she knew she was dreaming, she couldn't escape.

'It's all right, Anna, I'm here.' Mario kissed her gently on the neck. She clung to him.

'Don't ever leave me, Mario. Promise you'll never leave me.'

'You know I'd die rather than ever leave you, Anna, you know that. You are my world and I love you more than anything else.' He smiled down at her. She was asleep, carrying his babies. Mario didn't know when he had been so happy.

Fifty-Nine

Mary Rose was comforted by the happiness she heard in Anna's voice. She did not envy her her happiness because she knew she would find Anna's life suffocatingly boring. Still, she did envy her her pregnancy and, try as she did to get pregnant each month, it was a constant disappointment. She didn't actually want a child to take care of, rather one to secure her position within Crispin's family. Mary Rose felt the conflict in the Kearney family very keenly. She tried to get her mother-in-law to like her, but very soon realized that it was money – or rather lack of money – that held the family together. Neither of the girls was ever going to like her, and Amelia only responded when she thought she saw the colour of money in Mary Rose's eyes, or on her lips. Now, helping Travis, Mary Rose was actually making money for herself. Her shopping trip with Mrs Gulbenkian paid handsomely and she was offered a trip to Hong Kong to help redecorate part of her new house.

'I really want to go, Crispin. I think it will be very good for my business.'

'You don't need to work, Mary Rose. What on earth is the matter with you? Maybe if you could get pregnant you might be less of a flibbertigibbet.'

'It takes two to get pregnant, Crispin, remember?'

'I know it's not my fault, Mary Rose.' Crispin's tone of voice carried a warning. Mary Rose drew back. It was not worth a whole evening of sulking.

'Anyway, I'm going,' she said, tossing her head as she walked out of the bedroom. 'Not only am I going, but I'm going to give Justin a ring in New York and see if he'll meet me there,' she muttered as she stomped down the hall.

The journey to Hong Kong was long and boring. Mary Rose hated the stop in Delhi. She was appalled at the poverty in the streets, and at the number of beggars. She picked up a young boy on his way to visit his parents in Macao. She enjoyed his open, earnest, wide-eyed innocence. She decided after the first few, hot hours in the Imperial Hotel in the middle of the city, that they would both be much better off in her big mosquito-netted bed enjoying each other making love rather than toiling about the usual tourist sights.

'Beats temples and mosques,' she remarked as he'd come for the third time that afternoon.

She lay beside him, thinking how much this moment would shock Anna, and then she grinned. How much of her life was spent shocking people in order to annoy them? Or did she really want to be in this room with this young boy? She decided before she rolled over for a long, sweaty sleep that she actually did like the boy, and tried to remind herself to remember his name. Robin, she muttered. After they woke up she planned to make love in the big deep bath, followed by a cold shower. Then they would have to climb back on to the hot, sweaty plane the next morning.

When the British aeroplane was poised to make its precipitous landing in Hong Kong, Mary Rose thought they were going to crash into the mountain that stood like an imperious finger pointing at the sky. Robin, sitting beside her, took her hand.

'We'll be all right,' he said, his voice cracking with the strain of reassuring Mary Rose.

She laughed. 'We'll have to say goodbye now, Robin. I don't think your mother will want to meet me!' She grinned at him good naturedly. 'Now you know what sex is all about, you can get addicted and chase all the pretty little Chinese girls you can find.'

'I don't want pretty little Chinese girls, I want you, Mary Rose.'

'Now don't be greedy. I'm much too old for you, and besides, I'm married.'

'To a no-good bastard.'

'How do you know that?' Mary Rose was surprised.

'Because happily married women don't pick up people like me. You don't love him, Mary Rose.'

The plane was nosing towards the runway. 'I do in a way, Robin. You're too young to understand some of the complications of relationships. You'll find out in time. My husband and I understand each other very well, and that in itself is a sort of miracle. I only know two couples who are happily married, and although I love them all, I would be bored to death in that kind of a relationship. You go and have a wonderful holiday in Macao and always remember this trip with affection.'

She shut her eyes as the plane hit the tarmac. 'Oh, ten out of ten for effort,' she said, smiling brightly at Robin. The plane taxied to a stop and the stewardess opened the doors to a hot, wet day. A uniformed member of the airport came into the first class cabin.

'I'm here to collect Mrs Kearney.' The official was a tall, good-looking Sikh with a white turban wrapped around his head.

'Suddenly I'm a VIP,' Mary Rose giggled. She brightly said goodbye to Robin, patted him quickly on the shoulder, and was gone.

Robin looked longingly at her empty seat. She's not really as happy as she thinks she is, he told himself. He had been a virgin, but even he could tell that Mary Rose's bastard of a husband was no good in bed. Still – he leaned back and stretched – there were worse ways of not seeing Delhi. She was right about the Chinese girls.

Mrs Gulbenkian sat in the back of her Rolls looking like a well-brought-up Pekinese. Mary Rose sat beside her gazing out at the swarm of humanity that pushed by the car. At times the chauffeur hung out of the window and cursed the passing pedestrians. 'Mothers of whores, shit-eaters.' The flow of his curses continued almost all the way out to Repulse Bay. The car turned into a huge driveway. The gates were held open by two uniformed Chinese boys. The car cruised up the driveway with a satisfying scrunch of pebbles.

Mary Rose winced when she saw the house. It was a Hollywood blancmange of a building. Hideously pink. 'What an unusual colour,' she said weakly, feeling obliged to say something.

'Do you like it? Oh goody.' Mrs Gulbenkian seemed to have learned her English by reading Angela Brazil novels. 'I became very chummy with a splendid American interior decorator. He's the best in Hong Kong. And, my dear, he actually lives quite openly with his boyfriend. If you know what I mean?' She raised her heavily painted eyebrows and tried to look archly at Mary Rose.

'Yes, I do know what you mean.' Mary Rose tried not

to giggle. 'I know exactly what you mean. But that shade of pink is a little bright, don't you think?'

'D'you think so, Mary Rose? I'll telephone him when we get in and see what he thinks.'

'No! Don't do that, Mrs Gulbenkian.' Mary Rose had horrid visions of being chased around Hong Kong by a furious homosexual. 'I think I'll get used to the colour. It just took me by surprise, that's all.'

The car drew up at the imposing mock castellated front porch. Mary Rose couldn't for the life of her think how she was going to fit an English country interior into such a dreadful mess of a building. Mrs Gulbenkian hurried past her into the brightly gilded hall and grabbed the telephone.

'My English interior decorator has just arrived and she doesn't like the colour of the house, George. I'll put her on to you, darling.' She held the telephone out to Mary Rose. A servant padded past with her luggage.

'And what the hell is wrong with the colour of Mrs Gulbenkian's house?' A shrill whine bored into Mary Rose's ear.

'I'm sure it's lovely. I'm just not used to such a bright pink. After a few days it will probably look absolutely divine.'

'I'm coming over right away. Mrs Gulbenkian is one of my best customers and I don't want her upset.'

'Please don't come over. I'm sure we can work something out. After all, I work for an American firm in London.'

'Which one?' The voice was slightly mollified.

'Travis Mainwaring.'

'Yes. I know his stuff. OK, I'll make a date with Mrs Gulbenkian to have a look at the stuff she has brought back with her from London. I expect it will be completely wrong for the house.'

'Yeah, you could say that. It is very, very English.'

'Well, it can join the stuff from Thailand and Persia and wherever Mrs G. has bought from. I guess we'll have a different country for every room in the place.'

'We could do that. Or we could scrap the lot and set fire to it all and start again.' Mary Rose was sure that Mrs Gulbenkian had left the hall.

'You sound as though you have a sense of humour. What part of America are you from?'

'New York.' Mary Rose found herself smiling. 'And I'm homesick for the place already.' Damn, why had she flown in Justin when this man sounded such fun? 'Tomorrow I'm collecting a friend from the airport. After I'll give you a ring and we can get together.'

'What kind of a friend?'

'The carnal kind of a friend.' She enjoyed George's whinny of a laugh.

'Great, I'll see you after you've entertained yourself.'

After an excellent dinner, Mrs Gulbenkian was in a reminiscent mood. 'And I said to my third husband . . . or wait a minute, it might have been my fourth.'

'You did get married rather a lot, didn't you, Mrs Gulbenkian?'

'Of course, dear. It was *comme il faut* to be married. Anyway, I inherited each time. My fifth husband said I just wore him out. Now I've given up sex I go shopping.'

'I can see that.' Mary Rose tried not to gaze at a particularly ugly brass tray standing on several spindly legs in the middle of the room. A pendulous trail of haemorrhoidal chandeliers cast a gloomy light. I'll worry about all this tomorrow, she thought. She was tired.

'I have a friend called Justin Villias arriving tomorrow morning, Mrs Gulbenkian.'

'Ah, I see. Your lover, I suppose? You modern women don't waste much time. I'll send the chauffeur for him. Do you want him to share your room?'

'He's going to stay at the Pen. At least that's where he is booked into.'

'Stuff and nonsense! He can stay here. That way you can entertain yourself at night and not waste time travelling between here and the hotel.'

'If you say so, Mrs Gulbenkian. I must go to bed. I'm afraid I'm very tired.'

'I don't know what you young people do. When I was your age I danced the night away.'

Mary Rose left Mrs Gulbenkian sitting by her empty fireplace. Well, I sort of danced the night away, she thought as she climbed into her high brass bed. Where the hell did Mrs Gulbenkian get her terrible taste? She turned off the light and fell instantly asleep.

Sixty

Anna now felt she was truly pregnant. The day she felt flutterings was the day she realized that the babies inside her were real. Although she knew in her head she was pregnant, her heart was still frozen in terror at the thought that she might either lose the babies, or that it might all be an illusion.

Saying goodbye to her parents had been hard. 'Don't worry, Mom, Mario and his parents will take good care of me. And Fosca is like a sister. Anyway, I always have Pilar, the witch, and her awful concoctions. She is famous for taking care of pregnant ladies.' She kissed Mary and noticed that her mother had fine lines under her eyes now, and that her face sagged a little under the chin.

Daniel pulled Anna into his arms and hugged her hard. 'You take care of yourself, little honeybunch. I do miss you so. After the two babies arrive, I hope you'll soon fill our house with the sound of them and your laughter.' There were tears in his eyes. He brushed them away with the back of his hand and turned to Elisabetta. 'I'll be glad to get back here, Elisabetta. Apart from New England, this is God's own country.'

Elisabetta beamed at this good-looking Irish man. 'We love it,' she said shyly. She remembered the conversation they had had the night before with Anna's parents and Mario that war seemed inevitable. They had decided to spare Anna the bad news.

'At the least sign of trouble, send the children to me.' Daniel had been adamant. 'America won't go to war, and at least you'll know that Anna, Fosca and the babies will be safe.' Mario had made his position quite clear; he would stay with his parents to fight the Germans.

Now, as Daniel and Mary climbed into Francesco's car for the last time, the little group standing on the steps of the villa felt bereft and stranded. Mario wondered anxiously if he shouldn't bundle Anna and his sister up now and make them return to America with Anna's parents. The moment passed and he watched the car drive out of sight. He put one arm around Anna and the other around Fosca.

'Come,' he said. 'I've just taken down a new round of pecorino and it is in need of tasting. I'll open a bottle of Barolo and we will drown our sorrows.'

Francesco and Elisabetta had withdrawn to their bedroom. Francesco realized that the conversation of the night before had upset his wife deeply. 'I couldn't bear to lose Anna and the babies, and Fosca once more,' she said. 'Oh, when will it all end?'

'I wish I knew.' Francesco's voice was laden with bitterness. 'Mussolini makes speeches, he tells lies, he encourages people to tattle on one another. The prisons are full of our people being tortured. The Communists are fighting against us. We are divided and there is no truth. No light on the situation. I am a man who needs truth like some men need strong drink.'

He pulled Elisabetta to him and gently began to remove her dress. Stroking her full breasts, he then kissed her nipples softly. Time had been gentle with her. She still had very soft, honey-coloured skin. Where so many of her women friends had succumbed to fleshy old age, Elisabetta's body was still fine and strong.

'You have such beautiful skin,' he said wonderingly as she lay stretched out on their bed naked.

She stretched out her arms. 'Come here, my darling, and I will take away your worries about the war.'

Francesco smiled at her. 'You have always taken away all my worries, darling.' He slid gently into her, glorying in her well-loved body.

Downstairs, Mario sliced the pecorino with a long thin cheese knife. It was a breathless moment for Tommaso and himself. They had worked long and hard on this batch of cheese, and upstairs in the loft, forty rounded cheeses of differing sizes were laid side by side on shelves. For months they had moved the cheeses around every day to see that they received fresh air. The final operation after they had been carried up to the loft was to ensure that every one had been given a crusting of black pepper.

Mario was rightly proud of his cheeses. They sold all over the nearby villages and as far away as Pienza. Indeed, this batch would mostly sell at Christmas time. He cut a sliver of the cheese and poured a glass of the wine. He gently pared off the rind and took a bite. He handed another sliver to Tommaso. 'Try it. I think it's good this year.' A confident smile hovered around his lips.

Tommaso took the cheese between his thick, gnarled fingers. He smelled it and then he too bit. He grinned.

'It is good, signore, it's very good. I think it's the best we've done this year. Your father is good with cheese, but you, you are a maestro.' He sipped a little of the wine from his glass. 'A very fine wine.' Both men stood quietly in the kitchen, savouring the months of effort that had gone into the cheese.

'Do we get anything to eat or to drink?' Fosca laughed. 'You men, you are in love with your wines and your cheeses. What about ladies first?'

The post came late that day. Anna picked up a blue overseas airmail letter and saw that it was from Ralph. He was writing to say that he was in the Royal Horse Guards and had army business in Rome. He asked if he could come and visit for a long weekend. The letter had taken a while to arrive, and Anna realized that he was expecting to be there in two days' time. She called Lisa and gave her instructions to prepare a spare bedroom.

As she flitted about the big stone house, Anna was glad she had married an Italian man. She enjoyed living so closely within a big family. It reminded her of her days with her aunts, her grandmother and Father O'Brian. Life in America was losing the old tight family traditions. For the many years before Mario and Fosca joined her family, there had just been her two parents and herself. Now, she enjoyed the wider circle of her in-laws and the people that worked on the property. She recalled mentioning Pilar to her mother this morning, and the thought made her aware of just how much the old woman reassured and comforted her. She took off her pinafore and took the path to her cottage. 'Signora,' she panted as she got there. 'I have feelings in my stomach.' She made a circling motion with her hand. 'I can feel my babies move.'

Pilar grunted from her place by the fire. She got to her feet in jerks and starts and then shuffled into the sunlight in the doorway. She extended her knobbly, arthritic hand and touched Anna's belly lightly. Her head bobbed up and down with delight. '*Bene, bene. Lei avra due bambini. Un maschio e una femmina bellissimi.*'

'A girl and a boy.' Anna was delighted.

Pilar nodded and pulled her inside. The old woman's cottage always amazed Anna. In a world where all women gave their lives to their homes and their families, Pilar stubbornly resisted any attempts to conform. The little cottage was filthy. The chairs and the tables were dilapidated. After she had first visited Pilar, Anna had begged Mario to send some workmen in to paint the place and to deliver new furniture and a bed. But Mario wouldn't hear of it. 'You must remember you are American, and Americans interfere with everything. Nobody would dare tell Pilar what to do. She'd cast the evil eye on them.' He had laughed self-consciously then had crossed himself. 'You have no idea how powerful Pilar is. She is known and loved everywhere, but if you cross her . . .' He had shuddered.

Now, watching Pilar shuffling around the cottage, Anna remembered his words. She could hear the sound of cheeping under the woman's unmade bed.

'*SederLa,*' Pilar commanded, and pushed Anna down into a three-legged chair. She took an old green wine bottle from a dusty shelf and blew the cobwebs and the dust from it. Her breath was raw with onions and garlic. She handed Anna a filthy cup. The old woman stood over her, watching carefully while Anna gingerly drank the brew. It wasn't as bad or as bitter as the other cup she had had when she first visited Pilar's cottage. The woman pulled down her left eyelid and then grunted. She reached under her bed, scattering chicks like ping-pong balls all over the cottage. From the end of the bed, a black and white cat glared at Anna. Pilar pulled a handful of ferns from under the bed and handed them to her.

'*Prendere!*' she commanded. Anna took the foliage,

understanding that she should make an infusion with it. In her still rudimentary Italian, she thanked the old woman.

She wished her Italian was better, but the pregnancy had made her brains turn to caffellatte, the coffee mixed with milk that she now drank instead of the thick, dark black coffee that she loved. Lisa had absolutely forbidden her to drink coffee without milk until the babies were born.

Anna returned to the house dreaming of her babies, and went to find Mario to tell him they were going to have a girl and a boy. Mario, his expressive eyes full of joy, kissed her hard. 'That's marvellous,' he said, hoping that by the time they were born, the war would have receded. He very much doubted it.

Sixty-One

Mary Rose found shopping in Hong Kong an electrifying experience. She collected Justin from the airport. He was put out at having to give up his reservation at the Peninsular hotel.

'I don't want to stay with some boring old bag in a mansion,' he said playfully.

'She is not a boring old bag. Mrs Gulbenkian is one of my most important customers, and if she says you stay with her, you stay with her, Justin.'

'Since when did you do as you were told, Mary Rose?' he smiled.

'Since I started making lots of money. Now shut up and let's go and get some clothes for Anna's new babies.' They wandered down Nathan Road into a shop that was piled high with beautiful baby clothes. Mary Rose leaned over the tiny, delicate garments and inspected them with care. Only the best for her godchildren, she thought.

'Look at this, Justin. Isn't it beautiful?' She held a tiny embroidered vest up for him to inspect.

'Mary Rose, men find baby clothes boring, don't you know that?'

'Huh! You aren't bored trying to make babies.'

'Don't be gross.'

Mary Rose grinned. 'I like being gross and being in such a foul mood. I didn't bring Crispin because I won't put up with his boring crap. And I won't put up with yours. Either lighten up or fuck off!'

Justin could see the expression on Mary Rose's face: he didn't want to end up in Hong Kong on his own. His mood turned heavy. 'OK, OK. But can't we just buy the bloody clothes and then go and have some lunch?'

'Sure.' After another half an hour they left the shop with two large shopping bags. Justin resented having to carry bags advertising a fat baby with only a hat on its head.

'Bloody Chinese. Why does the brat have to have its willie hanging out?' he grumbled. The bags completely destroyed his cool image. Mary Rose laughed at him. They walked to the end of Nathan Road.

'This looks like a good restaurant.' Mary Rose pushed open the door and they were greeted with a blast of icy air. 'Whew, that feels better.' Justin handed the bulging bags with relief to a waiter. They were led to a small table.

Mary Rose picked up the menu. 'The jumbo prawns look good, and I love black-eyed pea soup.'

After half an hour of solid eating, Justin was a happy man once again. 'Ah . . .' He pushed back his chair and spread out his legs. 'That's better. Now we can go back to the house and go to bed.'

'You can. I can't. I'm off to Cat Street with Mrs

Gulbenkian to collect some decent antiques. She has the most terrible taste and much more money than sense.'

Justin was indignant. 'You . . . I've flown all this way to make love to you and you're going out shopping.'

Mary Rose smiled. 'I'm a working girl now, darling.' She stood up and smiled down at him. 'I'm off to powder my nose. You pay the bill.'

She grinned at herself in the bathroom mirror. I much prefer this life, she thought. Being married is really very boring. She was surprised at just how little she missed Crispin. Her face was flushed from the wine she had been drinking, and she felt an electric buzz of anticipation at the thought of making love with Justin. He was a much better lover than Crispin, and she was looking forward to some creative sex with him tonight. Keeping him waiting would make the experience all the better for both of them. Besides, she was looking forward to shopping with Mrs Gulbenkian.

They were in yet another antique emporium, and Mrs Gulbenkian was veering steadily towards still more brass trays. Mary Rose managed to head her off.

'Mrs Gulbenkian,' she said with an edge to her voice. 'You've bought all this stuff from England and it just doesn't go with Indian brass. No, I really don't think an elephant's foot is a good idea at all.' She could see Mrs Gulbenkian's raisin-black eyes surveying her coolly. For a moment Mary Rose thought she had blown it.

'All right.' Mrs Gulbenkian suddenly smiled. 'Let's go home. I'll leave the decorating to you and George. He should be there by the time we get back.'

'Deal,' Mary Rose said hurriedly. 'Here, let's take those wonderful alabaster vases and leave. I could do with a hot cup of tea.'

George was waiting when they got back. The scowl on his face was thunderous. 'I've been looking at the stuff you bought in England, Mrs G.,' he said with an easy familiarity. 'I can't see where it is going to fit in.'

Mrs Gulbenkian looked hopefully at Mary Rose. 'Ah, I was thinking in the back loggia. I was going to make an English country-style area. So far the effects are all so mixed I think I need a clear space for myself.'

George looked unconvinced. 'Maybe you and I could go somewhere quiet and discuss it.' Mary Rose realized that George was a past master at manipulating rich old ladies.

The potential conflict between Mary Rose and George made Mrs Gulbenkian decidedly uneasy. 'Why don't the two of you sort it out between yourselves? I'll entertain your friend Justin, Mary Rose. I met him for a few minutes before he went off to sleep off the jet-lag. A nice man, yes indeed he is.' She then strode purposefully up the stairs, leaving Mary Rose in the vast hall looking imploringly at George.

'Look,' she said. 'We don't have to fight over this. I am perfectly happy to stick to the loggia and leave you the rest of the house. She's a good client and I don't want to lose her.'

George stood in front of her. He was a chunky young man with a straight-edged moustache. He frowned, and then his face relaxed. 'We can try,' he said. 'Business is hard in this town. There are lots of rich old women, but Mrs G. takes the cookie when it comes to finding stuff. It's just like her to turn up with a pile of old Chesterfields and English curtains and expect it all to fit into the Hollywood-type decor she has demanded. It's nearly killed me doing this house. She has so much energy and so little to do all day. I feel as if I'm married to her. She hits the telephone whenever she feels like it, and she seems to have her best ideas at five o'clock in the morning. I'm exhausted. My partner works in the Hong Kong and

Shanghai Bank and he's pissed off with the whole deal.'

Mary Rose grinned at him. 'Then maybe I can take some of the strain off you. I'm here for a fortnight, so you can have a break. I'll keep her busy for you.' She put out her hand. 'I'm willing to be friends if you are. OK?'

'OK.' George had a nice smile and his blue eyes danced. 'You make your little England. Come to my party tomorrow night and meet Jonathan and my friends. Mrs Gulbenkian's friends are all too serious. I prefer to party hearty.'

'So do I.'

'Tomorrow night at my place then. I'm right at the top of the Peak. Mrs G. knows where. I'll ask her if she wants to come as well.'

Justin had been less than happy. 'You seemed to be getting on well with that decorator you were talking to this afternoon. I could hear you laughing from my bedroom.'

He was in a disgruntled mood. He liked his bedroom, but he had to wait until after one o'clock to get his hands on Mary Rose. Even then she had come very quickly, before he had, and had then fallen asleep.

Damn her, he thought as he looked at her lying contentedly, replete, by his side. That's bloody rude of her. But then he remembered he always enjoyed the way Mary Rose straightforwardly took her sexual favours. He sat up on the edge of the bed and stared out at the sea. The waves were rolling in on the beach. He stretched and walked to the window. Outside, the palm trees rustled in the wind and the night lay before him. For a moment he felt a pang of loneliness. Why did he not have a wife and family like all his other friends? He sighed. All those things he could have, but he knew he would never be faithful to one woman. It was far better

to be free to take an aeroplane anywhere in the world
to meet beautiful women like Mary Rose. She stirred in
the bed. He went back and gently shook her shoulder.

'I haven't come yet, remember, darling,' he said
tenderly.

She stirred, irritated. 'Fuck off, Crispin. I'm tired.'

Justin lay down again and wondered if this trip was
going to be worthwhile.

Sixty-Two

Ralph arrived, and at first Anna thought he seemed very
nervous. She tried her hardest to put him at ease, but the
particular circumstances made it difficult.

'Because I am pregnant I'm afraid I can't ride. But
Mario can take you out – if you can persuade him.
Unfortunately he's so busy he doesn't have much time
for the horses. They are mostly in the high pasture and
don't come down until the winter.'

Ralph thought she looked wonderful pregnant. Her
belly was beautifully swollen and she moved gracefully
to compensate for the weight. Most women embarrassed
him when they were pregnant, but not Anna. He thought
she looked more beautiful than ever. Why, he wondered,
did his heart break a little when he saw her gazing at
Mario with such adoration? There had been a time when
he could have asked her to marry him. Now she was
totally absorbed in this one great love of her life. He
had always known that Anna would be fiercely faithful
to whomever she married.

'He's a lucky chap that Mario of yours,' he said gruffly
as Anna led him to the door of his room.

'And I'm the luckiest woman in the world. The threat

of war did something good for both of us: without it we would never have met.' The once possible alternative hung between them. Anna smiled. 'Well . . .' She backed away from Ralph, who was still in his army uniform. 'We will all meet for dinner with the family at nine. Do you wish to change?'

Ralph would have liked to explore the issue further. But he realized it was futile. 'I do indeed. The journey was long and hair-raising. The roads were crowded with people fleeing. Don't you worry about the war, Anna?'

'No, not really. I suppose we are so cut off here in Asciano. There were Germans about, but they all left a while ago. I think we've all just tried to forget about it. Right now it is the really busy season of the year. The men are all rushing about getting in the harvest, and the women are in the kitchen bottling the fruit and vegetables for the winter. No sooner is that all over than we begin the olive harvest.

'Around Christmas the pigs are killed and I get to learn how to cure the salamis and the hams. I am really looking forward to learning how to make prosciutto. When I can do that I'll feel really Italian.' She sighed.

Ralph let her go. It didn't seem the right time to ask her if she was homesick for New York. The life of an Italian housewife was hard and she had come from a very luxurious background. Still, he reminded himself as he took off his uniform, she looks very good for it. He resolved to talk to Mario's parents about the war. Relaxing in a long, drawn-out bath, he remembered those lovely months when he did nothing but squire Anna around Dorset and Devon.

Ralph awoke next morning to the cacophony of the farmyard. At the breakfast table later that morning he sat looking at Anna, so prettily pregnant. He laughed. 'I now know what you mean when you wrote that you never knew the country could be so noisy. What is it about Italian animals? I've never heard such a din.'

Mario came in for his breakfast, having already toiled in the fields for three hours. 'Do you want a ride this morning, Ralph?'

'No thanks, Mario. You're far too busy, and besides, I think I'd just prefer to potter about with Anna.' He smiled at her. 'I get rather a lot of riding with the regiment, so if you don't mind, I'll spend some time on my own feet. I so rarely get to Italy. I do love it.' He didn't add that he was afraid he would not be seeing it for a long time once war was declared. He would doubtless be locked away in the basement of the War Office, working alongside his commander, Winston Churchill. For Ralph this was a tragedy: he wanted to be where the action was.

The weekend passed quite quickly for Anna. She had forgotten what good company Ralph was. They fed the chickens. He helped her hang out the sheets and the blankets and, now that the nights were colder, add extra blankets to the beds in the house.

Lisa liked him, and so did Tommaso. Anna realized that she had been quite lonely for someone who spoke English. Two days only partially satisfied her, and she was sorry when it was time for Ralph to leave.

When she said goodbye to him she clung for a moment. 'I'm just a silly, pregnant lady,' she said. 'Really, I'm fine. I just miss my mother and father a lot. But I'll get to see them soon.'

Before he left, Ralph took Mario aside. 'If I hear anything definite I'll ring you. I probably won't get through the censors, but if I say "the balloon is up", it means you must get the women out of here.'

Mario stood in the hallway looking at Ralph directly. 'You think it's going to get serious soon?'

'I know it's going to get serious soon, Mario. And I want Anna safe. She's very important to me.'

'And to all of us.' Mario's dark eyes were full of concern. 'Thank you, Ralph. I hope you will never have to make that call.'

'I hope so too.' Ralph farewelled both Elisabetta and Francesco.

'Goodbye all,' he said, and was gone.

Sixty-Three

The babies were born without major difficulty. Anna was surprised. When she had paid her usual visit to Pilar, she had asked in her halting Italian when they would be born. Pilar had told her on the full moon. Everybody had been alerted for the great event.

Lisa was midwife and she very firmly sent Mario away. 'None of your new-fangled notions,' she shouted at him. He stood in the doorway looking terrified.

'I'll be all right, Mario, really I will. We'll call you as soon as they are born. I think Lisa is right. Your mother will be with me. You take your father off into the village for a drink. I'll be fine. I'm as healthy as a horse. Go on.'

Once Mario had left the room, for a horrid moment Anna felt like panicking. Beside her bed she had a big jug of raspberry tea which would control any bleeding. Lisa tied a sheet to the bottom of the bed and smiled.

'When I tell you, take the end of this sheet and pull hard.' Anna nodded. They had been practising the birthing for many weeks.

Elisabetta arrived carrying fresh sheets and a lavender

341

pillow. 'I made this for you to lie on. The smell of the lavender is so soothing I think.'

There had been moments during her pregnancy when Anna had wondered if she would not have been safer in America. But then, even if her father had put her in a private hospital, she would have been among strangers. Here she was surrounded by her family and people who loved her. And Pilar and Lisa were famous throughout Asciano for their midwifery, and so far they had never lost a baby through any fault of their own.

After twelve hours, Anna was getting tired. Mario had been up and down the stairs countless times. Anna felt a change in the rolling intensity of the contractions. She began to panic. 'Mario!' she shouted. 'Mario!' She could hear him come flying up the stairs.

'What is it, Anna?' He ran into the room, pushing his way past Lisa.

'I need you here. Please don't leave me.' Mario threw his strong arms around her.

'I won't leave you,' he promised her. 'I'm staying, Lisa, and I'm not going away.' His voice was firm and decisive.

Lisa smiled. 'As you wish, but now we will have to work hard.' She put her hand on Anna's stomach. 'Now take a deep breath in between the contractions. And then when you feel the urge to push, bear down.'

Not long afterwards, both babies were born. Anna, lying in Mario's arms, was covered in sweat, but she felt wonderful. Elisabetta held the first-born child and Lisa the second-born.

'A girl and a boy, just as Pilar predicted,' Anna said happily. 'What shall we call them, Mario?'

'You choose, Anna. We've been playing with names for months.'

'Of all the names we've talked about, I think Giulio and Nicoletta are the nicest.'

'Why don't you wait until you get to know them both,' Elisabetta said. She kissed Anna's sweaty forehead. 'Mario, you go and open the champagne with your father. We'll clean Anna up and then you can bring Francesco up to see his grandchildren.' Both babies were bawling loudly. 'They've inherited their grandfather's great voice.' She gently washed Anna's face with a perfumed face flannel.

Anna, now holding a baby in each arm, felt radiant. 'Both perfect little babies,' she whispered, kissing the tops of the two wispy heads. 'Our own little babies.' She heard the sound of a sudden shout of laughter downstairs, then the champagne cork exploded. Then she realized she was very, very tired.

Shortly after, sipping the glass of champagne, she felt the urge for a cup of tea. But the sight of Mario and his father beaming at her over a silver tray filled with beautiful glasses and freshly made cakes, made her realize that she could not disappoint them both.

'I know how you feel.' Elisabetta smiled down at her. 'All I wanted was a hot cup of coffee. But still, all went well.'

'Could you tell Pilar that they are both perfect, Lisa?' Anna said sleepily, her eyes heavy. 'And that she was right in predicting a boy and a girl. Tell her I'll bring them for her to see as soon as I can get out of bed. And Lisa, really thank her for me, will you?'

Lisa hurried down the path. It was past midnight but she knew Pilar would be waiting for the news.

'All went well,' she reported to the old woman. Pilar's face broke into a smile.

'Good, I knew it would.'

Lisa could see that Pilar had a bowl of water on the table in front of her. 'I was looking into the water, Lisa, and war will be declared in the next few months. I can see it.'

Lisa was unwilling to be drawn into such a pessimistic discussion, but she dutifully leaned over the bowl. Although she could see nothing, she felt uncomfortable: Pilar was never wrong.

'Maybe it will not happen,' she whispered hopefully.

'It will, it will. And the world will never be the same again.'

Lisa crossed herself, then hurried back up the path. When she got to Anna's room, Anna was fast asleep with both babies in cots on either side of the bed. Lisa looked down on Anna's fair, golden hair and her long silky eyelashes. 'May God be good to her and her little ones,' she prayed.

The babies were christened in December, just before Christmas. Anna's parents were unable to come. Her father had had a slight stroke and the doctors recommended that he not travel.

Mary's voice was tense on the telephone. 'He's all right, Anna. We're both dreadfully disappointed, but it would be unwise for him to travel at the moment. Fortunately I haven't yet booked the flight. Darling, are you all right? The newspapers here make the war sound so imminent.'

'We're fine, Mom. And Mary Rose will be over for the christening at the end of the week, so I'm getting things ready for her. She's bringing Crispin, which makes her miserable. I'm worried about them both. She doesn't seem too happy with him. But I'm glad she is going to be godmother. Claude is standing in for Ralph who is in the Far East. He's written to say that he is getting married. I must say it was quite a shock. I've always sort of thought of Ralph as mine.'

Anna laughed. She knew she sounded ridiculous. 'Anyway, it will be marvellous to have Mary Rose here. Mario is decanting his best wine and bringing out a prosciutto. I am furiously piling up potatoes. The tobacco harvest is in and we got a good price for it. Now we have to slaughter the pigs, and then it will be Christmas. Do you think after Dad gets better you could come over?'

'We'll try to get over in the New Year, Anna. We both miss you lots. And thanks for the pictures of the babies. They are both so beautiful. Giulio is so dark, like his father, and Nicoletta is fair like you. Oh darling, I'm so glad you're happy and in love. It's just that I wish you weren't so far away.'

When Anna put the telephone down she had tears in her eyes. Mostly she shoved the pain of missing her parents into the back of her mind. But when she'd been in labour, she remembered, she had called out for her mother. Still, Regina d'Albro was arriving tomorrow and bringing her new lover. Apparently Tony was history. Anna smiled. The new lover's name was Orlando and he was a merchant seaman.

'I don't suppose he'll be any different from Regina's other men. I'll put them in the furthest bedroom so if they have to fight we won't have to hear them,' she told Mario as she recounted her telephone conversation with her parents to him.

'It's a shame your aunts can't come over,' he said. 'Maybe when the babies are a little older we can all make a trip to New York?'

'I'd love that. But I'd feel such a country bumpkin now, after all this time.'

Mario looked at her and smiled. 'You'll always be beautiful to me, and you will never be a country bumpkin. I know what you mean, though. But life is so good for us at the moment. I don't mind working hard or the long hours because it's all for us and the babies. Speaking of work, I must go off and join Tommaso and Nico in the fields.' Anna watched him stride back out

345

to the fields. The hard work had made him strong and confident. She loved the back of his neck where his hair grew in a straight line. He had the most kissable neck she had ever seen. She was glad they were now able to make love again after the last few uncomfortable months of her pregnancy. She was aware of the shine in both their faces whenever they saw each other. Her stomach now looked like an old hot-water bottle. The babies weighed nine pounds four ounces each. She would have to ride again to get her muscle tone back. But she didn't mind if Mario could take time off to ride with her. With the routine of the farm, they had little enough time to spend together, so riding would give them back those lovely, intimate days they had had at the Kearneys' house in Devon.

Sixty-Four

Anna couldn't help smiling at the odd crowd gathered around her babies for the christening. Regina did indeed drive from Genoa with her new lover. He looked as villainous as Anna had guessed he would, but he was handsome in a thick-set, burly way. He had black flashing pirate's eyes and a big, soup-stained moustache. He kept grabbing Regina, who shrieked with pleasure, making everyone in the house stop what they were doing and laugh. Elisabetta did not smile much at either of them. But she was her usual, gracious self, although Anna hoped Regina wouldn't notice her mother-in-law's lack of enthusiasm.

'I love this new man of mine,' Regina announced loudly and often. The third night she was there, Anna heard the usual sound of Regina screaming: she dreaded the thought of a heavy blow. At breakfast the following day she found herself staring at Regina, who was with her at the table.

'You think my Orlando hit me in the night time, huh, Anna?'

'Well, I must say I wondered.'

Regina shook her head. 'Orlando is too clever. He never hits me. He just laughs and goes to sleep.' She grinned. 'He is a good man and I want to marry him. But life is always a problem, no?'

At the christening, Regina stayed close to her lover. She was wearing a skin-tight red wool dress. The material was straining against her breasts and clung tightly to her buttocks. She was misty-eyed with the emotions of the moment. Anna envied Regina her ability to live so absolutely in the present. Many Italians lived that way, and it gave them an ability to share the moment with each other.

Beside Regina, Mary Rose was holding Nicoletta, and Claude, rather awkwardly, held Giulio. Anna noticed Fosca standing beside Claude, and rather hoped that her secret plans would come to fruition. The two certainly spent a lot of time together, and Claude played the guitar for Fosca most nights. She watched the smile on Fosca's face as she tried to help Claude adjust Giulio up on to his shoulders. The baby, once settled, obligingly regurgitated a large amount of vomit on to Claude's shoulder. Anna tried not to laugh. Her breasts were still full of milk and she hoped they would get through the service without leaking.

The priest blessed both the babies with holy water and then put a little bit of salt on each tongue. Nicoletta rather enjoyed the experience, but Giulio let out a loud howl of indignation. They were wearing the same christening dresses that Mario and Fosca had once worn. The long lace trains trailed to the floor and the little hats were tied under each plump baby chin.

347

Anna's heart ached with love for the two small, helpless beings. She took Mario's hand and squeezed it. 'It's all so lovely, darling,' she whispered.

He looked down at her. '. . . And so are you.'

Later that evening, the guests sat at the big wooden table in the loggia. The fire was roaring and their faces were flushed with the heat. The babies were upstairs and asleep. Lisa had taken up the 'silent priests', wooden hutches which were put in each big bed and from the ribs of which hung little iron pots of live coals. It was cold at night now, a searing Tuscan cold that ate at the bones.

The coffee and vinsanto were making the rounds. Mario had made a raspberry liqueur in honour of Mary Rose's arrival. He poured her a glass. Anna smiled across the table at her. So far they had had very little time to talk. The three days surrounding the christening had been taken up with friends and neighbours coming to pay their respects. Now the event was over, Anna looked forward to spending some time with Mary Rose alone. Crispin was sitting at the end of the table next to Regina, who rolled her eyes at him and patted his thigh.

'Crispin seems to be enjoying flirting with Regina,' Mary Rose snorted. 'She's much too much of a woman for him.'

Mary Rose was looking gaunt but lovely. 'It's really nice to be here, Anna. Tomorrow let's take a car and go to Siena together.'

'OK. I'll leave a couple of bottles of milk with Lisa and you and I can go and have lunch on the Campo. It's beautiful at this time of year. And because of the political situation, there are no tourists. Thank God.'

'It isn't just because of the political situation, Anna. It really looks as if there will be war. We had trouble getting enough money to get out here. All finances are now restricted. Don't you think you ought to consider coming to England for a while with Mario, or going back to your parents with the babies? Once war is declared you won't be able to get out.'

'Oh, Mary Rose, don't spoil the party. Here, have a swig of nocino. I made it myself from our own walnuts and alcohol. You can only make the drink on 8 June. That's when the walnuts are at their best. Here,' she pushed the drink across the table, 'try it.'

Mary Rose knew better than to push Anna. Anna seemed like all the Italians around her. Rather than believe it, they seemed far happier keeping their heads firmly in the sand and pretending everything would just go away.

Standing on the porch of the beautiful old farmhouse, Mary Rose could see why. All around her ducks and geese up-ended themselves looking for worms. It was evening, and the sun was setting slowly in the sky behind Mount Amiata. The shadows were long and Mary Rose could see the people sitting in the dining room, talking happily. Such a feeling of peace and contentment spread over her. Even Crispin seemed to have relaxed, although she was aware that he was watching her even as he flirted with Regina. She walked down the wide, shallow stone steps and breathed deeply. All the smells were of thyme and marjoram. Around her the gardens took on a different colour as the light faded. The late geraniums were almost purple in the dusk. The ducks were beginning to quack themselves off to their pen, and there were sleepy chirps from the chickens.

Mary Rose, driven by a force she did not understand, continued to walk down a long, shaded path. The path was striped by the shadows of the cypress trees standing along the edge of the road. She jumped when she saw a bent little figure in front of her. The old woman was hobbling towards the house. She gabbled something at Mary Rose, who did not understand. She shook her head helplessly in an attempt to convince the woman that her words fell on ignorant ears. This did nothing to stop the tirade. For a moment the old lady straightened up and stared intently at Mary Rose. Her eyes were huge and cat-like. Mary Rose swore that she saw an instant picture of herself being strangled by Crispin. For an awful moment she felt his hands around her neck and then blood flowed freely all around her. But Crispin wouldn't murder me, she thought. He loves me. The old woman shook her head and waved her finger under Mary Rose's nose.

I've had too much wine and I'm letting this old woman upset me, Mary Rose thought, and she pushed the old woman away with an impatient gesture. Caught unawares, the old woman fell to the ground. Mary Rose had had enough. She turned on her heels and stalked back to the house.

'Who on earth is that dreadful, smelly old woman I met on the path, Anna?'

'That's not a dreadful, smelly old woman, Mary Rose, that's Pilar. She's a witch and a wonderful woman.'

'Well, she wasn't wonderful to me!' Mary Rose recounted the fearful moment. 'Bloody silly really,' she said when she'd finished. She looked down the table where Crispin was soaking up the wine. 'He wouldn't hurt me. Without me he has absolutely nothing, and he's getting a bit too old to pull in the women.' She looked affectionately down the table and smiled.

Anna was glad to see her smile at Crispin, and she noticed that both of them seemed quite happy together. Later, in Mario's arms, she sighed. 'I think Mary Rose and Crispin are all right, actually. I think I worried too much about them.'

Mary Rose, full of wine and nocino liqueur, lay against

Crispin's back. 'You'd never hurt me, would you, darling?' She slid her hand between his legs.

'Of course not,' he said, rolling over to face her. 'I like fucking you much too much.' He appreciated her thin body. Let's hope she stays this way, he thought as he began to take his pleasure.

Sixty-Five

🍂

Mary Rose found a kindred spirit in Regina. They spent days after the christening gossiping in the loggia.

Orlando watched them and grinned playfully to Anna. 'One Italian woman, and one American. Both beautiful and both problems.'

Anna laughed. 'Yes, but I love them both. They are such fun.' She was glad that Orlando was able to understand English, even if speaking it was difficult for him. With both the babies to breastfeed, change and bath, Anna found herself very busy. Mario was out in the fields finishing the ploughing and came home tired and strained. She wished he did not have to work so hard. But she also realized that he was doing what he loved best in the world. Now he no longer talked of a shoe factory, just the land and the harvests.

He had Nico bring the sheep down from the high hills with the horses, and settled them in the fields behind the house. The sheep shed was cleaned and creosoted for the winter. Nico, the shepherd, was Sicilian and unpopular in Asciano. He was a big, slow, kind man with a smile that made Anna feel comfortable. She loved his hands. They were square and competent. Francesco told her stories of how, in the dead of winter, Nico would sleep out in the shed with his sheep. If one of the sheep became ill, Nico would lie with it in his arms. Watching Nico in the evening, with the sun going down, as he herded his sheep in front of him, Anna was struck how that sight could have taken place any time in the last two thousand years. Nico, walking tall and strong, gently flailing a whip with a long thin piece of string back and forwards over the sheep. They trotted, their bells tinkling, until they were settled in the shed, where he then milked them.

How timeless it all is, she thought. Even though she was busy with her babies, Anna had more time to herself. She sat in an old rocking-chair belonging to her mother-in-law and looked out at the mountains. She was lucky: while she breastfed one baby, Lisa took the other. Goodness knew how women managed in America. Here, there were endless pairs of arms and hands willing to take the children.

When she pushed the big double pram past the hideous new Fascist-style buildings in Asciano she shivered. Inside the police station that spread its ugly façade along the main road leading to Rapolano and Sinalunga, she knew innocent men and women were being regularly tortured. She always hurried back to the peace and safety of her life with Mario. Still, she could not ignore the radio and the ranting tones of Hitler. From England came a whining, inconclusive voice appeasing the monster. In Italy, Mussolini was still offering to save the world and to go and visit Hitler. He had the blessing of some of his people. But Francesco merely remarked that the man was mad and switched off the radio.

What Anna didn't know was that Francesco and Mario were having regular meetings with the men of the Resistance in Asciano. The family at the end of the road was going to be given an ultimatum. Either they fled their house and all they had, or they would be killed one by one by the partisans. Francesco knew this was a very dangerous move, but he and Mario agreed it was far too risky to have a bunch of Fascists spying on their every move.

'Don't tell Anna, it will spoil her milk,' Elisabetta said maternally when Francesco told her the plan. Mario hated keeping anything from Anna but he agreed reluctantly.

Anna nursed her babies and then in the evening joined Mary Rose, while Crispin found a group of old men that sat outside the bar in Asciano. Despite his lack of Italian he picked up their card game and was soon happily extracting small amounts of cash from, as well as losing regularly to one of the men who played cards like a demented fiend.

'You seem to have fitted very well into Italy,' Anna teased him.

Crispin laughed. 'I'm like a chameleon. I can fit in anywhere,' he said. But he was bored; very, very bored. Italian girls didn't seriously flirt with married men, and he couldn't take his wedding ring off without being obvious. He settled down, and like a snake in the hot summer sun, he waited for the time to pass so that he could return to England. The strain of being pleasant and nice to everyone was beginning to tell on him. Here in Mario's house, he couldn't scream 'fuck off', or slam doors, or hit the walls.

Mary Rose, however, seemed to come more alive as the days went by. Her eyes regained their sparkle and her throaty laugh was heard all over the house. Her hollow face filled out and her cheeks were flushed once more. Anna was pleased for her, but she was even more pleased with Fosca and Claude.

One evening, before Mary Rose left, she found Claude kissing Fosca in the garden. Unseen by them, she watched as Claude put his long, flute-playing fingers behind Fosca's neck and drew her to him. Anna slipped away, heaving a sigh. I am so sentimental, she thought to herself reprovingly. I'm now a married woman. But she remembered with a pang those magical moments between herself and Mario. There were still special moments between the two of them, but two demanding babies made the moments far fewer. Still, Mario loved the twins. He came into their nursery and played with them every night.

'Claude's in love with Fosca,' Anna told him.

'You're matchmaking again,' he replied playfully.

'No, I saw them kissing the other night. He looks so serious about her. And they're always together now.'

'I'm happy for her.' Mario smiled. 'She was very fond of Steven and he no longer writes to her.'

'Claude is still a student, but he's an excellent musician. When he goes back to Switzerland he'll find work in an orchestra.'

'If he ever goes back. I'll miss him if he does.' Mario's eyes were shaded with concern. He held Nicoletta in his arms and kissed her fair hair. 'Times are getting a little difficult, darling, but don't worry, we'll get through.' He put the baby into Anna's arms. 'I've got to go to Asciano now. Why don't you go down and spend the evening with Mary Rose? She'll be gone tomorrow. I gather Crispin's having his last evening playing cards in Asciano.'

Mary Rose was sitting in the corner by the big fire. All the windows had been shuttered for the winter, so the large square room was full of shadows. Once the room had been the stables and it ran the length of the house. Anna missed the perfect view of the Crete from the window. One low cypress stood sentinel, a solitary guard duty in the long months to come. Anna did not know that Mario had gone with his father to organize the death threat for the neighbours. Nor did she know that two men from Francesco's group had been taken into the police station at Asciano and tortured for the names of the rest of the members. People were splitting into many different factions. Francesco had heard that both men had died under torture, but neither had talked. They had left their dying messages in the hand of a man who had managed to talk his way out.

Anna, blissfully unaware, made plans for her Christmas. 'Mary Rose, I'm giving you my own dried porcini mushrooms to take home. You soak them in boiling water and they swell. Then you add both the mushrooms and the water to whatever dish you are making.'

Mary Rose made a face. 'I've given up cooking. When we get back I'm going to get a full-time cook and a housekeeper. Crispin is a messy little bugger and there's a list a yard long of food he can't eat. He's so boring.'

'I thought you both looked as though you were very happy together.'

'Only because he's in your house and can't scream at me.'

Anna looked very seriously at Mary Rose. 'If he's that bad, Mary Rose, have you ever considered leaving him?'

'Nope, not seriously, at least.' Mary Rose paused. 'I only know two happy marriages, and those are yours and your parents'. The fact is, maybe, that I'm too lazy to get rid of him. Anyway, I have two lovers. One is impotent and good fun, and the other is Justin Villias. You remember him?'

Anna nodded. 'Sure I do. Oh, Mary Rose, why can't you just settle down and be happy?'

'Darling, Regina and I agreed we'd die of boredom. Although this time she seems to have picked a man who can cope with her and she's very happy.'

'Who's talking about me?' Regina sailed into the room. 'Good, no men.' She plonked herself down on the sofa next to Mary Rose. 'Let's talk about men. How does your Mario make love, Anna?'

'I don't talk about that sort of thing, Regina. And you know that.'

'I know, but I like to see you blush.'

Anna took the opportunity to change the course of the discussion. 'Your English has improved greatly in the last week.'

'I should think so too!' Mary Rose's eyes were dancing a wicked dance. 'We've been comparing notes on our men and sex all week. Regina says Orlando can make her come a dozen times in one night.'

'Really, Mary Rose, you can get very boring when you talk about nothing other than sex.'

'What else is there to talk about?' She laughed heartily. 'Maybe we could talk about some of those beautiful little boys hanging around the streets of the village . . .'

'Mary Rose!' Anna's voice was like ice. 'Don't you dare touch any of those boys. Their mothers and their aunts and their grandmothers would be up here like a shot.'

'Don't worry, I have a policy. I don't fuck anybody whose mother I know. Or aunts or grandmother, come to think of it. I did once fuck a boy of sixteen. Oh boy, there was trouble. Crispin beat the shit out of me.'

'I didn't know that Crispin hit you, Mary Rose.' Anna's voice was scandalized. 'I knew you screamed at each other. You've always been a screamer. But he actually hits you?'

'Sure, most men do.'

'Then you've got to leave him, Mary Rose, you really must.'

Anna suddenly realized that both women were looking at her with near contempt in their eyes.

'Anna,' Mary Rose said gently. 'You'll have to wake

up and smell the coffee. The world is a very hard, cruel place. And so are relationships.'

Regina went over to Anna and gave her a hug. 'You are lucky, darling, you have a wonderful man and two beautiful babies. Life is not always so easy. I have Orlando now, and I hope we will be happy. But you cannot know this when you first meet a man. He will tell you what he wants to tell you, and when you find out it is too late, much too late.' She put out her arm. Down it Anna saw a long, thin silver scar. 'That was Giuseppe – very dangerous.' She grinned. 'I knifed him back. He went running.'

Anna shuddered. 'I don't want to live like that. I don't want to see people knifed and hurt, and blood. I like my life as it is.'

Outside she heard the high-pitched scream of a hare as it died in the jaws of a fox. Ugh, she thought, even my paradise has its violent moments.

Sixty-Six

Anna found she missed the company of both Mary Rose and Regina after they had gone. They had added so much to the cheery bustle of the house.

Orlando had kissed Anna on both cheeks and had grinned. 'I'm taking Regina away now so I can make a good woman of her,' he had announced with mock gravity.

'He may be able to make a good woman of me,' Regina had quipped, 'but never honest.' Then she had turned to Anna, her voice soft and gentle.

'He asked me last night, Anna. He said that see-ing you and Mario together and so happy convinced him that we should try.' She had shrugged. 'Why not, I try.'

'Good for you both.' Anna had hugged Regina, genuinely happy for her friend who had become even closer with this visit. 'When the children are older we'll come down and visit you.'

Anna, arm in arm with Mario on the front steps of the house, had watched in silence as the car took the two couples down the long, steep path.

Now only the cypress trees had foliage. Everywhere it was bare and cold, even though the sun was shining feebly, trying to warm the lizards in their winter sleep.

'It's so odd not to see lizards darting about the walls,' she said dreamily to Mario. 'I miss them. They're so colourful and so funny with their little swollen toes and their long tongues.'

'I miss them too. To me they mean summer.'

Mario held Anna while he stared into the distance. His mind was far away. Would the neighbours move once they got the anonymous letter? Or would they take it to the *carabinieri* for investigation? How many of the family would have to die if they decided to fight it out? Would he have to kill any of them? The answer to the last question was, sadly, yes. His father was too old to stalk in the dark, and he, Mario, was the only son. He would have to kill for the honour of his family and for the safety of his wife and children. He took no pleasure in the thought; in fact it horrified him. But it was an obligation that could not be broken. He had already talked to his father about the possibility that things might go terribly wrong and that he might be killed attempting to carry out his duty. He felt badly about not having told Anna, but his responsibility to her was uppermost in his mind. Hopefully, though, the family would move voluntarily and dramatic action would not be necessary.

'Come on, darling, it's getting cold,' he said, drawing her inside.

Later that night he made love to her as if it were the last time.

Anna, thrilled by the passion, responded. 'Darling,' she said breathlessly. 'What on earth has got into you?'

'I love you, Anna, that's all. I love you so much. I can't bear the thought of losing you.'

'You'll never lose me, Mario. You know that.' She felt him long and rigid inside her. Her hips rocked and her legs encircled him.

'Never, never,' she crooned in ecstasy. 'Always and for ever.'

God, if only, Mario thought miserably. He fell back finally, and slid into a disturbed, dream-torn sleep.

Christmas Day was a day of minor miracles, Anna thought. The fact that she was cooking the Christmas dinner by herself with only Fosca's help frightened her at first. Her mother-in-law was such a brilliant cook. Anna decided after a telephone call to her mother that she would cook a traditional American Christmas dinner and do without pasta. At times she really missed American take-away food. She particularly missed Chinese food, and she often cooked sweet-and-sour chicken for Claude, Fosca and Mario. Francesco made a face when presented with such foreign food, but he loved her hamburgers and French fries.

They sat on a mild and blue Tuscan day in front of the ever-smouldering fire. Anna held Nicoletta on her knee and Mario held Giulio. She smiled at Mario and blew him a kiss. Beside her, Fosca sat next to Claude. It was now no secret that both of them were very much in love. Lisa was serving the meal. She and the rest of the people in the house were looking forward to eating the foreign turkey dinner with the fresh peaches and the home-cured ham. Now the ham, studded with cloves and hung with rings of pineapples, sat proudly on the table.

Before the meal, Anna had run down to Pilar's cottage to take her a plate of food. The old woman had smiled her gummy smile. She loved Anna and was concerned at the hard times she knew were coming for this family and for herself. Her own death she contemplated without fear, but for Anna's family she was worried. She had tried to warn Francesco. He had only said that they would send away the women and the children, but that the men would stay and take their chances. Now, looking at Anna's radiant face, she hesitated. She knew that the laws of the universe could not be broken and that Anna must lead her life step by step, taking the consequences for her actions just like all other human beings. She trusted Anna, though. The birth of the babies had made a mature woman of her. Not like her friend, the old lady thought as she tottered back to her rickety table. That was no wise woman. Her life would be lived in darkness and in shadows. Her consequences would be filled with horror and terror. The old lady felt a great sadness sweep over her. Poor girl, she had so little chance to learn the right path. She could see in that lovely, dark, tormented face that there had been no shining light either from her mother or her father. Still, she comforted herself as she ate the delicious turkey, there was always hope and final redemption for everyone, especially for this woman. Even if she had cursed her at the time. Maybe now, as it was Christmas, she should lift her curse. Pilar smiled. She finished her plate of food and then moved arthritically towards her bed. She fished around under it, disturbing the nest of cats. They exploded out of the cottage in a ball of fur and fury. She grinned and pulled out a little wax doll. Carefully she removed the pin from the figure's chest and then threw it on the fire.

'Because of your friendship with the signora of my family,' she said slowly, 'I absolve you of your crime against me.' The crime Mary Rose had committed was the crime of disrespect. Pilar knew that Mary Rose respected no one but Anna, and that was to be her saving grace.

In the house, Anna was showing Francesco how they lit English Christmas puddings with brandy. She had made it her business to learn how to do it when they stayed with the Kearneys in Devon. Even though they hadn't spent Christmas there, the bad-tempered English cook had been making the Christmas cakes and puddings in October, just before they had returned to America. She couldn't believe how much alcohol went into the puddings and that they had to be hung from a rafter for three months.

But Anna much preferred Italian tradition. Just before Christmas, they had killed the pigs and made the prosciutto and the salamis which would hang all winter to be eaten with the fresh figs in the hot summer months. Everything provided by the farm kept them in such wonderful comfort. She sighed with pleasure. She hugged Nicoletta, who was now three months old and curious about everything. Her daughter was an electric wire, while Giulio was a far calmer baby. He smiled and gurgled at his father.

While Lisa was clearing the table and washing the dishes, Claude picked up his guitar and strummed it gently. Soon he was serenading Fosca. The babies had been taken by Francesco and Elisabetta to their part of the house to be spoiled by them. Mario took Anna's hand and they listened in a peaceful silence.

There was no peaceful silence in the Kearneys' house. Mary Rose spent Christmas dinner having a blazing row with Amelia.

'You will not take my present to you back to Marshall's store,' Mary Rose screamed at her mother-in-law. 'You always take anything I buy for you and change it. If you don't want it, give it back to me and I'll wear it! For a start, you can have your horrible bath cubes back.' She flung the box of offending lilac squares at her mother-in-law and stormed off to her house. She lay on the bed sobbing. She had no one to turn to and nowhere to go. She telephoned her mother in New York. A different voice answered. Her mother and father were both away. The voice was sorry, but she had no idea where they were. She thought of ringing Mary, but then she lay back; she had no right to destroy other people's happy Christmas.

'I say, you came on a bit strong then.' It was Crispin. 'The old thing is quite upset.'

'Well, so am I.' Mary Rose stretched. 'I've had a pain in my back ever since we came back from Italy. Today, for some reason, it's gone, thank God.'

'Don't change the subject, Mary Rose. You've hurt my mother's feelings.'

'Why don't you go fuck your mother, Crispin? I don't care about her feelings. If you cared about me a bit more and not your mother, we might make our marriage work.' She knew she was treading on dangerous ground, but she couldn't help pushing. Crispin was so easy to provoke. She got off the bed and began to undress.

'Don't talk about my mother that way!'

'What way, Crispin? You mean talking about the fact that you fancy her?'

She felt the blow to her face before she felt the pain. She stood still. Shit, she thought, I'll have a black eye and I've got to meet Mrs Gulbenkian in two days' time. She didn't show any fear. She turned and walked off to the bathroom.

'Only weak men and cowards bully women,' she said

quietly. 'And you're both, Crispin.' She gazed in the mirror at her rapidly swelling eye. He can break my bones, but he can't hurt me with his words any more, she thought. I'm over him and it's just a matter of time before I dump him. Fucking weedy neurotic.

'There is nothing erotic about a neurotic,' she remarked to the mirror. Now that she didn't bother to speak to Crispin that much, her mirror was rapidly becoming her best friend.

Sixty-Seven

The killing of the pigs had been all too much for Anna. She had wrapped her babies up against the freezing wintry weather and had taken off for Pilar's cottage. Now she could talk to the old woman with much more fluency.

She admired Mario's ability to take part in the killing. He had grown up on a farm and recognized the necessity of killing animals. He understood her fear and her reluctance to take part in the almost ritualized slaughter, but teased her in his good-humoured way.

'You'll enjoy eating the salami that we make afterwards, *cara*,' he had said.

'I know I will. But not the blood sausages and puddings.'

Mario had shrugged and kissed her goodbye, and now she sat in Pilar's crooked chair.

'You will be glad of the ham in the winter to come,' Pilar told her. What the old woman didn't tell her was that she would be eating the ham in very different circumstances. She could see the great light in Anna. For now it was partially extinguished by marriage and motherhood. There had not been time to keep it burning and bright.

Anna, watching Pilar scrutinizing her, felt embarrassed. Other Italian wives were out there at this time helping their men. Fosca was designated to hold the bowl that would catch the blood for the sausages. Anna knew that, after the pig was killed, a knife was inserted into its heart to bleed it cleanly to ensure the prosciutto would not spoil. All week Elisabetta had been arguing fiercely with Francesco over the fact that the pig he had chosen had been too fat. At breakfast she had still been arguing, even though the pig had already been penned awaiting execution.

Anna shuddered and then half smiled at Pilar. Pilar put a hand on her shoulder and then pulled a pot of thick black coffee from the fire.

'Have a coffee,' she said. 'And don't worry. It is not for everyone, this day's happening. You take care of your babies and maybe one day life will be different in Tuscany. Not so hard for the workers and the peasants. They have to work and work. There is not much time to rest or to play.' She sighed. 'My man died young from overwork.'

Anna felt a jolt of surprise. She had never thought that Pilar could have had a man in her life.

'You were married, Pilar?' she asked.

The old woman nodded and then a shy grin spread over her face. 'He was the love of my life. One winter he got pneumonia and he was gone. Your father-in-law got the best doctor from Siena, but it was too late.' She hobbled over to a corner of the room and carried back an old worn Tuscan roof tile.

'After he died, I found this outside in the garden.' She brushed the dust away and Anna could see writing etched on the terracotta. 'Oh that this life is hard,' he had written.

'He was fixing the roof the day before he died. It was so cold, Anna, so very cold.' Then the light in Pilar's face died. 'Those in your family are very different from most of the rich around here who come for the weekend from Rome or Florence. They pay their servants nothing. They ignore our tradition of sharing what they have with their peasants. They rob the poor and ill-treat those that work for them. I tell you, Anna, things will have to change around here. I'm not one for politics, but too many poor and only a handful of the rich makes for trouble.'

Anna went back to the house in a thoughtful mood. That night, with the pig butchered and hanging in the pantry, Anna sat watching the strings of sausages hanging over the fireplace in the kitchen. She liked the kitchen. Lisa had a big wooden table in the middle of the square room. There were benches running down the two sides. Now the family sat around the kitchen table planning the making of the prosciutto. Bowls of blood sat on the chest next to the bread box – a square cupboard on long wooden legs – which was full of Lisa's homemade bread. Nico and Tommaso were excited about the day's events. Anna, watching them, was aware that Francesco and Elisabetta ran a very different kind of farm.

'Whatever happened to the family that lived at the end of our road?' she said. 'I haven't seen them for some time now. Usually they lurk around if I am walking with the twins.'

There was a moment's silence.

'They decided to move away,' Mario said.

Anna looked surprised. 'Really, Mario? Why?'

Mario shrugged. He looked quickly at his father.

'Family problems,' Francesco said abruptly. Anna knew from the tone in her father-in-law's voice that she must ask no more.

'Yes, well . . . I must go upstairs and feed the twins.'

She felt excluded. Something was happening she knew nothing about.

Mario got up from the bench and put his arm around her. 'I'll come and help you,' he said gently. 'Don't worry, Anna.' He accompanied her across the kitchen and they climbed the stairs together. 'Things are happening all around us, darling. It is better for you to know as little as possible.'

'Why, Mario?'

He sighed, 'So that if the Guardia come to question us you have nothing to say. That's all. You are very well loved by everybody here, and what we want to do is to protect you.'

He stood looking down at both babies who were awake and smiling at him. 'I live only for the three of you, and I promise I will see that nothing can hurt you.' He kissed her. His mouth was full of longing for their future together. 'You'll see, darling, we will make the best prosciutto yet. This year will be a good one for us.'

Even as he hugged her, he knew he was lying.

In England, Mary Rose, driving up the busy road to London, wished she didn't have to face Mrs Gulbenkian with a black eye. She had carefully covered as much of the damage as she could with foundation cream, but it was very bruised. Why do I do it, she asked herself? Why don't I just get rid of him? She knew the answer. There was no getting rid of Crispin. He was in her life and he wasn't going to let go. Certainly not of the money. She would just have to make her life around him. Though, with Travis's help, she was now becoming very accomplished at getting away from him.

She was on her way to meet Mrs Gulbenkian who was again on the hunt for still more antiques, this time for a flat in Eaton Square. She had offered a room in the flat to Mary Rose, who was more than grateful to accept the gesture. Slowly, a great friendship was growing between the two women. Often she found the old woman understood her. Without ever complaining about Crispin, Mrs Gulbenkian seemed to understand her very difficult position.

As she drew nearer to London, Mary Rose knew that she wouldn't be able to fool Mrs Gulbenkian with her black eye.

'So he hit you,' was her comment as they met in the Tate Gallery. They were standing by one of the vast Turner canvases, and Mary Rose wished she could fade into the grey seascape.

'I fell over one of the dogs,' she said lamely.

'No you didn't. I had a black eye like that once, and I'll tell you, the bastard didn't do it again. I took a knife to him.'

The thought of Mrs Gulbenkian loose with a knife brought a smile to Mary Rose's face. There was not much else to smile at in London. Unfortunately Crispin hadn't been conscripted like all his other friends. There had been a procession of men in uniforms coming to the house to say goodbye. She missed Podge. And Ralph was now married and in the Far East. But Crispin stayed home. He had a weak chest and was refused duty. He was absurdly happy not to have to go to war, and seemed totally capable of doing nothing for the rest of his life.

Mrs Gulbenkian and Mary Rose set off for Peter Jones's to buy towels and bathroom fixtures. Over lunch and a good glass of wine, Mary Rose relaxed for the first time in months. Why was she keeping Crispin in her house on her money? She wasn't sure of the answer yet, and until she was she could do very little about it.

Sixty-Eight

ᨡ

'Anna, are you awake?' Mario was lying beside her, his forehead knotted with strain. He rubbed the back of his neck, hoping to ease the tension. They had managed to flush out the Fascists living at the bottom of the drive. The threats had finally driven them away. Generally, though, the tide of Fascism was rising. News came that the Germans had invaded Poland. Fear mounted as they began surrounding other countries and Hitler openly declared his intention of dominating Europe. England was digging in for war. Altogether the conflict was gathering momentum and, as in a tidal wave, it looked as if everybody would be swept away.

'Yes.' Anna was awake instantly. She could hear the tension in Mario's voice. 'I'm awake, darling. What's the matter?' She curled up close to him and put her arm around his neck.

'I think we should try and get through to your parents and get you back to America if we can.'

'Oh no, Mario. I don't want to leave you. I'll be all right, really I will.'

'The situation is much more serious than you think, darling. We haven't told you much about what's happening, but we are now at war. And if I don't get you out now I may never be able to do it.'

Anna felt tears welling in her eyes. She had never spent one day without Mario since they had married and she simply couldn't imagine what life would be without him. 'No, no, don't send me away,' she whispered.

'I'm not sending you away, darling. I'm saving your life and that of our babies. It will only be for a short

368

time and you will be back. It is much easier for me to concentrate if I know you're safe. Please, darling, think it over.'

'I will,' Anna said miserably. She sighed. Mario lay beside her until he heard her soft breathing and knew she was asleep. He leaned over and kissed her cheek. He couldn't bear the idea of being without her, but he also knew that the risks were great and that she would be better with her parents. He slipped out of bed and went down to the drawing room to telephone them.

'I'm sorry to wake you up at this ungodly hour,' he said, almost whispering, 'but I feel that I really must get Anna and the children out of here. Fosca says she will go to Switzerland with Claude, but I think Anna would be much better with you.'

'Of course.' Daniel's voice was concerned, but warm and welcoming. 'I'll look into it at my end. I was going to telephone you anyway. Things look real bad from here. It looks as if our boys are going to be called up. So far the average American doesn't want to have anything to do with the war in Europe, and Roosevelt is biding his time. I think he ought to go in behind the British and mop the whole thing up.'

Mario wasn't really listening. At least something was happening, and maybe Daniel could pull some strings and get Anna and the children safely out of Europe. There was a sense of heavy dread in his heart. It was not war that worried him as much as the rising tide of hatred for Jews and other ethnic groups. Each man's hand seemed to be against the other. The feeling in the streets of Asciano was running high. Yesterday, as he and his father had driven across to Sinalunga to get fresh fish for the children, they had seen the words 'Burn the Jews' scrawled on the wall of a building. The sight had shocked him, as had the whispered comments around the well at the bottom of Asciano. 'Down with the land-owners,' a man had hissed at them. It was really that comment that made Mario realize that he must make arrangements to get Anna and the babies out.

'Are you there, Mario?'

'Oh yes, I'm sorry, Danny. My head is in such a scramble.'

'Don't worry about a thing. I'll get going now and I'll ring back tomorrow. Stay by the phone.'

'I will. My love to Mary and the family.' Mario put down the phone and walked slowly back upstairs. Sliding in beside Anna, he pulled her into his arms and slowly began to make love to her. Asleep and quiescent, she responded. They seemed to come together and hang for an eternity in space. Between them was a moment of total communion, and Mario felt a lump beginning to form in his throat. This spiritual union is what he would miss the most. That and the delighted shine on Anna's face whenever she saw him.

That morning there were two letters for Anna. One from Kitty and the other from Martha. Kitty's was full of news about Joe and her friends. Martha's was a quieter letter. She wrote that she was worried about Anna and the babies. Anna, knowing that Mario had just spoken to her father, wrote back to both aunts and went into Asciano to post the letters. She paused for a cup of coffee with Lisa's grandmother, who lived in a little narrow house in the back streets of the town. When she got there, Lisa's Aunt Gina was sitting listening to the radio. There was loud martial music blaring from the set. Gina put up a warning hand.

'There is something big happening,' she said. 'There is to be an announcement from Il Duce in a moment. Take a chair and sit down.'

Anna watched the old lady. She had a long string of rosary beads in her fingers. On the wall behind her head was a framed photograph. It was a picture of

Lisa's father, who had died in the First World War, a handsome, dark-eyed man with a military moustache.

Il Duce's voice now began to speak in very fast Italian. Anna couldn't make out much of it, but it sounded as if Hitler had moved into another country. Suddenly Gina began to sob. Anna could hear feet pounding up and down the road outside. Doors were opening and slamming shut. People were shouting. 'War, war!' So this is what war sounds like, Anna thought, looking at Gina weeping on her chair. Men running and women weeping. She got up and squatted down beside Gina. She put her arms around the old lady, and for a moment or two they rocked together in sorrow. In sorrow for what was to come. The unknown future of a nation at war. Gradually, between Gina's sobs and Anna's patient demands, Anna gleaned the essence of Mussolini's bombastic announcement to Italians from his regal splendour in the Palazzo Venezia: that war had formally been declared between Britain and Germany. His arrogant words made it chillingly clear where his country stood and what sacrifices were expected of its citizens. The words floated outside and hung heavy like a prophetic pall in the mild September air.

Anna's shoulders drooped. 'I must go back to Mario and the babies,' she said, gently disentangling herself. She kissed Gina goodbye and wished she were not leaving her alone in this little house with the photograph of her dead son on the wall.

On the way back in the car she found herself crying. She would now have to leave Mario. She cried for herself and the people she loved in Asciano. For Tommaso, Nico and Lisa. She must say goodbye to Pilar. Goodness knows if the old witch would be there when she came back. She ran into the house to find the whole family and the others crouched by the radio.

Mario, white-faced, clutched Anna to him. 'War has

371

been declared,' he said. 'The Germans are on the move. I must get you out.'

Mario tried to telephone Daniel but the lines were solidly blocked. He went into Siena, and then on to Florence and the American consulate. There were queues of people ringing the building. Americans trying to get out, Mario supposed. He waited patiently, and in the evening he got to see a tired, harassed consul worker.

'Sorry.' The man shook his head. 'There is nothing going out of Italy for the next few weeks. All transport has been requisitioned for the duration of the war and we can't get anybody out. You should have come months ago, and then maybe we could have helped you.'

Mario returned home dejected, but then was slightly cheered as he saw the glow in Anna's eyes.

'At least I don't have to leave you, my darling,' she said contentedly that night.

Mario hugged her to him fiercely. 'I'll protect you with my life,' he said.

Sixty-Nine

Although the news that war had been declared seemed awful, Mary Rose felt a mounting sense of excitement in the chamber. They had been slightly late so they had to run the last few yards up the cloistered hall and then through the dark little back stairs that led to their seats. Mary Rose looked down on the mace lying on the long table, and at the Speaker of the House who sat in his wig and gown.

'Order! Order!' he said firmly as an electric buzz ran around the room.

Mary Rose looked at Travis. He put his arm around her and, his face grim, gave her a hug.

'So sad,' he said. 'All those young men who will die. There is nothing glorious about war. It just kills the brave and the best of each country.'

Mary Rose saw the cold blue eyes of the Whip gazing at them.

'Shhh,' she said, but Travis had broken the spell. No, she did not want war or even talk of war. Beside her, Mrs Gulbenkian was mopping her eyes.

'I have seen it all before,' she said. 'I hoped never to see it again. So many lovely young boys died in the First World War.'

The Whip was glaring. 'Let's get out of here,' Mary Rose said. 'I need a drink. Or lots of drinks.'

They pushed their way out, and silently the three of them walked down the now deserted halls. Sinister statues loomed out of the dark. Mary Rose walked past the great hall before she left the House. With a rising sense of shock she noticed that the windows of the houses around her had been blackened out. No lights shone in the street. There were people hurrying to and fro but they were mostly silent. Except for one man on a street corner.

'War's declared,' he screamed, waving his newspaper. ''itler's going to bash the British. The Eyeties won't fight. The Frogs don't know 'ow to. We're going to war.' Mary Rose realized the man was completely drunk. Then she saw that he had only one leg and one eye. From the eye that was unpatched she could see a single row of tears dripping down his face.

'Fucking Krauts! We should 'ave screwed 'em in the first war.'

Mary Rose, Travis and Mrs Gulbenkian walked on in silence.

When they got back to the flat in Eaton Square,

Mrs Gulbenkian got busy trying to improvise blackout curtains for the windows.

Mary Rose tried to telephone Anna, but all lines to Europe were blocked.

'I'm worried about her,' she told Travis.

He spoke to her gently. 'But she's probably safer where she is than trying to get out of Italy. I've been reading the newspapers and millions of people are on the move. I see that American residents are caught in the south of France trying to get across to England. I think she'd be better off if she stayed where she is. Look, I'm famished. I'll go into the kitchen and make dinner. Let me get you a drink: you look as if you need one.'

'Thanks, Travis.' Mary Rose was grateful. What a nice man he is, she thought as he poured her a large Scotch. 'I don't usually drink this stuff,' she said as she sipped the cool peat-tasting liquid. 'But I definitely need a shot of something.'

'How do you like your steak, Mary Rose?'

'Medium rare.' Odd how long it takes to find out about someone else's tastes. But Travis really was beginning to know hers. He was such a comforting person in her life. Justin was fun and perverse, but she was beginning to find herself looking forward more to being with Travis when she got to London. He was almost a refuge from Crispin's foul temper and bullying ways. Even if Travis could only make love to her in his flawed way, it was a gentle act.

Mary Rose felt very confused. Now, lying beside Travis, with Mrs Gulbenkian snoring very loudly next door, she wondered if she could seriously make an effort to get rid of Crispin. She fell asleep dreaming of guns and explosions.

Seventy

Life changed dramatically in Asciano. People no longer stopped in the streets to talk of the possibility of war. If there was any hope at all it flew out of the window when the Italian government ordered its delegation to turn its back on the League of Nations. War was now a reality and families lost their young men. So did the farms. The fields were now no longer ploughed to make ready for the Easter sowing. Tommaso and Nico were too old to go to war, but Lisa's brother, Emanuele, was called up and she was in tears daily.

Fosca kissed the family a tremulous goodbye. She and Claude were going to try and take the train over the Swiss border. She now wore an engagement ring and they planned to marry as soon as they got there.

'Take really good care of her for me, Claude.' There were tears in Mario's eyes. Shortly before, when they were alone, Anna took Fosca in her arms and said gently: 'Do you really want to marry Claude?'

Fosca looked steadily into Anna's blue eyes. For a moment brown eyes locked horns with blue and Anna could see the shadow of Steven's face in Fosca's soul. 'A woman only gives her heart once,' Anna said.

'I know that.' Fosca gazed at Anna. 'Claude is a good man and he loves me very much. Yes, I do want to marry him.'

Anna walked downstairs after that conversation, glad that she had found Mario and given her heart to him. Claude would be a good husband for Fosca, but that shadow would be there all her life. She wondered if Mary Rose, too, had given her heart to Crispin. Even if he did hit her. Thinking about it, Anna rather thought not. So far Mary Rose hadn't given her heart to anyone. And maybe she did not have a heart to give. Sometimes life is better that way, Anna thought. She quickened her pace to say a last goodbye to the departing couple. When they left she stood pressed close to Mario. 'They'll get there, safely, Mario, don't worry.'

'I'm not worried about them, darling. It's you I worry about. And the babies. Still, we'll do the best we can. I have to go out and help Tommaso.'

The men were still preparing the fields for the planting in April. The day the moon waned was the day to plant. The weeks slipped by and Anna tended to stay out of the town, leaving the essential shopping to be done by Lisa. This way she did not have to deal with the convoys of lorries carrying the soldiers backwards and forwards in the business that was now war. She helped Elisabetta pack provisions. She was there when Francesco said that they must take hams into the caves in the claylands and bury them along with turnips and onions. 'When the time comes, the women and children must go into hiding and there must be enough food to sustain them.' Even now there was a man living in the attic whose presence was, as yet, unexplained.

'Don't ask,' Mario told Anna when she finally mentioned him. 'The less you know the safer it is for you.'

Rumours and stories flew about the town. Lisa and Tommaso kept up with the news and imported every scrap they could hear.

One morning there was the sound of boots scrunching on the gravel. Mario was out of bed and into his clothes as if he had been practising for this moment for a long time. Anna lay still and hardly breathed. Then, hearing raised voices, she got out of bed and peeked out of the window. It was a platoon of brown-shirted soldiers with their guns pointing at Mario, who had been joined by Francesco. Anna tried not to scream. The argument seemed to go on for hours and then, as suddenly as they had come up the drive, they turned and marched down again. Mario and Francesco returned inside the house and Anna hurried downstairs.

'What was that about?' she demanded. She could hear the children crying in unison upstairs as if they, too, had felt the pall of evil that hung over the soldiers. Anna tried not to think of them as all evil. They, too, were men with families, wives and sweethearts at home.

'We must move him.' Francesco's lips were white. 'That was a near thing. Someone has denounced us. It's only because I know the *brigadiere* that the soldiers didn't dare insist on searching. But they will be back. This time the *brigadiere* will have to give them a search warrant. You take Anna and the children in the car and we'll put him bundled up in blankets under her feet. I hate to risk her and the grandchildren like this, but if either of us are alone we will be stopped. I'll get Elisabetta to put a picnic hamper in the back. Take him to the caves and leave him there.'

'I'm sorry, darling, to do this to you,' Mario said. 'I don't like the idea of you being in any danger. But if they come and find him here we are all in danger. There are no more safe houses left in which to hide him.'

'Don't worry, Mario, we'll all have to take risks now. I'll go and get the children ready.' Anna ran lightly up the stairs. She felt frightened, but she also felt a feeling of exhilaration. At last she was doing something.

They were stopped on the way out of Asciano. The *brigadiere*'s face loomed into Mario's window. He was a big man, but a friend.

'Mind if we look in your boot, sir?' he said somewhat diffidently.

'Not at all.' Mario handed him the key to the boot. 'Just taking some provisions for a picnic with the children. Such a lovely day, even if it is cold.' Mario realized he was chattering inanely.

The *brigadiere* opened the boot and poked about inside. 'It's all in order,' he said, smiling at Mario and Anna. 'How's your lovely wife?'

Restraining a desire to put his foot hard down on the accelerator, Mario answered reassuringly. 'Oh, she's fine. We're looking forward to our picnic, aren't we, dear?'

Anna turned her big blue eyes on to the *brigadiere* and smiled. 'Very much so. *Arrivederci.*' She waved at the *brigadiere* and his *carabinieri.*

Mario pulled away. 'Whew!' He tried not to brush away the sweat that poured down his brow even on such a cold day. They drove in a silence broken only by the gurgling of the two children sitting beside Anna in the back of the car. Under her feet she could feel the man relax. When the car had been stopped, Anna had felt him go rigid with fear. She tried to let her energy flow through her feet to tell him he would be all right. After half an hour, Mario took a right turn into an old cart track. As far as he could see there was no one around, but with all the hills and trees, someone could be watching and they would be none the wiser.

Finally, in a thick wood, he parked the car and got out. 'You carry the children behind those trees over there. I don't want them to see him. Then you get back into the car and I'll put him in the cave.' Mario helped Anna out of the car and watched her carry Nicoletta and Giulio away. Once they were hidden from sight, he lifted the blanket from the man. 'You're all right. We're here.'

The man, lying on the floor of the car, smiled up at him. 'Madonna,' he said. 'I thought we were all done for.'

'Madonna will protect us.' Mario held out his hand. 'You're too tall to be hiding in the back of my car.'

He hauled him out. 'What name are you using these days?'

'Luciano. My last cover was blown by a woman I was in love with, the bitch. She's dead now. I had to kill her or she'd have blown us all away.'

Mario carried the basket of provisions in front of Luciano. 'Here,' he said, pushing aside a thicket of brambles fashioned into a false screen. 'Here's a cave. Don't leave it. Tonight someone will come and lead you out of here to a safe house in San Giovanni d'Asso. Good luck, Luciano.'

'Thanks, comrade, and thanks to all your family for saving my life.'

Mario kissed the man on both cheeks and walked back to the car. War, terrible though it is, brings out the best in men, he thought. But obviously not all women! So far Mario was glad that he had not needed to kill anyone, but this morning, with the guns pointing at him and his father, he now realized that he could. That thought gave him some satisfaction.

On the way back they were stopped again, but this time it was the same group of soldiers that had come to the house. They were made to get out of the car and stand on the side of the road. Mario held Giulio in his arms and Anna held Nicoletta. Both children began crying loudly.

One of the soldiers came over and tried to placate them both. 'I have children at home,' he said, bringing out his pictures. Anna smiled gratefully at him as the most senior *carabiniere* and his subordinates pulled the car apart. Mario was glad that he had folded the blanket and left it on the seat. After fifteen heart-stopping minutes they were allowed to go on their way.

'Thank you, God,' Anna prayed as they drove back to the house.

When they got there, Francesco and Elisabetta were

waiting anxiously. 'The news is not good,' Francesco began without any preliminaries. 'There is a band of partisans coming down from the mountains. They have been blowing up trains to cut off the Germans on the French borders. We will have to meet them tonight and take them to Montalcino. I have a contact who will then take them on.'

Mario nodded. 'From now on things are going to get busy.'

Nicoletta was asleep in her mother's arms. Mario carried Giulio gently into the house.

That night, Anna sat up with Elisabetta while they waited for the men to come back.

'This is going to be the first of many long nights,' Elisabetta observed. Anna was grateful for her quiet, steady presence.

Seventy-One

The war was boring as far as Mary Rose was concerned. Now everybody fled London. Her friends, holed up in their country houses, talked of nothing else. Her main thoughts were for Anna and her new family, particularly after Italy's formal declaration of war on Britain in June. It seemed that Anna was imprisoned, forcefully chained to a country so far away, admittedly more politically than geographically. Mary Rose could only imagine what life was like for Anna in these moments, and it was a picture she preferred to cancel. The only excitement for her came with the beginning of large-scale bombing over London. Early in September German planes began vomiting tons of explosives on the city, creating an atmosphere she found perversely stimulating. The devastating explosions, the panic, the sirens, the sight and smell of fire. She dared not admit to anyone that such horror created in her a tingling high; even to Crispin, who was probably the most perverse person she knew. She covered her thrill and feigned boredom.

'If I hear one more story about "our boys overseas" I shall scream,' she said, lying in bed beside Crispin.

'People are dying out there, Mary Rose, and your fucking country is doing nothing about it.'

'That's not my fault. And anyway, why should we lose our lives to sort out a mess made by your leaders?'

'Roosevelt was part of making that mess. He could have come in at the beginning and we could have creamed Germany.'

Mary Rose rolled over. 'You're so provincial, Crispin.' She was bored and wanted to get back to London. 'I've got to get to Mrs Gulbenkian's flat tomorrow. They are delivering the curtains and I need to put them up.'

'This is your way of avoiding me, isn't it?'

'Of course not, darling.' Mary Rose rolled over and ran her hand down his thigh. I wonder how many women at this moment are seducing their husbands into believing they genuinely want sex with them when it's the last thing they want, she thought as she began the familiar motions. Millions, she thought, after Crispin had come loudly and strenuously. Why does it always take him so long?

Mary Rose got off the bed and went to take a bath. 'Marriages can die of boredom,' she announced to her mirror. 'Terminal boredom.'

Justin was in town. He'd left a message with Travis that he would like to see Mary Rose.

'Hey, great. What are you doing here, Justin?'

'I'm on army business and I want you to see me in my new uniform. I look great!'

Mary Rose had to laugh at the little boy in his voice. 'I'd love to see you in your new uniform. You can take me out to dinner tonight.'

She telephoned Travis. 'Have to cancel tonight, Travis. I'm going on a date with Justin.' She felt a pang of guilt when she heard the hurt in Travis's voice. She shrugged. It was just as well she had Justin in her life. She did not want to get too dependent on Travis. Besides, Justin was good fun and she needed some good fun. She put on her blue dress with a fishtail trail.

'My, Justin, you look positively divine.' She climbed into the taxi beside him. 'How about you take me to the River Room?'

'Sure thing, honey.' He eyed her carefully. 'You've lost a lot of weight.' He leaned forward in the cab and knocked on the glass partition. 'To the Savoy.'

The dining room was still as beautiful as ever, even if the windows were barred with thick, black curtains. Over the smoked salmon and oysters, Mary Rose began to relax. She had every intention of sleeping with Justin. It was a long time since she had had normal sex, and Justin was a good lover.

Back in her flat, he stripped off and walked naked into the kitchen. 'You know, Mary Rose, we're both so comfortable with each other.'

Mary Rose was in the bathroom. 'I know,' she said, coming out wrapped in her white towelling robe.

Justin pulled her to him and slid the towel off her shoulders. 'I've been waiting for this for a long time,' he said hoarsely.

'So have I.' Mary Rose fell into his arms.

Long after they had finished making love, they lay quietly beside each other smoking cigarettes.

'I do think it's important to have a lover that smokes.' Mary Rose drew deeply on her cigarette. 'Crispin doesn't smoke. He drinks like a fish, but doesn't understand wine. And he's a pig in bed.'

'Do I detect a disgruntled married woman?' Justin's voice was teasing.

'You do. I'm going to have to try and shift the bugger, but it's going to be difficult. It's not me he wants, but my money. That awful mother of his will insist that he stays because, without my money, they have nothing. But I don't want to support a bunch of layabouts for the rest of my life.'

'Boot him out and go back to New York. I'll be there and we can party.'

'Nah, I don't want to go back to New York. I like my life here. I'm perfectly happy in this flat. I love being so close to Sloane Square, and I have Travis as a friend and all the boys in the business. No, I don't want to go back. And anyway, I can't go back as long as there are no civilian passages for the duration of the war.'

Justin casually stroked Mary Rose's stomach. 'You're getting too thin,' he said.

Mary Rose obligingly opened her legs. 'And you're getting a hard-on. We ought to do something about that.' Both cigarettes smouldered in the ashtrays either side of the bed. The smoke curled high over their heads and blessed their labours.

'That was great,' Mary Rose breathed later. 'You were always such a good lover, Justin. It's a pity you're such a rat with women.'

'Not all women. I'm not a rat with you, am I?'

'I'd never let you get into a position where you could rat on me, Justin. I like men, but very few are faithful. Those that are are usually boring. So I take my choices and you're one of them . . . I need to sleep.' She flung her arm out and was asleep in minutes.

Justin looked at her tenderly. She looked so young and vulnerable lying there in her bed. The room had been decorated with blue wallflowers. The two small nursing chairs sat by a low coffee table. It was an elegant, comfortable room, rather like Mary Rose herself.

I wish I could be faithful to a woman like Mary Rose, Justin thought. But the world was so full of beddable women and he felt like a red setter let loose in a covey of partridges. When I'm much older I'll settle down with a young virgin and have children, he promised himself before he, too, fell asleep.

Seventy-Two

The men returned in the early hours of the morning.

Mario looked exhausted. 'We went around the back of Montalcino. I left Father with the partisans and walked down to the centre of the town where I sat at the bar we usually go to and ordered myself a coffee.' He grinned. 'I can say, now that I'm safe home again, that it was all rather exciting outwitting the Germans. So far they have had little to do except to get drunk and make passes at our women. I'm sorry to say, though, that some women have given in and can be seen on enemy arms. But most keep away. Anyway, I moved off and then walked up to the fort on the top of the hill. Around the back I was followed by a man who signalled his sign. We didn't talk, I just walked back down the road to the bottom of the hill and then we walked together like brothers. We found the men and Father where I had left them and he took them on. He can't betray me because we did not speak and I don't know who he is. It's far better that way.'

Mario was in bed, but too tense to sleep. Anna knew he was exhausted but that he also needed food. They had not eaten dinner. 'Come downstairs and I'll get you some prosciutto and a little bit of wine.'

He put his arm around her shoulders and they walked down the stairs. 'I was thinking of you all the time I was on the road, and of the little ones. More than anything else in the world I wanted to get back to you safely.'

'I'm glad, Mario.' He watched her carefully shaving the prosciutto and making him a sandwich. She poured him a full glass of wine and some for herself. She dipped her bread into the wine. 'It's rather fun having a five o'clock morning feast in the kitchen when everybody else is asleep,' she giggled.

By the time they got back into bed she had been revived by the wine. 'Let's make love, Mario.' He took her in his arms. Inside her he felt safe for the first time that night. They fell asleep, still joined in each other's arms.

The war progressed slowly in Asciano. Many faces were missing as the Germans urged the population to denounce one another. Now the Crete and the woods were full of people in hiding. Some in groups, others alone. Mario and Francesco were often out.

The Germans had an obsession with knowing where everybody was at all times. Now front doors were kicked in and people dragged from their beds. People were beaten with the butts of rifles in the street. Drunken German soldiers played football with any Jews they could find, and then took them to the Asciano train station where they were locked into guarded wagons and sent over the borders to Germany where they were never heard of again.

Six months later, once again first thing in the morning, there was the sound of troops coming up the drive.

'Are you hiding anyone in your cantina?' The fat German officer stood rocking on his heels at the front door.

'There's no one in our cantina at all. Go and see for yourself.' Mario was calm. The German officer stalked off with his men behind him.

'There go the hams,' Francesco remarked to Mario. They heard the sounds of shots. 'They're too lazy to pull up the floors so they're just shooting through the floorboards. They killed a whole lot of women and children that way in a village nearby.'

'The bastards,' Mario replied through gritted teeth.

Anna stood in the children's nursery, both babies in her arms. They were crawling now and were impatient to be put down.

'Move!' the officer screamed at her. 'And keep them quiet.' He strode through the room, poking at the furniture with his bayonet. He slashed the seat of an armchair in the drawing room. He grew increasingly frustrated as he found nothing. He climbed up into the storeroom and helped himself and his soldiers to piles of sausages and cheeses. Mario was glad that they had removed the bulk of food to the forest and, like many other people in Asciano, had only left sufficient to appease the soldiers' urge to loot and destroy. They all heaved a sigh of relief after the officer inspected their papers and then left.

Anna burst into tears. 'How could anybody be so awful?' she wailed. 'I must run down and see that Pilar is all right.' She handed Nicoletta and Giulio to her mother-in-law and fled.

Pilar was sitting by her stove. On her lap she was tending a cat. 'The bastards shot her,' she said, tears dripping down her face. 'Eh oh, little one. I will make you better.' But she knew she could not make this little animal live again. The bullet had torn through its stomach and blood was flowing freely into the towel that covered it. Anna put her hand on Pilar's shoulder. She could see the light dying in the cat's eyes.

'I'm sorry, Pilar,' she said quietly. 'Really I am.'

Pilar put the rapidly cooling body to her lips. 'Goodbye, little one,' she said.

'Here, give me the cat and I'll get Tommaso to bury it. The ground is so difficult this time of year.'

'Thank you, Anna.' Pilar was still crying, but she was calmer now.

Anna took the little cat in her arms and made her way to Tommaso's cottage up in the fields. 'It's a bad business, signora,' he said. He took the cat from her. 'It's a very bad business indeed.'

Seventy-Three

The dances and balls were muted that year. Mary Rose found herself attending boring cocktail parties in London and rather subdued dinner parties in the country.

Ralph's wife, Belinda, lived nearby. She was a quiet, gentle little thing and Mary Rose only saw her at odd intervals. But she envied her her swelling stomach.

'I'm pregnant,' Belinda had confessed when she had first come to Mary Rose's flat. 'Ralph is so thrilled. He managed to get to a telephone in GHQ in Shanghai. He just yelled to take care of myself and then the line was cut. But it was wonderful to hear his voice.'

The wistfulness in the woman's voice had torn at Mary Rose's heart. She did not feel like that about Crispin. In fact, these days she very much wished he'd move out of her life and leave her alone. While they were first married and when she had not known anyone in England, she had leaned on him heavily for support. Then, as she had expanded her interests and met other people, she had realized how spoilt and childish Crispin really was. His mother catered to his every whim and he had only to enter into a room for her to rise and hover like a bat until he had issued his instructions. Both the girls spoiled and resented him at the same moment, so that their family life was one of unending wars of attrition as the children fought for the attention of their mother. The colonel sat on the sidelines watching the proceedings with a glittering eye. Every so often he would come over to the dower house to moan about his wife. But Mary Rose knew it was pointless to reply. Anything she might say would be carried back and picked over like a dog with a bone. This was the family pattern, and by now Mary Rose was beginning to get heartily sick of it all. She couldn't simply take off for Anna's house as all traffic to Europe was blocked solid. She couldn't get back to her own house in New York for the same reasons. Besides, it seemed silly to mourn about an unhappy marriage when others were wounded and dying. Most days the Kearneys searched *The Times*' lists of the dead and missing.

'Peterson's bought it,' the colonel grumped over his tea and toast. 'Good job you have flat feet, my boy, isn't it? Otherwise you'd have to be out there like I was, in the mud and the –'

'Yes, yes, Dad. I know, with your men all blown away before your eyes. Is that why you've not done another day's work since?'

Both men squared off. 'I didn't mean anything.' Crispin, as usual, backed down from his father's simmering rage.

'Perhaps if you had a job, had something to do, you wouldn't be quite so bored,' the colonel retorted.

Catherine piped up and then grinned at her sister. 'Shut up, you two. Why don't you both find some war work to do like other people?'

Crispin's face looked horrified. 'I'm not rolling bandages or packing food parcels!'

Mary Rose gazed at both the girls with unconcealed dislike. Catherine turned to her. 'What are you doing about the war, Mary Rose?'

Mary Rose smiled. 'Actually, I'm off to St George's Hospital to offer to push books around on a trolley and dispense TLC with hot tea.'

'You're not, Mary Rose!' Crispin was appalled.

'Yes I am. Belinda visited me yesterday and she's going up as well. If that little scrap of a thing can do it, so can I. I'm designing a really sexy outfit for us both to wear.'

'My dear girl, the hospital uniforms have already been designed.' Amelia's voice was dismissive.

'Well then, I'll get Hartnell to redesign ours. Travis knows him.'

Crispin's eyes still held a look of amazement. 'Are you serious about this war work, Mary Rose? I thought you wanted to stay home and have a baby. We can't make babies long distance, you know.'

'I know.' Mary Rose's face was bleak. 'But you know, Crispin, you have to fuck to have babies, and lately there hasn't been any of that, has there?' A shocked, frozen silence fell over the room.

Most nights for the last few months, Crispin had been out and drinking. When he did come back, he would often climb on top of her, but he was mostly impotent. She hated the smell of alcohol on his breath and his fumbling attempts at entering her. The more she drew away from him and began to live her own life, the more desperate he became.

One night she had heard him enter the front door. Unsure if he were just drunk or on drugs, she had left the bedroom and crouched behind the locked bathroom door. She had heard him calling for her.

'Mary Rose, where are you? Come here.' He had

crashed around the drawing room downstairs and then up the broad stairs to the landing. 'Mary Rose!' he had screamed. 'I'm coming to find you.' She had stood in the bathroom, shivering with fear. He had lurched into the bedroom and, from under the bathroom door, she had seen the light go on. She had heard him grunt when he had realized she had not been in the bed. Then he had shuffled towards the door that protected her and had begun to beat his fists on it.

'Come out, you bitch, come out here.' Finally, exhausted, he had slumped to the floor. Gingerly, Mary Rose had opened the door. Then Crispin had leapt to his feet and had grabbed her shoulder.

'Crispin, what's the matter?' She could no longer be bothered to provoke him: she didn't care any longer. Then she had looked at him with disgust and he had seen that he no longer had a hold over her. To Mary Rose's amazement he had begun to jump up and down like a small boy throwing a tantrum.

'I want to be loved the way I want to be loved,' he had screamed as he had beaten the air with his fists.

'Nobody can love you the way you want to be loved, Crispin. Only your sick mother can do that.' Mary Rose had been amazed at how calm her voice had been. 'Now you go to bed and we will talk to each other in the morning.' She had lain for the rest of the night making her plans.

Now, as dawn flushed into a new day, she realized that these plans had been there for some while, probably from the first day that she had taken her car and had headed for her meeting with Travis. She watched his weak face as he slept beside her and a single tear slid down her cheek. She had never loved him, nor he her. But they had been drawn together out of different needs: he for money and she for stability. But neither of them had been satisfied. She felt an unsettling pall of failure.

Anna had Mario and Belinda was so happy with Ralph. She, the third, was not happy. Maybe she would not find happiness with a man in her lifetime, but now she knew she could at least have life. To live without fear of another human being. To live without criticism was something she hardly remembered. Maybe, she thought as she lay against her pillows, Travis had taught her acceptance. He, transfixed by the pain of his impotence, had taught her to be gentle when she was with him. Not for him the smart answer and the sharp reply. She found that when she arrived in London, still wired up from her fights with Crispin, she often hurt him with her broken glass remarks. Now she lay waiting for Crispin to rise out of his drunken sleep.

'How much, Crispin?' she said. He sat slouched over his coffee. She could hear the throaty sound of the Hoover downstairs. Mrs Birstall, the char, was bumping the furniture with her usual aplomb. Crispin's eyes flashed like stop lights. He straightened up and put down his coffee cup. Lighting a cigarette, he took a deep breath.

'I take it you mean for me to get out of your life.'

'Yes.' Mary Rose's voice was cold. She sat still. She knew that, now he scented the smell of money, he would snap to and begin to hustle.

'Well, I'll have to think about it, old thing. I mean to say, this has come as something of a surprise. I mean, we are talking about our marriage, you know.'

'I do know, Crispin. I'm sorry if it has come as something of a surprise.' Mary Rose knew that it was no surprise to him. His behaviour over the last few years had been designed to drive her away. She now realized that the violence was going to escalate until she was forced to buy her way out. Probably that was always what he intended. She had been the fool.

But there was a feeling of freedom as she watched him carefully.

'I can't give you an answer right away, of course.' Crispin had his self-important voice under control. Mary Rose could sense the excitement that he struggled to conceal.

'I'm going off to London this afternoon with Belinda. I'll be back in two days' time. Perhaps you can give me an answer then?'

She knew that would give him time to get together with his mother, and between the two of them they would come up with a package that would keep him in cashmere and silk shirts for life. She could then go back to the States, leaving him the dower house. 'Thank you, Crispin,' she said firmly. She rose out of bed and walked naked to the bathroom.

'Are you sure you don't want a quickie just for old times' sake?' The thought of money had given him an erection.

'No thanks, Crispin.' Mary Rose walked into the bathroom, closing and then locking the door. She leaned against the door exhausted but triumphant. She was free at last. Now all that remained was for her to negotiate carefully.

Seventy-Four

Pilar took the death of her little cat very hard. It was strange to see the usually fiery little woman looking so whipped by the loss. 'My cats are my children,' she tried to explain to Anna.

'I know that, Pilar.' Anna put her arms around the old lady's shoulders and hugged her thin little frame. 'They all love you and protect you, especially that little one. She always reminded me of a grey scarf the way she weaved around your legs.'

Now Anna tried to visit Pilar every day, bringing the children with her. The town was no longer a harmonious cluster of families. It had been split by fear and the anxiety of self-preservation. People no longer dared come to Pilar for help. But they protected the old woman, not wanting her denounced as a witch. Francesco had offered to house her on the farm with the rest of the family, but she had shaken her head.

'Here I was born and here I shall stay. Let them kill me if they will. I am old and have lived my life.' She had glowered fiercely at Francesco and her chin had wobbled with hate. She had spat derisively. 'Sons of whores,' she had muttered as she hobbled back into her cottage.

Francesco had laughed. 'I like her spirit.'

In spite of Pilar's gutsy stand, Anna found life difficult. Much of the time, Mario could not tell her why he was out and about at night. Sometimes he and Francesco were gone for days. Anna felt disconcerted. She so belonged here in this family with Mario, but she was still in exile from a country she loved and from her parents. No news, nothing, was coming through.

At times all were aware that there were people hidden in the top part of the house. Then Lisa's voice would hush and she would pass by silently carrying bowls of food. The children, almost by a kind of osmosis, knew not to ask. The lists of the names of people who had disappeared grew daily. Many of Elisabetta's Jewish friends were now in hiding in Florence. Anna knew of the blood-bath outside, but the family was kept strangely separated from the events. It was as if a Pathé newsreel was running in her head and she could see England under siege by bombing.

She wondered about Mary Rose. Was she still over

there, or had she gone back to America and safety? She knew France was overrun and that people were dying like flies. Those who hadn't collaborated had lost their souls. America was teetering on the edge of openly joining the conflict. Then came the news of Pearl Harbor.

Waves of euphoria washed over the whole family after the news was picked up on a secret radio in the forest.

'The Americans are coming in now!' Mario's face was alight as he burst through the front door. 'It won't be long and we will be rid of the Germans. We will grind their faces in the dust.'

Anna looked at her beloved husband and was appalled to see how much he had absorbed the blood-lust and hatred of war. She knew he had witnessed atrocities that he had not – and never would – discussed with her. She knew because she had held his shaking, nightmare-ridden body in her arms and heard his garbled words to shoot. One night he had screamed: 'Don't shoot, don't shoot', and then he had sobbed.

She had woken him up gently. 'Darling, what was that you were dreaming about?'

He had wakened and had then said: 'You don't want to know.' He had then fallen back asleep, senseless.

Now Mario took out a good bottle of wine. 'I have been keeping this wine for a special occasion, and this is a special occasion. Not long now.'

The next day in Asciano, Anna noticed people walking around with a revived spring in their step. Having left the children at home, she walked carefully. She did not want to excite the attention of the Germans standing in sullen groups on the corners of the streets. In the bar by the church where the Germans had pushed out all the old men, soldiers sat with their helmets balanced on the end of their rifles.

'Don't think that the Americans can save you now,'

they jeered at the passing population. 'Just gives us more bodies to burn. American boots, American uniforms.' Anna went past, her eyes to the ground. The news had obviously shaken the German soldiers and she was anxious to get home. She noticed a small knot of uniformed men pointing at her. They were standing by the well. Hopefully they were just commenting on the fact that she was known to be the town's only American. She hurried back to the house to tell Mario.

'Tomorrow,' he said firmly, 'we send you with the children to the caves. But tonight we practise as soon as it gets dark.'

At ten o'clock, after the dinner dishes had been washed and put away, Mario and Francesco lined up Elisabetta, Lisa, Anna and the children and distributed clothes and food among them.

'Now go to the far end of the woods and don't come back until I call the all-clear,' Mario instructed.

Obediently, Anna led the way carrying Nicoletta. Lisa carried Giulio. Quietly they fled across the lawn and into the trees. As they reached the deep shadows of the trees, they saw headlights coming up the path. The two men stood transfixed in the glare. Anna made a move to go back, but Elisabetta held her tightly.

Lisa took the children and whispered to them to follow her. 'I will go fast now,' she said, and began to run.

Elisabetta, her arms around Anna, could feel her daughter-in-law's heart beating fast.

'It's the Germans,' Anna said, her voice breaking with fear. 'They've come to arrest me. I must go back or they'll take Mario and Francesco and torture them to find me.' She pulled away but Elisabetta held her tight. Anna was surprised at the strength in the woman's arms.

'You cannot go back, Anna. They will kill us all if they see that you have come from the forest. We must go now because soon they will start to look for us.'

'I must go to Mario.' Anna struggled.

'It is not what Mario would want, Anna. He would want you to take care of his children. Listen,' she hissed. '*Noblesse oblige*. You know our family motto. We must go.'

Anna could hear the Germans shouting and the word '*Amerikaner*' was often repeated. Elisabetta flinched as she saw a rifle butt raised in the air. She saw one of the men on the ground. She gasped and hid Anna's head in her arms.

'Come, Anna,' she said, pulling at her daughter-in-law. 'We must go now.'

Anna held firm. 'Mario,' she pleaded. 'God please save him.' She found herself gasping with pain and fear. Then they heard a shot ring out. The man on the ground convulsed and then lay still. The other man, they realized, was Francesco. He stood tall and bare-headed in the moonlight. He turned his face briefly to the woods and Elisabetta knew he was thinking of her.

'Goodbye, my love,' she whispered, tears pouring down her face. 'I'll love you for ever.' For several moments she stood frozen, her eyes transfixed at the horror in front of her. Then she jolted.

'Come.' She pulled Anna's now acquiescent arm. 'We must go to the children.' Both women stumbled and wept as they ran down the trail. Behind them they could hear the thick sound of men's boots and ribald laughter. For Anna, the last thing she remembered was Mario's body convulsing on the ground. Mercifully, her mind snapped with the strain.

Seventy-Five

🖋

'Darling?' Elisabetta was crouched on the ground in front of Anna who was sitting quietly, her hands in her lap. Beside her, Lisa held Nicoletta on her lap while Giulio played nearby.

'What is the matter with her?' Lisa asked.

'I don't know.' Elisabetta's voice was fearful. 'I think the shock has temporarily taken her mind away.' She tried again. 'Anna, look, this is Nicoletta, your little girl. Nicoletta, give your mother a kiss.'

Lisa held the girl up to her mother's face. The child pursed her lips and kissed her mother, babbling affectionately. There was a slight smile at the corners of Anna's mouth, but her huge blue eyes, now empty, continued to stare vacantly into space. Elisabetta pushed back a strand of hair and looked around the cave. They were deeply entombed in the larval cavity. The men had done their work well. There were rudimentary beds made from split logs, thick blankets, piles of wood for burning, and tins of provisions. They would be able to stay here for a long while.

'Please God it's not a long while,' Elisabetta whispered to herself. Her own fears for Francesco now flooded back and she tried to suppress tears. Lisa had been crying on and off since they had arrived the night before. Now the children were grubby, although not hungry. Elisabetta had cooked a large pan of pasta early that morning. Big demijohns capable of holding fifty litres of water were standing in rows against the walls of the cave. Elisabetta knew there were other caves dotted around the area and supposed that someone would contact them. She desperately needed to hear news of her husband and she tried to believe that her son was still alive. In her heart of hearts she knew it was not possible. Having nursed so many people on their death beds, she knew by the way his body crumpled in its final convulsion that he was no longer alive.

'Maybe it is better for Anna that she is not with us for a while,' she said to Lisa. 'But she will come back. I know she will.' Her voice sounded hollow. How on earth would they manage, two women with two children and Anna only there in body? Elisabetta steeled herself. She straightened her shoulders and smiled. 'All right, children, let's all get washed.' She heaved at the big demijohn. A flood of water ran out, missing the bucket that Lisa was holding under the jar. Elisabetta lost all control and began to cry.

Lisa righted the demijohn and held her in her arms. 'You cry, signora. We will be all right. God will take care of us.'

At that moment Elisabetta wished she had Lisa's simple faith. She wiped her eyes and tilted the demijohn again. 'Isn't it funny, Lisa, I can take the awful things happening and suffer in silence. But it is when a little thing like spilling water happens that I go to pieces. Oh Lisa, I can't believe this is not just a terrible nightmare and we are really all in our beds.'

'I'm afraid this is a nightmare, but it is real.'

The bucket was now full and Lisa took it to the fire that was glowing in the middle of the cave. Someone – probably Francesco – had created a hood over the fire that took the smoke away from the centre of the cave and funnelled it outside. Elisabetta walked to the door of the cave and slid around the big boulder that hid the opening. The cave was far down a steep ravine. High walls hid it from view. Because it was still winter, the surrounding landscape was bare and lunar. She pulled her shawl around her and shivered. The wind was bitter. The *tramontana*, the suicide wind, she reminded herself. She went back in. The smoke was not going to give them away. How like Francesco to think of such a clever device. Her eyes filled again and she gave a long, sobbing sigh.

Two days passed. Elisabetta and Lisa had taken shovels and dug small pits for a lavatory outside, behind a small, straggling tree that clung to the outside wall of the cave. Nearby there was a small spring which cheered both women with its serene activity.

Elisabetta, repressing a wish to collapse and mourn her son's death, and trying to ignore the thoughts that crowded into her mind of her husband's probable torture at the hands of the Germans, threw herself into work. She dug up six of the massive hams that the men had buried so long ago. She strung them from a pole she found outside.

It was a gnarled and twisted tree trunk. To Elisabetta, it looked just as she now felt; but she endured, knowing that her survival was the only way to keep the children safe. Her heart was in such pain she had to move, and keep moving. The hams swung from the pole slung in a corner of the cave. Strings of onions and a pile of potatoes rested in another.

'At least we have wood, fire, and water,' she consoled herself.

On the fourth day Elisabetta washed Anna and put her on a plank. There she knew she would sit until someone led her outside for some fresh air.

'Anna!' She tried but now she knew it was useless. The most response any of them could get was a slight smile. Nicoletta and Giulio climbed on their mother's lap and played with her hands and her fingers. They kissed her and were puzzled at the lack of response. Lisa would gently take them away and busy them with a game.

Elisabetta was outside filling in the ablution holes and preparing for the back-breaking job of digging some more. Suddenly she heard the sound of feet crunching on the clay surface. Instantly she ran into the cave, her hand across her mouth and her right arm waving a warning.

'Someone is out there,' she hissed. The children stopped doing what they were doing and clung to her. Lisa took Anna's hand. Anna was beyond fear, she realized as she stood shaking and waiting. A man slid around the rock.

'It's all right,' he said, coming straight to Elisabetta.

'Tommaso!' She put her arms around his thick neck. 'Oh, Tommaso, is it you?'

Tommaso's eyes took in the cave, the provisions and the frightened women and children. He stared at Anna. 'What is the matter with Signora Anna?' he whispered, horror-struck at her vacant face.

'We saw Mario shot by the Germans. He is dead, isn't he?'

Tommaso nodded solemnly. 'I waited until they left and then Nico and I buried him. They will not find his body.' His face went blank for a moment. 'Now they are hanging bodies from trees to frighten the people into denouncing on pain of being exposed for all the town to see. But there is hope for some people, despite the Germans. I know a fellow who comes to the café. He whispered to me that Signor Francesco is safe, although he is wounded and has been tortured. But he has been sent to Germany. At least he is still alive.' His eyes filled with tears. 'Oh *Dio*, we so much want him back. He was . . .' He corrected himself. 'He is such a good man.'

Elisabetta smiled sadly. 'Thank you for that news, Tommaso. I feel I can live again. I know my Francesco will be all right. He is tough and hardy and used to the cold.' He was pleased to see a smile break through her wintry countenance.

Lisa clasped her hands. 'At least one of them is alive,' she said. She looked down at Anna. 'It is better that she cannot hear this conversation. Maybe when we can take her out of here we can find a doctor.'

'I don't think a doctor can help her,' Tommaso said. 'I've seen grief do this before. Hopefully time will tell.'

They spent the rest of the afternoon sharing news with Tommaso. 'The Germans are in the house,' he told them. 'You have officers, so hopefully they will not be the filthy pigs the soldiers are. But then there's no knowing. The Americans are in Paris but the city has not fallen yet. There is fighting in all the streets. News is hard to get, but my friend Heinz says that there are orders to pull back if the Americans take Paris. He says he is tired of war and just wants to get home to his sweetheart. I don't blame him. He's a nice, honest lad and hates what he sees going on. He told me that he used to watch Anna and Mario and envy them their love. He hopes he will be that happy. He was sad when he knew Mario was shot. I was coming to find you anyway, but he warned me not to come back. Nico is making his way back to Sicily. He sends his love and prayers for you all.'

He smiled at them. 'So you have my company. You will need a man to take care of you all.' He tickled Nicoletta's grubby cheek. 'Come on, little one, you come outside with your Uncle Tommaso while I dig some holes. It's not work for a signora.'

Elisabetta watched his round, honest figure leave the camp, with Nicoletta hanging off his arm. Giulio followed them. Underneath the unbearable pain of the death of her son was the quiet relief that Francesco was still alive. She crossed herself as she hurried to help Lisa prepare the evening meal.

'God is good,' she said, smiling at Lisa.

'*È vero*. God is good. It is human beings who let

him down. At least Anna will eat, even if we have to feed her.'

'That's a blessing.' Elisabetta realized that blessings were going to be far from numerous, and that every one that came along must be treasured.

Seventy-Six

'You must be out of your mind, Crispin.' Amelia's face had assumed a dull red flush. 'You haven't agreed to anything, have you?'

'Well, not really. I said I'd have to give it some thought. I don't see why it's such a bad idea. We're both bored with each other. She's away all the time and I just hang around here. I'm getting older by the minute and I want to get out and live a little. I thought marriage to Mary Rose would be swanning about the world for the rest of my life. But in fact she changed almost overnight with this damn job, and now she's off to do her precious good works. I'm sure she's having an affair with that Travis chap. I call him Randy Travis just to annoy her.'

There was a pout on Crispin's face. Amelia looked carefully at her oldest child. He was now thirty-four and no longer had the shine of youth about him. His hair was still thick and blond but there were one or two flashes of silver. Amelia knew her son well. He was worried that he was getting too old to 'pull the girls'. Amelia found herself smiling faintly at the slang used by her daughters. There was an airforce base further up the road and both girls were in great demand.

'I think you'd be a damn fool if you let her get away. This place costs a fortune to keep up, and how would you pay for your lifestyle? She'll give you a large lump sum and you'll run through it like hot gravy. And talking about gravy, Crispin, you climbed on board that train and you'd better stay there. No, I don't think it's a good idea to agree to a divorce because she's got banks of lawyers at her fingertips and we only have old Mr Ryder. He's all we can afford.'

Amelia was lost in thought. 'I suppose if you could catch her with a man you could sue for adultery.' She raised one eyebrow. 'Or just threaten to splash her name in the papers. "Mrs Kearney found in bed with Randy Travis" type of stuff in the *News Chronicle*. She might pay up, then again she might not.'

Amelia had to admit Crispin's voice sounded almost arch. 'You do know me very well, don't you, Mother?'

'I do, Crispin. And sometimes I'm not sure that I like what I see.'

'Tough. It keeps you in rhododendrons and pays for the cook. We'd all keel over if we had to stomach your cooking.'

Amelia watched him stomp out of the house and sighed. She would not repeat this conversation to her husband. He tended to take Mary Rose's side. It embarrassed him to have a son with flat feet and a wonky chest. Still, she was glad that she'd probably managed to stop Crispin running out of his marriage. She knew all too well whatever money he got out of Mary Rose would soon be gone on gambling and womanizing and then she would be left yet again struggling to keep the house going. Oh no, Amelia told herself firmly, those days are over, never to return again. Hopefully the two girls would find rich American husbands from the base and go off to America after this blasted war was over. Then she could have the place to herself with her dogs and her garden. Her husband was not a nuisance. He could continue to sit in a corner like a stuffed corn doll.

In his way he was company for her. She wandered out to the rose garden with her secateurs.

Upstairs in the dower house, Crispin was lying across his bed telephoning the family lawyer.

'Mr Ryder,' he said in hushed, sad tones. 'I need to be sure that this conversation will remain absolutely confidential. My mother would break her heart if she ever found out.'

Mr Ryder rolled his eyes. He'd been having these confidential conversations with Crispin for many years now, and they largely covered women and gambling debts. He had hoped that Crispin would settle down with his rich American bride.

'What is it, Crispin?' Mr Ryder's snuff-stained moustache assumed a disapproving bristle.

'I think my wife is having an affair.' Crispin found himself feeling genuinely upset. How could Mary Rose do this to him, he wondered.

'I see. And what sort of evidence do you have of this affair?' The old man wanted to chuckle.

'Mary Rose is in a business with a man called Randy . . . er . . . I mean Travis Mainwaring. She is hardly ever home and now she has moved into a flat in Eaton Square owned by a client of hers. I feel so devastated I want to set my mind at rest. I want to get a private detective on the case. A divorce detective, you know, one of those people who check up on adulterous wives. Or husbands of course.'

'Right ho. We have quite a good fellow in Exeter. I'll give you his telephone number. If he finds that your wife is having an affair, he'll get the evidence and photographs. No doubt you'll want a divorce?'

'I haven't made that decision yet, Mr Ryder. I'll need time to think about it.'

'Well, let me know what you decide.' Mr Ryder put the telephone down and sighed. He hated these cases.

Usually the sinner was so much nicer than the so-called saint, and in Crispin's case, it couldn't happen to a nastier fellow. Poor woman, she will have to pay through the nose if she gets caught. He called for a cup of tea and then exploded with a double pinch of snuff from the back of his hand.

'Rodney March, Private Detective,' said the card that was thrust into Crispin's willing hand. The office was suitably cloistered and dark. Crispin found himself rather excited by the visit. His role as the wronged suitor was beginning to take shape.

'She ignores me completely now, you see.' Crispin put his tweed-jacketed elbows on the desk and rested his aquiline head on his fists. He stared at Rodney March with, he hoped, hard-done-by blue eyes.

'That's women, innit?' Rodney's boot-button eyes, deeply set in a badly shaved face, stared at him. His teeth were broken and decayed. Why can't the English working classes take care of their teeth, Crispin wondered.

'I'm not absolutely certain, but she's away a hell of a lot. He's always on the telephone to her when she's at home, and well . . . things haven't been going too well between us.'

'I know what you mean. Not too much of the old . . .' Rodney made a gesture with his elbow.

'Quite.' Crispin felt embarrassed. The man was really very perceptive in a horrible, vulgar way. But then, what can one expect from a man who makes a living peeking into other people's private lives, he told himself sternly.

'OK, guv. My parish used to be the Old Kent Road. Although Eaton Square is up-market, I'll 'ave a look about. That's the address, is it?'

Crispin nodded. 'And this is the telephone number. When do you think you're likely to go? She's up there now and for the next three days.'

'I'll go up and watch tomorrow. And then when I get an idea of who she is seeing and where, I'll go in and nab them at it.' He leered. 'That's the best bit. Catch them at it.'

Crispin left the office, glad to be away. He climbed into his car and revved the engine. He made a face. He didn't much like the idea of anybody 'at it' with Mary Rose. He didn't want her, but he didn't want anybody else to have her either, and particularly not her money. He fell asleep that night dreaming of Rodney's eyes staring at him while he was trying to make love to a red-headed girl with no pubic hair.

Seventy-Seven

The moon was full and hung over the bare, undulating Crete, casting mysterious shadows outside the caves. Tommaso lay on his back, blessing the fact that the day had been hot. April was here and he longed to be back in the fields planting the grain. For him the planting season on the first day the moon waned was full of confused feelings. First, there were the months that he devoted to the digging of the fields. Then there was the preparing and tilling of the soil. He loved the earth with a passion. He loved the thick clay that stuck to his boots and fingers. He loved the warm, brown smell of the earth as he turned it in huge chocolate coloured slabs. He moulded and tended his fields like he would a woman. The planting he did as his father had done before him, in the light of the mother moon. Now, he gazed up at her craggy face. He watched her pocked countenance and he wished with all his heart that he was in his fields with his satchel slung over his shoulder and his right hand full of seeds. For Tommaso, planting a field was analogous to making love to a woman. And right now he very badly wanted a woman. Normally, after planting his fields, he made a trip to Buonconvento where there was a convenient local 'brothel'. Maria, a big fat warm woman, always made him welcome. Over the years, not only did she satisfy his deepest urge to fuck himself dry, but she was also a friend. Sometimes he would take her out to dinner in the family restaurant behind the whorehouse. Now he missed her dreadfully. Sensing a foreign presence, he looked up and saw Lisa standing beside him, gazing at his prone form.

'Are you all right, Tommaso?' she whispered, the moonlight casting red glints on her long, dark hair.

'I guess so,' he grumbled. 'Here, sit down and talk to me.'

Lisa heaved a sigh. 'I am so worried about Signora Anna. She does not get better. She is like a doll.'

'There is nothing we can do about it, Lisa. She will come back in time, God willing. We can just take care of her and trust that the people that come to take care of us do not betray us. It feels so odd to have news that the war now is raging around us. The Germans are in retreat. Our people are tortured and dying, but we are here, cut off from everything, just waiting. It is the waiting that makes it all so difficult for a man like me. I'm used to activity.'

Lisa sat down beside him. He smelled the clean, freshly washed smell of her body. He, who had always taken Lisa's presence for granted, had been surprised at the strength in her little body. She heaved and dug and cooked and washed without complaint. She smiled and never showed grief or anxiety, even though she must be worried about the fate of her mother. She took care of all the children and served both the other women faithfully. Now she had discovered many different ways to cook the grains that they had in the cave. Privately, Tommaso swore that once this blasted war was over, he would never eat another bean as long as he lived. Now, looking at her gentle face and big brown eyes, he felt a surge of tenderness. He had to restrain himself from touching her cheek. He wondered if his feeling was a genuine attraction to Lisa or a result of the lust engendered by the moon. Making love had always made him feel at peace and in unity with the world. And God knows how the world had been raped and torn by this war. He wished Lisa was not a good Catholic girl. He wished she was a wild and willing woman. He wished many unsayable things. He turned on his stomach so that she could not see his erection. What it is to be a man, he thought bashfully. He heard a little giggle at his side. He looked up sharply, affronted by the intimacy of the giggle. 'What's the matter, Lisa? Why do you laugh?'

'Because,' she said, throwing back her head, her hair hanging down her back, 'you want a woman.'

'How do you know that?' he asked, amazed at her percipience.

'I can smell it,' she said. She bent over and kissed him hard on the mouth. 'A pity I'm not Maria from Buonconvento, huh?'

She rose gracefully to her feet, still giggling, and left Tommaso stretched on the ground, racked in pain. 'Madonna,' he swore. 'The little witch!'

Seventy-Eight

Rodney March wore his best raincoat for spying on Mary Rose Kearney. After all, it wasn't every day that he was asked to go on a job in a posh part of town.

'Bye, sweetie,' he said, as he pinched his wife's bottom affectionately as he passed through the front door.

'Fuck off. And keep your 'ands to yourself and your willie in its proper place.' Amy, Rodney's wife, was a long-suffering woman, and she had two whining kids to take to school.

Rodney climbed into his Austin Seven and prepared to hit the road. Once on the open road, he was free to dream his dreams. They were not big dreams of amazing adventures or piles of money. Rather, they were dreams of him fornicating with lots and lots of women. Now, sealed inside his Austin Seven, he had hours ahead of him to lust his life away. With his foot down on the accelerator, he imagined he was driving a Rolls-Royce convertible. The leather was cream and the smell of it was nearly as sexual as the raven-haired beauty who lay with her head on his lap and gently sucked him off as he drove. Following that little adventure, he put himself into a harem, where he was making love to one woman with his mouth and copulating with a black woman at the same time. Time passed swiftly for Rodney.

When he reached the outskirts of London, he almost hit a big red bus and decided he ought to concentrate. Soon he was passing through Chiswick, and then Hammersmith, before turning south from Knightsbridge down Sloane Street. This part of London was new territory for him. When he saw Eaton Square his broad brow furrowed.

''Ow in the 'ell am I going to 'ang out 'ere waiting for the chick to meet 'er fellow?' he inquired aloud to himself.

There was no comforting answer. He couldn't face parking his Austin Seven in among the Rolls and the Bentleys, so he parked it down a side alley and patted the neat little roof. 'We don't belong 'ere,' he said affectionately. 'We're better off down the Old Kent

Road where a broad can 'ave a bit of fun and I can 'ang out and look like one of the locals. Blimey, what am I going to do?'

He sauntered down to Sloane Square and stared into the windows of Peter Jones. He bought himself an evening newspaper, then returned to Eaton Square and leaned against the gate of the first house, pretending to read. He did not have long to wait. A car pulled up. He turned the page and looked over the top. Yes indeed, he was in luck. Crispin had given him a picture of Mary Rose. He didn't need to consult it. I'd like to get that bit of crackling between the sheets, he thought. I could show her a thing or two. Married to that wet twit it's no wonder she's looking elsewhere.

Mary Rose parked the car and for a moment stood looking down the road. Rodney lifted his newspaper again.

She carried her Fortnum and Mason's shopping bags into the kitchen. She loved Mrs Gulbenkian's kitchen. Designed by Mary Rose, it was tiled with yellow and blue Portuguese tiles. The wall was painted a clear Mediterranean blue, and there was a bright, fire-engine-red Aga sitting against the back wall. Everywhere the surfaces were white marble. Sets of shelves were filled with cooking utensils. In the middle of the kitchen was a big, low cooking table, also covered in white marble. At home with Crispin she couldn't really be bothered cooking. Crispin was such a neurotic about food. But here, with guests like Travis and Justin, cooking was a pleasure.

Tonight she was making an Italian dish for Travis. Rolled stuffed beef with ham and ricotta cheese, baked in a dish of fresh green beans and potatoes. She added the garlic to the smoking pan and then, when everything was frying nicely, she finished the dish with a tablespoon of thick red tomato paste. Soon she was ready to shower and get changed.

She loved her shower. Apart from the Savoy, nowhere else seemed to have showers. The English preferred to bathe in their own dirt. She wrinkled her nose and laughed as the hot water splashed over her head. She also enjoyed the fact that she had a bidet. She washed herself luxuriously in scented rosewater. Now she was ready to put on her silk underwear and a long, loose top that just covered her thighs. Travis liked to finger the silk when he was coming.

After dinner and making love, Mary Rose sat up in bed and reached for a cigarette. She lit one for Travis and they lay beside each other smoking. 'I think Crispin is going to let me go this time. We've never really talked straight about splitting up, but I asked him directly and he says he'll think about it.'

'I sure hope he will. That bastard is no good for you, Mary Rose. You always look so strained when you get here. I used to think it was the drive up, but it's not that, is it?'

'No, it's not that, Travis. I realize now that I've had time to get away from him and be on my own. Looking after somebody as neurotic as Crispin is a twenty-four-hour-a-day job and I'm not up to it. I want a man in my life that can take care of me. Not a wimp that can't get out of bed and do a day's work.' She drew deeply on her cigarette. 'If you'd told me before I was married that I'd love working hard I would have laughed in your face. I guess that's where we went wrong. I married Crispin when I knew he was a layabout. So was I, but I grew up and he didn't. Still, it's not my bag any more. He's somebody else's nightmare, thank God.'

Outside, Rodney was shifting uncomfortably. He had nipped down to the pub for several pints, banking on the fact that Mary Rose and the man who had joined her would be eating from seven until eight. Now he urgently needed to pee. Eaton Square did not appear to have any urinals, and he didn't dare risk leaving his post to search for some. Posh people must be able to hold their drink, he thought. He hiked himself over the fence, scratching himself on a rose bush as he did so. Little whimpers of pain escaped from his mouth. Shit, shit, shit, he cursed silently. He took a surreptitious look around the now deserted streets. At six o'clock the cocktail crowd had swarmed the streets. Short dresses and minks had joined suits and ties. At eight, the dinner and dance set had left their houses in bouffant frocks and white ties. Now there was nobody left. The only signs of life were the nanny lights in the nurseries that blazed from the top dormer windows. One day, Rodney promised himself, me and Amy and the kids is going to live here and then I won't have to pee in the hedge. The smell of his urine mixed with the smell of cats in the privet hedge. He leaned back against a willow tree and let the long green fronds hide him. He lit a cigarette and tried to keep his mind off sex so he could concentrate on the job. Once, wallowing in a luscious sexual fantasy, he'd lost a man and it had cost him the job.

He was rewarded for his patience by seeing Travis leaving the house at six o'clock in the morning, just as dawn was breaking. He snapped the man coming towards him and was glad that he was hidden by the tree. Though it was winter, the falling branches of the willow were thick enough to cover his whereabouts. Satisfied, he put his camera in his pocket. Travis was snapped leaving the house; hopefully the number would show up clearly. Now all he had to do was to get it printed and then call his boss. Nice-looking man, her lover. Much better to get shafted by him than by her gigolo of a husband, Rodney thought as he headed for home and Amy.

Seventy-Nine

At the end of April, a thin man in a trilby slid into the cave. 'We have to move you,' he told Tommaso.

Tommaso's face drained of all colour. They had become used to their cave and their way of life.

'The Germans are fighting a rearguard action and they are slaughtering anybody in their path. We have to get you out of here because they will go to ground in these caves. I've heard that they now know they're here.' He produced a small, crumpled letter. 'This is a letter for Signora Anna.' He glanced at the still, quiet figure. 'She is sick?'

'No,' Tommaso said shortly. 'She lost her husband. He was shot in front of her. Her mind has snapped like a twig.'

The man handed the letter to Elisabetta who opened it. 'Oh dear,' she said, 'it's from Ralph. He is back in England. His wife died in childbirth, leaving him with a little boy. How sad. How terribly, terribly sad.' She looked at Anna. 'At least she won't have to suffer this fresh piece of news.' Giulio sat next to his mother on the ground, talking baby-talk to her.

Elisabetta looked at the well-ordered cave and dreaded the move. 'When must we go?' she asked the man.

'Tomorrow night. I will send three men to guide you. Can the signora walk?'

'Yes, she can walk,' Lisa said. 'Signora Elisabetta and I can take the twins.'

'My men will help you carry provisions. What you can't carry, burn. We don't want to feed the bastards.'

'If it weren't for my friend Heinz, I'd hate all Germans,' Tommaso observed as he began collecting the hams.

'Don't hate anyone,' Elisabetta said sadly. 'Most people the world over are quiet, loving and kind. They are the ones you don't hear from. There are as many good Germans as there are Nazis. I am proud of Italy. We do have our Fascists and our collaborators, but they are few.' She stroked Giulio's soft, fair hair. 'Poor fatherless boy.' Tears welled in her eyes.

Lisa took Giulio. 'Come on, little one. Let's go outside and play.' Tommaso watched them go and realized that he had fallen in love with Lisa. So far he had said nothing, but her joy in life, and her ability one moment to be a child and another a mature woman full of fun and sexual passion, transfixed him. He had never forgotten the warmth and promise of her kiss that night under the full moon. But now was no time for talking of love: he had a job to do.

The next night, six men filed into the cave. They were wearing black clothes and had stocking caps which made their eyes look cold and dangerous. They were all armed to the teeth.

'We have come to take the family away,' one of them snapped unceremoniously.

'Where are we going?' Elisabetta asked anxiously.

'Don't ask,' was the reply.

They handed over black shawls and black stocking caps for the little party. 'Take off your rings, ladies, please. We don't need anything flashing in the moonlight.'

The man who had been there the night before squatted down and gathered the children in front of him. 'Now children,' he said, 'I want you to be very, very quiet. Not a sound. Here . . .' He put a handful of sweets into Elisabetta's hands. 'Give these to the children to suck.'

The children's eyes grew wide with wonder. They had not seen sweets for a very long time. They filled their mouths and followed the men outside.

They walked for what seemed like hours. Two of the men carried the children after the first twenty minutes, and soon they were asleep over their bearers' shoulders. Elisabetta was grateful to hand over the twins. The climb up the Crete was steep and hard.

'*Ora basta*,' the leader said after dawn was breaking, stopping suddenly. He pushed back a big limb of a tree. Behind it lay another cave. 'We'll stay here for the day-time and tonight we move again.'

That night they left the Crete and moved along mountain roads. They seemed to be heading south. The weather was getting warmer and the terrain softer than the dramatic sweep of the Tuscan highlands. As they travelled, Tommaso kept up the spirits of the little party. He carried a large flagon of wine. Everywhere they stopped he disappeared and came back with it full, as if by magic. He teased Lisa unmercifully, and she had to stifle her giggles. By the end of the week it was obvious they were a long way south of Tuscany. They seldom saw anybody on these tiny little trails. The men of the Resistance knew their way like mountain goats. Elisabetta was amazed at how efficiently they found enough hidden rations, so that they were never short of food.

Through all this travelling, Lisa led Anna by the hand. She washed her, changed her, and helped her go to the lavatory. Still, there was no sign that Anna understood anything. Elisabetta worried for her and prayed for the life of her husband. They travelled until, on the last Sunday of the month, they came to a mountain and began to climb.

The children thrived on the enforced march. The men now loved them both. They carried them on their shoulders, and in their arms when they slept. They told them stories and played football with Giulio. The twins now talked with thick Tuscan accents that made their grandmother laugh. Travelling became a way of life for them.

'I don't know what it will be like when we settle down again,' Elisabetta joked. Tommaso smiled, glad that she could laugh again. The travels had made Elisabetta as slim as a rush in a frog pond. The sun had browned her skin. She looked beautiful as she struggled to keep up with the men.

Lisa sang and danced her way to the top of the mountain. When they arrived, exhausted, Tommaso put the flagon of wine to his lips and sank to his knees.

'You are old, Tommaso,' Lisa teased. 'Look, I can still dance.' She kicked her heels in the air.

'I'll show you who's old,' he grumbled. 'Just you wait, my girl.'

'I am waiting,' she said. And there was a passionate, smouldering silence between them. Tommaso, tired as he was, had a vision of Lisa without clothes, lying beside a rushing stream and he inside her. Stop that, he commanded himself. I've got to make camp.

Later, before the sun was up, the men slid away into the shadows and the little family was alone again.

Eighty

🖋

'Yes, that's Travis Mainwaring.' Crispin held the photograph in his hand. Despite the poor quality of the print, and the fact that it had been taken in poor light, fortunately a nearby street-lamp had illuminated the necessary, incriminating details. Crispin knew that he was going to see the image of the man who was a friend and colleague of his wife's, but he hadn't expected to have quite such a reaction. Rodney March had telephoned and had said triumphantly: 'I got a picture of the bloke that stayed the night with your wife.' The detective's description of the man certainly fitted Travis, but even then Crispin didn't want to believe it.

'How could she?' he said, holding the photograph in his hand. 'The bitch. The prize rotten disgusting whore.' He knew he had to get out of Rodney's office before he was sick. He paid the fee and then left the building. He stood for a moment by his car, shaking with anger. Then he made for the nearest pub.

It was a brown, fly-speckled little tavern. The woman behind the bar was skinny with bleached blonde hair and a slash of bright red lipstick.

'A gin and tonic,' he said, sliding on to the brass bar-stool.

'With ice?' she inquired in a high, reedy voice.

'Yes.' Crispin was in no mood to talk. He gazed at himself in the mirror behind the bar, and between the greasy smears he wondered if he were losing his looks. God knows, Mary Rose had told him enough times that he was too old to be a gigolo. The rest of his life yawned emptily ahead of him. What was he going to do? He'd never thought further than the day ahead, and now that he was forced to think he didn't much like what he saw. Another woman was the obvious answer. Or maybe he should reconsider and stay with Mary Rose.

The idea that he should be responsible for himself from now on terrified him. Yes, he would have her money, or as much of it as he could claw away. But that did not deal with the acres of time he would have on his hands.

Crispin was horrified to find that he and Mary Rose were the only ones of his married friends without children. Everyone he knew seemed to be into whelping and had reached middle age within a matter of a few years. The talk among his male friends that used to be about sex and horses now took a mind-boggling, boring turn into what schools the children were down for, and management courses. Is this, he thought in absolute despair, what happens to the world of men when women get their hands on them? Remembering Podge's very staid stag night last year he rather thought that yes, it was exactly what happened when women get their men tied down. The thought that he was about to throw off the shackles cheered him up.

Somewhere outside there must be lots and lots of randy, nubile women simply waiting for Crispin to turn up. He would bag as much money as he could and then decamp from rural Devon and hit London, Paris and New York. Somewhere along the way he could pick up another rich woman and move in. Women were so easily fooled, especially New York women with their meagre little bodies and wizened faces. American women needed men, unlike English women who were more reticent.

'Another gin,' he said, pushing his glass across the counter. He watched with glittering eyes as the girl poured the tonic into the glass. Not a bad arse, he thought. She was thin, and had pouting little breasts, the kind he liked to nibble. He smiled at her.

She grinned back. Not bad looking in a ratty kind of way, the girl decided. His eyes were a little pink around the rims, but he wore expensive clothes. She watched him carefully. He might be good for a fiver, she thought. And she could do with some extra money for the weekend. She pushed the glass towards him and her fingers touched his. He left his hand on the bar and watched her carefully. 'You got a name?' she said.

'Yes, I have.' Crispin smiled winningly. 'My name is Travis ... Travis Mainwaring. I'm known as Randy

Travis to my friends.' And to my wife, he thought viciously. Sod the bitch. He tossed back the gin. 'Give me another. Better make that a double.'

She deliberately filled the glass to the top with gin and then added a tiny bit of tonic. 'There you are,' she said, pushing the glass towards him. 'Compliments of the house.'

Crispin felt a surge of lust sweep over him. 'Are there any other compliments I can pay you, other than to tell you that you are beautiful?' He immediately wanted to kick himself at the crassness of it all.

The girl grinned an experienced grin. 'Wanna come round the back for a knee tremble?'

Crispin looked at her. 'I haven't tried one of those,' he said, returning her grin. He was aware that he hadn't been propositioned by a strange woman in a bar ever. Maybe he wasn't as middle-aged or as unattractive as Mary Rose thought. OK, I'll try anything once, he thought. He slid off the stool and stood uncertainly by the bar. She flipped up the flap of the counter and motioned for him to follow her. She led him into a small, square, ill-lit storeroom which smelt powerfully of beer.

''Ere,' she said, 'let me.' And she expertly unbuttoned his trousers. For a moment he stood in his expensive cords, looking down at his dangling prick. 'We're not getting much action 'ere, are we?' she said reprovingly. She took his limp penis in her hand and began to pump it up and down. Nothing happened, except that Crispin began to feel the dawning of a horrible feeling of shame and panic. What the hell was he doing behind some dingy bar in Exeter? She dropped to her knees and began to suck him enthusiastically like a Hoover. Crispin gazed warily at the door, which was open, and wondered what he should do if they were interrupted by the owner of the bar. A fly buzzed inquisitively against the window. He looked down at the busy convolutions of the woman's head. In the dim light, her dyed roots showed up against the aggressive blonde tips of her hair.

'It's no good,' he said softly. 'I can't come. I've just found out that my wife's having an affair, you see.' Tears filled his eyes. The woman pulled herself back and sat on her heels.

'You been up the road to see Rodney, then.' She wiped her mouth with the back of her hand. Crispin nodded. 'Oh well, you'll probably be off sex for a while. Most men are when they find out about their wives. I don't know why. After all, men aren't faithful anyway.' She put out her hand. 'That'll be a fiver,' she said matter-of-factly.

Crispin felt a lurch in his stomach. She was a whore. Well, I knew that anyway, he told himself as he peeled off a five-pound note. He pushed her hand away and buttoned himself up. He spared himself the final humiliation of having her tuck his unresponsive penis away. They walked back into the still empty bar and he smiled at her as best he could.

'Thank you,' he said, finding nothing else to say.

'Don't worry about it,' she said nonchalantly. 'You'll get it up again soon.'

Crispin bowed his head and ran for his car. He very much wanted to get back to the dower house and his mother. She would know what to do. She always did.

Eighty-One

🙙

Elisabetta smelled the wind of May and recalled how she would watch Francesco and Mario work in the fields planting the tobacco crop. The pain of Mario's death was slightly less agonizing as the weeks passed, and she still prayed daily for her husband's safety. Lisa and Tommaso now spoke of both men less. They were all so intent on survival. Alone in this seemingly empty mountain they were still alert for any signs of other people. Sometimes Elisabetta felt so alone she would not have minded passers-by.

'How odd to be here, just the few of us, when Europe is crawling with the dead and dying,' she said to Lisa. 'Refugees trying to escape.' She shook her head. She knew all these things were happening, because the men had told her. She, too, had more than paid her dues for this war. A dead son, an imprisoned husband, and now the remainder of her family in hiding. She clutched her arms around her body and realized that for her, any happy thoughts had been dead since that terrible scene so many weeks ago. Still, she mustn't complain. They were alive and they had food, although she yearned endlessly for some fresh salad, or even a tomato. She didn't know she could become so passionate about a tomato.

It was the last days of May. Elisabetta had told Tommaso and Lisa to take a day off. 'I'll be fine looking after Anna and the children myself,' she said, smiling at them. 'You are both tired and you just need a day away. Why don't you take a picnic with you and come back in the evening? We'll be perfectly safe where we are.'

At first Tommaso was worried. 'The master wouldn't like me to leave you alone.'

'Don't worry, I'll be fine.' Elisabetta realized that she too was looking forward to a day alone, with just the children and the ever-silent Anna.

'Thank you,' Lisa said simply. 'Come on, Tommaso, I'll pack some lunch.'

They set off down the path, Tommaso carrying a long stick to deter the newly waking vipers. Lisa covered her head with a shawl and shivered. 'I've always been frightened of the vipers, ever since one fell from a tree in May after laying its eggs. It fell right on top of my mother.'

'I'll protect you,' Tommaso said stoically. He very much hoped the vipers would all stay in their holes this morning: he was terrified of snakes. He fingered the hunting knife that lay against his thigh. The edge was razor sharp. He took a swig from his flask of wine. The men had left him several bottles which he would have to ration carefully. To be without bread for a Tuscan was a tragedy, but to be without wine was unthinkable.

Finally they came to a clearing. The grass was just poking its tiny, delicate green fronds through the brown, dry earth. A tree hung over the stream, its newly hatched leaves shining silver in the sunlight. The stream danced merrily over the stones.

'This looks lovely,' Lisa said. There was a hint of nervousness in her voice. Tommaso, too, felt uncharacteristically nervous. They had been surrounded by the children, Anna, and Elisabetta for so long that now they found the silence between them awkward.

Lisa busied herself arranging the meal. She had cooked a bowl of chickpeas with pasta. Tommaso put the wine on the ground between them. He sat down and put his stick beside him. It's a pity I always have to feel on guard, he thought to himself, even now when there is nobody around. He looked across the valley. Around them he knew there were impenetrable mountains known only to the partisans, men who grew up in these forests. These men had played and swum and climbed these mountains and knew them like a man knows a woman's body. He glanced at Lisa and found himself blushing. He knew he so much wanted to know Lisa's body. Seeing his look she smiled gently at him and put her hand on his.

'Let's have some wine,' she said, pulling two wooden

bowls from her sack. They sat, Lisa cross-legged, opposite each other and drank their wine.

After a moment's silence, Tommaso stretched out his hand and gently stroked Lisa's cheek. 'I've been wanting to do that for weeks,' he said quietly.

'And I've wanted you to do that also,' she replied. Lisa's face was serene. 'Tommaso, I want you to make love to me. I've thought a lot about it; actually all the time. This war will go on for a long time and maybe we will both be killed. I don't want to leave this life without knowing what it is to be loved by you.' She paused. 'I don't mind that you don't love me or that you won't marry me. I just want to feel your arms around me and your mouth on my mouth.' She dropped her gaze.

Tommaso felt a lump in his throat. 'I do love you, Lisa, I really do. And I have for a long time.' He pulled her to him. 'After this war is over we will get married. I can't imagine life without you, without your joy and your energy.'

He found himself kissing her soft lips, and such a happiness welled up in him that he thought he might cry. Lisa lay back in his arms and returned his kiss with a fire and enthusiasm that surprised him. He was used to Maria's matter-of-fact love-making. Other girls he had talked into bed usually displayed all sorts of delaying tactics. But here Lisa offered herself fully and frankly to him. He lay beside her on the grass and wished this moment could last for ever.

When he entered her, Lisa gave a gasp of pain. 'Do you want me to stop?' he asked, concerned.

'No, don't stop, please don't stop.' And Tommaso made love to Lisa, the stream rushing by in full approval.

Elisabetta sat by the opening of the cave in the hot sunlight. She very much hoped that Lisa and Tommaso were somewhere in the mountain making love. She had watched them both over the weeks and it was not normal for two such healthy people not to make love. Even at her age she enjoyed sex, probably more than she had when she was younger. Now, at her age, it brought no fear of pregnancy with it, and Francesco was such a good lover. She grinned. The children were playing around her, and Anna sat still and quietly. Soon she would take Anna by the hand and walk with her and the children. But for the moment she was enjoying the silence in the forest, disturbed only by the children's voices and the chattering of the birds.

Eighty-Two
❧

'Had a good time?' Crispin asked Mary Rose innocently as she came swinging through the front door. He had heard the wheels of her car ploughing through the gravel as usual as she slammed on the brakes, no doubt narrowly missing the front doorstep. Bits of chipped stonework from the steps littered the drive, testimony to her previous miscalculated entries.

'Yes, thanks, wonderful.'

Crispin found himself wincing at the light tone in her voice. For a few days she would be happy and hum about the house. Then the old familiar sullen Mary Rose would re-emerge. Crispin felt betrayed: where was the young, gorgeous, fun-loving Mary Rose? What had happened to her in his life? He had been a good husband to her. OK, he had knocked her about a bit, but most men do that. It's part of the warp and the woof of marriage, he told himself.

'Have you thought any more about our separation?' Mary Rose asked.

'Yes,' Crispin replied nervously. 'I think I should get a drink before we get down to business.' Indeed, he had spent the night pacing up and down the bedroom, wondering how much he could legitimately get out of Mary Rose without seeming to be too greedy. He'd come up with the figure of one hundred and fifty thousand pounds in cash, together with the house and his car. He could invest the cash and live quite comfortably. This all sounded fine. Maybe he could even buy a small bachelor flat in Dolphin Square. Those flats were just the ticket for seducing women. Right across from the White Elephant. Very seductive, with the doorman standing by to usher the women out.

'I think if you could let me have a hundred and fifty thousand. I keep this house and my car. I could get by with that.' All through this, mice were running around his head. Had he asked too much? Should he ask for more?

Mary Rose smiled at him. 'I'll talk to my accountant in the morning.' She turned and left the room.

Crispin went downstairs, high on the thought of all that lovely money. He headed for his mother's house.

'You damn fool,' Amelia hissed through clenched teeth. 'You told me that you have a picture of a man coming out of her flat at six o'clock in the morning. You've got her cold. You can take her for six times that amount of money if you divorce her for adultery.'

'I don't really want to do that, Mummy.'

'Whyever not? She cuckolded you, didn't she?'

Crispin made a face. 'Well, I don't really want to be held up in public as a man whose wife had an affair.'

'You won't have to be held up in public once she sees the evidence. She'll back down. She's got her own position to protect: her precious clients won't want to be seen consorting with a loose woman.'

'Mother, times have changed and the world is full

of perfectly acceptable loose women. No, that's not the point.'

'The point is, Crispin you fool, a hundred and fifty thousand is not going to keep you in peanuts for long. You have never had to be responsible for anything: her solicitors and accountants saw to it all. The bills for your house alone will eat a huge hole in that amount in no time at all. You'll need at least half a million.'

'I don't see her accountants going for that at all.'

'Nor will Mary Rose, for that matter, unless she knows she has to come up with the goods. Is that man still on the case?'

Crispin nodded. 'Yes. Mary Rose goes back to London at the weekend and Rodney is going to try and get into the flat. He is a specialist at getting into buildings, so it won't be much of a problem for him. He just has to get a picture of them in bed together. After that I can go ahead.'

'Now you're talking, Crispin. In future, don't be so wet. It's not as if you love the little tramp.'

As Crispin walked across the lawn back to the dower house, he decided he agreed with his mother. He didn't love anybody but himself. Still, life was going to be awfully dull without Mary Rose.

'Don't give him anything,' was the accountant's advice. Mary Rose could hear the concern in Mr White's voice over the telephone. He acted as her international accountant now, and she imagined his offices in Grosvenor Square.

'I'd rather pay him off just to get him off my back, Mr White . . . If he signs a piece of paper saying he's accepted the money . . .'

'Well, do what you think fit, dear, but the man's a cad.'

Mary Rose was surprised at the anger in Mr White's

voice. He was normally a placid man, not given to insults.

'I know that.' Mary Rose made a face. 'I seem to specialize in shits.'

Mr White laughed. 'Next time you get a man who will look after you.'

'There's not going to be a next time.'

Mr White put down the telephone and stared at it. 'I hope there will be, for your sake,' he said to no one in particular.

Mary Rose was delighted to be going back to London. Upon presenting Crispin with the news that he could have his one hundred and fifty thousand, the car and the house, she was surprised at the cool reception.

'Now we are officially separated,' she said firmly, 'I expect you to move out of the bedroom.'

'It's my house,' he said sulkily. 'You move out.'

'OK, I will.' Mary Rose spent the rest of the week setting herself up in a guest bedroom at the other end of the house. 'I'll pack and get out of your hair after I finish the house I'm doing up in Belgrave Square. Travis and I are flat out at the moment.'

Yes, flat out screwing, Crispin thought savagely. Suddenly he realized with an enormous sense of rage that he did not want to be pushed out of her life like an empty beer bottle with a return deposit. He was going to extract his revenge. She couldn't two-time him and get away with it. Lying and cheating was his province: what right had she to think she could do it too? Once this thought had taken hold of him he felt an enormous surge of power.

'Mother,' he said on the telephone from his room, the door shut so Mary Rose could not hear. 'You are absolutely right. I will sue her for a divorce. Whatever was I thinking of: that little bitch deserves all she is going to get.'

'I'm so glad you've come to your senses, Crispin.'

Now he couldn't wait to get the final piece of evidence. When Mary Rose left for London on Friday, Rodney was already concealed in his willowy coffin. The leaves were now fully out and he felt quite safe. I 'ope the bleeder is planning to fuck 'er tonight, he thought. I'm missing Fulham playing Arsenal. He knew it was useless to ask Amy to listen for him. No good in bed and no good at football. Still, he mused, she cooked a good egg and chips and that took some doing. Getting the egg just right with the middle bit still wobbly and the chips fat and just about to brown. That took art. He very much wished he had a plate of egg and chips in front of him. He was so hungry he could almost taste them. Time for the Spam sandwich. How many times in his life, Rodney wondered, had he stood outside some house in the dark munching a Spam sandwich while, inside, somebody was climbing into a woman's knickers? Still, he supposed it was a living. And if he could pull this one off, he could take Amy and the kids on a holiday. While the little bleeders were enjoying themselves he could try and get Amy to act a bit more willing. A pity really, she'd been such a little goer when he first met her.

Travis was at Mary Rose's door within minutes of her pulling up. He carried with him lists of the clients' new orders. Swathes of material bulged in his briefcase, and under his arm he had a bottle of Lanson champagne. Mary Rose, he knew, was bringing up a big Devon crab, and those crabs were succulent at this time of year. He felt happy that he was here in this beautiful square. Mary Rose and he had a loving friendship. He realized that he was unable to make love fully to her, but he pleased her with his mouth and his hands and he enjoyed the release she was so easily able to give him.

He rang the doorbell. Rodney took a picture. Capital, he thought, a picture of a man with a bottle of champagne entering the love nest. Men, in his opinion, didn't bring a bottle of champagne to a woman unless they wanted one thing, and one thing only.

Once Travis was inside, Mary Rose fixed dinner. After dressing the crab she put it and its pretty coral roe back in the shell. She grated fresh cheese on top and then put the dish under the grill. When the cheese was a light, golden, frothy brown she pulled it out.

'You can open the champagne now, Travis,' she sang.

He laughed at the sound of the cork popping. 'Oh, well done, girl,' he said in a mock English accent.

After dinner, Mary Rose cleared the table and they began in earnest to complete the loose ends on the house.

'Once we finish the house, Crispin agrees we can separate. But I'm slightly worried about him. He wasn't so gung-ho to get rid of me by the end of the week. I think he is having second thoughts, not because he wants to stay with me, but more because he won't have much of a life without me. Still, I see little of him now. We're almost like strangers, so I expect it will be all right.'

'It will be painful, Mary Rose. Any break-up is painful, even if you are glad to get away. Old habits die hard.'

Mary Rose looked seriously at Travis. 'Actually, Travis, I've never discussed my marriage with anybody. But Crispin is a bully and a liar. The last years have been hell for me. If he doesn't get what he wants he throws tantrums like a small kid. Which is really what he is. He brags that he'll never grow up.' She paused. 'Anyway, he hits me.'

'He hits you?'

'Yeah. I know I used to provoke him. But I stopped that a long time ago and still he hits me. I'm scared of him actually.' She gazed at Travis. 'Oh come on, let's finish this. I'm really tired. And talking about Crispin just depresses me.'

They worked until one o'clock. Travis took off his clothes and fell into bed. Mary Rose followed him, too tired even to put on her nightie. She slid into the sleeping Travis's arms. She liked his arms. They were safe arms.

Rodney finally found a big drainpipe at the back of the house. He'd seen the final light go out in the flat. So the bedroom was on the right side of the house. Not too difficult to reach. All he needed now was a window with a latch that he could manoeuvre off with his thin shield of plastic. If not, he had a tennis ball and some sellotape. That was slightly more risky: when the ball broke the glass pane the tape would hold the splinters long enough for him to put his hand through and lift the latch. Rodney grinned. He was glad that house-breaking had been one of his specialities as a kid. He climbed steadily until he found a ledge. Then, thanks to some careless person leaving a window conveniently unlatched, he slid into the flat and found himself in the kitchen. Now to unlatch the front door quietly. When he took a photograph of the guilty couple, Travis would no doubt give chase. Seeing the front door open, Travis would run outside after him. But by that time Rodney would be shinning down the drainpipe at the back of the house and away with the final piece of evidence.

Camera in hand, he gingerly pushed open the bedroom door. Perfect. The sleeping couple could not have incriminated themselves more thoroughly if he'd rehearsed them himself. He aimed the camera at Mary Rose and Travis and the flash went off.

'What the hell . . . !'

Travis was up, but Rodney had already fled. He rounded the corner to the kitchen as he heard Travis pounding out of the bedroom. With a nimble leap,

Rodney was out of the window and sliding down the thick gutterpipe. He reached the bottom as he heard Travis open the front door. He waited, breathing hard. Travis couldn't go very far: he hadn't had time to put on any clothes. Soon Travis would realize there was no one on the street and he would have to go back upstairs. He could not call the police because then he would have to explain what he was doing in a flat with another man's wife.

Rodney smiled. Sometimes his job was better than sex, he thought. Well, almost.

Eighty-Three

They were going to have to move again. This time different men came to help them. It was always different men, Elisabetta thought wearily. She ached for some order in her life, for familiar faces that she had known since early childhood. She had grown up in Asciano, gone to school in Asciano, and now all those years and relationships seemed lost. She felt violated and almost raped by the knowledge that German officers were in her house, no doubt sleeping in the bed she had shared with her husband.

'Hurry, Tommaso,' she said. 'We must get packed and be on the move tonight. Such a shame. The children love this mountain. But as the Germans are pulling back, and will probably be hiding here, we must go on down south. The leader tells me that he has had an offer from a friend of Anna's who will meet us and then take us to her house to hide.' She frowned. 'I can't imagine who it could be unless . . .' Her brow cleared. 'It might be Regina. That's the only friend of Anna's in Italy I can think of.'

Lisa hummed contentedly, even though she didn't want to leave. Making love with Tommaso in the evenings when the children were asleep had become addictive. He was a good lover. He did not seem to want to satisfy just himself, a complaint she had heard from many of her friends. He wanted to satisfy her to the point where she moaned with pleasure in his arms. Gently and surely he taught her the art of making love, and she blessed him for it. At nights they slipped away into the cool maw of the mountain and there, in the silence broken only by nightingales, they exercised their passion for each other. Still, she didn't mind what happened as long as she had Tommaso. She was in love for the first time in her life. Even though it had come late, it was all the better for the waiting. She smiled as she packed. She kissed little Nicoletta on the head and tweaked Giulio's cheek. And sighing as she raised Anna to her feet, she gazed deep into the still empty eyes. Would she ever come back? All they could do was to pray and hope.

As they filed out of the cave for the last time, the leader whispered quietly to Elisabetta that their solitary incarceration was now over. 'We will be taking you down the mountain and then you must join the queues of other refugees travelling south. Your friends will meet you in Naples. They have a house there.'

Elisabetta nodded. 'The only friend that Anna has is a woman called Regina, and she lives in Genoa.'

The leader shook his head. 'No names.' He smiled. 'The way will be difficult and there is much bombing and killing. Where we are heading is chaos, but soon that's where the Allied troops will be. A lot has happened in the past months, but because we have little time I will be brief. It looks like the Fascists are well and truly on the run and I wouldn't be surprised if they're soon overthrown and the country surrenders. But it's the

Germans who are now causing all the trouble: they've decided to dig in and fight the Americans on their own. But the Allies have already landed in Sicily and it won't be long before they're on the mainland. What we want to try and do is to get you past the German lines and closer to the Allies as soon as possible, because when the real conflict starts it is going to be furious and everyone will be in the crossfire. There are Germans all over the place. We will follow behind you and try to give you some protection, but if the Germans close in on you we will have to disappear. None of us minds dying, but the fear is giving information under torture.' Elisabetta could see the worry in the man's eyes.

'To die is not so bad,' he continued. 'But to give way under torture, to betray your fellow comrades . . . it is not possible. So better that I warn you now and you think of an explanation. Here are your papers.' He passed her a sheaf of papers. 'I have made out your papers putting the fair-haired woman as your daughter and the two children as hers. She lost her husband in the war.'

'That part is true.' Elisabetta felt her voice shake. She was furious with herself. How dare she lose control when these men were risking their lives for her? The man's face was rigid with obvious disapproval at her weakness.

'The man and the other woman are married. Your daughter is Swiss, which will explain her blue eyes and fair hair. It is important that the Germans never find out that she is American. If you are stopped, I can do no more than say that it is important that you teach the children to call you by your new names.' He stood outside the dark cave. 'I wish you luck. Now we go.'

'I must say thank you to you and to your men. I know you are risking your lives for us.'

The man stared at her intently. 'I knew your son,'

he said curtly, almost unwillingly. 'And I know your husband.'

The fact that he spoke of Francesco in the present tense gave Elisabetta a jolt of pleasure. 'Thank you,' she stuttered. She knew better than to ask the questions about Francesco's whereabouts that thronged her lips.

'Now we go,' the man repeated. And they began the most gruelling part of their journey.

For days they trudged wearily along the packed roads south. The weather was blazingly hot and the children cried. The three adults carried them as best they could. At night they made the most distance because only then did the aeroplanes cease their almost continuous strafing. Elisabetta came to know death intimately. Initially Lisa cried whenever she saw a dead child, but then she too set her face in a stern silence.

They were all bruised from throwing themselves into the ditches. Scratched from the brambles and the bushes, their clothes were torn apart and rent. After a while they could tell who had been on the road the longest. Many of the refugees had no food and their mouths were stained green from eating grass and roots. Elisabetta was grateful for the fleeting visits of one of the men who would deposit morsels of prosciutto or a few cooked potatoes. Once there was a treat of a bowl of rice with peas and pancetta.

'What a feast,' Lisa had exclaimed, her eyes shining. They had sat protected in a small huddle on the ground. Elisabetta had worried that one of the starving refugees might raid their little hoard of food, but she had been amazed at how gentle the people were with each other. There were so many different types of fleeing people. The gypsies were the most efficient at travelling. They helped and advised the doctors, the shopkeepers, the carpenters and the other city dwellers totally unused to country life.

'There is a German guard-post outside the city of Naples,' one of the gypsies informed Elisabetta. 'Beware. They shoot first. And they will stop all of us.'

'How do you intend to get by?' She was curious, knowing that gypsies, like Jews, were rounded up and either shot on the spot or sent to the camps in Germany. No one really knew what happened in these camps but, throughout the war, rumours had been rife of mass exterminations. Elisabetta prayed that Francesco would survive in such camps and, as she struggled along the roads, in a strange way she was glad that she was suffering. The thought of Francesco suffering alone horrified her. They were both in this nightmare together. Yet she was certain the day would come when they would be back in each other's arms. It was that thought that kept her going.

'We will slip away before we get to the guard-block,' the gypsy replied. 'I am here to ask if you want to come with us? I don't give your companion much of a chance if the soldiers see her. They rape most women they come across. I have seen your daughter's face and she is very beautiful. I think she would be taken away to be placed in one of the German brothels.'

'What a people.' Elisabetta shook her head. 'What makes them so savage?'

'Oddly enough,' the man replied, 'it's the Aryan blood they so much admire. They are descendants of the most dreaded warriors of all time. The same people that decimated most of Europe and England hundreds of years ago.' He shook his head. 'We gypsies are experts at breeding dogs and horses. We know that you not only breed for the body but you also breed for the spirit of the animal. These people are worse than any ill-bred animal I have ever known!' He spat on the ground. 'Anyway, I have made my offer.'

He stood gazing at Elisabetta. 'Thank you,' she said

simply. 'I will take you up on your offer.' How is it, she wondered, that in the time of war people are so magnificent? She smiled at a woman trudging past her with a baby in her arms.

'Have you come far?' she asked.

'From Florence,' the woman replied. 'I am a Jew. They have taken all the rest of my family. Only I am left with my baby, so I fled. We have been on the road for three months.'

She smiled briefly and Elisabetta was struck by the gentle light in her eyes. She realized that the woman was beyond suffering. She was not cut off from her feelings like Anna, but still, there were no more tears to flow. Elisabetta had noticed this in so many of the people, even in the children that struggled beside them. Even her own grandchildren and the others with them no longer smiled or played when they stopped. The few snatched moments of rest were used almost exclusively to prepare for the next nightmare struggle of bound feet and blisters on the road to possible hope and freedom.

Elisabetta set her mind on Regina's face. If they were heading for Regina's, then she knew they would find help. Orlando was the sort of resourceful man who would protect them. Now all they had to do was to survive the journey.

Eighty-Four

🪶

'Crispin.' Mary Rose sat up in bed, frozen with misery. 'Oh Travis, I'm so sorry. Remember I told you that there was something odd about his behaviour before I left? It must have been that shit of a mother of his. Crispin is too weak ever to do anything like that off his own bat.'

She made a smile. 'So he and his mother are going to try to blackmail me.'

Travis was now sitting on the edge of the bed, wrapped in a towelling dressing-gown. 'What are you going to do, Mary Rose?'

'Wait and see how the cookie crumbles. If Crispin wants to make a fight out of it, then we'll see who wins.'

'I want you to know that I don't want you to give in to blackmail on my account. I'm American and I don't give a shit what the English newspapers do to me. It will be harder for you because you're well known in the society pages.' He shrugged and then grinned. 'The funny part is that we haven't technically committed anything.'

'I know,' Mary Rose said thoughtfully. 'And that will be our trump card if we have to use it. I hope Crispin backs off. When I get back to Devon I'll find out what he actually wants. I have a feeling his mother has talked him out of getting rid of me because she knows that my accountants won't go for the amount of money she wants. Crispin's one hundred and fifty thousand pounds is cheap at the price. And he can have the fucking house. I don't want anything to do with them any more, anyway. I just want my freedom and to be shot of the whole family. They can rot in hell down there in their dank way of life.'

She had been very moved by Travis's remarks. She realized he was more than just protecting her; he was prepared to allow the whole of England to know he was impotent.

'Thank you, Travis,' she said, her eyes unexpectedly full of tears. 'You restore my faith in men.'

'You weren't married to a man, Mary Rose. You married a defect.'

'I know. I'm such a damn fool. Today I have to go to the hospital to do my war-time duty. Actually, I'm enjoying being there very much. The soldiers are so brave and they have such a funny sense of humour.' She sighed. 'Damn all this, just when my life was going so well. I wonder what Mrs Gulbenkian will say?'

Travis grinned. 'Whatever it is, it will be worth hearing. She's had a lot of practice with shits.'

'Yeah. I'm picking her up at Harrods later this evening. She has Jonathan and George with her and we're going out to dinner. Want to come?' Mary Rose realized with a start that she very much wanted Travis to come with her. She now relied on him quite heavily. They worked well together, she reasoned, and he liked Jonathan and George.

'OK.' Travis smiled, a dimple briefly denting his left cheek. 'I might as well hear what Mrs G. has to say about our possible exposure to the gutter press.'

'I hope it doesn't come to that.' Mary Rose's voice was doom-laden. She very much feared it *would* come to that. Mrs Kearney, as she would call her from now on, was way out of touch with the real world, imagining that, from their vantage point as members of the British establishment, she could do what she wanted with impunity. After all, the old cow would reckon that, even if the colonel had not gone to an English public school, he was now firmly embedded in the London Club syndrome, thanks to her connections. England, of all places, Mary Rose realized to her cost, was a country that had – and always would have – a rigid class structure. At the bottom of the heap for the English were Americans. Well, she would show Crispin, his mother, and those bloody spiteful girls. She had not lived in England for long without realizing that the English parochialism could be turned to her advantage.

'I'll telephone my solicitor and tell him what is happening.'

* * *

'The bitch will be on to me by now.' Crispin laid his head on his arms and raised his eyebrows.

Amelia sat in the chair opposite him. 'Yes, she probably is by now, if what that detective said was right about an incriminating photograph. Serves her right if she wishes to commit adultery. I have always been faithful to your father, always.' She blew a gust of wind through her large nostrils.

Crispin smiled. The idea of any other man being attracted to her bulky, dog-smelling body amused him. It wasn't always that way, he remembered, and was surprised at the rising blush that stained his cheeks.

Amelia looked at her son and sighed. What a dear loving little boy he had been, always snuggling into her in bed when the colonel had left to attend to the gardeners. Now he was in such trouble. His wife had cuckolded him and was trying to deny him his financial rights. Amelia knew she would fight for her son.

'I'll telephone Mr Ryder and we'll make an appointment to go down there together at once,' she said. 'You collect the photograph from your private detective.'

Amelia realized as they trudged across the lawn to her house that she was rather enjoying the excitement of this moment. 'And by the way, I don't think you should say anything about this to your father. He was always taken with the little whore, you know.'

Crispin felt his heart lurch. Even if Mary Rose was behaving like a whore, she was his little whore – or was she? He felt confused.

A few days later he left in his car, his mother beside him. He had tried to ditch her. 'Mother, I'm a grown man. I should be able to go and see our family lawyer about my divorce without my mother! Please.'

'Crispin, you couldn't organize yourself out of a paper bag. I need to see that your future is secure. What happens if you fall in love with a nice lass and have children? How could you afford ever to get married again? No, she has taken years off your life and you must protect yourself.'

Crispin sank into the driving seat. It was bad enough to have to tow your mother around at his age, but must she wear that dreadful old felt hat?

Mr Ryder made a face when he saw the photograph. 'Well, no doubt about it,' he said uncomfortably, 'the photograph is incriminating.' He gazed at Mary Rose's sleeping face and the man who lay with his arms around her. He's a much better bet for Mary Rose than this little blackmailing cad sitting before me, he thought. As for the horror of a mother, he'd had dealings with the litigious Mrs Kearney before. 'What do you intend to do?' he asked her.

'Divorce the woman, of course. Crispin must be compensated for all the years he looked after his wife so wonderfully.'

'What did you actually do, Mr Kearney?'

'Well, I ... er ... I administrated her business affairs. Very complicated actually. She had a very large portfolio.'

'I see.' Mr Ryder knew very well what Crispin had been up to over the years. He had a sheaf of cheques with Crispin's signature on them. Mostly for clothes, all the latest dance records, endless amounts of restaurants. And he had a record of all the cash payments to Jimmy Leadbetter for gambling debts. He gazed at Crispin with ill-concealed distaste. 'Presumably she has nothing she can enter into the courts about your behaviour.'

'Absolutely nothing at all,' Amelia butted in. 'He's been an excellent husband to her.'

'I would like to hear from Mr Kearney,' Mr Ryder said sternly. 'After all, it's Mr Kearney divorcing his wife, is it not?'

Amelia blushed and sat back, fussing with her brown

gloves. She must really get a new pair for the court case, she thought. She liked the idea of being the injured party's mother. She would get a new hat and suit.

'No, my mother is right. She has absolutely nothing to hold against me.' Crispin's voice choked. 'I tried my best to keep my marriage vows. She wasn't an easy woman to live with, you know . . .'

Mr Ryder's face again registered the smell of very dead fish. 'I don't need to know those sort of details, Mr Kearney. I take it you want to divorce your wife on grounds of adultery with this man in the picture?'

'I think so, Mr Ryder. I'm going to have one last chance at talking to her when she comes back in the next few days to see if we can't sort something out.'

Half a million to be exact, Amelia wanted to stress to her son, but she kept the thought to herself. She must look up the divorce judges in the High Court on the Strand. She probably knew most of them anyway.

'Well, Mr Kearney, let me know your decision in the next few days.' He handed back the photograph.

'No, you can keep that one. I have had several made,' Crispin said.

Mr Ryder put the photograph on his desk and, after shaking the hands of his clients, stared at it. Poor woman, he thought. His heart ached for Mary Rose. He knew what an ordeal she would face. At least I hope the man stands by her, he thought.

At the Pot-Pourri, Mrs Gulbenkian listened to the morning's events in silence. 'What a ratty-arsed little shit,' she remarked uncharacteristically. 'That's what you get for marrying a gigolo, Mary Rose. Fight it, darling, fight it all the way. It will be a horrible experience, but I don't think any judge in London will find for him. At least the newspapers certainly won't. A gigolo is a gigolo and not liked by anybody. Men who prey on women are two-a-penny, but usually they have the decency to get out when the going gets rough. But Crispin has his mother behind him. And he's afraid of her.' Mrs Gulbenkian's voice turned world-weary. 'He is a mother's boy and they love their mummies more than anything else on earth.'

'Mother – son incest, it's the Englishman's disease.' Jonathan laughed and finished his glass of wine. 'It's all that being sent away to boarding school and being beaten on the bottom: it's so erotogenic for the bastards. The worst S. and M. queens are the English. They are so cruel.'

'I know that,' Mary Rose said with a shiver. 'Try living with Crispin.' She remembered the pinching and the bruises. Travis put his hand over hers. He was sad to feel her hand shaking. He really must have done a number on her, he thought. She's scared of him.

They finished dinner. 'I'm coming back to the flat with you tonight,' Travis said firmly. 'He can't do us any more harm. He has the picture he wanted and good luck to him.'

Mary Rose smiled at him.

'That's the spirit, Travis,' Mrs Gulbenkian said. She ordered a taxi. 'Let's open a bottle of champagne when we get back and celebrate our premature victory.'

She waved at Jonathan and George who were getting into another taxi. 'Good-night, boys, I'll see you at eight-sharp tomorrow.'

Mary Rose settled back in the taxi.

'Now, when I was divorcing my third husband . . .'

Mary Rose smiled. Thank goodness for Mrs Gulbenkian's wealth of marital experience. She let the old lady cruise through her memories: she was comforted by the conversation but had no real desire to listen. Most of it she'd heard before, anyway. She gazed out of the taxi window at London as it hobbled by, hideously crippled by the bombing and deprivation. How it had changed. She recalled her first days here and how she was both intimidated and enthralled by the haughty architecture and the sheer sensation of history. London had been a regal lady: a little frayed around the edges, admittedly, but still elegant and cultured, while at the same time capable of unpredictable high spirits. But those long years of violence and sacrifice had turned the city decrepit. Horrifying scars violated every vision, causing her almost to wince in sympathy. The damage to the monuments such as Guildhall, St Paul's and other of Wren's masterpieces were sacrilegious. But what affected Mary Rose more were the slabs of ignoble terraced houses, levelled useless, yet unmourned by all but those who once considered them home. She had seen them burned by the ferocious incendiary bombs, and with them the familial security and hopes of the humble people within them. These people had willingly, or stoically, or blindly, sacrificed their sons and husbands to the cause. And now had not even a hearth of their own to take away the chilling, empty reality. But somehow they rallied, and in many cases soared above it. Mary Rose, with all her dollars and good fortune, couldn't fathom where the courage came from, how these people could sob at the loss of their home one moment, and whistle while clearing away the rubble the next. She had seen swarms of women, old men, and children restore order to a just-bombed neighbourhood with a collective efficiency which left her perplexed, humiliated even. And somewhere in the working throng there was always someone whistling, or singing some cheerful ditty, as if to act as a talisman of sorts. Such scenes awed Mary Rose, but she felt depressingly detached, because she knew her personal strengths were of no use here. London, she knew, would recover without her help, bless it. And damn it.

Eighty-Five

*

'Will this nightmare ever end?' Elisabetta was terrified. All day she had been rehearsing her little band in the likely event that they might be stopped and questioned. The gypsy, whose name turned out to be Nino, followed gravely behind. A last visit from the partisan leader before the men peeled off to return to the battles in Tuscany revealed that they had already talked to Nino who had promised to take care of them.

'Thank you a thousand times,' Elisabetta said, gratefully accepting a gift of eggs and potatoes.

That night she invited the gypsy and his imposing wife to share their meagre meal. For them it was truly a feast. Elisabetta reflected on her situation. Under normal circumstances she would be helping in the fields. The vines would be heavy with black and green grapes, the tobacco plants bent down with the weight of their huge leaves, the fruit trees full of plums and cherries. Still, she thought, sending up a grateful prayer of thanks, the eggs tasted marvellous. And Nino's wife Seraphena had conjured up a dish of anchovies fried with sweet parsley.

Nino grinned. 'My wife is a terror. Some German is going to do without his tin of anchovies tonight. She tells their fortunes, you see. In return they let her go. They are afraid of her, the superstitious bastards.'

Seraphena grinned. 'I tell them I will give them the evil eye and that their dongs will drop off.' She gave a howl of laughter. Elisabetta watched Lisa and Tommaso sitting quietly together with the children either side of them. Little Nicoletta and Giulio were now so thin it broke her heart. Nicoletta sat by Lisa eating the food that Lisa poked into her mouth. They were all dirty and dishevelled, but for the moment Elisabetta didn't care. The salt of the anchovies was in her mouth. She had not tasted salt for many a month. The nights were getting colder now, but as they continued south the days were still blindingly hot.

Ten kilometres before the German road-block, Nino ordered Elisabetta and Tommaso to follow him. Elisabetta had the twins. All of them carried what little they had left on their backs.

Nino obviously knew the trail well. He walked sure-footed and confident, away from the road and the milling crowds, into the forest. Behind him, as they made a distance between themselves and the roads, they could hear the planes coming down low over the struggling refugees. By now, after so many weeks, Elisabetta was numb to the horror of it all. She held her breath and walked in prayer that, at the end of it all, Regina would be waiting for them. To keep herself going she imagined hot meals, steaming soups and, above all, a hot bath. She could not get used to the smell of her own dirty flesh. Her hair was caked with grease and dust, her face dry, and her lips parched. What little water was available was carried by Nino, and every so often, one of the lucky members of the party was allowed to wet their lips. She often did without her turn, instead motioning to one of the children. They walked by night and lay under bushes most of the day.

After the fourth day, when they could see the city lying on the curve of a hill, they came across a small group of German soldiers sitting on the ground around a blind corner. Elisabetta, walking ahead with the twins, saw them first.

'Oh God,' she screamed, both in fright and also to alert the others. But the warning was too late for

Tommaso and Lisa who were coming around the corner with Anna. But Nino and Seraphena, at the rear, melted away. There was nothing Elisabetta could do. She stood frozen in the clearing, surrounded by the soldiers. One man who seemed to be in charge put on his army cap and stood up.

'Who are you?' he asked in German.

'I do not speak German,' Elisabetta replied, trying to keep the fear out of her voice. One of the soldiers put his rude hand under Anna's chin.

'Here's a fine catch,' he said, staring at Anna. The officer looked around and stared at Anna's face.

'She is very beautiful,' he said in faultless Italian.

'She is my daughter,' Elisabetta said. 'She cannot speak. She lost her husband at the beginning of the war and she also lost her mind.'

The officer's face showed no sign of emotion. 'Your papers, please,' he said, holding out his hand. Elisabetta fumbled in her bag and drew out the sheaf of papers she had been given. The officer stared at the documents and then flicked through them. In between gazing at the papers he looked carefully at the children. 'Where are you from?' he asked.

'Asciano in Tuscany,' Elisabetta answered.

'You are a long way from home, are you not?'

'We are trying to get to Naples where I have an aunt who can take care of us. We have been burnt out of our farm and there was no food.' She was amazed at how fluently she lied. Little Nicoletta, afraid of the soldiers, was clinging to Anna and, crying, Giulio joined her. Both children were pulling at the unresponsive figure of their mother.

'How sad,' the officer remarked. 'She really is deranged.'

'Yes.' Elisabetta found her eyes filling with real tears. 'Let us hope we can find a doctor to help her in Naples.' She was determined to let the officer know that she intended to leave this knot of soldiers and continue on her way.

The man stood for a moment lost in thought, and then he yelled something loudly to his soldiers, who stood staring at him. He gestured with his arm. 'You can go now,' he said in Italian.

Elisabetta looked at him gratefully. 'Thank you,' she said humbly, real gratitude in her voice.

'Not all Germans want to hurt innocent women and children,' he said. 'Besides, I have a little girl with blue eyes and blonde hair like your daughter. I'd like to think that, if ever she were in trouble, someone would give her a break. Think yourself lucky, signora, that it is me you bumped into.'

'I will. I will always. Bless you. Would you tell me your name?'

'My name is Gustavenson. I'm from Berlin. You . . .' He pointed at one of the soldiers. 'Give the signora some bread and some coffee for her journey. Also see if you have some fruit for the children.'

Elisabetta pressed on with her charges. The children were whooping and shouting, clutching apples and pears in their hands. That night when they lay down to sleep, Tommaso made three cups of precious coffee.

'Real Italian coffee,' Elisabetta said gratefully. Wishing her absent husband good-night before she fell asleep, she realized how grateful she had learned to be for very small mercies.

Eighty-Six

🖋

'I don't see why you should discard me like an old jumper, Mary Rose.' Crispin was sitting sulking on the armchair of her bedroom.

'I didn't discard you like an old jumper, Crispin. You asked to go, remember?'

'No I didn't. You asked me how much money I'd take to go. That's different. I felt hurt and rejected. And then to find you were two-timing me with that Travis creep . . .'

'He is not a creep. And you had no right to put a private detective on to me. We were separated, we already had separate bedrooms. So, anything I did was perfectly legitimate.'

'You are still married to me, Mary Rose.'

'Oh no, not for long. I just have to pack my things and leave you once and for all. Sod all of you! You are a really nasty, unpleasant family and you are welcome to each other.'

'Well then, if you refuse to be my wife and insist on moving out, then I will have to divorce you for adultery. You know what sort of scandal that will make.'

'Sure I do. And since when have I been afraid of a scandal?' She forced herself to smile coolly at him.

'Are you sure you won't change your mind? After all, half a million is not that much to you in the long run. It might leave you a bit short for a while, but you have plenty of money to come in after this war is over. There will be a boom while America rearms the whole of Europe, and you have stock in munitions.'

'My finances are none of your business any more, Crispin.'

'OK then, have it the hard way. Your picture in bed with Travis will make the rags.'

Mary Rose shrugged. 'So? At least he's more of a man than you'll ever be.' She stomped off to the attic to drag down some more suitcases. By tonight I'll be out of this dump, she thought.

When she finished packing she went to the drawing room where she knew Crispin would be drowning his sorrows.

'Goodbye then, Crispin. And please serve any papers on Mr Simpson in London. He will act for me.'

'My, we have been busy.' Crispin's voice was heavy with sarcasm. 'Well, thanks for everything.' He stood up, swaying on his feet.

Mary Rose let herself out of the front door and banged it for the last time. Thank God I'm free, she thought as she climbed into the car. The roof-rack was piled high with her clothes. That was all she had taken, apart from a few pictures of her house in New York and some small silver items. The rest she had left behind. She wanted nothing of her past life which would remind her of Crispin. He was now someone else's nightmare. Grimly she put her foot on the accelerator and fled for London.

Back in the drawing room, Crispin sat with tears rolling down his face. Quite how he'd got himself into this position he wasn't sure. He sat quiet and confused. The house reverberated with silence. He drank the rest of the bottle of whisky and then smashed the glass into the fireplace. Much later he found himself half awake on the chair in front of a dead fire. He stood up swaying and, as he stumbled to bed, he wondered where Mary Rose was. Probably in the arms of that American Johnny. The thought made him cry again.

'Sod it,' he mumbled. 'I was a good husband to her and she betrayed me. I'll show the bitch that you can't mess with a Kearney!'

Alone in her bed in London, Mary Rose very much wished she could talk to Anna. Only Anna would understand her lonely predicament. She could confess to Anna the horror that her life had become with Crispin. Anna would understand and believe her. After all, it was Anna who had warned her not to marry Crispin. It was Anna who had seen her bruises and had been horrified. Where was Anna when she needed her?

Eighty-Seven

Anna was still a long way away. Occasionally she had the feeling that a face was gazing at her with great compassion. She knew the face very well. It had a gentle expression and a broken-mouthed smile. The eyes were luminous. The face made Anna feel not quite so alone. She was down a long, dark tunnel. There was some light at the top, but not much. She kept straining to see if she could reach the light, but she couldn't. She would fall back exhausted, only to try again.

Elisabetta arose from a good night's sleep, brought on by good food and fresh coffee. They had enough left for a mug of coffee each before moving on. The sugar invigorated all of them and they set off in high spirits.

Once in Naples they moved aimlessly towards the heart of the city. Elisabetta had been given instructions to look for Piazza Giovanni Bovio. Once there they were to stand by the Neptune Fountain and wait. Finding the piazza was a nightmare of dodging patrols of German soldiers who took little interest in the chaos in the teeming streets. Elisabetta was grateful that the army of Germans seemed more intent on filling the cafés and the bars. Most of them had Italian women on their arms. Elisabetta made a face.

'Collaborators,' Lisa hissed in disgust.

Tommaso shrugged a shoulder. 'Who knows, *cara*? They too have children and grandmothers. In this war you survive any way you can.'

Elisabetta was appalled at the damage the Germans had done to the once beautiful city. Naples was where she had come with Francesco for their honeymoon. She considered the city to be the most romantic in Italy after Siena. Nothing could beat Siena, but now, looking at the rubble, she ached for those long-ago days when they had made love on the sands of a deserted part of the bay. She shook herself and lengthened her stride. They must find their hosts before dusk.

It was almost dusk when they reached the piazza. She had been looking forward to washing her face in the fountain, but predictably enough, there was no water, just chips of rubble from the bombing. The air-raid sirens sounded. People fled from the centre of the piazza, taking refuge in the colonnades under the tall houses. With a mixture of relief and horror she gazed up at the aeroplanes and saw Allied insignia on their wings. But while they were bombing Germans, they were also killing innocent Italians. The women and children always seem to die first in a man-made war, she observed. Now almost immune to the dead and dying, she smelled the familiar smell of cordite in the air and saw the helpless, writhing bodies. Wailing and shrieking was now a coda to the crump and banging of the bombs landing. The sound of war was a horrendous concerto of its own composing. The smell of war was the rich, sour smell of blood. The paintings of war were the green slime of decomposing flesh and the bright crimson

451

of the blood spilt by the yellow glare of the explosions. Over all the city there hung a yellow pall of dust and debris. And the crying, always the crying. Elisabetta didn't think she could ever forget the crying. They were crouched against a wall. The three adults covering the bodies of the children for safety.

After the final bomb shook the building she looked up. She saw a tall, red-headed woman standing in front of her. She looked again and then she smiled.

'Regina,' she said. 'Oh, I knew it must be you.'

Regina smiled a tired smile. 'I've been praying you'd get here safely.' She gazed at Anna. 'What happened?' Her voice was weary, resigned, fine-tuned to misfortune.

'Mario was shot in front of her. Her mind has gone.'

Regina stared at Anna. 'How awful,' she said. 'Damn this fucking war!' She put her arms around Elisabetta and hugged her tenderly. 'I'm sorry about Mario, Elisabetta.' They remained in an embrace for a moment, oblivious to the surrounding chaos. Then Regina said suddenly: 'Orlando is waiting for us in a truck down that side street over there. Come!' She quickly shook hands with Tommaso and Lisa. 'It's good to see you again,' she said, taking Nicoletta's arm. 'Let's hurry! I don't want the Germans to requisition the truck. It's our only transport. Everything else has been blown to bits.'

Orlando was waiting and grinned broadly when he saw them. Elisabetta was pleased, not only to see his reassuring face, but also to have another man to protect them. They were loaded unceremoniously into the truck and Orlando pulled a big tarpaulin over them.

'The less the Germans see, the less likely they are to ask questions,' he said. He got back into the truck, Regina at his side.

Elisabetta was conscious of the cold and the discomfort as they swayed around corners. But already, in her heart, she was allowing for a bit of confidence in the future. No longer was it her leading the others to safety. Although as the wife of the *padrone* she was well used to responsibility, it had always been shared with her husband. So far, since they had been separated, Lisa and Tommaso had looked to her for guidance. As she held the twins against the bumping of the truck she realized that she was tired, really tired, and needed to hand everything over to Regina and Orlando.

It was dark when they pulled up outside a big square house set in the deepest woods Elisabetta had ever seen. It was now early January and cold. She drew her rags around her and shivered. The children lifted their bandaged feet from the cold ground.

'Don't you worry,' Orlando said genially. 'We have everything you need, food, hot water, and clothes. How does that sound?'

'It sounds marvellous,' Elisabetta said wearily. 'Just marvellous.' She fainted, falling limp to the ground. There was a moment's consternation and then Orlando picked her up in his arms.

'Come everybody, she's just tired. She'll be fine in a moment.'

Inside, a young girl led the procession into a big room. There in the grate was a leaping, orange fire. The little group gathered gratefully around the flames.

Elisabetta was stretched out on the sofa. She came to. 'I'll go and get the first bath ready for the children.' She forced herself on to her elbows.

'No. Don't you move, signora. You've done your bit. Now I'll take over.'

Elisabetta fell back gratefully. 'Don't worry, Lisa, I'm all right.' She looked at Anna who stared into the fire. 'Look, Anna is watching the flames.'

Tommaso nodded. 'She is, I can see her eyes moving.

They are not blank as they have been for so long. I hope she will come back, signora.'

'So do we all.' Then Elisabetta fell asleep.

She felt as if she had been asleep for weeks when she awoke. Regina was sitting in a chair by the now spent fire. 'Come, Elisabetta, I have prepared a bath for you and some clean clothes. But first let me give you some hot soup. This is just some chickpea soup with peas. It will be good for your stomach. The children ate well and they are now asleep with Lisa and Tommaso. Once you have eaten and have cleaned yourself you can sleep for a very long time. Orlando and I will take care of the children. You have nothing to worry about. The news is that the Germans are leaving. It seems the war is really coming to an end. We are very isolated here, so we are safe.'

Elisabetta fought to swallow the first spoonful of soup. Apart from the two mugs of coffee it had been a long time since she had tasted hot food: probably her last hot meal had been the eggs they had been given by the partisans. The effort of eating was almost too much for her, but she forced herself. She felt her stomach tighten in shock at the unaccustomed food.

Later she sat in a big, old-fashioned hip-bath in front of the fire in Regina's bathroom. 'This is a luxury,' she said shyly, covering her breasts with her arms.

'Don't mind me.' Regina laughed. She took a big sponge and nimbly washed Elisabetta's back.

'Regina, do you think there is any way I could get news of Francesco? I'm sure he's alive and in a camp in Germany.'

'Sure. We can contact the Red Cross. It's good at finding people. I know it's difficult, but for now you must sleep and get your strength back. You want to look your best for your husband, yes?'

Elisabetta nodded. Regina saw the sorrow for the loss of her son in the stoop of her shoulders. Many years had been added to the woman's face. Still, Regina comforted herself, the smile will come back now that there are others to carry the responsibility for a while. The poor woman had borne an enormous load, and bravely. She handed Elisabetta a towel and tried not to wince as she raised her skeletal body from the hip-bath. The children did not look much better. Lisa and Tommaso seemed to have fared the best, but then they were *contadini* and used to the hardness of life on a Tuscan farm.

Regina sighed as she pulled back her bed-clothes. At least they all were safe now. She no longer had to sit bolt upright staring into the dark, worrying about them. By her side, Orlando was snoring. She kissed the top of his balding head. He had looked long and hard for the Biancharini family. He had heard on the Resistance grapevine that Mario had been killed and that Francesco had been taken prisoner. The rest, he had heard, had escaped. Orlando had been tireless in his search. Finally, all those weeks ago, they had had word that the family was safe and in the care of the partisans.

Regina settled down to sleep. Anna's face haunted her for a moment. You'll come back, Anna, that's a promise. Back to what, though, was a question she dared not answer.

Eighty-Eight

Mary Rose awoke with a hangover. Travis was beside her. She watched him sleeping, his arm outflung, the hand open and innocent. What a mess, she thought. I'm going to win this case because Crispin's picked the one man who can't screw. So technically we can't be accused of adultery. Poor Travis. She wished her head did not ache so much. She wished it was a man like Justin Villias who was tough and could take whatever happened to him and laugh. Travis was very vulnerable, and that made her feel guilty. Why did I get him into this mess, she wondered. She was still wondering when Travis woke up.

'What is it, Mary Rose?'

'Nothing. I have a terrible hangover. We must have had an awful lot of champagne.'

'Two bottles, but who's counting? You drank most of it. Are you wondering about me having to explain my impotence?' She nodded miserably. 'I don't mind that much, Mary Rose. You see, before I met you I didn't have a sex life at all. What on earth was I going to say to a girl? I can't make love to you, but you can go down on me? Not much of an invitation. Besides,' he said grinning, 'we have had the best inventive sex ever, haven't we?'

Mary Rose found herself smiling. 'We have indeed. How about some foot-fucking to cure my hangover?'

'Invitation accepted.' Travis knelt at the end of the bed and Mary Rose grasped his erection with her elegant arched feet. Her feet were soft and the fit was tight. Travis felt his breathing increase: the tension was almost unbearable. Leaning forward as Mary Rose began to move her feet backwards and forwards, he slipped his fingers into her. She was moist and waiting. Both of them groaned in unison and then collapsed.

He lay on top of Mary Rose, who was covered in sweat, her legs splayed. For once he felt comfortable. He was not revolted by the feeling of her lying under him. Mary Rose, too, recognized the change in him and lay still, not wishing to frighten him. He rolled off her and was surprised to find himself crying.

Mary Rose put a hand on his shoulder. 'Travis, what's the matter?'

'I don't know, Mary Rose, I really don't know. I don't know if I'm crying for me or for you or for the whole fucking mess.' He wiped away his tears. 'How's your headache?'

'It's gone.' She stretched. 'Let's go back to sleep and wake up to a new day.' She snuggled into her sheets. There is life after Crispin, she thought.

During the next, befuddled week, Mary Rose wondered about Anna. So far any attempt at finding out about the Biancharini family met with no answer. Mary Rose telephoned the Foreign Office, only to be met with a snooty voice. 'There is a war on, madam.'

'I know there's a fucking war on!' She was furious. 'But she's probably in danger. Isn't that your job? Isn't there a British Embassy in Rome or a Consulate in Florence?'

'We will see what we can do. Why don't you try the Red Cross?'

She slammed the telephone down in disgust. She was sitting in the flat sorting out wallpaper for the house in Belgravia. She heard the snap of the letterbox. She rose to her feet, tightened her towelling robe around her waist and went downstairs. She liked the thick, white carpet that clung so luxuriously to the shallow staircase. She loved the sweep of the spiral staircase that led down to the massive oak front doors. She appreciated the big rooms, so lavishly furnished, and the bathroom which, beside her bedroom, was her own. After the dower house, half finished but still uncomfortably a monument to mid-Victorian vertical architecture, she felt so much more at home in the Georgian squareness of this house.

She opened the letterbox and stared at a long manila envelope. On the outside was stamped 'Ryder and Sons, Solicitors'. Yuk, she thought, Crispin's divorce papers. She took the envelope, along with several other letters, up to the flat. She sat on the sofa, wishing Travis were with her. She did not really want to open the envelope alone. She got to her feet and made herself a cup of strong coffee. Just for luck she threw a slug of brandy into the cup. The smell of the brandy steadied her. She sat down and opened the other letters. Two bills: one for a hundred and eighty pounds from Harrods, and another for a side of fresh smoked salmon from the fruit and vegetable department at Fortnum's. There was also a letter from Martha saying that they were all desperate about Anna and had she had any more news since she had last written? No, she hadn't. But Mary Rose was glad she could report that the Foreign Office had at least agreed in principle that it would look into the matter. She took a second sip of coffee and the brandy burned her tongue. She opened the manila envelope and pulled out the document. For a moment she admired the pretty piece of ribbon that ran down the middle of the pages. The document was short and simple. Travis Mainwaring was named as the co-respondent and Crispin was asking for a divorce on the grounds that his wife had been photographed in flagrante delicto. In other words, she thought, we were caught with our knickers down. She found herself laughing. Despite the pompous accusations in front of her, the fact was that she and Travis had only slept in each other's arms that night, nothing more. Crispin's devious, delinquent need to destroy her and satisfy his lust for money was taking up all his time and effort. A private detective, two lawyers, courts, judges, all the unnecessary paraphernalia just to blackmail her. She was not going to be blackmailed. She reached for the telephone and called Mr Ryder.

'Look, Mr Ryder,' she said somewhat nervously. 'We have known each other for some time now.' She could hear an embarrassed silence at the other end of the telephone. 'Mr Ryder, I know you can't talk to me and that you represent my ex-husband. But please, for all our sakes, could you just try and get him to back off? I'm not the sort of person who gives in to blackmail. I have offered to give him a hundred and fifty thousand pounds and my share of the house. Please could you try and save everybody a lot of embarrassment? I know this is just a draft copy of the divorce papers: I appreciate you sending them, and I intend to write back and agree to the divorce. But I will contest the grounds. I'm sorry it has come to this.'

'Believe you me, dear lady, so am I.'

Mary Rose was comforted by the sincerity in the man's voice. She put down the telephone and wept. 'Oh dear,' she whispered, 'first Travis and now me "blubbing", as Crispin would say in his horrid, sneering way.'

'Your wife will not contest the divorce, Mr Kearney, but she will not accept the grounds.' Mr Ryder had telephoned Crispin immediately.

'She must be mad.' Crispin was very upset. 'We got a picture of her in bed with the bastard.'

Mr Ryder winced. 'I'm sorry, sir,' he said stiffly, 'that's all I can tell you. Are you sure you want to go on with this suit? The usual way is for a gentleman to offer a compromise.'

'I know that.' Crispin's voice was cold. 'But in this case I don't have to be a gentleman. My wife certainly did not behave like a lady, more like a whore.'

'As you wish. I'll draw up the papers now that we know where we stand. I will have the divorce papers served on her at her solicitor's office. Less embarrassing than at her private address.'

'Whose side are you on, Ryder?'

'I represent your interests, sir, but I rather think we'd be better off if you didn't sue her for adultery. If you give her grounds it will make a small splash in the newspapers. But if you sue her for adultery, I'm afraid she will counter-sue and there will be a most unholy row.'

'Well, she should have thought about that before she bedded that chap. She's ruined my life. Nothing will ever be the same. I am heartbroken, Ryder, absolutely heartbroken. You have no idea.'

Mr Ryder put the telephone down and muttered to himself, 'This feels like a bad 'un, you mark my words.'

Travis came by to take Mary Rose out to dinner. Mrs Gulbenkian was at a dinner party and Mary Rose was glad. She needed to sit quietly to regain her equilibrium. It was one thing to talk about divorce, even to leave Crispin. She had been living apart from him for so long it was not much of a shock. But to see the words written down . . .

She showed Travis the draft divorce papers. 'It was good of Mr Ryder to send me a draft. Usually they just send a man around with the final papers and you have to go from there. I spoke to my lawyer, Mr Ridgeway, and we have to go and see him tomorrow afternoon. I am really sorry to drag you in like this.'

'Don't be.' Travis leaned forward and poured Mary Rose another glass of thick, red Barolo. Mary Rose wrinkled her nose. The wine was full of the smell of a hot Italian summer. At the back of the taste were burnt fields, yellow and umber from the hot summer sun.

'Hmmmmm,' she sighed, forgetting her worries for a moment.

'Anyway,' Travis said, 'we'll get over this awful business and then I think we ought to consider doing a house in New York. The Del Morenos have written to me. The war is now ending and things will loosen up. I'd like to spend more time in America. I need to get away from the claustrophobia of this country. It's too small and too parochial. Sometimes I feel like screaming and taking off for the big, wide Arizona deserts. A man can breathe in America.'

'I know what you mean. For me it is that everything's stacked against you if you don't arselick the great British middle classes. You have to have the right voice and the right clothes and be seen at the right places. I don't know how much chance we have with this court case, but I'm glad we are going through this together. Anyway, I'm waiting to see the look on Ridgeway's face when he hears the defence.'

'I'll drink to that.' Travis lifted his glass. 'Come on, I'll get you home. Tomorrow we have a lot of explaining to do.'

Travis dropped her off at her front door. 'Are you sure you're all right? If you want me to stay, I will, but I could do with a change of clothes.' He grinned. 'And I know you will want your bathroom to yourself. One day when I design a house for you, I'll design you a perfectly wonderful personal bathroom. And I'll make a door that is sculpted to your body: that way only you will be able to enter. Or your children.' He saw a look of pain in her eyes. 'I'm sorry, Mary Rose, I didn't mean to hurt you.'

'It's OK. Maybe if we had been able to have children . . . ?' But then Mary Rose knew that was not true.

'Nah,' she said, kissing Travis gently on the cheek. 'Crispin is a rat, and he'd be a rat of a father. And anyway, I wouldn't want those awful people to be grandparents to my child.' She smiled tremulously under the porch light.

How vulnerable she is, Travis thought as he walked back to his car. He cursed the English, and the Irish for good measure. He was not looking forward to tomorrow.

Eighty-Nine

The days in the house in the forest passed slowly. Sadly, the leafy oasis surrounding the farmhouse only shielded them from the chilling unreality unfolding less than twenty miles away; it didn't eliminate it. After all she'd seen and experienced on the long march south, Elisabetta tried hard to ignore the terrifying sounds of war virtually on her doorstep. But it took more than she had left in her. She consoled herself with the fact that these were the sounds of victory. And that soon silence would mark a new beginning. The Allied troops had just liberated Naples and were consolidating their control over the south, driving the never-say-die Germans to the north. Elisabetta hadn't ventured out of the house since they arrived and had no intention of doing so. But Orlando and Regina had described to her the rape of Naples, the devastation of this once glorious Mediterranean paradise, the utter humiliation of its colourful inhabitants. Neapolitans had paid dearly for the freeing of their country, and Elisabetta couldn't help wondering whether freedom at all costs was worth such a price. Was there a rational balance between political liberty and civilian devastation? It was doubtful that such a question even entered the heads of the crazed combatants presently locked in furious battle not far away. Their motivation was victory at all costs. Elisabetta had no objection to that either. She couldn't wait for the rumoured Allied landing further up the peninsula, and for the Allies to march triumphantly into Rome. Nearly five years of war had eaten away a valuable part of her, like an acid silently devours silk.

Elisabetta lay still, exhausted. Sometimes she wondered if she'd ever get her strength back. Now she had time to mourn, to feel the fierce pain of the loss of her son. When there was no one to see her she rolled on the floor. It embarrassed her, but the pain drove her to the ground. She had never experienced anything like it, not even when she gave birth to the twins. The death of a child, her only son, was such quivering agony. And the fact that she could not be there to hold him, to bury his body. 'Ayyeeeeee,' she shrieked. And she howled.

When Regina heard the cries she quickly took the children out into the garden. Lisa also took Anna's hand. On one or two occasions it seemed to Lisa that Anna's brow furrowed at the feral sounds that came from Elisabetta's room.

'She will get better in time, Lisa, don't worry.' Tommaso tried to comfort her. Often they slipped away in the now-cold forest and made love wrapped in Tommaso's coat. 'Grief takes time, just lots and lots of time. Slowly the rents and the wounds in her soul will recover. It is like growing scar tissue. Now the wounds are open and gaping, but in a year or two she will be able to know joy, not just grief and sorrow.'

'What's going to happen to all of us, Tommaso?'

'We're going back to Asciano. I'm going to marry you and we will all live happily ever after.' He repeated his mantra, as he had done many times. 'Signorina Fosca will come back married to Claude and we will be one big happy family. With my boss back at the *fattoria*, I want more than anything to plant the corn and tend the vines. And I want to make lots and lots of *bambini*.' He hugged Lisa to him. 'And that's not a bad ambition for a man, eh?'

Laboriously Regina began to make inquiries of all the agencies now working in the camps in Germany.

'There are two gunshots that have changed the world

as we know it,' she told Orlando. 'The assassination of the Archduke Ferdinand in Sarajevo was one shot that travelled round the world and meant the world was never the same again. The other shot was the one which that mad creature Hitler aimed at himself in his bunker: from that moment on the world was a safer place. Now the Allies are in the camps and maybe we can find Francesco.'

Regina badgered and bullied. Then finally she got word that a camp of Italians had been discovered over the German border. The men had been used to work the local farms and, though in bad condition, many were still alive.

'I must go and see for myself,' Regina told Elisabetta. 'And no, you can't come. It would not be easy for you. You are still very weak and your chest is bad, and now it is freezing in Germany. As soon as I have word I will telephone you.' She held up an imperious hand. 'Elisabetta, there is no point in you trucking all that way to die just as you find your husband. We are not playing *La Bohème* here. My tiny hand is going to be freezing so I'm taking Orlando to keep me warm. Besides, Orlando can hustle his way out of a worm hole. He is so gifted.'

Weakly Elisabetta agreed. She was too tired, she knew that. And her chest hurt when she breathed. She did not know if it was the crying or a virus. She subsided, resigned, into her bed.

That week Regina and Orlando were gone. Tommaso and Lisa took care of the house with the help of the young serving girl. Elisabetta lay in her bed and prayed. She was glad to hear the sound of the children laughing again: it had been a long time. She was also glad to see that she had some colour back in her face and that her limbs were beginning to become rounded again. Anna, too, had filled out and seemed to have regained some light in her eyes. Elisabetta dreaded the moment when her daughter-in-law would come back to life and have to face the pain of Mario's death. Maybe her loss of memory had been God's way of protecting the young girl's mind during the long journey to freedom.

Anna's room was big and square. It had the family silver stored on the polished wooden cupboards. There was a big gilt mirror on the wall over the fireplace. It was a beautiful room, its windows overlooking a long rambling meadow. Anna sat for hours there in silence.

Just in the last few days, Lisa had found her with tears running down her face. No expression, just the slow, silent drip of tears. Lisa put down her silver tray and touched her mistress gently. 'What's the matter, *cara*?' she whispered.

Anna couldn't tell her, but she saw the face more clearly now, and she knew it was her Aunt Martha. Aunt Martha had something in her hand, something that she was going to send to Anna. That something would release Anna from the tunnel. But Anna didn't know if she wanted to be released. She was comfortable in her tunnel. Everything around her was soft and furry. Kind hands stroked her. Little hands played about her lap and her knees. Little pecks of kisses fell on her cheeks and the water ran down the sides of her face. Anna didn't know what she wanted. Better to sit still and wait.

For three weeks, Elisabetta waited for news from Regina, frantic with worry. At two o'clock one morning, the telephone rang. She was instantly awake, and collided with Lisa who was gingerly making her way down the stairs in the dark.

'Yes,' Lisa said excitedly. 'It's Signora Regina,' she whispered. Her cheeks were flushed with excitement. She could hear Tommaso getting up in his bedroom next door and scrabbling for his shoes.

'Elisabetta,' Regina's voice crackled over the phone. 'I've got someone here for you.'

'Oh no.' Elisabetta steadied herself with her hand on the telephone table.

'Elisabetta . . . Elisabetta. It's me, Francesco.'

Elisabetta was sobbing so hard she was almost speechless. 'Is it really you? After all this time. Darling, darling, are you all right?'

'Yes, I'm fine. Oh Elisabetta, I've dreamed of this moment all the time I was away from you. I'm coming home. Wait for me. Only a week and I'll be back. Darling, I love you and want to put my arms around you more than anything in the world. Whatever has happened, nothing can take away my love for you.'

Regina came back on the line. 'Elisabetta, we have to go now. But as soon as his papers have cleared we're on our way. We'll ring you before we set out so you can tell Lisa and Tommaso to prepare a feast, yes?'

Elisabetta was laughing. 'Surely,' she said. 'Surely.'

Ninety

Silas Ridgeway was not at all happy with the conversation with his client. 'I see, or I think I understand what you are saying, Mrs Kearney. You were in bed with Mr Mainwaring, and on the instructions of your husband, you were photographed by a private detective. Yet you claim you had not committed adultery?'

'That is right.' Mary Rose looked sideways at Travis. His face looked miserable, but his chin was firm.

'Let me read the definition of the word "adultery". "Voluntary sexual intercourse between a married person and a person (married or not) other than his or her spouse." Now, did you or did you not have sexual intercourse with each other? I am sorry to be so blunt, but if you are to be divorced on these grounds we must be very sure of our case before we refute what seems to be evidence that you did indeed experience sexual intercourse with each other.'

Travis leaned forward. 'Mr Ridgeway,' he said earnestly. 'I am incapable of having normal sexual intercourse.' He could see a puzzled look on the lawyer's face. 'I am clinically impotent, and have always been. I have all my medical records to prove it.'

Mr Ridgeway leaned back in his padded chair and regarded his steepled fingertips. 'Now, is that a fact?' He wished he'd not had lox and bagels for breakfast: it was too heavy a meal. This sort of a case really needed a comfortable stomach. Anyway, sex in the afternoon – even the contemplation of it – was exhausting. Certainly Mrs Kearney was a beautiful woman. And the man was not bad for a goy. But this case ... Why do I always get the odd ones? He knew the answer to that. He was the best divorce lawyer in the business. Sometimes he wondered if it was because he so dreaded the loss of his beloved wife that he put everything he had into defending women from men who ill-treated them. He prized his wife and his children and, as he watched the light and the shadows move over Mary Rose's face, he realized that she must have suffered. His heart went out to her.

'Tell me,' he said. 'Tell me everything.' For now he just wanted to listen to her story as it poured from her lips: he would make notes later. As he listened he began to form a concept of how to run the trial. All trials were like theatre. Everyone in the court acted a part. He evaluated Mary Rose and knew she would be magnificent. Now, as she recounted the fights and the insults she had received from Crispin, Ridgeway looked at Travis.

Travis, he felt, would play the part of the honourable man who rescued a damsel in distress. He looked calm and dependable. Hopefully, this Crispin, whose photograph he had seen occasionally in the *Tatler*, would be more dodgy. He needed the opposition to be very dodgy indeed. A pity his clients were both American. English judges didn't like Americans. They thought of them as vulgar and unclubbable. Mary Rose faltered to the end of the story.

'Thank you, my dear. I think I have a pretty good idea of how to proceed. I'll arrange to have the papers delivered here as you agreed with the other side, and then I'll telephone you. I don't expect much to happen until the New Year. But I'll take a full and formal statement from you both.'

He looked at Travis. 'You will collect as much medical evidence as you have, will you not?'

'Do you want both the medical evidence and psychiatric reports?'

'We'll need everything we can lay our hands on. This will be, er, a rather unusual case.' He stood up and left his desk. He shook hands with Mary Rose and clapped Travis on the shoulder. 'This is not going to be pleasant for either of you, and I can't let you underestimate the damage the tabloids are going to do. I only hope you can gain their sympathy. If not . . .' He shrugged. 'Remember it is all tomorrow's fish and chips.'

'Thank you, Mr Ridgeway,' Mary Rose said. 'Thank you very much indeed.'

When they left his office, Ridgeway shook his head. What an odd situation. An adulterer who technically has committed no crime? Without the full act of sexual intercourse there can be no adultery. Well, this will be one for the books, he said, addressing the bank of law books standing in neat shelves behind his desk. He could see it now, '*Kearney vs Kearney*. Solicitor Silas Ridgeway and Sons'. I wonder what they did get up to in bed? Anyway, that was none of his business, and it surely was nothing he could discuss with his wife. She was a good and virtuous woman.

'At least we didn't have to tell him what we do do in bed, Travis.' They had returned to their Eaton Square cocoon. 'And that's a relief.'

Travis made no reply.

'What's the matter?' Mary Rose rolled on to an elbow and gazed down at him.

'It's going to be a bitch, isn't it?'

'Look, Travis, you can always back out. At any time. I'll understand, I promise you.'

Travis shook his head. 'No, Mary Rose, I'm not going to let you be blackmailed by that bastard. Anyway, I'm not ashamed of our love for each other.'

Mary Rose's eyes widened. 'You love me, Travis?'

'Sure I do. Don't think I'd be here all the time if I didn't. OK, I'm damaged goods, but you make me very happy.'

'You're not damaged goods, Travis. We have much better sex than I ever did with Crispin.' She shivered. 'He needed to hurt me to come. I know there's a dark side in all of us, but I don't want to get pushed down that hole. Sex should be a communion and good fun, not something that is twisted and perverse. Anyway, I'm not worried. Whatever happens, I'll be rid of him once and for all. Until I'm divorced from him he feels like a noose around my neck. I'm tired of his whining phone calls and his self-pitying letters.'

She lay back on the pillow. 'I guess I'm real good at hiding from reality, and this flat is such a safe cocoon. Even from the chaos outside. I realize now that I've used this haven not only to escape from having to deal with my personal marital problems, but also with facing Britain being at war. I know it's

469

been incredibly cowardly, but it's been my only form of self-preservation. I've seen the devastation outside, the misery and the suffering. I've seen the people begging in the streets, the young men on crutches, the families without homes, the buildings razed to the ground ... And you know, Travis, I simply haven't been able to cope with it emotionally. Do you understand ... am I making sense? I know I should be out there, but the best I can do is spend a few days in the hospital smiling a lot and handing out food trays. I've always been an escapist, a fun-seeker. But it's no fun out there. Here, in this apartment, in bed with you, I can cope. We will have to face the real world, but not until after Christmas. Let's make the best of that time together.'

Travis held her in his arms. She slowly began to stroke his face with light, feathery touches. 'Tell me,' she said gently, 'about the first time you tried to make love to a girl?'

Travis buried his head in her shoulder. 'Well, it was when I was sixteen. She was the homecoming queen and I was the homecoming king. I was the best ball player they had: I had an offer to go professional, but I didn't want to. I wanted to decorate houses more than anything else in the world. I told you we were poor and Mom had to bring us up on nothing. Dad left me when I was young, so there was just Mom, my sister and me. I loved my little sister. She was the only person in the world that I did love.'

'You mean you didn't love your Mom?'

'I didn't. Well, it's not as simple as that.'

'Life never is, especially at sixteen.' Mary Rose sighed. Memories of her mother weeping over her father intruded for a moment.

'Anyway, I was all Mom had. Gradually I found myself comforting her, taking care of her ...' He hesitated for a moment. 'She insisted I slept in her bed. We only had two rooms, and I suggested that my sister slept with her. But after she drowned – ' his voice shook ' – I had no choice. A boy shouldn't have to share his mother's bed, not at sixteen, anyway.'

He recounted to Mary Rose his first high school infatuation. It was a story like many others, one of pubescent exploration into a realm of innocent romance, built by fumbling and embarrassment, giggling and tears, joy and humiliation.

'I remember the girl trying to help me get it up,' he said, recalling the night after the school dance when they had decided to take that daring, trembling step into full sexual intimacy. 'It was as if a large, invisible hand was holding it down. I couldn't do anything. I felt so dreadful. She dumped me after that. I stayed away from girls for a long time. I wondered if I were homosexual. But I knew I wasn't because I was fully sexually attracted to girls, but just impotent. I think it was losing my sister, and then having to sleep in the same bed with my mother. I remember so clearly the smell of her. She used to enfold me in her arms and sleep with me tightly wrapped to her body. I don't know. It was a choking sensation; I always felt as if I needed fresh air, to breathe.'

Mary Rose lay quietly. She felt her nightdress wet against her shoulder. All his pain was leaking out. This case, she thought, will tear him apart.

'Travis, all this sort of stuff is going to be flying around during this case. Are you sure you can cope?'

'Yeah, I'm sure. It's nothing I haven't had to put up with before. There you are, bollock-naked in front of doctors and students. They discuss you like you're not there. At least I get to keep my clothes on this time. Anyway, when our barrister gives the judge my files and there is no case, I want to be there to see Crispin's face. That will be worth a load of shit.'

'I'm looking forward to seeing his mother's face. Even

if I am plastered all over the *Morning Echo* it will be worth it. Oh Travis, why do parents fuck you up?'

'I don't know; I think they do the best they can. My Mom had no education. She didn't know anything about anything, except survival. As soon as I made some money I got her a nice place and put money in the bank for her. She lived well in her old age. The one thing I never did, though, was to spend the night in that house. It hurt her, but I couldn't risk her demanding that I got into bed with her.'

Mary Rose rolled over. 'You know,' she said, 'I was thinking the other day. Because you can't make love to me in the biblical sense, in a way I've learned a lot more about sex. We invent new ways of giving each other pleasure. I am much happier with you than I was with so many men who only understood about screwing a woman. That was Crispin's problem. Apart from the fact he was – and is – sadistic, he can only jerk off. He can't give any of himself to anyone. I suppose his mother holds his balls, really.'

'Yeah, that's true. But so do most mothers, or at least they try to. I just pulled away.' He shrugged. 'I guess she took them anyway.'

'Nah, Travis, don't worry about it. The day will come when you'll break that curse. You don't belong to her any more.'

'Then who do I belong to?'

The question went unanswered. Mary Rose was afraid of that one.

Ninety-One

'We will all be home by Christmas, you'll see.' Elisabetta's voice was confident.

'I hope so.' Lisa smiled. 'I pray every day that my mother is well and safe.' She sighed and said shyly, 'It would be so nice to spend Christmas with her and Tommaso.'

Elisabetta looked at her. 'Is Tommaso going to marry you?'

'Yes, we will be married when we get back. It's such a funny thing that a dreadful war like this should bring Tommaso and me together.'

'Sometimes I wonder if it is the only time people stop taking account of themselves and find their more noble natures. But certainly not the Nazis. Yet then I think of that officer who let us go and gave us food, and Tommaso's friend who warned us in Asciano.'

That afternoon the telephone went, and once again Elisabetta heard her husband's voice. 'I'm ready to leave, darling. Not long now and we will be in each other's arms.'

'I shan't believe this is happening until I feel you next to me.' She was shaking. 'It's been so long. Too long.'

'Don't expect much when you see me. I'm skinny, like a rat, but at least I'm clean.'

'I don't care what you look like, I just want you home.'

'Regina reckons we will be back in five days. The roads are still congested, but they are clearing.'

'Take care, darling, and be careful. I'll start making your favourite tortellini in brodo.' She put the telephone

473

down and danced into the kitchen. 'Lisa,' she said as she grabbed her by the waist and waltzed her around the kitchen. 'He's going to be back in five days. We must prepare.'

Giulio and Nicoletta heard the truck before anyone else. They were playing in front of the house. 'Truck, truck,' they shrieked as the old Fiat jolted and grunted to the front door. Francesco looked down at the children and instantly recognized his grandson's fair hair. Both Nicoletta and Giulio stood back, holding hands. Who was this thin, ugly stranger who seemed to want to talk to them?

'They don't recognize me,' Francesco said sorrowfully to Regina.

'They will. Give them time. Elisabetta, we're home!' she bellowed.

Orlando unloaded extra food and wine from the back of the truck. Elisabetta came flying out of the front door and fell into Francesco's arms.

'Oh, *caro*. At last.' She pulled away and looked at him. 'You are so thin.' She ran her finger down the creases that knifed his cheeks. 'But you are still my Francesco; that hasn't changed.'

He smiled down at this vision that had never left his mind in all the time he was in the police station, and later in the Italian work camp. When they beat him he called her name, when they took the fingernails from his right hand he blessed her, when they kicked him he called for her until he was unconscious. She was the one thing that had made his life worth living. And now he was back with her. He would have lost his mind but for this icon, this woman. He sighed as he held her close and whispered into her ear. The other adults took the children by their hands and melted away, leaving the two of them alone in the driveway.

'I have to take you to Anna, Francesco.'

'I know. Regina told me she has lost her mind.'

'Sometimes I, too, wished I'd lost mine. But I had no choice: the children needed me. Still, Anna has all that pain to come.' They walked, Francesco's arm around his wife's waist. She took him to Anna's beautiful room.

'We tried to make the room as lovely as possible. We talk to her all the time. Anna,' she said, walking across the room, 'here is Francesco. He's back, Anna.'

She took Anna's hand in hers and drew her to her feet. Francesco's eyes filled with tears. He, too, had suffered horribly following his son's death. But before him stood this woman who did not recognize him or anybody else.

'Anna,' he said, touching her gently. 'It's me, Francesco.' He stroked her face. Unlike his, it had no deep indentations, and the recent weeks of good food had smoothed her cheeks and rounded her body. She stood glowing in the evening light.

'We can only go on trying,' Elisabetta said, suddenly tired with all the overflowing emotions. 'Come, Anna, we will go downstairs and celebrate Francesco's return.'

During the meal, Elisabetta looked at all the faces around the table. The one obvious absence caused her a pang of agony, but she blessed them all and thanked God for their safety. Thanks to Orlando, the table was piled high with black market food. Bananas, steak grilled in olive oil and leaves of fresh sage. Guinea-fowls, brushed with olive oil, rosemary and lemon juice, and grilled on the fire. Orlando had also brought a bag of flour, so Lisa was able to make fresh Tuscan pizza.

'None of that Neapolitan muck,' she sniffed.

Francesco was busily talking to Nicoletta. He put his hand on top of her head. 'I am proud of you,' he said.

Little Giulio, sitting by his mother, piped up. 'And of me?'

'Especially of you, my darling. Your father would have been thrilled to be here on this night. Who knows, I believe he probably is.' He raised his glass of wine to the rest of the table. '*Salute*,' he said, smiling broadly.

'*Salute*,' they chorused back.

Francesco's resolve stayed firm until he got into bed with Elisabetta. Then he broke down and cried all the tears he had held for so long. Lying quietly in her arms he sighed. 'We will have to build our lives again, darling.'

'I know.' Elisabetta felt a growing sense of confidence. 'We will build our lives again. At least we have each other. Without you I don't think I could build anything.' She fell asleep. Francesco lay awake beside her. He knew that she could rebuild her life, time and time again. Women could. They were the strong ones. Without her, however, he would have nothing to build for.

Ninety-Two

Ralph was having breakfast in the nursery with his son Edgar. He was amused to watch his nanny trying to spoon a boiled egg down the child.

'Here, Edgar,' the nurse said, lifting up a thin piece of toast, wet with the yellow yolk of the egg. 'Here's a soldier.' She ineffectually tried to push the toast into the boy's mouth. Ralph laughed.

'Don't hound him, Nanny. You'll put him off boiled eggs for life. That's what my nanny did to me. Give the boy some toast and lemon marmalade. That's what he likes.'

'You'll spoil him, Major Fanshaw. Then what'll we do?'

Ralph looked at his son. He always felt a deep sense of guilt and pity when he looked at the child. Guilt because Belinda had died in childbirth. However he tried to rationalize it, he felt both responsible for her death and that his son was motherless. Could he have done anything about her death had he been in England at the time? Was it true that she had overdone the hospital visiting with Mary Rose? It was time he came out of his reclusive lifestyle and caught up with Mary Rose. That decided, he went to his study and telephoned the Kearney house.

'She's not here.' Amelia's voice was stiff with hostility.

'Are they away?' Ralph asked. 'Because if they are I'll leave a message for them.'

'Where have you been, Ralph? Everybody knows that Mary Rose left my son and went off and committed adultery in London with this American man. There is to be a court case.'

'Surely not?' Ralph said, taken aback. 'There'll be a horrible scandal.'

'Well, she should have thought of that before she went running off with that awful, vulgar American.'

'I do understand your position, Amelia, but is it possible that you might have her address? I have a question I would like to put to her about my wife. I mean my late wife. I don't know if you know.'

'Yes, I do know. And I'm sorry.' Amelia's sympathy was perfunctory. 'Ask Mr Ryder, our solicitor. He will have it. Tell him I said you could take her address. Though why you should want to ask that lying little bitch anything, I don't know.'

After a few polite remarks, Ralph hung up and sighed. Why he had decided to rejoin the human race he knew not. Perhaps it was something to do with the fact that, in the last few weeks, he had been dreaming again, and in one of the dreams he had seen a very clear picture of Anna. He felt compelled to see her again.

He telephoned Mr Ryder. 'I'm an old friend of Mary Rose Kearney. Mrs Amelia Kearney said I could ask you for her daughter-in-law's telephone number.'

'If she said so, then that's all right. I'll give you her solicitor's number in London. I do have her London address, but I'm afraid it's under a pile of papers somewhere.'

Ralph telephoned Mr Silas Ridgeway. 'I'll tell Mrs Kearney that you called and she can call you back,' he said.

Ralph put the phone down and smiled grimly. It's a bad business when you get into the hands of those lawyer-wallahs, he observed, passing his black labrador lying on the mat. He felt restless and went out to the stables to collect his horse. Soon he was cantering down the orchard before extending his horse into a full gallop. He realized that he very much wanted Anna to be at his side. The thought made him feel guilty, but it wouldn't go away.

Ralph had rarely seen two more gloomy people. Mary Rose and Travis seemed spent, devoid of enthusiasm, blank. It was obvious they had to force themselves to observe even the most basic courtesy. His attempts to break the stretches of painful silence had been clumsy and in vain. He realized that it was no time to ask Mary Rose about Belinda, her last days. His private grief would have to remain private, at least for the time being.

'Well, I gather things are a little difficult at the moment. Mary Rose, I'm sorry.'

She smiled back at him wanly. 'We're not always this miserable. Travis and I had to give formal statements today. It was very difficult and unpleasant, especially as we know they will be read out in open court. They don't leave much to the imagination. The details of why I wanted to leave Crispin are difficult. Except for Anna, I didn't show anybody my bruises or my black eyes. And I wouldn't involve her in a case like this. Anyway, most of what he did was mental. It was like living in my own personal concentration camp. Ugh, I hate even thinking about it.'

Travis put his hand on her arm. 'Don't, Mary Rose. It's all over now bar the shouting, as the British say. They can shout and sneer, but the day after the case we'll be out of here and back to the States. We may have a lot of faults, but at least we are an up-front nation.' He shook his head. 'This place stinks! I've never seen such hypocrisy.'

Ralph looked down at his plate of oysters and at his Guinness laced with champagne. 'In many ways you're right. But remember, you don't hear from the decent, quiet people in England. They just get on with their lives. I can defend the country because I'm one of the lucky ones born with a silver spoon in my mouth. For anybody else, it is difficult. We can only hope the old dinosaurs die out and their children replace them. A decent bunch of men and women who don't want an exclusive lifestyle.' He smiled. 'But then I'm a little cynical about altruism these days. The war did that for me. I saw unspeakable things done to human beings, but also great kindness.

'I don't know what I want any more. Maybe just to run my estate, to ride my horse, and fish for salmon in the river. Nothing complicated.' He paused. 'By the way, Mary Rose, do you know anything about Anna and her family?'

'No, not really. I went over just before war was declared. In fact, Crispin and I were among the last over there. Then we lost touch. I did try on the phone and she sounded all right. But nothing now for ages.'

'I'll try and give her a buzz. I have to go to Rome in the spring anyway. If I can't get a reply I'll take the embassy car and drive up there.' He smiled. 'I have had an absolute yen to see her. We used to get on so well. We were really good friends. It's tragic how the war separates people. Now I feel an urge to harmonize myself, to try and get back all the life that I lost. I'm really pleased to see you, Mary Rose. And to meet you, Travis. If there is anything you want me to do . . .' He fiddled with his last oyster, carefully dripping the lemon juice on to it. 'I mean, I'll always go into the dock and give you an absolutely splendid character reference. You see, I knew Crispin very well indeed, as you know. I know what he's capable of doing to a woman. Looking at you today, I can see what he must have done.'

Mary Rose fiddled with her bread. She badly needed to hear those words. So far she could only tell Travis her impressions of what had happened. It filled her heart with certainty to have Ralph confirm what she knew to be true.

'I don't mind the divorce part of this,' she said. 'I just want to get as far away from Crispin as I can. And his bloody family. What I do mind is being dragged through the mud, and I want to fight back.'

'Good for you, Mary Rose. Just remember, you're one of the fighting Irish. Good luck, and don't let the bastards get you down.'

'I won't,' Mary Rose said, smiling for the first time that evening. She lifted up her champagne glass. 'Here's to us, Travis.'

Travis's eyes sparkled. 'Hey,' he said. 'Bottoms up.'

Ninety-Three
♪

By the autumn Elisabetta and Francesco had led their little family home in triumph. But the joy was muted by the condition of the house and estate. The Germans had wrecked the buildings, particularly the main villa. It looked as if tanks had deliberately mowed down the cypress trees. As they walked in silence through the open front door, Elisabetta put her hands over her mouth: she feared she might be sick. A terrible feeling of violation caused her to shake. The last time she had seen her house it had been a quiet haven of great beauty. All her married life she had sought to make it a fit place for her beloved family. Now it was desecrated.

'Don't worry, signora.' Lisa put her hand on Elisabetta's arm. 'Tommaso and I can get this cleaned up in no time.' But even as she spoke she knew she couldn't ever make up for the damage done to the paintings, or to the smashed light fittings. The great chandelier in the hall was blown to pieces: obviously drunken German officers had used it for target practice.

The children ran around obliviously. Giulio found a little felt rabbit out in the laundry. He came back into the house grinning broadly. Elisabetta, with tears streaming down her face, had to laugh. Then she became hysterical.

Francesco took her in his arms. 'Hush, darling,' he said gently.

'I'm such a fool,' she said. 'I'm so stupid. How can I make a fuss like this about the house when you survived the camp and the children are well and happy?'

Anna sat vacantly on a broken chair. It all goes by her,

Elisabetta thought as she calmed down. The good and the bad. She collected herself. 'Come along, Tommaso and Lisa, let's get to work.'

'I'll go and look at the damage to the outside.' Francesco strode off. He understood his wife's feelings, but he was so glad to be back he didn't care if there were only two bricks left standing. He stood out in the belt of the woods where Mario had died and prayed to the Madonna to save his daughter-in-law.

'We're back, Mario, wherever you are. I will take care of her and your little ones.' He crossed himself and allowed the grief to surge over him. So far, during all the hectic times, he had had little time to grieve, but now he knew the pain would hit him. Yet he could bear it with Elisabetta beside him. He had not known that you could defer grief, but he realized that was what he had done in the camp. With only Elisabetta in front of him he had excluded everything else from his consciousness. Even eating the meagre rations had afforded him no pleasure. Now he was going to have to learn to live again.

The idea of making love to Elisabetta made him nervous. Would he ever feel a sexual urge again? It surprised him how, when he was hungry – and that was all the time – he felt nothing. He had been too shy to check with the other men whether they felt the same. Maybe time would tell. Probably if he ate well he would get his strength. He frowned. His dreams had been about holding Elisabetta in his arms, yet last night he had been far too tired and too upset to make love. He wondered if she had been disappointed. They had been separated for so long. She had her torments and fears to go through, as did he. He would take time to get to know his wife again. For tonight, he decided to take the best of the food they had brought with them and to make a feast. When life gets tough, he reminded himself, that is the time to celebrate.

He went around to the back of the big cellar and felt along the back wall. No, the Germans hadn't found his father's secret stock of Barolo wine. Tonight they would drink the finest wine Italy could offer. He was glad that they had some prosciutto from Parma. There was nothing to pick in the garden, even though the weather was mild. There had been no olive-picking or harvesting of the grapes this year. Everything had been senselessly, and needlessly, neglected or destroyed. He wandered back into the house.

Elisabetta had put Anna on the terrace for some sun. Her face was pale from sitting for so long in Regina's forest. She obviously felt the sun because she lifted her eyes to the horizon.

'Well, that's something to celebrate.' Francesco took Anna's hand in his. He looked down at the ring that had bound his son to his daughter-in-law. Gentle thoughts filled his mind, of Mario as a little boy playing here on the terrace. He had been a terror as a child, always climbing and running. A nervous live wire with big gentle eyes. He had had girlfriends. Many of them. There was the one from Asciano he had nearly married. Francesco was glad he let that one go. She had gone off with another man. Just as well: he could not have loved Anna more. She brought such a different current of air into the family. She came with all the bounce and enthusiasm of a brash American. Anna was not nearly as brash as most of the Americans he had met, but still, there was that puppyish likeability about her. Her willingness to give everybody the benefit of the doubt. Her laughter, which was constant. Her optimism which came from living in a huge, open, affluent society.

It was all such a contrast to the closed, secretive, Tuscan way of life. Trust nobody but the family, and not them either, could well be a Tuscan motto. Every man's hand against all. Francesco smiled. Life in the concentration camp had taught him that none of that was true. The Tuscans in the camp had got on together and were like brothers to each other. True, they had had little time for the Romans who had whined most of the time, and the Neapolitans who had been far too cunning. He laughed out loud and went to find Elisabetta. He must tell her of life in the camp.

Later in the evening, Elisabetta stood up and smiled at the people around the table. Giulio was asleep, his fair hair silvered in the light of a candle. They had made a big fire in as many rooms as they needed to use. Tommaso and Lisa were in one room, and the twins were sleeping in Francesco's dressing room. The fire played shadows against the kitchen wall. The windows were broken and let in the cold night air. But their stomachs were full and their faces flushed with the Barolo wine.

'I'll take Anna to bed,' Elisabetta said. She put her hand on Anna's shoulder and the woman stood up like an obedient child. 'Good-night, everyone,' Elisabetta said. 'And thank you all for the hard work. You were magnificent.' She gently led Anna away.

'Thank God.' Francesco slipped inside his wife.

Elisabetta tightened her arms around his neck. 'Did you miss this?' she murmured as Francesco's body gathered speed. He couldn't reply: his need was too urgent. Finally, spent, he lay beside her.

'How could I not miss it?' he said gently, kissing her eyelids. 'But more than this I missed simply holding you. The feel of you against me. The softness of you and your breasts. I think I missed your breasts most of all.' He looked down at her naked body. 'Your breasts are so beautiful.' He tickled her inky-brown nipples. Then he lay back on his pillow and realized he really was home. Home was Elisabetta. The rest didn't matter. He fell asleep.

Ninety-Four

1

'I suggest you wear something very plain. A black suit and a string of pearls.' Mary Rose's barrister, Lord Kelston, was a sharp-nosed, pursed-lipped man. He hadn't wanted much to take the case. But he was hard-pressed for money. There was his house in Scotland and another in Holland Park to maintain. And three of his children were in boarding school, while the fourth was about to come out. A chap didn't have much choice these days. Besides, the woman was rich. But he realized that she was also quite vulnerable, squeezing from him that tiny, single drop of compassion which remained in him after all his years at the Bar. It surfaced rarely these days, almost involuntarily. He hoped that he could at least get the charge of adultery thrown out. A lot would depend on the judge. After all, in English law, judges decided whatever they wished.

' "Judges' rules" means that there are no rules,' he explained patiently to Travis for the umpteenth time. Travis simply could not grasp the idea that there was a world of difference between American law and the English legal system.

'In America we have a Constitution,' he said. 'I have my legal rights protected.'

'Of course you do. But that's America. We don't have a constitution because we have every intention of seeing that nobody has any rights. Just think of the fuss if everybody felt they could defend themselves, or refused to give evidence against themselves. Why, it would be anarchy, wouldn't it?'

'No.' Travis stared blankly at the barrister. 'It isn't anarchy if everybody gets a fair trial.'

'You shall have a fair trial, Mr Mainwaring, that's what I am here for.' Lord Kelston swung his robe over his shoulder, tugged at his wig and left his chambers. Damn! he thought. I have to leave my own chambers to get rid of the man. Poor fellow. He has no idea what's coming to him. He went round to the chambers next door to see how the opposition was getting on.

'Piece of cake.' Ratty Radcliffe, Crispin's barrister, was sitting back in his chair, his highly polished shoes on the table. 'She doesn't stand a chance. We've got the evidence in the bag. Fella in bed with his wife, picture to prove it . . . what more do we need?'

'Ah, my dear fellow, never think the case is closed until it really is. You never know, I might have something up my sleeve.'

'Hopefully a bottle of whisky. How about a quick one before we head for home?'

Lord Kelston chuckled. 'Only you're not heading for home, are you?'

'No, I'm off to spend the night with Bunty. What a good little girl she is. So kind, so very kind.'

Lord Kelston sipped his whisky and wished he was not a Catholic. Somehow the thought of lying with a woman other than his wife made him feel so guilty he didn't feel it was worth it. It took a trial like this to make him realize even more urgently that it wasn't worth it, even if his wife's body resembled an ageing hot-water bottle. Such a shame that six children should take such a toll on her. When she was young she had seemed all acres of gleaming skin to him. Still, Ratty was always one for the ladies, and he was married to a fearsome woman. 'Fearsome Fanny', she was known as in the shires.

On the way home, Travis was largely silent. 'I can't

486

get the hang of English law. As far as I can see there is no law.'

'Yeah, I guess you can say that. There really is one law for the rich and one for the poor. That's what Robin Hood is all about. Nothing much has changed.'

They had a miserable Christmas. The flat seemed small and cramped. The end of the war meant that Mrs Gulbenkian had headed for Hong Kong. The streets were thronged with servicemen who were out of work and begging.

'I can't believe that the English government would allow all these men the privilege of dying for their country and then bring them home to nothing,' Mary Rose said as they strolled through Hyde Park. 'No jobs, no money. I just can't believe it.' She was upset.

'Here, take it.' She pushed a five-pound note into a man's hands. He had one leg and the other was grafted to a white stump.

'Thank you, lady,' he said, his eyes red from the alcohol that was obviously the only thing keeping him warm.

'You'd better believe it.' Travis was very frightened.

Now the trial lay directly ahead of them. So far they had both put a wall up between it and their everyday lives. Christmas was the wall. They had refused to think past that. Now Christmas Day had come and gone, as had a joyless New Year's Eve. They hadn't even bothered to go out. They had sat grimly facing each other, a bottle of champagne and the remains of the Christmas pudding in front of them. Travis's Christmas hat had slid over his ear.

'Oh, Mary Rose, this is a bitch of an evening. We said we'd hold the Christmas crackers and pudding for New Year's Eve in case we found our sense of humour again. But it doesn't look as if either of us are up to much.'

Mary Rose sat in her chair and made a face. 'Look,

Travis, why don't we just get smashed and forget the rest of the world?'

'Good idea.'

They were both rolling drunk when they managed to heave themselves into bed.

Travis felt unaccountably happy. 'I am so drunk,' he began.

Mary Rose made a dive for him. 'I'll stop the room spinning,' she said, pinning him down across the bed. She lay on top of him, laughing.

'Wheee, I'm flying,' Travis said, and bucked her off. They slid inelegantly on to the thickly carpeted floor.

'Travis . . .' Mary Rose was suddenly no longer drunk.

'Don't say anything . . .' Travis felt himself engorged. He pulled off Mary Rose's silk underpants. 'Quick.' He was trembling with a mixture of lust and fright. Mary Rose, with willing fingers, guided him between her legs. He felt an unfamiliar sensation. No longer the thick tissue of fingers, or the rough embrace of a towel, but a gentle, silken warmth. He tried to keep his mind alert to the sensation, but soon rolls and heaves of pleasure overcame him and he succumbed to the rhythm and sensations that pulled him down, and then further down, until he was no more.

When he opened his eyes he was stricken with remorse. 'Oh darling, are you all right? That was so selfish of me.'

'No it wasn't,' Mary Rose said dreamily. 'It was the nicest thing that has happened to me in many years.' She propped herself up on her elbow. 'Do you realize you have just demolished our case?'

'No I haven't. At the time I was impotent, but I'm not any more. Give me a few minutes and we'll try again. I couldn't bear it if I only had one shot.' He lit a cigarette for himself and then passed one to her. 'To think I've been missing this for so long. Still,' he said cheerfully. 'I'm going to make up for lost time, you'd better believe it. Mary Rose,' he said, putting down his cigarette and taking hers. 'Will you marry me?'

Mary Rose looked at him uncertainly. 'I don't know, Travis. So far I've made rather a mess of marriage. I don't know if I want to do it again. Ask me after the trial.' She kissed him gently. 'And now, if you don't mind, let's try again. After all,' she said in a mock schoolteacher's voice, 'you might only have one shot and that would be a pity.'

Ninety-Five

Looking back at Christmas, Elisabetta realized that news from Daniel and Mary had made the whole thing bearable. The pain of missing Mario came back with full force – the poignant moment when she was aware his stocking was not hanging on the fireplace mantel. She talked about it with Francesco.

'No,' he said firmly. 'We must let him go.'

'But even when they were both away in America we hung their stockings.' She tried to argue, but it was useless.

'Darling, then they were both alive and coming back to us. Now we must accept that he is dead and will not come back. We will mourn for him always, but don't hold on to the past. I will get the stonemason to make a memorial for him and we can honour his grave. Tommaso buried him deep in the woods. Maybe one day when we have some money we can build a little chapel there. But we must let go.'

The news from Mary and Daniel was that they were

thankful that they were all safe. They had heard the news about Mario in stunned silence. From the Post Office phone, Francesco had told them simply that Anna had had a rough time, but that, hopefully, she would soon be back to normal. He had left the phone with promises of a visit in the near future.

'I didn't really tell them anything,' he told Elisabetta later. He felt his words coming out awkwardly. 'I will try this week to get Dr Roselli to come and have a look at her.' He sighed. 'I don't know what he can do. Or anyone else.'

Ralph's letter arrived. He had tried to telephone, but of course he had no way of knowing that all the telephones around Asciano had been smashed by the Germans. Only a few were working, and they were used for news of the dead and the dying. He said he would be in Rome in a couple of months' time and would try and get up to see them if he could get some extra petrol. He asked after Anna.

Elisabetta wrote back in her strained, neglected English, sympathizing with his loss and telling him of their own. Of Anna, she just said that she was not herself and maybe he could help them when he came for a visit. She wondered whether, if the doctor in the village could do nothing, there might be a specialist in London who could help.

All through the Christmas period, Elisabetta tried to make the occasion fun for the children. They had been through so much that, now they were safe, she would try to make amends to them. It was hard when news from Arezzo told of how the Germans had shot all the men and boys between the ages of seven and seventy. How, near by, a group of partisans were found by the Germans in the corn, taken to a house where they were barred in, and then blown sky-high. One man, lodged under a crossbeam, lived to tell the tale. A pall hung over Asciano. Nearby in San Giovanni d'Asso, many a family wore a black band of mourning. The streets grieved for voices that would never be heard again. Boys who had grown to men in the shadow of the castello were now lying somewhere in hostile fields.

Francesco forbade the women and the children to go into Asciano: savage reprisals were taking place. Partisans fighting with the Communists, Fascists killing and being killed summarily, old scores between families being settled.

'Bad blood,' Francesco muttered as he climbed wearily from an old car he had managed to buy. 'Better you stay home with the children.'

Slowly, in the weeks after Christmas, the work progressed. Everyone pitched in. Soon the windows were boarded up for the winter. Lisa scrubbed and polished.

At last the day came when she and Tommaso were married in the little chapel attached to the farm. It was an ice-cold Tuscan day. The sun shone in recognition of the event and the girls were dressed as bridesmaids. There was no material in the town to make the dresses, but Elisabetta had found her old ballgowns tucked away in the attic and had thanked her lucky stars that the Germans had not seen them.

'Look,' she had said, delighted with the silks and the satins. 'We're in luck. You will have the best wedding in Asciano this year.' For days and nights both the women had hung over the dresses, cutting and reshaping them. Lisa was to be married in thick cream taffeta.

'It couldn't be white, could it?' Tommaso had remarked one night. Lisa had leaned over in bed and boxed his ear. 'I'll buy you a red garter for the honeymoon.'

'What honeymoon?' Lisa had asked.

'Just you wait until you are my bride and I can ravish you on our first night.'

'Tommaso,' Lisa had laughed. 'You're such a fool.'

'I know. Men are fools. That's why women love them.'

The wedding was a huge success. The town needed to celebrate. All the usual signposts of the passing of the seasons had been ruined by the Germans. There were no strings of onions and garlic hanging from the rafters. No dried figs, split and stuffed with almonds. No tomatoes wrinkled by the hot sun. No hams, no pecorino cheeses. Years of provisioning had been swept away and it would take many years to bring it back. They all knew that, but they needed to draw together as a community.

The communes in Tuscany go back a thousand years, was the first bit of local history Anna had learned from Mario. And the commune is the centre of our lives, he had said. Now Elisabetta remembered this conversation and the enraptured look in Anna's eyes as she had tried to absorb her new way of life.

They made Anna the bridesmaid of honour, as befitted her rank as the last married woman in the family. On the day she looked beautiful in her tightly waisted dress with six panels reaching to the floor. Nicoletta was dressed in a miniature copy of her dress. Lisa's bridal veil was made from an old lace altar cloth Elisabetta had found in the chapel. It was yellow and crumpled when she had found it, but she had bleached it in the sun and had ironed it gently with the charcoal iron.

The town stood respectfully as Lisa and Tommaso came up the small path to the chapel. Lisa's mother, thankfully alive, came next on the arm of her neighbour. They were followed by Francesco and Elisabetta. Francesco held Anna by the hand and gently led her through the ceremony. The children behaved beautifully. As Lisa walked down the aisle with her veil pulled back, Elisabetta caught Francesco's eye. She squeezed his hand.

'Everything will be all right,' she said. 'We'll hear about Fosca and Claude soon.'

'I hope so,' Francesco whispered back. 'We've lost a son and I couldn't bear anything now to happen to my daughter.'

The feasting went on well into the night. Everybody had brought bowls and plates and anything they could contribute to make the wedding a success. Table after table was filled with people eating and talking. There was little talk of the past atrocities. The Fascists knew they were not welcome, so none came. Instead, children ran madly around the tables, shouting and playing. The elderly looked on fondly, and often a wrinkled hand would reach out to pat or slap a child as it tore past. The candles glimmered on the tables, but were unnecessary on such a starlit night.

At twelve o'clock exactly, Tommaso drove up in Francesco's car. 'Come along,' he said to Lisa, who looked surprised. 'We are going off for our honeymoon.'

'You must be joking,' she said. 'Besides, I have to help to clear up.'

'No you don't. This is your wedding. You are coming with me.' He lifted her up in his arms and carried her to the car. There was a roar of good-natured laughter from the crowd.

'I must at least change my clothes.'

'Your clothes are all in a suitcase in the back of the car.'

'Where are we going?'

'You'll see.'

They drove down darkly wooded lanes until they came to a drive. Tommaso turned right and then stopped the car outside a little cottage. He got out and pushed open the front door. Inside was a softly shining lamp. Lisa, intrigued, climbed out, carefully holding her train above the thick, damp grass.

'Where are we?' she asked.

'Somewhere in the universe,' Tommaso replied, playfully laconic. Nearby they could hear the rushing of a stream.

For a moment Tommaso seemed almost nervous. He fiddled about in the little kitchen behind the small sitting room. There was a fire in the grate. Lisa slipped off her wedding gown and removed her headdress. She sat on the sofa in her underwear. Tommaso returned carrying a bottle of wine and some little soft amaretto biscuits.

'You look so beautiful in the firelight,' he said quietly. He poured two glasses of wine and handed her one. 'I can't believe that I'm so lucky.'

'Neither can I.' They were both strangely shy.

'We don't have to do anything tonight, Lisa. I was only joking the other day.'

Lisa smiled gently at him. 'Tommaso Roselli, are you going to leave your wife a virgin on her wedding night?'

Tommaso grinned and put down his glass of wine.

Ninety-Six

Lord Kelston was not in a good mood when he telephoned Mary Rose at eight o'clock in the morning. 'How the devil,' he demanded, 'did the *Morning Echo* get a picture of the two of you in bed?'

'Oh, shit . . . I'm sorry, Lord Kelston, I didn't mean to swear.' She felt Travis wake with a start by her side. 'I can only think that Crispin gave it to someone. He's vindictive, but I didn't think that vindictive. Wait. Yes. The only person who could be low enough to do that would be his mother.'

'Well, it's not going to do us much good. You'd better go out and get a copy and read it before you arrive in court. The whole place will be buzzing with the scandal.'

'I'm sorry.' Mary Rose knew she sounded ineffectual. She put the telephone down and looked miserably at Travis. 'I'm afraid the old bitch has done us in. That rag, the *Echo*, has a picture of us, the one taken by that private detective.' She shrugged. 'Well, at least I get to see it.'

Travis pulled on his trousers and a polo-necked sweater. 'I'll go down to Sloane Square and get a copy. Don't worry, darling, they would have got a copy sooner or later anyway. These scandals always involve everybody behaving like lice. I don't expect anything but treachery from Crispin and his mother, so let's not get depressed. We've nothing to lose. As soon as this is over we're out of here.'

That's not the point, Mary Rose thought as she lay in bed waiting for him to come back. The point is, how can you marry someone and share their bed and their life and then be betrayed like this? What sort of man did I marry? She walked to the window, impatient for Travis to come back. Finally, after what seemed like an age, he turned the corner and was walking back, his head down reading the front page of a newspaper.

'Not on the front page as well! Holy shit.' She and Travis stared transfixed at their three-column image. 'If I was going to make the front page of the *Echo*, at least it could have been because I had won the pools or something. Not a picture of me in bed with another man.' She felt an awful wave of embarrassment wash over her. 'I hope the New York newspapers don't pick this up. My mother would have a fit. Not because she would disapprove, but because it was made public.' My parents, she wryly observed, sinned their share, but always in private. Oh well, today is the day.

She mentally went through the list of clothes she would be wearing. She had chosen a very plain, black suit. The jacket was tight at the waist and then flared into a small peplum flounce. The skirt was pencil slim with a split at the back. She chose a black crocodile handbag with matching shoes. For her head she selected a hat with a dark veil to cover most of her face. She knew she would look perfect for the part, but just to make her inner world feel a little less exposed, she decided to wear her sexiest black silk underwear.

'It could be worse,' Travis said later, trying to smile. She looked at the photograph again.

'Well, I've been more photogenic in my time,' she said. 'Actually we both look rather vulnerable.'

The private detective had caught them just before they had been woken by the flash. She was sleeping in Travis's arms. As a piece of superficial evidence it certainly looked incriminating.

Mary Rose grinned. 'What the hell,' she said finally. 'Let's milk it for all it's worth. We're stuck with the whole caboodle. Let's just get on with it and pretend we are in a play. I think Ridgeway was quite right when he said to remember that we're playing a part. We are playing a part. I'm guilty of adultery, at least in a spiritual sense, and I know it. But I'm just not prepared to be blackmailed by an arsehole like Crispin. So I'm going to fix you some champagne and orange juice and scrambled eggs and then we'll go in to fight. What Crispin hasn't reckoned is that I'm OK until I get my back up against a wall. Then I come out fighting.'

'Yeah, well I can see the fire in your eyes, Mary Rose, and I think I might end up feeling quite sorry for Crispin.'

'Don't,' she said tersely. 'He deserves all he gets.'

They walked in through the gates of the Matrimonial Courts in the Strand. Mary Rose had often driven past the courts. She had always admired the architecture because it reminded her of the box of bricks she had had as a child. Lovely ornate windows with deep embrasures.

'Give us a story, love. Come on, what happened?'

'Hey Yankie, what's with the other man's wife?'

Mary Rose was appalled and restrained herself from taking Travis's hand. Reporters pushed and jostled all around her. They shoved with their elbows, their big flash cameras exploding. Finally she and Travis were through the gauntlet and in the quiet well of the huge central room that was the heart of the court. Mary Rose stared down at the black and white checked floor, then looked up and saw Mr Ridgeway coming towards them.

'Ah, you made it I see. I tried to telephone, but you had left. I'm sorry about the welcoming committee, but I'm afraid we'll have to accept that it will be there for the duration of the trial. Be careful where you go and what you do. Obviously you can't be seen with each other at night, and you must not discuss anything over the telephone. It would have been better if you had come separately, but as we are claiming that you are business partners – which you are – there really is no harm done.'

Lord Kelston was in a more positive mood. 'I say, your medical evidence is quite impressive. I think we can win this one. What a knock out for Radcliffe.' He harrumphed into his cup of coffee. They were sitting in the refectory, which amused Mary Rose. The place looked like a cheap cafeteria. Her coffee was dreadful, but at least it was black and hot. She sipped and tried not to catch Travis's eye. There had been a major change in the medical evidence, but that was their intimate secret.

Down at the far end of the room she could see Crispin, neat in his grey cashmere and wool suit. His fair hair hung over his forehead. She wondered if he was hating this as much as she was. Probably not, she decided. He liked to be the centre of attention and was probably banking on a great deal of sympathy. Amelia was sitting next to him in an absolutely hideous fustian blue wool suit. She had a black hat clamped to the side of her head with a feather looming over her brow. No marks for good taste. Of the rest of the family there was no sign.

'I can't see why Mary Rose is looking so jolly,' Crispin complained to his mother. 'You'd at least think she'd have the grace to look embarrassed. I'd be embarrassed if I had my photograph plastered all over the front page of the *Morning Echo*, to say nothing of being called an adulteress. She has no shame. But then, she's American I suppose, and they are animals.'

'Yes, dear.' Amelia was trying to humour her son.

All night long he had paced the sitting room in the Savoy. He had insisted they stay in Mary Rose's original suite. 'This is where she betrayed me,' he had kept muttering. Amelia had ordered a bottle of whisky and had hoped he'd drink himself to sleep. But it had been morning when he had finally dropped into his bed, leaving her awake and sweating.

'I do hope this all goes well,' she muttered to herself. She was still shaken at her husband's disapproval of the whole event.

'I wash my hands of this whole affair, Amelia,' he had told her. 'This is no way for a gentleman to behave. You have always encouraged the boy to be an absolute cad, and by jove this time you've gone too far. I shan't be able to hold my head up in London again. To think that a son of mine has ratted on his wife. It is one thing to have an affair, everyone does at some time or another. But to go public . . . ! Disgusting, absolutely disgusting. I'll have nothing to do with it.' He had stomped off, and since then had slept in his study.

Amelia had looked at the ceiling of the suite and had remembered that, now Mary Rose had left, they really did not have the money to throw away on a suite in the Savoy. And if the case went badly wrong, there might not be any money anyway. Eventually she had fallen into an uneasy sleep.

The judge sat on the raised platform under a carved wooden canopy. He gazed out at the human figures before him with an implacable expression of hatred.

'Oh dear,' Ridgeway whispered to Mary Rose. 'It's Judge Henry Saltash.'

'What's he like?'

'Very fierce. But he can be very fair. We'll have to see.'

'Your Honour.' Radcliffe was on his feet, his nose twitching eagerly. He scented a coup. It always helped if there were plenty of journalists to bias the public and to fill the newspapers and air-waves with information against the other side. He presented the heartbreaking case of a man from a good family rescuing an American damsel with an offer of marriage, only to find his heart broken by her perfidious wooing of another American behind her loving husband's back.

'And here,' he said, reaching the peak of his oration, 'is the evidence.' He motioned to the clerk of the court to put the incriminating evidence before the judge.

Judge Saltash gazed wearily at the photograph. He looked as if this unpleasant task was one that was forced upon him most mornings at far too early an hour. Other people in bed with each other was not an edifying sight.

He heaved a very audible sigh. 'Yes, I take your point, this certainly is evidence. But if this is the case, why is the other side contesting the grounds for divorce?'

He gazed at Lord Kelston. He knew the man well. He played a good stroke of golf and wouldn't have taken on a case like this if he had thought he was going to lose. Besides, Kelston and Radcliffe had been at each other's throats since they had gone to *the* school together. Radcliffe had always bullied Kelston, who had been rather a swot. There was more to this than met the eye. Hope he gets on with it, though. Judge Saltash looked surreptitiously at his watch. He wanted to leave London at four. He had a fishing date with his gamekeeper.

'Your Honour,' Lord Kelston began. 'I agree that these two people before you are guilty of sleeping in each other's arms.' He said the word 'sleeping' very deliberately and slowly. 'There is no excuse for their behaviour. But they are business partners. They do much of their work interior decorating the great houses of London.'

'What's the name of the partnership?' the judge inquired.

' "Mainwaring and Buchanan", Your Honour.'

The judge nodded. 'Ah yes, indeed.' He nodded cordially at Mary Rose. What a fine-looking girl, he thought. He cast a look at Crispin. Kearney, he wondered. Don't know that name. Must be a Johnny-come-lately. Irish. Of course, would have to be. He gazed at Amelia's hat with intense dislike. How could a woman come into my court dressed like that, he wondered. Shouldn't be allowed.

'Mrs Kearney had separated from her husband and was suffering a great deal,' Lord Kelston continued. 'Mr Mainwaring was working late in her flat and attempted to comfort her. They did not ever suspect that they were being watched because they had nothing to hide.'

Judge Saltash interrupted. 'Nothing to hide, Lord Kelston? Surely a married woman entertaining another man in her bed warrants an attempt at secrecy?'

'Not, Your Honour, if the other man's intentions are purely platonic.'

'Purely platonic, Lord Kelston? I take it you are a married man?'

Lord Kelston tried not to smile. The court reporter was scribbling faster than a drowning mouse paddles. The judge knew damn well he was married. He had dined with them often enough.

'Yes, My Lord, I am a married man.'

'What would your wife say if you told her you were not spending the night with another married woman, merely platonically comforting her?'

'She would not believe me, My Lord.'

'I should think not,' the judge snorted.

'But then I have six children.'

'By jove you do. But what's that got to do with it?'

'Everything, Your Honour. This gentleman here is afflicted with a medical condition that makes it impossible for him to commit adultery.'

The judge's eyebrows shot up under his wig. 'He what?'

'Mr Mainwaring is impotent, Your Honour.'

'You mean . . . ?' The judge leaned forward, breathing heavily.

Mary Rose saw that the whole court was leaning forward, hanging on Lord Kelston's every word. Travis was looking fixedly at the floor. His hands were knotting and unknotting. Lord Kelston passed the bundle of medical papers to the judge. After briefly thumbing through them he said with a puzzled frown: 'Completely and absolutely impotent.'

'Completely and absolutely. Not a centimetre of action.'

'No, not even a millimetre.'

Judge Saltash looked at Travis with something resembling sympathy. 'Well, in my long years on the divorce bench, never have I been presented with a case like this. I think, gentlemen . . .' He gestured at the two barristers. 'I think we had better repair to my chambers.'

'Court in recession!' bawled the clerk of the court. The two barristers left the court with the judge.

'Now we go and have some lunch.' Ridgeway was grinning.

Mary Rose swept past Crispin and his mother. She restrained herself from putting out her tongue.

'I'm going to the loo,' she whispered to Travis. 'Now it's all so funny. I think I'm going to crack up. We know what they know, but they don't know what we know.'

Travis grinned. 'I just keep thinking we'll be out of this damned country this time next week.'

Mary Rose stopped grinning. 'Sure, Travis, this whole courtroom farce makes me realize I have to get out of here. I'll go potty like the English if I stay.'

They waited most of the afternoon, sitting at the tables outside the court. At one point Radcliffe came out of the judge's chambers and called Crispin and Amelia who were sitting in silence several tables away. Mary Rose heard Amelia's voice rise in high protest.

'This is an outrage,' she yelled.

Ridgeway grinned. 'I think we've got them on the run. And the later it gets, the less old Saltash will want to waste time. He'll want to go fishing.'

Crispin and Amelia came back into the room, followed by Mr Ryder who was puffing and ingesting yet more snuff. Throughout the whole day he had seemed to want to absent himself from the entire case. He bore down on Mary Rose.

'Hello, my dear,' he said, smiling at her with genuine affection. 'Well, it looks as if we will have to withdraw the case, I'm afraid.'

'We still want an independent medical witness,' Amelia yelled from behind him. Mr Ryder's eyebrows went up. 'That is not possible,' he said. 'All the best experts in this country have been presented with this case, so there is no point.'

He turned his attention back to Mary Rose. 'Now, my dear, if we withdraw the charge of adultery, will you keep your promise to give your ex-husband the one hundred and fifty thousand pounds you promised him? And the house, of course.'

Mary Rose looked across at Crispin, who sat with his head bowed. 'I promised Crispin that he could have the money and my share of the house. I will keep that promise. Here, if you like I will write you out a cheque now.' She pushed her chair away from the table. She heard both the barristers come into the room. 'Here is the cheque. Now in return, I never want to see him or his family again.'

She faced the barristers and smiled. 'I think we have settled our differences,' she said. 'Crispin can now do the decent thing, which he should have done in the first place. It is a sad day when a man forgets his chivalry. I think if Travis and I slip away through a back door before the verdict, we can miss the press.'

She shook Lord Kelston by the hand. 'Thank you for everything.' She then kissed Mr Ridgeway lightly on the cheek. 'By the way, Travis and I are going to be married as soon as I get my divorce.' She took Travis's hand. He was beaming.

'This way,' the clerk of the court beckoned. 'I'll show you how to get out.' He too was smiling. All the world loves a lover, he thought, slightly shocked at his own sentimentality.

The evening papers carried the headlines. 'Mary Rose cleared of adultery', said one; 'Man in case can't get it up', said another.

Mary Rose lay in bed with Travis beside her. 'Let's show them just how wrong they are.'

'Willingly.' Travis smiled down at her. 'You really will marry me, Mary Rose? I've been too nervous to ask, in case it was just your little joke.'

'I don't joke about things like that, Travis. I will gladly marry you.'

They fell asleep in each other's arms.

Ninety-Seven

The doctor in Asciano couldn't find anything wrong with Anna. He knew that she had somehow cut herself off from real life, but he had no idea of how to get her back. He brought several specialists from Rome and one from Milan to see her, but they too were baffled.

'A great tragedy,' they pronounced, and left.

'Something will jolt her back into reality,' Lisa prophesied. She was a happy, smiling woman, holding the knowledge that she was probably pregnant. They no longer lived with the Biancharini family, but in their own cottage.

One day in March there was the grinding of wheels on the gravel path that led to the house. Elisabetta went to the door to see who it was. She was stunned to see Fosca climb out of an old, battered taxi. She was carrying a small suitcase tied with string. Her body was extremely thin. But what tore at her mother's heart was the sorrow on her face. Gone were the sparkling eyes and the sweetness that, in the past, had shone around her. In its place was a drab, depressed person. There was a feeling that this girl had gone away radiantly in love and was now returning defeated.

Elisabetta ran to her and enfolded her daughter in

her arms. 'Fosca,' she said, bursting into tears. 'Is it really you? We've been worried sick about you. We tried asking the Red Cross for your whereabouts, but they couldn't find you.'

Fosca, too, was crying. 'I got dreadfully lost at the border. It's taken me months to get here. I left Claude in Zürich and tried to make my way back as soon as the border opened. But what little money I had was stolen. I lost my other suitcase and this is all I have in the world.'

'Darling,' Elisabetta said, not wanting to ask about Claude so early on, 'your everything in the world is us. Come, your father will be over the moon that you are back again.'

'Where is Mario? And Anna?'

Elisabetta's heart immediately began racing. She had dreaded this moment for months. But she tried to calm herself, to pass on a gentle air in the face of a reality which was beyond change.

'Mario is dead, Fosca,' she said simply, looking her daughter directly in the eyes. 'He was shot by the Germans. And Anna is suffering a mental breakdown. I'm afraid she won't recognize you.'

Fosca's face remained unchanged, frozen in its exhaustion. Her expression reflected a weariness of life, a resignation, a surrender to misfortune. Only deep in her eyes was it possible to detect the massive blow which her mother had just dealt her. Flashes of horror.

'Will this suffering ever end?' she asked blankly after several moments' silence.

'It will, darling, it will.' Privately Elisabetta doubted that. For the vast majority of people the war would be a time in their lives when so much damage was done that probably the suffering would never end. She took Fosca by the hand and led her into the drawing room. Francesco was sitting at his desk doing the accounts.

When he looked up and saw his daughter he gave a loud, spontaneous shout of joy.

'Fosca!' he said, running across the long room. He swept her into his arms and covered her with kisses. 'I've waited for this moment for so long, darling.'

Fosca relaxed in his arms and wept. He carried her to the sofa and sat with her on his knee, just as he had done when she was a little girl. 'I've left Claude, Daddy. I had to. I couldn't live like that. We moved all the time. He wants a musician's life and I can't live like that. Once the war was over he wanted to go to Bolivia and live among the gypsies. I wanted a little house and children. So I had to go. It hurts, it hurts so very much. And now I find that Mario is dead.'

There was a moment's silence, then the sound of children running. Giulio burst through the door demanding supper.

Fosca dried her tears and began to smile. 'Giulio,' she said, looking at the square, strong child. 'He is so like Mario it is uncanny.'

Elisabetta broke the silence. 'All right, we'll get supper together for you soon. But for the moment give me some time with your aunt.' She turned to Fosca. 'It's Lisa's day off. She married Tommaso and is expecting a baby, so I suppose not all the news is bad. They are very happy together. They were both wonderful when we were on the run. Let's go up and get Anna from her room. Don't be shocked, Fosca. If anything, Anna is more beautiful than ever.'

Fosca stood by the door of the room and watched shyly as Elisabetta took Anna's hand and gently got her out of her chair by the window. Anna had been crying.

'This is new,' Elisabetta said. 'I hope maybe she is beginning to feel something.'

Fosca stroked Anna's face with her hand. 'Anna,' she said softly. 'Don't you remember me?' There was no recognition in Anna's eyes, only a blank wall of blue. Fosca took Anna's other hand, and together with her mother, they walked down the stairs to the kitchen.

Two weeks later, Ralph arrived. He strode into the house wearing his uniform. His bulk filled the kitchen. He smiled at the family, all seated for lunch. His eyes sought out Anna, and then he stood puzzled. She only stared at him.

'What's wrong?' he said, looking at Elisabetta.

'I couldn't explain properly in my letter, Ralph, but she went into shock when Mario was shot in front of us. She has never recovered. We have had specialists look at her, but they say there is nothing they can do. We just have to wait and pray she comes back . . .' Her voice trailed uncertainly.

Ralph sat down heavily. Lisa brought him a plate of Tuscan bean soup. 'Oh God,' he said miserably. 'Not Anna.' He sat for a moment in stunned silence, realizing just how much he had banked on this moment. 'I'm sorry, Francesco. It was very rude of me just to turn up. I tried to call from Rome but there were no lines. So I just came on.'

'We were wondering if perhaps there might be a specialist in England that we could consult,' Francesco said.

'I am sure there is. I'll check into it immediately I'm back.' He picked up his spoon and dug it into the thick Tuscan bread that lined the bottom of the bowl. He was not hungry, but he would not insult Lisa's cooking.

'I have news of Mary Rose,' he said, trying to strike a less gloomy note. 'She was almost divorced for adultery by that rat of a husband of hers but, being Mary Rose, she found a way around it. She is off to New York with a really nice chap and they will get married as soon as she is free. So that's a bit of good news.'

'How's your son?' Elisabetta asked.

'Funny you should ask.' He took a photograph of Edgar out of his top pocket. 'Noisy little brute, but great fun. He's going to be very good at games, a bit like his father, I'm afraid. Not much upstairs, but a good seat on a horse.'

Later in the afternoon, Ralph asked if he might visit Anna in her room.

'Of course,' Elisabetta said. 'It's on the top floor on the right.' Walking to her room, he thought of his resolve of years before, to distance himself from Anna and allow her to flow freely, undisturbed, in her relationship with Mario. It had been far from easy to maintain. His feelings for Anna had continued to simmer warmly, comfortingly deep inside him, even during his relationship with Belinda. Sometimes they began to boil and it took all his emotional force to restore them to a controllable level. But he had never been able to deny the fact that he adored the woman. Slowly climbing the time-worn steps to her room he felt a mixture of shame and guilt at what was plainly his present opportunistic intent. He felt a bit like a carrion crow, but there was an undeniable, very human force which drove him on. Only he knew its history and how much he wanted to give it a future.

Ralph knocked gently on the door but, after waiting, realized that Anna could not respond. He pushed the door open very gently.

'Anna,' he said. She was staring out of the window. He crossed the room and sat down in a chair next to her. 'Anna, it's me, Ralph.' She gazed at his face. Again he saw no change.

All afternoon he talked to her. He knew she was not responding, but he hoped that somewhere deep inside her there was a glimmer of understanding. He held her hand, he patted her cheek.

Day after day of the week he was there he spent all his time with Anna. Elisabetta and Francesco watched him with sympathy. On the fifth day when he knocked on the door, he thought she turned her head when he walked into the room. He was not sure, so he said nothing. On the sixth day he was beside himself with grief. He had been sitting beside her telling her of the death of his wife. Then, to his surprise, he found himself crying as he had never cried before. Harsh sobs tore at his chest and throat. He tried to apologize, but the sobs were too strong. They choked him. He finally laid his head on her lap and let the sounds of grief flow. After a moment he felt a hand on his head. He froze. He lay still. Again he felt a light, feathery touch. He lifted his head and looked into Anna's eyes. For the first time since he had reached the house he could see that Anna was returning to reality. He tried not to react, or to frighten her.

'Anna,' he said wonderingly.

'Why, Ralph, what are you doing here?'

'I'm just visiting, Anna.'

She looked around the room. 'What a beautiful room. Where is everybody?' Then Ralph realized that she had indeed come back, but back to a world that was no longer. She had lost time and was still living before the dreadful shot that flung her so far away.

Ralph was afraid. 'Anna,' he said. 'You wait here for a moment and I'll go and tell Elisabetta to come and get you.'

'All right.' Anna sat looking out over the fields. 'What a magnificent view. But I thought it was late summer now; this is spring.'

'I'll get Elisabetta.' Ralph hurried down the stairs. He quickly explained the situation to Elisabetta, who ran up the stairs as fast as she could.

'Anna,' she said, opening the door.

'Elisabetta?' Anna replied uncertainly.

'Yes, darling.' Elisabetta slid on to the floor beside her. 'Anna,' she said gently, 'you've been away for many, many months. An awful lot has happened since you went, and some of it is very painful.'

'They shot Mario.' Anna's face was suddenly a mask of horror. 'I remember that now.' She frowned. 'We were running away to the woods with the children.'

'Yes, that's right.' Elisabetta was relieved that she did not have to break the news of Mario's death to her. She was afraid that Anna might relapse. But she knew already.

Anna stood up, breathing unsteadily. 'That moment was so awful I couldn't bear to go on living. I suppose my mind snapped, but my body wouldn't die. I couldn't communicate with anybody. I survived, I suppose, just because you and Lisa helped me. I knew I was eating, but not what I was eating. I felt as though I was down this big, black hole. I wondered about the children, but I seemed to walk, or rather to be led here and there. Sometimes I knew that I was crying. Oh Elisabetta, how can I live without Mario?'

Elisabetta pressed her daughter-in-law's hands. 'Anna, we will have to go on without him. I know how you feel, but you have his little ones. Francesco, too, was devastated, but slowly we will all recover. We are a big, warm, loving family and together we will survive. That's the strength of family life.' She hugged Anna to her. 'Darling, it will take time, just give life time.'

Anna smiled wanly, wishing she did not feel such pain. 'I'll be all right. Now I must see the twins. Where are they?'

'In the garden,' Ralph said. 'I'll go and get them.' His heart was pounding. Anna was going to be all right.

'It was the sound of those sobs,' Anna continued. 'Ralph's sobs. They sounded so much like my own.

But I couldn't let anybody know I was suffering.' She paused. 'Why was he crying?'

'He lost his wife, Anna,' Elisabetta replied. 'She died in childbirth.'

'Oh, poor Ralph.' Anna stared out of the window for a moment, her attention fixed on her own thoughts. 'Let's go downstairs and find the children together and see Francesco.' She walked steadily down the stairs by herself, Elisabetta behind her. At the bottom of the stairs the twins bounded into their mother's arms.

'Giulio . . . Nicoletta,' Anna exclaimed, hugging the children. Francesco, hearing the commotion, came running, joined by Lisa and Tommaso.

'Anna,' he cried, his face alight with joy. He bent over her small frame and picked her up. Swung off her feet, she snuggled into the deep, simple love that Francesco felt for the wife of his son. 'I knew you'd come back, Anna, I just knew it.'

Lisa was smiling through her tears. Anna, a bit at a loss with all the fuss, held her children securely. 'I am back at last. That dreadful nightmare is over.' She looked about the hall, frowning at the broken windows and the damaged furniture. 'We'll make this place beautiful again, won't we?' she told her father-in-law.

'Certainly we will, Anna. In a year's time, no one will know that this house, its gardens and fields, were ever destroyed by the Germans.'

Anna stood quietly, listening to his firm voice and the promise of a new tomorrow. 'Only Mario won't be here to see it,' she said softly. She looked over Francesco's shoulders at Ralph who was standing in the shadows of the room.

'Ralph,' she said. 'Shall we go and see Mario's grave?' She wondered if, by sharing her grief with Ralph, it could lessen his.

Ralph opened the front door for her and they walked

out to the garden together. Ralph followed the same path through the chestnut and oak woods shown to him by Francesco several days before.

Standing by the grave, as yet innocent of a headstone, Anna's tears fell down her face. Ralph, standing beside her, put his arm around her frail shoulders. It was far too early now, but in time he hoped that Anna would come to love him. He could not offer her the first taste of love. That she had shared with Mario, and it could not be found again. But he could offer her a steady love and his heart for the rest of his life. Standing in the promise of an early April, he felt the breeze brush his cheek. He had time on his side, plenty of time.

They walked back to the house together, his arm still around her shoulders.

Nicoletta and Giulio were standing on the doorstep. 'Read us a story, Mummy.'

Anna smiled through her tears. 'All right, darlings, what's it to be?'

'When Pooh Bear helps Eeyore to find his tail,' Nicoletta said.

Ralph watched her as she walked off with her children. One day the two of them would be together. That is a promise, he told himself, and went inside the house to celebrate his secret with a glass of Brunello wine.